NOT A VERY SMART BOMB

Major Pitak's reaction, when Esmay finally got her on the other end of the connection, was hardly reassuring.

"Now I'll go tell *Wraith*'s captain," said the voice in her pressure helmet, "that a totally inexperienced junior officer on her first real EVA thinks she saw an enemy mine stuck to his ship and while she didn't get any good pictures the first time, she is now taking pictures which, if the mine doesn't blow her up, may show us whether she's right. And give us a clue how to do something about it. Suiza, can you think of any mistake you haven't made yet?"

"I didn't set it off," Esmay said, before she could stop herself. A harsh bark of laughter came over the com. She began retracing her route.

The edges of the shattered shield nodes cast jagged shadows that striped the hull's dull black. Things looked different now . . . she couldn't see the mine, but it had to be close.

EEEEERRRRP! Esmay jerked to a halt. She leaned her chin on the comunit switch. "Don't move," a voice said in her ear. "Look down, knee level, 10 o'clock, . . . but don't move." Esmay looked down. Something . . . something *moved*. Something small, rising on a thin wire stalk that gleamed in the searchlight. "Just don't move," the voice said again. "With any luck it will think you're part of the ship."

She tried not to breathe as the sensor swayed nearer. It could already have matched her thermal profile to that of "human in EVA suit" if that was part of its programming.

And if it had done all that, she was already dead, she just hadn't been killed yet.

BAEN BOOKS by ELIZABETH MOON

ONCE A HERO

ELIZABETH MOON

BAEN

ONCE A HERO

This is a work of fiction. All the characters and events portrayed in this book are fictional, and any resemblance to real people or incidents is purely coincidental.

A Baen Books Original

Baen Publishing Enterprises
P.O. Box 1403
Riverdale, NY 10471

ISBN: 0-671-57842-1

Cover art by Gary Ruddell

First paperback printing, April 1998
Second paperback printing, February 1999
This limited edition, December 1999

Distributed by Simon & Schuster
1230 Avenue of the Americas
New York, NY 10020

Typeset by Windhaven Press: Editorial Services, Auburn, NH
Printed in the United States of America

Dedication

For James, the newest Marine in the family.
Semper Fi.

Acknowledgements

As usual, many people helped with the details. Tim
Bashor, Major U.S. Marine Corps, retired, and presently
an exemplary bookstore owner, offered innumerable
good suggestions on how to cause trouble aboard a large
ship. If you think that part of the book makes sense,
it's thanks largely to him. Richard Moon, Malcolm
McLean, and Michael Byrd also helped out on specific
details. Judy Glaister kept me from making a worse
hash of the role of nurses in therapy. Any mistakes are
my own (I don't need help to make mistakes . . .).
R.S.M. provided the medical texts; the Tuesday Lunch
& Ice Skating Club approved the ship design (approved
may not be the right word for "collapsed in helpless
giggles"). Consultants for various bits who would prefer
not to be named include the ubiquitous M.M. and E.M.
and T.B.

CHAPTER ONE

R.S.S. *Harrier*, near Xavier

Esmay Suiza had done her best to clean up before reporting as ordered to the admiral aboard her flagship, but the mutiny and the following battle had left her little time. She had showered, and run her uniform through the cycler, but it wasn't her dress uniform—the fight aboard *Despite* had put holes through interior bulkheads and started innumerable small fires, including one in the junior officers' storage compartment. She herself, though clean, had not slept well in . . . however many days it had been. She knew her eyes were bloodshot and sticky with fatigue; her hands trembled. She had the stomach-clenching feeling that her best wasn't good enough.

Admiral Serrano looked like an older edition of Captain Serrano, the same compact trim frame, the same bronze skin. Here the dark hair was streaked silver, and a few lines marked the broad forehead, but she gave an impression of crackling energy held just in check.

"Lieutenant Junior Grade Suiza reporting, sir." At least her voice didn't shake. Those few days of command had ironed out the uneasy flutter she used to struggle against.

"Have a seat, Lieutenant." The admiral had no expression Esmay could read. She sat in the appointed chair, glad that her knees held and she made it a controlled descent. When she was down safely, the admiral nodded, and went on. "I have reviewed your summary of events aboard *Despite*. It seems to have been a very . . . difficult . . . time."

"Yes, sir." That was safe. In a world of danger, that was always safe; so she had been taught in the Academy and

1

her first ship postings. But her memory reminded her that it wasn't always true, that a "Yes, sir," to Captain Hearne had been treason, and a "Yes, sir," to Major Dovir had been mutiny.

"You do understand, Lieutenant, that it is mandatory for all officers participating in a mutiny to stand before a court to justify their actions?" That in a voice almost gentle, as if she were a child. She would never be a child again.

"Yes, sir," she said, grateful for the gentleness even though she knew it would do her no lasting good. "We— I—have to take responsibility."

"That's right. And you, because you are the senior surviving officer, and the one who ended up in command of the ship, will bear the brunt of this investigation and the court." The admiral paused, looking at her with that quiet, expressionless face; Esmay felt cold inside. They had to have a scapegoat, is that what it meant? She would be to blame for the whole thing, even though she hadn't even known, at first—even though the senior officers— now dead—had tried to keep the youngsters out of it? Panic filled in a quick sketch of her future: dismissed, disgraced, thrown out of Fleet and forced to return home. She wanted to argue that it wasn't fair, but she knew better. Fairness wasn't the issue here. The survival of ships, which depended on the absolute obedience of all to the captain . . . that was the issue.

"I understand," she said finally. She almost understood.

"I won't tell you that such a court is merely a formality, even in a case like this," the admiral said. "A court is never a mere formality. Things always come out in courts to the detriment of everyone concerned—things that might not matter ordinarily. But in this case, I don't want you to panic. It is clear from your report, and that of other personnel—" Which, Esmay hoped, might mean the admiral's niece, "—that you did not instigate the mutiny, and that there is a reasonable probability that the mutiny will be held to be justified." The knot in Esmay's stomach loosened slightly. "Obviously, it is necessary to remove you from command of *Despite*."

Esmay felt her face heating, more relief than embarrassment. She was so tired of having to figure out how to ask the senior NCOs what to do next without violating protocol. "Of course, sir," she said, with a little more enthusiasm than she meant to show. The admiral actually smiled now.

"Frankly, I'm surprised that a jig could take over *Despite* and handle her in battle—let alone get off the decisive shot. That was good work, Lieutenant."

"Thank you, sir." She felt herself going even redder, and embarrassment overcame reticence. "Actually, it was the crew—'specially Master Chief Vesec—they knew what to do."

"They always do," the admiral said. "But you had the sense to let them, and the guts to come back. You're young; you made mistakes of course—" Esmay thought of their first attempt to join the fight, the way she'd insisted on too high an insertion velocity and forced them to blow past. She hadn't known then about the glitch in the nav computer, but that was no excuse. The admiral went on, recapturing her attention. "But I believe you have the root of the matter in you. Stand your court, take your medicine, whatever it is, and—good luck to you, Lieutenant Suiza." The admiral stood; Esmay scrambled up to shake the hand extended to her. She was being dismissed; she didn't know where she was going or what would happen next, but—but she felt a warm glow where the cold knot had been.

As the escort outside made clear, where she was going was a quarantined section of officers' country on the flagship. Peli and the few other junior officers were already there, stowing their duffels in the lockers and looking glum.

"Well, she didn't eat you alive," Peli said. "I suppose my turn's coming. What's she like?"

"A Serrano," Esmay said. That should be enough; she wasn't about to discuss an admiral's character on board a ship. "There's a court coming—but you know that." They had not so much talked about it, as touched the subject and flinched away.

"At the moment," Peli said, "I'm just as glad you had the seniority and not me. Though we're all in trouble."

She had been glad to lay down command, but just for a moment she wanted it back, so she could tell Peli to be quiet. And so she would have something to do. It took only a minute or two to stow her own meager duffel in the compartment she'd been assigned, and only another to wonder how much the officer evicted from it would resent having to double up with someone else. Then she was faced with blank walls—or an empty passage—or the cluster of fellow mutineers in the tiny wardroom which was all the common space they would have until the admiral decreed otherwise. Esmay lay back on her bunk and wished she could turn off the relentless playback in her head, that kept showing her the same gruesome scenes over and over and over. Why did they seem *worse* each time?

"Of course they're listening," Peli said. Esmay paused in the wardroom entrance; four of the others were there, listening to Peli. He looked up, his glance including her in the conversation. "We have to assume they're monitoring everything we say and do."

"That's standard," Esmay said. "Even in normal situations." One of her own stomach-clenching fears was that the forensic teams sent to *Despite* would find out that she talked in her sleep. She didn't know, but if she had, and if she had talked during those nightmares . . .

"Yes, but now they're paying attention," Peli said.

"Well, *we* didn't do anything wrong." That was Arphan, a mere ensign. "We weren't traitors, and we didn't lead the mutiny either. So I don't see where they can do anything to us."

"Not to you, no," Peli said, with an edge of contempt. "From this, if from nothing else, ensigns are safe. Although you could die of fright facing the court."

"Why should I face a court?" Arphan, like Esmay, had come to the Academy from a non-Service family. Unlike Esmay, he had come from an influential non-Service

Family, with friends who held Seats in Council, and expected family clout to get him out of things.

"Regulations," Peli said crisply. "You were a commissioned officer serving aboard a vessel on which a mutiny occurred: you will stand before a court." Esmay didn't mind Peli's brutal directness so much when it was aimed at someone else, but she knew he'd be at her soon enough. "But don't worry," Peli went on. "You're unlikely to spend very long at hard labor. Esmay and I, on the other hand—" he looked up at her and smiled, a tight unhappy smile. "Esmay and I are the senior surviving officers. Questions will be asked. If they decide to make an example, we are the ones to be made an example of. Jigs are an eminently expendable class."

Arphan looked at both of them, and then, without another word, squeezed past two of the others, and Esmay at the door.

"Avoiding contamination," Liam said cheerfully. He was another jig, junior to Peli but part of Peli's "expendable class."

"Just as well," Peli said. "I don't like whiners. D'you know, he wanted me to press the admiral for damage payments to replace a ruined uniform?"

Esmay could not help thinking what the necessary replacements were going to do to her small savings.

"And he's rich," Liam said. Liam Livadhi, Service to the core and for many generations, on both sides of the family. He could afford to sound cheerful; he probably had a dozen cousins who had just outgrown whatever uniforms he needed.

"Speaking of the court," Esmay made herself say. "What *are* the uniform protocols?"

"Uniforms!" Peli glared at her. "You too?"

"For the court, Peli, not for display!" It came out sharper than she intended, and he blinked in surprise.

"Oh. Right." She could practically see the little wheels flickering behind his eyes, calculating, remembering. "I don't really know; the only things I've seen were those cubes back in the Academy, in military law classes. And that was usually just the last day, the verdict. I don't know if they wore dress the whole time."

"The thing is," Esmay said, "if we need new uniforms made, we have to have time for it." Officers' dress uniforms, unlike regular duty uniforms, were handmade by licensed tailors. She did not want to appear before a court in something non-regulation.

"Good point. There wasn't much left of the stuff in that compartment, so we have to assume that all our dress uniforms were damaged." He looked up at her. "You'll have to ask about it, Esmay; you're still the senior."

"Not any more." Even as she said it, she knew she was, for this purpose. Peli didn't quite sneer, but he didn't offer to help out, either.

"On this, you are the one. Sorry, Es', but you have to."

Asking about the uniforms brought her to the notice of the paper-pushers again. As captain—even for those few days—she had the responsibility to sign off on all the innumerable forms required.

"Not the death letters," Lieutenant Commander Hosri said. "The admiral felt that the families would prefer to have those signed by a more senior officer who could better explain the circumstances." Esmay had completely forgotten that duty: the captain must write to the family of any crew members who died while assigned to the ship. She felt herself blushing. "And there are other major reports which the admiral feels should be deferred until Forensics has completed its examination. But you left a lot of routine stuff undone, Suiza."

"Yes, sir," Esmay said, her heart sinking again. When could she have done it? How could she have known? The excuses raced through her mind and out again: no excuses were enough.

"Have your officers fill out these forms—" he handed her a sheaf of them. "Turn them in, completed and countersigned by you, within forty-eight hours, and I'll forward them to the admiral's staff for approval. If approved, that will authorize officers to arrange for replacements of uniforms—and yes, that will include Fleet authorization to forward measurements to registered tailors, so they can get started. Now, we need to deal with the basic reports that *should* have been filed, or ready to file, at the time when you were relieved of command of *Despite*."

The junior officers were not delighted with the forms; some of them procrastinated, and Esmay found herself having to nag them to finish the paperwork by the deadline. "None too early," grunted Hosri's senior clerk, when Esmay brought the reports in. He glanced at the clock. "What'd you do, wait until the last minute?"

She said nothing; she didn't like this clerk, and she had had to work with him for two straight shifts on the incomplete reports Hosri thought she should do. Just let it be over with, she told herself, even though she knew that the reports were the least of her problems. While she worked on those, the other young officers faced daily sessions with investigators determined to find out exactly how it was that an R.S.S. patrol ship had been captained by a traitor, and then embroiled in mutiny. Her turn would come next.

Forensics had swarmed over the *Despite*, stripping the records from the automatic surveillance equipment, searching every compartment, questioning every survivor, examining all the bodies in the ship's morgue. Esmay could only imagine that search, from the questions they asked each day. First with no visual cues at all, when they asked her to explain, moment by moment, where she had been and what she had seen, heard, and done when Captain Hearne took the ship away from Xavier. Later, with a 3-D display of the ship, they led her through it again. Exactly where had she been? Facing which way? When she said she saw Captain Hearne the last time, where was Hearne, and what had she been doing?

Esmay had never been good at this sort of thing. She found out quickly that she had apparently perjured herself already: she could not, from where she remembered she'd been sitting, have seen Lt. Commander Forrester come out of the cross-corridor the way she'd said. It was, the interrogator pointed out, physically impossible to see around corners without special instruments. Had she had any? No. But her specialty had been scan. Was she sure she had not rigged something up? And again here—lines of her earlier testimony moved down the monitor alongside the image of the ship. Could she explain how she had gotten from her own quarters back *here* all the way forward and down two decks in only fifteen seconds? Because there was a clear picture of her—she recognized herself with familiar distaste—in the access corridor to the forward portside battery at 18:30:15, when she had insisted she was in her own quarters for the 18:30 duty report.

Esmay had no idea, and said so. She had made a habit of being in her quarters for that duty report; it had meant that she didn't have to linger in the junior officers' wardroom and join the day's gossip, or make her report with the others. Surely she would have done so even more readily with the rumors then sweeping the ship. She didn't like rumors; rumors got you in trouble. People fought over rumors and then were in more trouble. She hadn't known that Captain Hearne was a traitor—of course she hadn't—but she had had an uneasy feeling in the pit of her stomach, and she had tried not to think about it.

Not until she'd been dragged through it again did she remember that someone had paged her and told her to come initial the daily scan log of the warhead lockers. Checking the automatic scans had been part of her daily routine. She'd insisted that she had done it, and whoever it was had insisted she hadn't, and finally she'd gone down to see. Who had called her? She didn't remember. And what had she found when she got there?

"I'd made an error entering the scan code," Esmay said. "At least—I guess that's what it was."

"What do you mean?" This interrogator had the most neutral voice Esmay had ever heard; it made her nervous for reasons she could not define.

"Well . . . the number was wrong. Sometimes that happened. But usually it wouldn't enter; it would signal a conflict."

"Explain, please."

Esmay struggled on, caught between the social desire not to bore the listener, and the innocent's need to explain fully why she wasn't guilty. She had entered, during her rotation, thousands of scan log codes. Sometimes she made mistakes; everyone did. She did not say what she had long thought, which was how silly it was to have officers entering codes by hand, when there were perfectly decent, inexpensive code readers which could enter them directly. When she made a mistake, the coder usually locked up, refusing entry. But occasionally, it would accept the error code, only to hang up when the next shift compared its code to hers.

"Then they'd call me, and I'd have to come myself and reset the code, and initial the change. That must be what happened."

"I see." A pause during which she could feel the sweat springing out on her neck. "And from what station did you make the 1830 report, then?"

She had no idea. Going from her quarters—she could see the route clearly in her mind, but she could not remember calling in. Yet if she hadn't, someone would have logged it . . . except that was when, up on the bridge, the mutineers made their move against Captain Hearne. Sometime around then, anyway.

"I don't know that I did," she said. "I don't remember that I didn't. I got to the weapons bay, reset the codes, initialed them, and came back to my quarters, and then—" By then the mutiny had spread beyond the bridge, and the senior mutineers had sent someone down to keep the juniors out of it if they could. That hadn't worked; there had been more traitors than that.

The investigator nodded shortly, and went on to something else. To a series of somethings else. Finally, over many sessions, they worked their way up to the time when she herself was in charge.

Could she explain her decision to return to Xavier system and try to fight a battle against odds, with no senior officers and substantial casualties?

Only briefly, and obliquely, had she allowed herself to think of her decision as heroic. Reality wouldn't let her dwell on it. She hadn't known what she was doing; her inexperience had caused too many deaths. Even though it came out all right in the end, in one way, it was not all right for those who had died.

If it wasn't heroic, what was it? It looked stupid now, foolhardy. Yet . . . her crew, despite her inexperience, had blown away the enemy flagship.

"I . . . remembered Commander Serrano," she said. "I had to come back. After sending a message, so in case—"

"Gallant, but hardly practical," said this interrogator, whose voice had a twang she associated with central Familias planets. "You are a protégé of Commander Serrano?"

"No." She dared not claim that; they had served on the same ship only once, and had not been friends. She explained, to someone who surely knew better than she, how wide the gap was between a raw ensign of provincial background, and a major rising on the twin plumes of ability and family.

"Not a . . . er . . . particular friend?" This with a meaningful smirk.

Esmay barely kept herself from snorting. What did he think she was, some prude off a back-country planet that didn't know one sex from the other? That could not call things by their right names? She put out of mind her aunt, who certainly would never use the terms common in the Fleet.

"No. We were not lovers. We were not friends. She was a major, command track; I was an ensign, technical track. It's just that she was polite—"

"Others weren't?" In the same tone.

"Not always," Esmay said, before she could stop herself. Too late now; she might as well complete the portrait of a provincial idiot. "I'm not from a Fleet family. I'm from Altiplano—the first person from Altiplano to attend the Academy. Some people thought it was a hoot." Too late again, she remembered that expression's Fleet meaning. "A regrettably laughable imposition," she added, to the raised eyebrows. "In our slang." Which was no stranger than Fleet slang, just someone else's. Which was the point: Heris Serrano had never laughed at it. But she wouldn't say that to those eyebrows, which right now made her wonder which great Fleet family she had just insulted.

"Altiplano. Yes." The eyebrows had come down, but the tone of condescension hadn't. "That is a planet where the Ageist influence is particularly strong, isn't it?"

"Ageists?" Esmay scrambled through what she knew of politics at home—she had not been home since she was sixteen—and came up with nothing. "I don't think anyone in Altiplano hates old people."

"No, no," the man said. "*Ageists*—surely you know. They oppose rejuvenation."

Esmay stared at him, now thoroughly confused. "Oppose rejuvenation? Why?" Not her relatives, who would be only too happy if Papa Stefan lived forever; he was the only one who could keep Sanni and Berthol from each other's throats, and those two were essential.

"How closely do you follow events on Altiplano?" the man asked.

"I don't," Esmay said. She had left it behind gladly; she had discarded without watching the newscube subscription her family sent her. She had finally decided, in the bleak aftermath of a nightmare in which she was not only stripped of her commission but sentenced to a term of hard labor, that she would never go back to Altiplano, no matter what. They could throw her out of Fleet, but they couldn't make her go home. She had looked it up: no judicial action could force someone to return to their planet of origin for crimes committed somewhere else. "And I can't believe they really oppose rejuvenation . . . at least, I can't imagine anyone I know thinking that way."

"Oh?"

Since he seemed interested, the first person in years who had shown any interest at all, Esmay found herself telling him about Papa Stefan, Sanni, Berthol, and the rest, at least insofar as it bore on their likely attitude towards rejuv. When she slowed down, he interrupted.

"And is your family . . . er . . . prominent on Altiplano?"

Surely that was in her file. "My father's a regional commander in the militia," she said. "The ranks aren't equivalent, but there are only four regional commanders on Altiplano." It would be the height of bad manners to say more; if he couldn't figure out from that where she stood socially on her home planet, then he'd have to suffer in ignorance.

"And you chose to go into Fleet? Why?"

That again. She had dealt with that in her first application, and during the entrance interviews and the military psychology classes as well. She rattled off the explanation that had always seemed to go best, and it sank into the investigator's unresponsive gaze.

"Is that all?"

"Well . . . yes." The smart young officer did not talk about wish fulfillment, the hours she'd spent in the manor orchard staring up at the stars and promising herself she'd be there someday. Better to be matter-of-fact, practical, sensible. No one wanted wild-eyed dreamers, fanatics. Especially not from worlds that had only a couple of centuries of human colonization.

But his silence dragged another sentence out of her. "I loved the thought of going into space," she said. And felt herself flushing, the telltale heat on her face and neck. She hated her fair skin that always showed her emotions.

"Ah," he said, touching his stylus to his datapad. "Well, Lieutenant, that will be all." *For now,* his look said. It could not be the end of questioning; that wasn't how things worked. Esmay said nothing except the polite formula he expected, and went back to her temporary quarters.

She had not realized until the second or third shift aboard the flagship that only she, of the young mutineers, had a private compartment. She wasn't sure why, since there were three other women, all crammed into one compartment. She'd have been happy to share—well, not happy, but willing—but the admiral's orders left no room for argument, as Esmay found when she asked the officer assigned as their keeper if she could change the arrangement. He'd looked disgusted, and told her no so firmly that her eardrums rattled.

So she had privacy, if she wanted it. She could lie on her bunk (someone else's bunk, but hers for the duration), and remember. And try to think. She didn't really like either, not alone. She had the kind of mind that worked best alongside others, striking sparks from her own and others' intransigence. Alone, it whirred uselessly, recycling the same thoughts over and over.

But the others did not want to talk about what bothered her. No, that was not quite honest. She did not want to talk to them about those things either. She did not want to talk about how she felt when she saw the first casualties of the mutiny—how the smell of blood and scorched decking affected her, how it brought back memories she had hoped were gone forever.

War isn't clean anywhere, Esmay. Her father had said that, when she'd told him she wanted to go into space, wanted to become a Fleet officer. *Human blood and human guts smell the same; human cries sound the same.*

She had said she knew it; she had thought she knew it. But those hours in the orchard, looking up at the distant stars, clean light on clean darkness . . . she had hoped for something better. Not security, no: she was too much her father's child to wish for that. But something clean-edged, the danger sharpened by vacuum and weapons that vaporized . . .

She had been wrong, and now she knew it in every reluctant cell of her body.

"Esmay?" Someone tapped on her door. Esmay glanced at the timer and sat up hurriedly. She must have dozed off.

"I'm coming," she said. A quick glance in the mirror; she had the flyaway sort of hair that always needed something done to it. If it had been acceptable, she'd have cut it a centimeter long and let it be. She swiped at it, both hands, and palmed the door control. Peli outside, looking worried.

"Are you all right? You weren't at lunch, and now—"

"Another interview," Esmay said quickly. "And I wasn't

really hungry anyway. I'm coming." She wasn't hungry now, either, but skipping meals brought the psychnannies down on you, and she had no desire to be interviewed by yet another set of inquiring minds.

Supper sat uneasily in her stomach; she sat in the crowded little wardroom not really listening to the others talk. It was mostly guesses about where they were, and when they would arrive, and how long it would take to convene the court. Who would sit on it, who would represent them, how much trouble this would cause them in the future.

"Not as much as being under Captain Hearne if she'd gotten away with it," Esmay heard herself say. She hadn't meant to say anything, but she knew she was the only one really at risk in court. And here they were chattering away as if all that mattered was a possible black mark that might keep them from promotion ahead of their group.

They stared at her. "What do you mean?" Liam Livadhi asked. "Hearne couldn't have gotten away with it. Not unless she took the ship straight over to the Benignity—" He stopped, looking suddenly pale.

"Exactly," Esmay said. "She could have done that, if Dovir and the other loyalists hadn't stopped her. And we could all be Benignity prisoners." Dead, or worse than. The others looked at her as if she had suddenly sprouted a full suit of battle armor with weaponry. "Or she could have told Fleet that Heris Serrano was the traitor, that the accusations were false, and she had fled to save her ship and crew from a maniac. She could have assumed that no one could defeat a Benignity assault group with only two warships." And even Heris Serrano had not done so; Esmay had recognized the peril even as she ended it. Without her own decisive entry into battle, Serrano would have perished, and all witnesses to Hearne's treachery with her.

Peli and Liam looked at Esmay with more respect than she'd had from them yet, even in battle. "I never thought of all that," Peli said. "It never occurred to me that Hearne could have gotten away with it . . . but you're right. We might not even have known—only those on the bridge actually heard Captain Serrano's challenge. If one more bridge officer had been a Benignity agent—"

"We'd be dead." Liam rumpled his Livadhi-red hair. "Ouch. I don't like the thought that I might have disappeared that way."

Arphan scowled. "Surely they'd have ransomed us. I know *my* family—"

"Traders!" Liam said, in a tone that made it sound like a cognate of traitors. "I suppose your Family does business with them, eh?"

Arphan jumped up, eyes blazing. "I don't have to be insulted by people like *you*—"

"As a matter of fact, you do," Liam said, leaning back. "I outrank you, trade-born infant. You're still just an ensign, in case you hadn't noticed."

"No quarreling," Esmay said. This she could handle. "Livadhi, he can't help who his family is. Arphan, Livadhi is your senior; show respect."

"Whooo," murmured Peli. "The ex-captain remembers the feel of command." But his tone was more admiring than scornful. Esmay was able to grin at him.

"As a matter of fact, I do. And keeping you juniors from messing each other's uniforms is easier than fighting a battle. Shall we keep it that way?"

Expressions ranging from surprise to satisfaction met her gaze; she kept the smile on her face and eventually they all smiled back.

"Sure, Esmay," Livadhi said. "I'm sorry, Arphan—I shouldn't have chosen this time, if any, to slang your family. Lieutenant Suiza's right. Friends?" He held out his hand. Arphan, still scowling, finally shook it, muttering something about being sorry. It did not escape Esmay's notice that he had chosen a combination of address which claimed her as a friend, while emphasizing her authority to Arphan. She could do that sort of thing if she thought of it, but she had to think; Liam Livadhi, and the others born into Fleet families, seemed to do it as naturally as breathing.

CHAPTER TWO

Harborview Industrial Park, Castle Rock

The conference room had been swept and garnished, ensuring that it was empty of the security demons whose probing eyes and ears, and busy tongues, would have had a field day. Outside, two offices away, an efficient receptionist would deal with any calls; the rest of the staff were busy on assigned projects. The three partners who had formed Special Materials Analysis Consulting looked at the moment more like business rivals than old friends. Arhos Asperson, short, compact, dark-haired, leaned forward, elbows on the polished table, as Gori Lansamir reported on the results of clandestine research. Across from him, Losa Aguilar lay back in her chair, consciously opposing him in gesture as in attitudes. The lounging posture did not suit her; with her lean body went an energy usually expressed in action.

"You were right, Arhos. In-house projections at Calmorrie are that demand will rise steeply, especially for repeat procedures where the last procedure used drugs from a questionable source." Gori scowled, an unusual expression on his normally amiable face. Arhos nodded.

"In other words, last week's blip in the price of a first-time rejuvenation wasn't a blip at all."

"No." Gori pointed to details in the chart he'd displayed. "Ever since the king resigned, there's been talk about adulteration of the components. The shakeup in the Morreline family holdings suggests to me it may be even bigger than what's alleged in the suits already filed."

"I suppose we should be glad we didn't get ours done last year," Losa said. Arhos looked at her; had there been

16

a hint of smugness in her tone? Probably. Losa enjoyed rightness as a personal fiefdom. Usually he didn't mind, but when she disagreed with him that buzzsaw certainty hurt.

"Not to our credit, since we couldn't afford them last year—or this, with the price increase. I suppose we could get one of us done—" Arhos glanced at his partners. Gori might go along with that, but Losa never would. Nor would he himself, u iess he was the one to get rejuv.

"No," Losa said quickly, before Gori could say anything. "For the same reasons we didn't pool funds to do one of us last year."

"You don't have to make your distrust quite so obvious," Arhos murmured. "I wasn't suggesting it—only pointing out that we could afford only one this year, too. It's taken us five years to save up that much—and with the price expected to rise steeply—"

"We need more contracts," Gori said. "Surely with all that's happening in the Fleet right now, we can find a niche?"

"We should have an advantage," Losa said. "We shouldn't be under any suspicion, like the major suppliers and consulting firms."

"That might help." Arhos had his doubts. Somehow even when the witch-hunters were out, the good old firms seemed to find a safe hideout. "We do good work; we've had Fleet contracts through Misiani . . . if anyone notices the sub-sub-contractors at a time like this."

"That's what you're worried about? That we're not noticeable enough?"

"In a way. The thing is, they have no way of knowing whether we subs perform well because we're good, or because we're under the thumb of the main contractor. Thus no reason to trust us on our own."

"We've had a few . . ." Losa began. Then she shrugged, before Arhos could say it. "But not enough of the juicy ones. Our profit margin's too low."

"No, and the real problem, I'm convinced, is that we aren't rejuved yet. The big firms all have rejuved executives now."

"We're not that old."

"No, but—Gori's not as boyishly cute anymore. None of us look like bright young kids. Look, Losa, we've been over this before . . ."

"And I didn't like it then . . ." She had abandoned the fake slouch for her more normal upright posture; he had never seen anyone but a dancer with such a back and neck. He could remember the feel of it under his hands . . . but that had been years ago. Now they were only partners in work. He pulled his mind away from the thought of Losa rejuved to . . . perhaps . . . eighteen . . .

"Look, it's simple. If we want to survive in this field, we have to convince clients we're successful. Successful consultants are rich—and rich people are rejuved. We're still getting contracts, but not the best contracts. In ten years, the kind of contracts we're getting will go to the new bright young things—or to our present competitors who've managed to afford rejuv."

"We could cut back—" That was Gori, with no conviction in his voice. They had discussed this before; even Gori didn't really want to live like an impoverished student again.

"No." Arhos shook his head. "It's suicide either way. To save out enough for rejuv, even one at a time, we'd have to cut expenses—this office for one—and that would make us look like losers. We need to rejuv—all of us—within the next five years. With the revelations about those contaminated drugs, the price will go up and stay up just when we need it most."

"Which comes down to more contracts," Losa said. "Except that we can't do more without hiring more—and that drives our cost up."

"Maybe. We need some new ideas, contracts that will give us a higher margin of profit, and not require any more expenditures."

"From your tone I'd gather you already have some."

"Well . . . yes. There are specialties which pay a much higher rate . . . for which we are already qualified."

Losa's lip curled. "Industrial sabotage? We don't want to try *that* with Fleet . . . not with the current mood."

"Public opinion's on their side right now because of the Xavier affair—that Serrano woman is a hero—but in the long run what they'll remember is one hero and three traitors."

"And we're to be traitors too?"

Arhos glared at her. "No, not traitors. But—none of us got into this work because of any particular love for the Familias bureaucracy. Remember why we left General Control Systems. And then, as subcontractors, we've had the same piles of paperwork—"

"You're talking about working outside Familias space? Won't that just mean a whole new set of paper-pushers to contend with?"

"Not necessarily. Not everyone outside is as tangled in red tape as the Familias. And it isn't necessarily against Familias interests . . . at least I don't see it that way."

"You want rejuvenation," Losa said sharply, leaning forward.

"Yes. And so do you, Losa. So does Gori. None of us have been able to increase our profits within the confines of Fleet contracts and subcontracts: too many fish in this pond, many of them with more teeth. So either we give up our ambitions, which I for one am not willing to do, or we find another pond. Ideally a pond that connects with this one, so we don't lose all the goodwill we've built."

Losa heaved a dramatic sigh. "All right, Arhos . . . just tell us."

He let himself smile. "We have a potential client who would like to have us disable a self-destruct device on a service ship."

"Whose service ship? Fleet's?"

Arhos nodded.

"Not blow it up—disable its self-destruct?"

"Right."

"Why?"

Arhos shrugged. "In this kind of situation it's not my business why . . . though I could speculate, I'd rather not."

"And who is this potential client?"

"He didn't say whom he worked for, but a little discreet

data probe allowed me to estimate a very high probability
that he's an agent for Aethar's World."

Losa and Gori stared at him as if he'd sprouted horns.
"You were talking to the Bloodhorde?" Losa asked, having
beat out Gori by a breath.

"Can we trust him?" asked Gori.

"Not really," Arhos admitted, spreading his hands. "But
the offer was . . . generous. And I suspect we can work
up from it—he didn't sound as firm as he thought."

"What kind of service ship?" asked Gori.

"A deep space repair ship, one of those floating ship-
factories crewed like an orbital station. Why anyone would
put a self-destruct on it in the first place, I can't understand—it sounds dangerous to me; what if the captain goes
crazy? And they want it disabled, is all."

"I hate the thought of dealing with the Bloodhorde,"
Losa said. "And here we're talking about twenty or thirty
thousand people—"

"Military personnel," Arhos said. "Not ordinary people.
They signed up for the risk. That's what they're paid for.
And we need the cash. If we don't get the new rejuv
procedure soon—"

"But the *Bloodhorde*, Arhos! All those hairy, beefy types
with their Destiny garbage! They belong back on their
home planet, whacking each other with clubs and sitting
around drunk singing . . ."

"Of course they do." Arhos grinned at her. "They're
barbarians, and we all know it. That's why I'm not worried
. . . Fleet will be able to contain them just as they always
have. And this job doesn't require us to damage Fleet—"

"Disabling a ship system—"

"A system that's never been used and never will be.
DSRs never get into combat anyway, so I don't know why
they even have self-destruct devices. I'd think they'd go
the other way, make it impossible to blow them up. But
apparently they do have such things, and the person who
contacted me wanted it turned off."

Losa sat up straight. "It's obvious, Arhos you can see—"

He held up his hand. "I don't want to see—speculate,

rather. It will have no effect on the DSR's function as a repair and maintenance facility; it won't kill anyone; it won't do anything but keep some ham-handed ensign from blowing the ship up by accident. In a way, you could think of our action as damage control . . ." Losa snorted, but he ignored her and went on. "And the good news is . . . they offered, before I started dickering, a fee that will cover rejuvenation for two of us." Into the silence around the table, he dropped the last piece of bait. "I got them up another half mil, and that means we have enough for all three of us. Net, not gross. After the job, of course."

"The complete—"

"New, with the newest, certified drugs. A margin for inflation while the job's on."

Losa's thin face glowed. "Rejuv . . . just like that Lady Cecelia . . ."

"Yes. I thought you'd see it that way." Arhos cocked his head at Gori. "And you?"

"Mmm. I don't like the Bloodhorde, what I've heard about them, but . . . probably most of it's propaganda anyway. If they were so quarrelsome and technologically backward, they wouldn't have been able to hold their empire together the past century. I suppose it's in a solid currency?"

"Yes."

Gori shrugged. "Then I don't see a problem, as long as it's within our technical expertise. As you said, it's not like we're actually doing any damage to a ship, or to peoples' lives. A self-destruct isn't a weapon; we're not really depriving Fleet of anything." He thought a moment, then added, "But how're we going to get aboard the ship? And where is it?"

Arhos grinned, this time more broadly. "We're going to get a contract. A *legitimate* contract. There's one up for bid, just posted this morning in fact. All the Fleet weapons inventory needs recalibration—the word is, they're afraid more traitors like Hearne could have diddled the guidance systems codes. It's such a big job, they've decided to put it out to all qualified consultants with the right clearances, regardless of size. I put in our bid on the way back."

"But what if we'd said no to the other—?"

"Then we'd have had a legitimate job. I bid for the contract in Sector 14 only, giving as a reason our small staff. It was listed as a bonus project, because of the distance from major nexi. I think we fit that profile very well—and besides, we can dicker with whoever gets it if we don't."

"As long as we *do* get paid," Losa said, with an edge of fierceness.

"Oh, we will. The Bloodhorde representative is coming tomorrow—standard first-visit negotiations, but I want full security backup. He's likely to turn mean, for all that he's wearing a suit. He won't know about the other contract, and I'm going to try to get an additional travel and expense budget out of him."

"Who else are we taking in on this job?" Gori asked.

"The Fleet part of it, the usual team. This part—only the three of us. We don't want to share the fee, after all."

"There's only one tricky point," Arhos said. "That's the civilian/Fleet interface on Sierra. It's the Sector HQ of a red-zoned sector . . . they do more than just glance at ID there." He glanced across the broad desk at the blond man in the expensive business suit.

"Your IDs will be in order," the blond man said. He lounged back in his chair as if it were a throne, a posture which made the suit look as if it had been made for someone else, someone who knew how to sit without sprawling.

"We could avoid the problem entirely by traveling with Fleet from somewhere else—Comus, for instance."

"No." Flat, rude, arrogant.

"Explain."

"It is not my place to explain. It is yours to comply with the contract." The blond man glared at the others.

"It is not my place to be stupid," Arhos said. With a flick of his gaze, he ensured the blond man's continued existence for a space of time. How long depended on his mood, which the blond man was not helping. He reminded himself that the consulting fee transferred to the firm's account would pay for three and a half rejuvenations at the rate Gori had calculated would apply when they were through with the job. Fleet's fee for recalibrating all those weapons would give them something to live on. If they killed this messenger, they would have to deal with someone who might be worse. "If you want this done neatly, as you said, then you should listen to the experts."

"Expert sneaks." That with the trademark Bloodhorde sneer. Clearly the blond man had no respect, a condition dangerous in itself, beyond unpleasant. Arhos allowed an eyelid to droop. Before it rose again, the blond man was gasping for breath, the noose around his thick neck grooving the skin. The chair in which he sat had flipped restraints onto his arms, and tightened them. Arhos did not move.

"Insults annoy us," he said mildly. "We are experts— that's why you hired us. It is part of our expertise to travel unnoticed, accepted. It is my opinion that waiting until Sierra Station to enter Fleet jurisdiction will bring unwelcome notice. Civilian contractors, special consultants, normally join up with Fleet transport closer to their point of origin." He smiled. The blond man's face had turned an ugly puce; he made disgusting noises. But the blue eyes showed no fear, not even as they dulled with oxygen deprivation. He nodded, and the noose sprang away from the blond man's neck as if someone had pushed it. Someone had, remotely. . . .

"Mother-devouring scum—!" the blond man croaked. He yanked hard, but the chair restraints held his arms down.

"Experts," Arhos said. "You pay us, we do your job— cleanly, thoroughly. But don't insult us."

"You will regret this," the blond man said.

"I don't think so." Arhos smiled. "It is not my neck which has a mark from a noose. Nor will it."

"If I were loose—"

Arhos cocked his head to one side. "I would have to kill you, if you attacked me. It would be most unfortunate."

"You! You are too little—"

"Bloodhorde barbarian!" That from the other person in the room, the woman who had said nothing before, whose quiet demeanor fit the subordinate role she had seemed to have. "Do you still think size is everything, after all your defeats?"

"Peace, Losa. It is no part of our contract to instruct this . . . individual . . . in the realities of hand-to-hand fighting. We have no reason to give him gratuitous data."

"As you wish." She sounded more sulky than submissive.

"Now," Arhos said. "We will expect half the fee on deposit with our bankers by midday tomorrow, the next fourth when we arrive at Sierra Station, and the final fourth when we have completed the task. No—" as the blond man started to speak. "No, don't argue. You lost your bargaining advantage when you insulted us. You can always hire someone else if you don't like my terms. You won't find anyone as good—you know that already—but it's your choice. Take or leave—which?"

"Take," the blond man said, still hoarse from the noose. "Greedy swine . . ."

"Very good." No need to mention that every insult now—after that warning—would raise the price of the job. One did not have to like one's customers if they produced enough profit, and Arhos—the best in his field—knew to a single credit how much it took to satisfy his feelings.

Though the job itself was intriguing, a challenge he would not have thought of by himself, but one well worth the attempt. Not attempt, he thought . . . the achievement. He had no doubts; they had not failed in an assignment in years. Getting this buffoon out of the office quietly was the only problem that concerned him, once the buffoon had thumb-printed a credit authorization.

"Nasty," Losa said, after the man had left. "And dangerous."

"Yes, but solvent. We don't have to like them . . ."

"You said that before."

"It's true."

"He scared me . . . he wasn't afraid, he was just angry. What if they want revenge for the insult?"

Arhos looked at her, and wished she'd make up her mind what kind of person she was. "Losa . . . this is a dangerous business, and it's never bothered you before. We have good security; we'll be taking precautions. Do you want that rejuvenation, or don't you?"

"Of course I want it."

"I think you're just annoyed that I found the contract, and not you."

"Maybe." She sighed, then grinned, as she rarely did now. "I must need one, turning into a cautious old lady before my time."

"You're not an old lady, Losa, and now you never will be."

R.S.S. *Harrier*

By the time the flagship reached sector headquarters, Esmay had begun thinking of the court as a door to freedom—freedom from the tensions and rivalries of a cluster of scared junior officers with not enough to do. While it made legal sense, she supposed, to keep them all isolated and relatively idle, it felt like punishment.

Even the largest ship has limited resources for recreation; duties normally fill most of its crew's time. Esmay tried to make herself use the teaching cubes—she encouraged the others to use them—but with a knot of uncertainty lodged in the middle of her brain, the rest of it couldn't concentrate on anything as dry as "Methods for back-flushing filters in a closed system" or "Communications protocols for Fleet vessels operating in zones classified F and R." As for the tactical cubes, she already knew where she'd gone wrong coming back to Xavier, and there was nothing she could do about it now. Besides, none of the tactical cubes considered the technical problems she'd faced in starting a battle with a ship which had suffered internal damage in a mutiny.

She could not work hard enough by day to ensure restful sleep at night. Physical exhaustion might have done that, but her share of the gym time wasn't enough to achieve that. So the nightmares came, night after night, and she woke sweat-soaked and gritty-eyed. The ones she understood were bad enough, replays of the mutiny or the battle at Xavier, complete with sound and smell. But others seemed to have drawn from memories of every training film, every military gory story she'd ever heard . . . all jumbled together like the vivid shards of a shattered bowl.

She looked up at a killer's face . . . she looked down to see her own hands slimy with blood and guts . . . she stared into the muzzle of a Pearce-Xochin 382, which seemed to widen until her whole body could slide down inside it . . . she heard herself begging, in a high thin voice, for someone to stop. . . . NO. That time when she woke, tangled in damp bedding, someone was pounding on her door and calling for her. She coughed a few times, then found voice enough to answer.

It was not a door, but a hatch: she was not home, but aboard a ship, which was better than home. She took the deep breaths she told herself to take, and explained to the voice outside that it had been just a bad dream. Grumbles from without: some of us need our sleep too, you know. She apologized, struggling with a rush of sudden, inexplicable anger which urged her to yank open the . . . hatch, not door . . . and strangle the speaker. It was the situation; tempers would naturally flare, and she must set an example. Finally the grumbler left, and she lay back against the bulkhead—the safe gray bulkhead—thinking.

She had not had such dreams in years, not since leaving home for the Fleet prep school. Even at home, they'd been rarer as she got older, although they had been frequent enough to worry her family. Her stepmother and her father had both explained, at tedious length, their origin. She had run away once, after her mother died, a stupid and irresponsible act mitigated by youth and the fact that she was probably already sick with the same fever that killed her mother. She had found trouble, a minor battle in the insurrection now known as the Califer Uprising. Her father's troops had found and rescued her, but she'd nearly died of the fever. Somehow, what she'd seen and heard and smelled had tangled with the fever during the days in coma, and left her with the bad dreams of something which had never really happened. Not as she dreamed it, anyway.

It made sense that being in a real battle would bring back those old memories and the confusion the fever engendered. She really had smelled spilled guts before; smells were particularly evocative . . . that was in the psychology books she had read secretly in Papa Stefan's library, when she had believed she was crazy as well as lazy and cowardly and stupid. And now that she understood where the nightmares had been leading, trying to link her past experiences with her present, she could deal with this consciously. She had had nightmares because she needed to make the connection, and now that she had it, she would not need the nightmares.

She fell asleep abruptly, dreaming no more until the bell signaled the time to wake. That day she congratulated herself on figuring it out, and instructed herself to have no more nightmares. She was tense at bedtime, but talked herself out of it. If she dreamed, she did not remember it, and no one complained of the noise she made. Only once more before they reached Sector HQ did she have a nightmare, and that one was even easier to understand. She dreamt she came into the court-martial and only when the presiding officer spoke discovered that she was stark naked. When she tried to run out, she could not move. They all looked at her, and laughed, and then walked out, leaving her alone.

It was almost a relief to find she could have *normal* nightmares.

At Sector HQ, her replacement uniforms were ready, delivered directly to the quarantine section aboard the ship by guards who clearly felt this beneath their dignity. The new clothes felt stiff and awkward, as if her body had changed in ways that measurements could not reflect. She had used the minimal fitness equipment in the quarantined section daily, so the difference wasn't flab. It was . . . something more mental than physical. Peli and Liam groaned dramatically when they saw their tailors' bills; Esmay said nothing about hers, and only later realized they assumed she had no resources beyond her salary.

For the first time, the young officers were called before the admiral as a group. Esmay wore a new uniform; so did everyone else. An armed escort led them; another closed in behind. Esmay tried to breathe normally, but could not help worrying—had something else gone wrong? What could it be?

Admiral Serrano waited, expressionless, as they all filed into the office, packed in so close that Esmay could smell the new fabric of their uniforms. The admiral had responded to each formal greeting with a little nod, and a flick of her eyes to the next in line.

"It is my duty to inform you that you have all been called before a court to explain, if you can, the events leading up to the mutiny aboard *Despite* and the subsequent involvement of that ship and crew in action at Xavier."

Esmay heard nothing from behind her, but she felt the reaction of her fellow officers; though they had known it must happen, the formal words delivered by an admiral of the Fleet struck with awesome force. Court-martial. Some officers served from commissioning to retirement without being threatened with an investigation, let alone a hearing before some Board . . . and certainly without standing a court-martial. A court-martial was the ultimate disgrace, if you were convicted; it was a blemish on your career even if you were acquitted.

"Because of the complexity of this case," the admiral went on, "the Judge Advocate General has chosen to handle it with utmost circumspection but also utmost gravity. The precise charges have not been determined for each of you, but in general, the junior lieutenants can expect to see charges of both treason and mutiny, which the JAG is not considering mutually exclusive defenses, one for the other. That is, if you were a party to treason, this does not defend against a later charge of mutiny, and vice versa." The admiral's bright black eyes seemed to bore into Esmay's. Did she mean something *particular* about that? Esmay wanted to blurt out that she was not and had never been a traitor, but discipline kept her jaw locked.

The admiral coughed delicately, clearly a social cough, a punctuation in what she said. "I am authorized to tell you that the reason for this is the high level of concern about Benignity influence in the officer corps. It would not have been feasible to ignore that possibility in this case; your defense counsels will explain it to you. The ensigns are being charged with mutiny only, except in one case where investigation is still in progress."

"But we haven't even seen a defense lawyer!" complained Arphan from the back. Esmay could have swatted him; the idiot had no right to speak.

"Ensign . . . Arphan, isn't it? Did anyone give you leave to interrupt, Ensign?" The admiral needed no help from a jig to squash a feckless junior.

"No, sir, but—"

"Then be silent." The admiral looked back at Esmay, who felt guilty that she had not somehow gagged Arphan, but the admiral's look conveyed no rebuke. "Junior Lieutenant Suiza, as the senior surviving officer, and former captain of a mutinied ship in combat, your trial will necessarily be severed from that of the officers junior to you, although you will be called to testify in their trials, and they in yours. Additionally, you will face a Captain's Board of Inquiry to investigate your handling of *Despite* in battle."

Esmay had expected this, in one way, and in another had hoped that one investigation and judicial ordeal might subsume the other.

"Because of the unusual circumstances of the Xavier situation, including the actions taken by Commander Serrano, it has been determined that you should all be transported to Fleet Headquarters for these courts-martial on another vessel."

Esmay blinked. They didn't trust Admiral Serrano because of her niece? Then she remembered all the rumors—now demonstrably untrue—about Heris Serrano and her departure from Fleet.

"Commander Serrano will of course be facing a Board of Inquiry herself, and three of you will be called to testify to that Board." Esmay could not imagine who might be thought to have useful information there. "You will be allowed communications access to notify your families, and if possible speak with them directly, but you are not to communicate with anyone other than your families. Specifically, you are ordered, under penalty, to avoid discussion of this case with anyone in or out of Fleet except your defense counsel and each other. I strongly recommend that you not discuss this among yourselves any more than you already have. You will be closely observed, not always by those who have your interests at heart. You will be met at Fleet Headquarters by your assigned defense counsel, and you will have the usual resources then to prepare yourself for court." The admiral's gaze raked the lines for a moment; Esmay hoped no one would ask stupid questions, and no one did.

"You're dismissed," the admiral said. "Except for Junior Lieutenant Suiza." Esmay's heart sank through her boot-soles and the deck she stood on. She stood while the others shuffled out, watching the admiral's face for any clue. When they had all gone, the admiral sighed.

"Sit down, Lieutenant Suiza." Esmay sat. "This is going to be a difficult time for you, and I want to be sure you understand that. Yet I don't want to panic you. Unfortunately, I really don't know you well enough to know how much warning it takes to scare you too much. Your record, as an officer, doesn't help me along. Can you?"

Esmay kept her jaw from dropping with an effort. She had no idea what to say; for once *Yes, sir* wasn't enough. The admiral continued, more slowly, giving her time to think.

"You did very well at the Academy prep school; you were rated high, not brilliantly, in the Academy itself. I would guess you're not the sort to look up your own fitness reports—is that right?"

"Yes, sir," Esmay said.

"Mmm. So you may not know that you've been described as 'hard worker, willing, not a leader' or 'steady, competent, always completes assignments, shows initiative with jobs but not people, leadership potential average.'" The admiral paused, but Esmay couldn't think of anything. That's about what she'd thought of herself. "Some of them say you're shy, and others just say quiet and nondemanding . . . but in a lifetime in the Fleet, Lieutenant Suiza, I've never seen this sort of fitness report—one after another, from the prep school all the way through—coupled with the kind of decisive leadership you showed with *Despite*. I've known some quiet, unassuming officers who were good in combat—but there was always, somewhere in the background, at least one little glint from that undiscovered diamond."

"It was an accident," Esmay said, without thinking. "And besides, it was the crew who did it, really."

"Accidents," the admiral said, "do not just happen. Accidents are caused. What kind of accident do you think would have resulted if Junior Lieutenant Livadhi had been senior?"

Esmay had wondered that; in the aftermath of battle, Liam and Peli both had been sure they would have chosen a different insertion velocity and vector, but she remembered the look on their faces when she'd announced they were going back.

"You don't have to answer," the admiral said. "I know from his interviews. He would have sent the same message you did, then hopped back to Sector HQ, hoping to find someone handy. He would not have taken *Despite* back, and although he can justly critique your tactics on system entry, he himself would have been far too late to save the situation."

"I . . . I'm not sure. He's brave—"

"Courage isn't the whole issue here, and you know it. Prudence and courage make good teammates; cowardice can be as rash as storycube courage." The admiral smiled, and Esmay felt cold. "Lieutenant, if you can puzzle me, I assure you that you are puzzling the rest of Fleet even more. It's not that they don't want you to have done what you did—but they don't understand it. If you can hide that level of ability, all these years, under a bland exterior, what *else* are you hiding? Some have even suggested that you are a Benignity deep agent, that you somehow set up Commander Hearne and engineered a mutiny, just to get yourself known as a hero."

"I didn't!" Esmay said without thinking.

"I don't think so myself. But right now there's a crisis of confidence all over the Familias Regnant, and it has not spared the Regular Space Service. It was bad enough to discover that Lepescu was making sport of killing Fleet personnel, but to find that three traitorous captains could be dispatched to something like Xavier—*that* has shaken the confidence of Fleet Intelligence, as well it should. By all rights, you should be whisked through the obligatory court as quickly as possible, and then hailed as the hero you are—and don't bother to deny it. You are. Unfortunately for you, circumstances are against you, and I expect you and your defense counsel will have a rugged few weeks. Nor is there anything I can do about it; right now my influence could only harm you."

"That's all right," Esmay said. It wasn't all right, not if she understood Admiral Serrano's implications, but she could certainly see why the admiral couldn't change reality. Growing up a senior officer's daughter had taught her that, if nothing else. Power always had limits, and banging your head on them only hurt your head.

The admiral was still looking at her with that intense dark gaze. "I wish I knew you and your background better. I can't even tell if you're sitting there complacent, reasonably wary, or terrified . . . would you mind enlightening me?"

"Numb," said Esmay honestly. "I'm certainly not complacent; I wasn't complacent even before your warning. I know that young officers who get involved with mutinies, for whatever reason, always have a stained record. But whether I'm reasonably wary or terrified—that I don't know myself."

"Where did you develop that kind of control, then, if you don't mind my asking? Usually our intakes from colonial planets are all too easy to read."

It sounded like genuine interest; Esmay wondered if it was, and if she dared explain. "The admiral knows about my father . . . ?" she began.

"One of four sector commanders on Altiplano; I presume that means you grew up in some kind of military household. But most planetary militia are less . . . formal . . . than we are."

"It began with Papa Stefan," Esmay said. She was not entirely sure it had really begun there, because how had Papa Stefan accumulated the experience he passed on? "It's not like Fleet, but there's a hereditary military . . . at least, the leading families are."

"But your file says you were raised on a farm of some sort?"

"Estancia," Esmay said. "It's—more than a farm. And fairly big." Fairly big hardly described it; Esmay didn't even know how many hectares were in the main holding. "But Papa Stefan insisted that all the children have some military training as they grew."

"Not all military traditions value the absolute control of facial expression and emotion," the admiral commented. "I gather yours does."

"Mostly," Esmay said. She couldn't explain her own aversion to unnecessary display of emotion, without going into the whole family mess, Berthol and Sanni and the rest. Certainly Papa Stefan and her own father valued self-control, but not to the degree she practiced it.

"Well . . . I wanted you to know that you have my best wishes in this matter," the admiral said. She was smiling, a smile that seemed warm and genuine. "After all, you saved my favorite niece—excuse me, Commander Serrano—and I won't forget that, no matter what. I'll be keeping an eye on your career, Lieutenant; I think you have more potential than even you suspect."

CHAPTER THREE

Esmay had time to meditate on those words as the long arm of the Fleet's judicial branch separated her from the other junior officers, put her aboard a courier-escort, and whisked her to Fleet Headquarters a full eight days before the others arrived. She met her defense counsel, a balding middle-aged major who looked more like a bureaucrat than an officer; he had the incipient paunch of someone who avoided the gym except in the last few weeks before the annual physical fitness test.

"It would've made sense for them to link the cases," Major Chapin grumbled, poring over Esmay's file. "Starting at the back end, you are the hero of Xavier; you saved the planet, the system, and an admiral's niece's ass. Unfortunately—"

"It was explained to me," Esmay said.

"Good. At least none of the records are missing. We'll need to prepare separately for the Captain's Board of Inquiry and for each of the main threats of the court martial. I hope you have an organized mind—"

"I think so," Esmay said.

"Good. For the time being, forget military protocol, if you can; I'm going to call you Esmay, and you're going to call me Fred, because we have too much work to let formalities slow us down. Clear?"

"Yes, sir—Fred."

"Good. Now—tell me everything you told the investigators, and then everything you didn't tell them. The whole story of your life isn't too long. I won't get bored, and I don't know what's useful until I hear it."

In the next days, Esmay found that Major Chapin meant what he'd said. She also found herself increasingly

34

comfortable talking to him, which made her nervous. She reminded herself that she was a grownup, not a child who could throw herself at any friendly adult when she needed comfort. She even mentioned the nightmares, the ones connected to Xavier.

"You might want to consider a psych session," he said. "If it's bothering you that much."

"It's not now," she said. "It was those first days after . . ."

"Sounds normal to me. If you're sleeping well enough to stay alert . . . there's an advantage in not going for a psych evaluation now, you see, because it might look as if we're going to plead mental incompetence."

"Oh."

"But by all means, if you need it—"

"I don't," Esmay said firmly.

"Good . . . now about this petty thievery you said was plaguing the enlisted lockers . . ."

Circumstances conspired to shift the date of the court martial so that the Captain's Board met first. Major Chapin grumbled about this, too.

"You don't take counsel to a Board of Inquiry, so you'll have to remember everything we've talked about by yourself. You can always ask for a short recess and come ask me, but it leaves a bad impression. Damn it—I wanted you to have experience before you went in alone."

"Can't be helped," Esmay said. He looked mildly surprised, which almost annoyed her. Had he expected her to complain when it could do no good? To make a useless fuss, and to him?

"I'm glad you're taking it that way. Now—if they don't bring up the matter of the damage to the nav computer, you have two choices—" That session went on for hours, until Esmay felt she understood the point of Chapin's advice, as well as the advice itself.

The morning the Board hearing began, Chapin walked her into the building and all the way to the anteroom where he would wait in case she asked for a recess and his guidance. "Chin up, Lieutenant," he said as the door opened. "Keep in mind that you won the battle and didn't lose your ship."

The Board of Inquiry made no allowances for the irregular way in which Esmay had arrived in command of *Despite*, or so it seemed from the questions. If a Jig commanded in battle, that jig had better know what she was doing, and every error Esmay made came up.

Even before the next senior officer died of wounds, why had she not prepared for command—surely that mess on the bridge could have been cleaned up faster? Esmay, remembering the near-panic, the need to secure every single compartment, check every single crew member, still thought there were more important things than cleaning blood off the command chair. She didn't say that, but she did list the other emergencies that had seemed more pressing. The Board chair, a hard-faced one-star admiral Esmay had never heard anything about, good or bad, listened to this with compressed lips and no expression she could read.

Well then, when she took command, why had she chosen to creep into one system—the right move, all agreed, given what she found—and then go blazing back into Xavier, where she had every reason to believe an enemy force lay in wait? Didn't she realize that more competent mining of the jump point entry corridor would have made that suicidal? Esmay wasn't about to argue that her decision made sense; she had followed an instinct, not anything rational, and instincts killed more often than they saved.

And why hadn't she thought of using a microjump to kill momentum earlier, when she might have saved two ships and not just one? Esmay explained about the nav computer, the need to patch a replacement chip from one of the missile-control units. And on and on, hour after hour. They seemed far less interested—in fact, not interested at all—in how the *Despite* had blown the enemy flagship, than in her mistakes. The Board replayed surveillance material, pointed out discrepancies, lectured, and when it was over at last Esmay went out feeling as if she'd been boiled until all her bones dissolved in the soup.

Major Chapin, waiting in the anteroom where he'd watched on a video link, handed her a glass of water. "You probably don't believe this, but you did as well as you could, given the circumstances."

"I don't think so." She sipped the water. Major Chapin sat watching her until she had finished that glass.

"Lieutenant, I know you're tired and probably feel that you've been pulled sideways through a wire gauge, but you need to hear this. Boards of Inquiry are supposed to be grueling. That's part of their purpose. You stood up there and told the truth; you didn't get flustered; you didn't waffle; you didn't make excuses. Your handling of the nav computer failure was perfect—you gave them the facts and then dropped it. You let Timmy Warndstadt chew you up one side and down the other, and at the end you were still on your feet answering stupid questions in a civil tone of voice. I've worked with senior commanders who did worse."

"Really?" She wasn't sure if it was hope she felt, or simply astonishment that someone—anyone—could approve of something she did.

"Really. Not only that, remember what I told you at the beginning: you didn't lose your ship and you made a decisive move in the battle. They can't ignore that, even if they think it was blind accident. And after your testimony, they're much less likely to think it was accidental. I wish they'd asked more about the details; you were right not to volunteer it, since it would've sounded like making excuses, but . . . it annoys me when they ignore briefs. I put it all in; the least they could do is read it and ask the right questions. Of course there will be negative comments; there always are, if something gets as far as a Board. But they know—whether they're willing to admit it or not—that you did well for a junior in combat for the first time."

The door opened, and Esmay had to go back. She

returned to her place, facing the long table with the five officers.

"This is a complicated case," Admiral Warndstadt said. "And the Board has arrived at a complicated resolution. Lieutenant Suiza, this Board finds that your handling of the *Despite* from the time you assumed effective command after Dovir's wounds rendered him incapable of taking the bridge, to your . . . precipitous . . . return to Xavier, was within the standards expected of a Fleet captain." Esmay felt the first quiver of hope that she was not going to be tossed out on her ear, just before being imprisoned as the result of the court-martial.

Admiral Warndstadt went on, this time reading from notes. "However, your tactical decisions, when you returned to the Xavier system, were markedly substandard. This Board notes that this was your first experience of combat and your first time in command of a ship; the Board makes appropriate allowance for these circumstances. Still, the Board recommends that you not be considered for command of a Regular Space Service vessel until you have shown, in combat situations, the level of tactical and operational competence expected of warship commanders." Esmay almost nodded; as Chapin had warned her, and she already understood, they could not ignore her mistakes. Such Boards existed to point out to captains that luck, even great good luck, was no substitute for competence.

Warndstadt looked up at her again, this time with one corner of that lean mouth tucked up in what might almost be a smile. "On the other hand, the Board notes that your unorthodox maneuvers resulted in the defeat of an enemy vessel markedly superior in firepower and mass, and the successful defense of Xavier. You seem well aware of your shortcomings as commander of a ship in combat; the Board feels that your character and your deportment are both suitable for command positions in the future, as long as you get the requisite experience first. Few lieutenants junior grade command anything bigger than a shuttle anyway; the Board's recommendation should have the effect of giving you time to grow into your potential. Now—a complete transcript of the Board's recommendation will be forwarded to you and your counsel at a later date, should you wish to appeal."

She would be crazy to appeal; this was the best outcome she could have hoped for.

"Yes, sir," she said. "Thank you, sir." She got through the rest of the ritual, the dismissal of the Board and the necessary individual acknowledgement of each member, without being fully aware what she said. She wanted to fall into a bed and sleep for a month . . . but in three days, her court-martial would begin. In the meantime, she had to record her initial statements for the other courts-martial, including Commander Serrano's.

"Everything's unusual about this," Chapin said, as one who disapproved on principle of the unusual. "They had a time finding enough officers to sit on this many different boards and courts at once, and they're short of space, too. So they're shuffling people and spaces, and decided that since you're in such demand they can, after all, accept recorded testimony for some of it. With any luck, you won't actually have to appear in person in all of them . . . they certainly can't yank you out of yours just to answer two questions in some other jig's trial. It rushes you right now, but then your defense is simple anyway."

"It is?"

"In principle. Were you a conspirator, intending to commit a mutiny? No. Were you a traitor, in the pay of a foreign power? No. Simple. I expect they'll ask all the awkward questions they can think of, just so it looks good, and in case the original investigators forgot to check . . . but it's clear to me, and should be clear to them, that you were an ordinary junior officer who reacted to a developing situation—luckily, in the best interests of both Fleet and the Familias Regnant. The only problem I see . . ." He paused, and gave her a long look.

"Yes?" Esmay finally said, when waiting produced nothing but that steady stare.

"It's going to be difficult to present you as the ordinary

junior officer—although your fitness reports support that, putting you right square in the middle of your class—when you became the very unordinary youngest-ever captain to blow away a Benignity heavy cruiser. They're going to want to know why you were hiding that kind of ability . . . *how* you hid that kind of ability. Why were you denying Fleet the benefit of your talent?"

"That's what Admiral Serrano said." Esmay forced her shoulders back; she wanted to hunch into a little ball.

"And what did you say?"

"I . . . couldn't answer. I don't know. I didn't know I could do it until I did it, and I still find it hard to believe."

"Such modesty." Something in the tone chilled her. "I'm your defense counsel, and more than that I'm an attorney with many years of experience—I was in civil practice and Fleet reserves before I went full-time into Fleet. You may be able to fool yourself, young woman, but you don't fool me. You did what you did because you are unusually capable. Some of that capability showed up on the screening exams you took to get into Fleet in the first place—or had you forgotten your scores?"

She had; she had dismissed them as a fluke when her grades in the Fleet prep school came out only slightly above average.

"I'm now convinced," Chapin went on, "that you were not hiding your talents for any obvious reason—such as being a Benignity agent—but you were hiding them. You avoided command track as if it had thorns all over it. I pulled your file from prep school and talked to your instructors in the Academy too. They're all kicking themselves for not noticing, and nurturing, such an obvious talent for command—"

"But I made mistakes," Esmay said. She could not let this go on. She had been lucky, she had had outstanding senior NCOs who had done most of it . . . she rattled this off as fast as she could, while Chapin sat watching her with the same skeptical expression.

"It won't do," he said finally. "For your own good, Lieutenant Suiza—" He had not called her that from the first day; she stiffened. "For your own good," he repeated more softly. "You must face what you are; you must admit how much of what happened was your doing. Your decisions—good ones. Your ability to take charge, to get that performance from those you commanded. It was no accident. Whether the court dwells on this or not, you must. If you truly did not know what you were capable of—if you didn't know you were hiding your abilities— then you must figure out why. Otherwise the rest of your life will be one mess after another." As if she had spoken, his finger came up and leveled at her. "And no, you cannot go back to being just another ordinary junior officer, not after this. Whatever the court decides, reality has decided. You are special. People will expect more, and you'd better learn to handle that."

Esmay struggled to keep calm. One corner of her mind wondered why it was so hard to believe she was talented; most of it concentrated on the need for control.

The Board, technically considered an administrative and not a judicial procedure, had attracted no media attention, but the multiple courts martial of junior officers involved in a mutiny—and then in the successful defense of Xavier—was too juicy to miss. Fleet kept the defendants isolated as long as it could, but Chapin warned Esmay that politics demanded the courts be open to selected media coverage.

"Usually no one much cares about courts-martial," he said. "The rare one that has some publicity value is usually kept closed, on the grounds of military necessity. But this case—or rather, all your cases—are unique in Familias history. We've had to court-martial groups of officers before—the Trannvis Revolt, for instance—but we've never had to court-martial a group that had done something *good*. That has the newshounds baying for blood . . . not yours, yet, but any blood that happens to hit the ground. And in a situation this complex, someone's going to bleed."

Esmay grimaced. "I wish they wouldn't—"

"Of course. And I don't want you sitting over the screens keeping track of the media; it will only tie you in knots.

But you needed to know before you went in that there will be media there, and they'll try to get statements from you between sessions, even though they have been told you are forbidden to give them. Just don't say anything, anything at all, while you're going from the courtroom to the rooms where you'll be sequestered between sessions. I don't have to tell *you* to keep a composed face; you always do."

Despite the warning, the mass of video and audio pickups, the competing voices of the media interviewers, were like a blow to the face on her first trip between the defendants' suite and the courtroom.

"Lieutenant Suiza, is it true that you killed Captain Hearne yourself—?"

"Lieutenant Suiza, just a word about Commander Serrano, please—?"

"There she is—Lieutenant Suiza, how does it feel to be a hero?"

"Lieutenant Suiza, what will your family think about your being court-martialed—?"

She could feel her face settling into a stony mask, but behind that mask she felt helpless, terrified. A murderer? A hero? No, she was a very junior lieutenant who could happily have stayed in obscurity for decades yet. Her family's opinion of courts-martial . . . she didn't want to think about that. Mindful of the publicity problem, she had sent only the briefest message to them—and asked them not to reply. She didn't trust even Fleet ansibles to keep such messages secure under the pressure of every news service in the Familias.

Inside the courtroom, she faced another bank of media pickups. Even as she followed the ritual of the court, she could not fail to be aware that every word, every fleeting expression, would be broadcast across the worlds for all to see. Chapin, waiting at the defense table, muttered "Relax, Lieutenant; you look as if you were about to try the court and not the other way around."

All the cases were linked by the need for officers to testify about each other's behavior—because of the need to determine whether the mutiny resulted from a conspiracy. But Esmay, as the senior surviving officer, had been nominally charged with additional violations of the Code. Chapin had emphasized that the charges were required— that he expected a fairly quick dismissal of most of them, given that no evidence supported them. "Unfortunately," he'd said, "just because Hearne was a traitor doesn't mean that you mutineers are out of danger: if there's any evidence that there was a conspiracy to mutiny before there was clear evidence of Hearne's treachery, then that conspiracy, by itself, is cause for a guilty verdict on that charge."

But as far as Esmay knew, none of the subordinates not in the pay of the Compassionate Hand had suspected Hearne or the others. She certainly hadn't. Hearne had seemed a bit slapdash in some ways, but she was rumored to be brilliant in combat, and rumor also linked a mild disregard for "unnecessary" regulations with superior combat ability.

Now she found herself retelling the story of her assignment to *Despite* all over again. Her duties, her usual routine during time off-duty, her responsibilities to officers even more junior, her evaluation of her peers.

"And you had suspected nothing about Captain Hearne, Major Cossordi, Major Stek, or Lieutenant Arvad?"

"No, sir," Esmay said. She had said this before, about each one separately.

"And to your knowledge, no one else suspected that they were in the pay of the Benignity?"

"No, sir."

"Did you have a particular relationship with Dovir?" The idea was so ludicrous that Esmay nearly lost control of her expression.

"Dovir, sir? No, sir." Silence lengthened; she was tempted to explain Dovir's preferences in particular companions, and decided better not.

"And you never heard anything of a plot to mutiny against Captain Hearne?"

"No, sir."

"No grumbling of any sort, from officer or enlisted?"

That was a different matter. Grumbling filled ships as air did; people had grumbled about everything from the food to the shortage of gym slots; people always did. Esmay picked her words with care. "Sir, of course I heard people grumble; they do. But not more than on any other ship."

A huff of annoyance from one of the officers. "And you have so much experience on so many ships!" he said, dripping sarcasm.

Chapin stood up. "Objection."

"Sustained." The chairman gave the speaker a disapproving look. "You are aware of the standards, Thedrun."

"Sir."

The chair peered at Esmay. "Please discuss the nature of the grumbling, Lieutenant Suiza. This court is not sure that an inexperienced officer is fully aware of the amount of grumbling that is normal."

"Yes, sir." Esmay paused, dragging up from the depths of her memory a few instances. "When *Despite* was in the yards, before I joined her, the recreation area had been cut by about thirty percent, to allow retrofitting of the enhanced charged beam generator on the portside. That meant losing fifteen of the exercise machines; it would have been nineteen, but Captain Hearne approved a tighter spacing. However, this meant shortening the exercise periods, and some crew could not get their required exercise without getting up on their down shift. Some complained that Hearne should have relaxed the exercise requirements, or installed the other machines elsewhere."

"What else?"

"Well, there was apparently a sneak thief pilfering from enlisted lockers. That caused a lot of annoyance, because it should have been easy enough to catch, but the scanners never caught anything."

"They'd been tampered with?"

"Chief Bascome assumed so, but couldn't prove it. It went on for . . . perhaps twenty or thirty days . . . and then it never happened again. The items taken were rarely of great monetary value, but always personal treasures." Should she mention that they'd been found after the battle, in the cleanup phase, in the locker of someone killed? Yes; she had been taught that withholding information was the same as lying. "We found the things after the battle," she said. "But the person whose locker they were in had died in the original fight."

"The mutiny, you mean."

"Yes, sir. Under the circumstances, we just gave the stuff back to the owners—the surviving ones, that is."

A grunt from the chairman, which she could not interpret.

The trial went on, hour after tedious hour. Most of the time the questions made sense, examining what she had known, what she had witnessed, what she had done. Other times the court seemed determined to follow some useless thread of inquiry—like the kinds of grumbling she'd observed—into a thicket where they would lodge until one of them kicked free and returned to the main issues.

One of the side-issues turned nasty. The hectoring Thedrun had continued to ask his questions as if he was sure she was guilty of something dire. He began asking her about her responsibility in regard to supervising the ensigns. "Isn't it true, Lieutenant Suiza, that you were charged with ensuring that the ensigns carried out their duties and put in the required hours of study?"

"Sir, that duty rotated among the four senior lieutenants junior grade, under the supervision of Lieutenant Hangard. I was assigned that duty for the first thirty days after *Despite* left Sector HQ, then it devolved onto the next senior, Lieutenant Junior Grade Pelisandre for thirty days, and so on."

"But as the senior, you were ultimately responsible—?"

"No, sir. Lieutenant Hangard had made it clear that he wished the jig—sorry—"

"Never mind," the chairman said. "We do know what the word means."

"Well, then, Lieutenant Hangard wanted the jig in charge of the ensigns to report directly to him. He said we each needed to feel the responsibility alone for a short time." Where was this leading?

"Then you are not aware that Ensign Arphan was engaged in illegal diversion of military equipment?"

"What!" Esmay couldn't keep her voice from reacting to that. "Ensign *Arphan*? But he's—"

"Ensign Arphan," the chairman said, "has been convicted of diversion and illegal sale of military goods to unlicensed buyers—in this case, his father's shipping company."

"I . . . it's hard to believe," Esmay said. On second thought, she could believe it, but still . . . why hadn't she noticed? How had someone else found out?

"You haven't answered the question: were you or were you not aware that Ensign Arphan had illegally diverted military equipment?"

"No, sir, I was not aware of that."

"Very well. Now, about the mutiny itself—" Esmay wondered why they bothered to ask questions which the surveillance cubes had already answered. Hearne had attempted to destroy all the records of her conversation with Serrano, but the mutiny erupted before she could. So the court had seen the playbacks, from several angles . . . for Serrano had of course recorded Hearne's transmissions, and the transmissions agreed.

What seemed to worry the court most was the possibility that the junior officers had been plotting even before Hearne defied Serrano. Esmay repeated her earlier statements, and they picked them apart. How was it possible that she had not known Hearne was a traitor before? How was it possible that she had been party to a successful mutiny, if she had not been involved in some plan with the other mutineers ahead of time? Was it really that easy to produce a spontaneous mutiny?

By the end of the second day, Esmay wanted to bang heads. She found it hard to believe that a whole row of senior officers were so incapable of recognizing what lay in front of them—so insistent on finding something other than the plain, obvious truth. Hearne had been a traitor, along with a few others of the officers and some of the enlisted. No one had noticed because, up until the moment she defied Serrano, her actions had not been suspicious.

"You never had any suspicion that she was using illicit pharmaceuticals?" one of them asked for the third time.

"No, sir," Esmay said. She had said that before. Captain Hearne had never appeared under the influence, not that Esmay would have been able to recognize subtle effects of drugs . . . even if she'd seen that much of Hearne. Esmay had no way to know what she was taking. Nor had she investigated Hearne's cabin after the mutiny to find out. She had had a battle to fight.

More questions followed, on Hearne's motivation; Major Chapin cut those off repeatedly. Esmay was glad to sit and let him handle it; she felt stale and grumpy as well as tired. Of course she didn't know why Hearne might have turned traitor; of course she didn't know if Hearne had been in debt, had had political connections to a foreign government, had harbored some grievance against Fleet. How could she?

Her own motivations came into question; Esmay answered as calmly as she could. She had harbored no grievance against Captain Hearne, who had spoken to her only a few times. When Hearne's private log came into evidence, she found that Hearne had described Lieutenant Junior Grade Suiza as "competent but colorless; causes no trouble, but lacks initiative."

"Do you feel you lack initiative?" asked the board chair.

Esmay considered this. Were they hoping she'd say yes, or no? What hook did they plan to hang her on? "Sir, I'm sure Captain Hearne had reason to think that. It is my habit to be cautious, to be sure I understand the situation fully before stating an opinion. I was, therefore, not the first to offer solutions or suggestions when the captain posed a problem."

"You didn't resent her opinion?"

"No," Esmay said. "I thought she was right."

"And you were satisfied with that?"

"Sir, I was not satisfied with myself, but the captain's opinion seemed fair."

"I notice you use the past tense . . . do you still feel the captain's evaluation of you was accurate?"

"Objection," Chapin said quickly. "Lieutenant Suiza's present self-evaluation and its comparison to Captain Hearne's prior evaluation is not an issue."

At last it wound down . . . all the evidence given, all the questions asked and asked again, all the arguments made by opposing counsel. Esmay waited while the officers conferred; in the reverse of the Board procedures, she stayed in the courtroom while the members withdrew.

"Take a long breath," Chapin said. "You're looking pale again . . . but you did very well."

"It seemed so . . . so complicated."

"Well, if they let it look as simple as it is, they'd have no good reason for a trial, except that it's the regulations. With all the media coverage, they don't want to make it look easy; they want it to look as if they were thorough and demanding."

"Can you tell—?"

"How it will come out? If they don't acquit you of all charges, I'll be very surprised . . . they have the Board report; they know you've been chewed on about mistakes. And if they don't acquit, we'll appeal—that'll be easier, actually, out from under the media's many eyes. Besides, they found themselves a bad apple to squash, that young Arphan fellow."

The officers returned, and Esmay stood, heart beating so that she could scarcely breathe. What would it be?

"Lieutenant Junior Grade Esmay Suiza, it is the decision of this court that you are innocent of all charges made against you; this court has voted unanimously for acquittal. Congratulations, Lieutenant."

"Thank you, sir." She managed to stay on her feet during the final ceremonies, which again included greeting each officer on the court, and the prosecuting counsel, who—now that he wasn't badgering her with questions—seemed friendly and harmless.

"I knew we didn't have a chance," he said, shaking her hand. "It was obvious from the evidence, really, but we had to go through with it. Unless you'd come in here blind drunk and assaulted an admiral, you were safe enough."

"I didn't feel safe," Esmay said.

He laughed. "Then I did my job, Lieutenant. That's what I'm supposed to do, scare the defendant into admitting every scrap of guilt. You just didn't happen to have any." He turned to Chapin. "Fred, why do you always get the easy ones? The last fellow I had to defend was a mean-minded SOB who'd been blackmailing recruits."

"I'm rewarded for my virtues," Chapin said blandly, and they both laughed. Esmay didn't feel like joining in; she felt like finding a quiet place to sleep for a week.

"What'll you do now, Lieutenant?" asked one of the other officers.

"Take some leave," she said. "They said it'd be awhile before they had a new assignment for me, and I could have thirty days home leave plus travel. I haven't been home since I left." She wasn't that anxious to go home, but she knew no other way to escape the media attention.

CHAPTER FOUR

Altiplano

Esmay thought she had outdistanced the last of the newshounds two stops before her homeworld Altiplano. When she came out of the arrival lounge into the main concourse, the bright lights blinded her for a moment. They had figured out where she was going, of course. She set her jaw and kept going. They could have all they liked of her walking from one side of the station to another. They might even get someone on the down shuttle, but once she hit the dirt, they would find themselves blocked. That would be one good to come out of this misconceived homecoming.

"Lieutenant Suiza!" It took a long moment, several strides, for her to realize that one of the yells wasn't a newshound's demand for a comment, but her uncle Berthol. She looked around. He wore his dress uniform, and Esmay groaned inwardly, thinking ahead to the reaction of her Fleet acquaintances when they saw the newsclips of this. When he caught her eye, he quit waving and pulled himself rigid. Sighing, Esmay stopped short, bracing against the expected crunch from behind, and saluted. When her father had sent word that he could not meet her at the station, she'd assumed that meant no one would . . . she hadn't expected Berthol.

"Good to see you, Esmaya," he said now, opening a path between them with a glance that sent the newshounds scurrying out of the way.

"And you, sir," Esmay said, very conscious of the scrutiny of the cameras.

"God's teeth, Esmaya, I'm not a sir to you." But the twinkle in his eye approved of her formality. The stars on his shoulders glittered as the cameras shifted for better angles, their spotlights crisscrossing. Esmay had told Fleet that her father was one of four regional commanders . . . she had not reminded them what must be in her file, that her uncles Berthol and Gerard were two of the others. "I guess you didn't starve in Fleet, after all. You know Grandmother is still convinced you can find nothing legal to eat . . ."

Esmay found herself grinning even as she wished he hadn't brought that up. Grandmother was his grandmother, not hers—well over a hundred, and an influence as potent in her way as Papa Stefan in his. "I'm fine," she said, and turned, hoping to convince Berthol not to grandstand for the cameras.

"More than fine, Esmaya." He sobered, and touched her shoulder gently. "You give us pride. We are more than glad to have you home." Now he turned; his aides, she noticed now, had been scattered in the crowd and now came together at his back. The glaring lights receded behind them despite raised voices. "When we get down, we will celebrate."

Esmay's heart sank. What she really wanted was a quiet drive out to the estancia, and a room with windows open to the rose garden . . . and a full night's sleep, a night that fit her body's rhythms.

"We can't waste this," he said more quietly, as they walked straight past a departure lounge full of people she didn't know, who were giving her the soft tongue-clicking applause she remembered so well. Berthol ushered her into the waiting shuttle, and into the rear compartment which his aides closed off as they came through.

"What's going on?" Esmay asked. Tension curdled her stomach; she did not really want to know.

"What's going on . . . you'll be fully briefed later," Berthol said. "We didn't reserve a full shuttle—we thought it would be too obvious. Natural enough to have a private compartment. And there's no way out of the welcoming celebration, though I'm sure you're ready for a vacation at home, eh?"

Esmay nodded. She glanced around at Berthol's aides.

The militia ranks were not those of Fleet, exactly; the insignia, except for stars marking flag rank, were completely different. It came back to her in a rush. Infantry, armor, air, navy—what her Fleet called, somewhat disparagingly, "wet-fleet." All four branches here, all of them older than she was. The one wearing armor tags had an ear-wire, and now he turned to Berthol.

"General Suiza says it's all ready, sir."

"Your father," Berthol said. "He's in charge down there, for reasons that will become clear later. In the meantime, there'll be a formal ceremony at the shuttleport—blessedly brief, if I know your father—then a parade into town, and a formal presentation at the palace."

"Presentation?" Esmay squeezed that in when Berthol took a breath.

"Ah—" He seemed embarrassed a moment, then lowered his voice. "You see, Esmay, when it was your action that saved an entire planet, and then you don't even get a token of recognition from your Fleet . . ."

Dear God. Esmay scrambled through all the possible explanations she could make—that he would not understand—and realized it was no use. They had decided that *her* Fleet had not sufficiently honored her, and it would do no good to point out that her acquittal was itself acknowledgement and reward. Besides, she knew that someone had put in a recommendation for a medal—which made her skin itch to think of it. She wished they'd just forget it. But this—

"And it's not like you're just any shaggy pony out of the back lots," Berthol went on. "You're a Suiza. They're treating you—"

"Very well, Uncle Berthol," she said, hoping to stop him, if she couldn't stop the ceremony.

"No—I don't think so. Nor does the Long Table. They've voted to give you the Starmount—"

"No," Esmay breathed. She was uneasily aware that something deep inside disagreed, and breathed *yes*.

"And a title of your own. To be converted if you marry on Altiplano."

Dear God, she thought again. She didn't deserve this. It was ridiculous. It would cause . . . immense trouble either way. No matter that Fleet would not realize it had been intended as a rebuke—they would find it awkward, and that made her awkward.

"Not much of a steading with it," Berthol said. "In fact, your father said he'd provide that; it's that little valley where you used to hide out . . ."

Despite herself, Esmay felt a stab of pleasure at the memory of that little mountain valley, with its facing slopes of poplar and pine, its grassy meadows and clear stream. She had claimed it years before in her mind, but had never thought it would be hers. If it could be . . . she remembered some R.S.S. regulations she was afraid might interfere.

"Don't worry," Berthol said, as if he could read her mind. "It's under the limit—your father ran a new survey, and chopped it short at the upper end. It's under the glacier there. Anyway, if you need to refresh yourself on the protocol of the award ceremony . . ."

She did, of course. The data cube the major with the armor insignia handed her contained not only the ceremony, but a precis on recent political developments, and her family's position on all of them. The Minerals Development Commission was still squabbling with the Marine Biological Commission over control of benthic development. Some things never changed, but in the years she'd been gone the focus of the battle had shifted from the Seline Trench, as the colonies of interest to the biologists died, and were mined for their rich ores, to the Plaanid Trench, where new vents nourished new vent communities. That quarrel would have been unimportant on many worlds, but on Altiplano the Minerals Development Commission represented the Secularists, while Old Believers and the Lifehearts controlled the Marine Biological Commission. Which meant that an argument over exactly when a benthic vent community was dead and could be mined might erupt in religious riots around the entire planet.

"Sanni," Berthol said, when she had clicked off the cube reader, "is involved with the Lifehearts again."

Esmay remembered vividly the moment when her romantic feelings about the night sky became utter certainty that she would have to leave her home forever. Her aunt Sanni— Sanibel Aresha Livon Suiza—and her uncle Berthol, screaming at each other across the big dining room at the estancia. Sanni, a Lifeheart as rigid in her piety as any Old Believer. Esmay found the Lifeheart philosophy attractive, but Sanni in a rage terrified her. Yet it was Berthol who had thrown the priceless chocolate pot, shattering its painted water lilies and swans, scarring the wide polished table. Her own father had walked in on the end of that, with Sanni scrabbling on the floor for shards and Berthol still yelling. And Papa Stefan, two paces behind him, had shamed them both into apologies and hand-shakings.

Esmay hadn't believed it. Whatever was wrong between Sanni and Berthol stayed wrong, and was still wrong, and here she was back in the middle of it.

"It's not my problem now," she said. "I'm only here for a short leave—"

"She likes you," Berthol said. His gaze flicked to his aides, who were studiously ignoring this. "She says you're the one sane member of your generation, and now you're a hero."

Esmay felt herself reddening. "I'm not. All I did—"

"Esmay, this is *family*. You don't have to pretend. All you did, you babykin, was survive a mutiny, come out on top, and then defeat a warship twice your size."

Bigger than that, Esmay thought. She didn't say it; it would only make things worse. "It didn't know I was there until too late," she said.

"So you were smarter than its captain. Hero, Esmay. Get used to it. You're carrying our flag out there, Esmay, and you're doing very well."

She was not carrying *their* flag, but her own. They would not understand that, even if she dared say it to them. And Berthol sounded too much like Major Chapin, too much like Admiral Serrano. She had been a hero by accident— why wasn't it as obvious to the others as it was to her?

"And Sanni's very proud of you," Berthol went on. "She wants to talk to you—ask you all about Fleet, about your life. If you're meeting anyone eligible, if I know Sanni." He laughed, but it sounded forced.

She had left for a good reason. She should have stayed away. Yet at the thought of the whole family for once approving, for once seeing her as an asset rather than a very chancy proposition, her heart beat faster. The Starmount . . . when she'd been a little girl, she remembered the first soldier she'd seen awarded the Starmount, a lean, red-haired fellow who walked lopsided. She had stared and stared at the medal on its blue and silver ribbon that dangled around his neck until a disapproving grownup made her apologize and then quit following him. No one from Altiplano could be indifferent to the Starmount . . . and she didn't have to tell Fleet how she felt.

At the shuttlefield, the only media wore the green and scarlet uniforms of the Altiplano Central News Agency. No one tried to speak to her; no one tried to crowd close. She knew that her walk from the shuttle through the terminal to the waiting car would be only one clip in the finished story, narrated by a senior "analyst." No one would try to interview her; here that was considered rude and disrespectful.

Her father, backed by a wedge of other officers, gave her the same formal salute Berthol had; she returned it, and he gave her the semiformal hug and kisses, not fatherly, but from commander to junior about to be honored. She was introduced to his senior aide, to the next senior; she was led through a corridor where a solid block of militia provided complete privacy—in their terms, which meant from civilian eyes—for her few moments in the ladies' retiring room, where she found two tiring maids ready to apply fresh makeup and attempt to do something about her flyaway hair. That ended in a spritz of scented stuff which would leave her scalp itchy for two days—but this once, she didn't mind. In moments they had whisked off her R.S.S. uniform jacket, pressed it, and after a look at the shirt beneath, insisted on replacing it with a clean one from her luggage.

Refreshed, and to her surprise cheered by these ministrations, Esmay came back out, into the midst of a low-voiced argument between her father and her uncle.

"It's only one cloud," her uncle was saying. "And it might not rain—"

"It's only one bullet," her father said. "And it might miss. I'm not taking the chance. When her hair gets wet— Oh, there you are, Esmaya. There's a line of storms moving into the city; we're going to go by car—"

"It's not nearly as impressive," Berthol grumbled. "And it's not as if you expected her to do any *real* riding."

She had assumed by car; she'd forgotten that on Altiplano all ceremony involved horses. She thanked some unknown deity for the gift of a possible rainstorm and her father's distaste for the frizzy mess her hair became if it got damp. At least no one from Fleet was here, to make a joke about a backwoods military that still used horses.

Of course the parade still had horses, even though she was in a car. From the protection of the car, she watched the perfectly drilled cavalry swing into position before and behind, the horses moving in unison, their glossy haunches bunching and relaxing. The riders, their backs upright, hands quiet, faces set in a neutral expression that would not vary if a horse stood up on its hind legs . . . not that one of those well-trained animals would. Beyond the horses, a crowd on the sidewalks, faces peering from the windows of the taller buildings. Some of them waved the gold and red Altiplano colors.

She had not been home for just over ten standard years. She had left as a gawky teenager, who in memory seemed the very model of adolescent incapacity. Nothing had fit, not her body nor her mind nor her emotions. From not fitting at home to not fitting in the Fleet prep school had been a tiny, natural transition. By the time she had graduated from the Academy, she had expected to be the odd one out, the one whose reactions were not natural.

She had not realized how much those feelings had been due to age and then the real displacement of leaving her home world before her adult identity had solidified. Now, in the light of Altiplano's sun, with her body held by Altiplano's gravity, she began to relax, feeling at home in a way she had not since she was a little girl. The colors were *right* in a way they had not been for years; her very bones knew that this gravity, not one standard G, was the right gravity.

When she stepped out of the car, and walked up the red stone steps of the palace, her feet found the right intervals without effort. These steps were the right height, the right depth; this stone felt solid enough; this doorway welcomed; this air—she took another long breath—this air smelled right, and felt right all the way down to the bottom of her lungs.

She looked around at the people now crowding into the hall around her. Humans were humans, but the shapes of humans varied with their genome and the worlds they lived on. Here the bone structure looked familiar; these were the faces she had known all her life, prominent cheekbones and brows, long jutting chins, eyes set deeply under thick eyebrows. These long arms and legs, big bony hands and feet, boxy joints—these were her people, her look. Here she fit in, at least physically.

"Ezzmaya! S'oort semzz zalaas!" Esmay turned; her ears had already adapted to the Altiplano dialect, even in her family's less-obvious form, and she had no trouble understanding the welcome she'd just been given. She didn't immediately recognize the wizened old man in front of her, stiffly upright and wearing the brilliant braid of a former senior NCO, but her father's senior aide murmured into her earplug. Retired master sergeant Sebastian Coron . . . of course. He had been part of her life as far back in childhood as she could remember, always crisp and correct, but with a twinkle for his commander's elder daughter.

Her tongue, hearing the familiar speech, curled into the trills without her having to think of it. She thanked him for his congratulations in the formal phrases that brought a broader grin to his face. "And your family—your bodysons and heartdaughters? And don't I remember that you have grandlings now?"

Before he could answer, her father had extended his own

hand to Coron. "You can come visit later," her father said. "We need to get her upstairs—" Coron nodded, gave Esmay a stiff short bow, and stepped back. As her father led her away, he said "I hope you don't mind—he's so proud of you, you'd think he was your father. He wanted to come—"

"Of course I don't mind." She glanced up the green-carpeted stairs. She had always loved the stained glass window on the landing, that poured rich gold and blood-colored light onto the carpet. Palace guards in black and gold stood stiff as the banister rails, staring at nothing. As a child, she had wondered whether they would be so stiff if tickled, but she'd never had the chance . . . or the daring . . . to try it. Now she climbed past them, bemused by the mixture of memories and present feelings.

"And he wants to hear about it direct from you—at least some of it . . ."

"That's fine," said Esmay. She would rather tell old Coron than any of the fresh-faced young militia officers now surrounding them. Coron had taught her more of the basics than her father probably knew; she had pored over the handbooks on small-unit tactics under his watchful eye all one summer down in Varsimla.

"He does get a bit carried away," her father went on. "But he saved my skin often enough." He looked ahead to the upper hall, where a cluster of men in formal dress waited in a semicircle. "Ah . . . there we are. The Long Table advisors—did you have time in the car—?"

She had not, but that's what the earplugs were for. Most of them were men she had met before, in the way that the children of a household meet distinguished guests. She would not have remembered that Cockerall Mordanz was Advisor on Marine Resources, but she did remember that he'd once fallen off during a polo game and her uncle Berthol's pony had neatly jumped over him. The current Long Table Host, Ardry Castendas Garland, had once slipped coming into their dining room, and knocked over the little table with the hot towels on it; her great-grandmother had scolded her for staring.

"Esmay—Lieutenant Suiza!" the Host said now, catching

himself and returning to the formality appropriate to the ceremony. "It is an honor . . ." His voice trailed away, and Esmay allowed herself an interior smile. Altiplano lacked the right honorific for someone like her: female, a military officer, a hero. She felt conflicting impulses to help him out, and to let him stew in his problem: they, after all, had wanted to make her a hero. Let them come up with something. "My dear," he said finally. "I'm sorry, but I keep remembering the sweet child you were. It's hard to grasp what you've become."

Esmay could cheerfully have slapped him. Sweet child! She had been a sulky, awkward teenager, the successor to an awkward child . . . not sweet, but difficult and strange. And what she was now should be simple enough to grasp: a junior officer of the Regular Space Service.

"It's clear enough," said another man, one she didn't recognize. Opposition Leader, her earplug said. Orias Leandros. He smiled at her, but the smile was intended for the Host. He would make political profit of her . . . he thought.

"Host Garland," Esmay said quickly. She didn't like either of them, but she knew where her family duty lay. "You can be no more amazed at my present predicament than I am. My father tells me you plan an award—but, you must realize, you do me too much honor."

"Not at all," Garland said, back in balance again. He shot the briefest glare at his rival. "It's obvious that your family inheritance of military ability continues down the generations. No doubt your sons—" He stopped, trapped again in the assumptions of Altiplano and the usual phrases. What would have been a fine compliment to a man sounded almost indecent applied to a woman.

"It has been so long," Esmay said, changing the subject before Orias Leandros could say anything damaging. "Perhaps you would introduce me to the other advisors?"

"Of course." Garland was sweating a little. How had he ever been elected Host, when he was still as clumsy in word and deed as ever? But he got through the introductions well enough, and Esmay managed to smile with the right intensity at all the right people.

The award ceremony itself felt odd, because Esmay could not feel anything at all. She was too aware of the faint murmur of the earplug, coaching her through the required lines, of the expressions on the faces around her . . . the embarrassment she'd felt when first told of the award could not penetrate the concentration needed to do it right. The Starmount itself, a disk with the blue and black enamel representing a mountain against the sky, the little diamond glittering at the peak, aroused neither pride nor guilt. She bent her head to let the Host put the wide blue-and-gray ribbon around her neck; the medal felt lighter than she'd expected.

Then it was only a matter of standing in the line, saying the ritual greetings and thanks to those who filed past her: pleased, how kind, thank you, how lovely, how kind, thank you so much, very kind, how pleased . . . until the last of the line, a white-haired old lady related to Esmay's grandmother in some complicated way, had passed from her father to her, and from her to the Host. She had a few minutes to sip the tangy fruit juice and taste the pastries, then her father hurried her into the car again for the trip home.

She would like to have stayed longer; she was still hungry, and some of the faces that had blurred past had been friends once. She would have liked a chance to shop in town, to get herself some new clothes. But she had no more to say about it than when she'd been a schoolgirl. The general said it was time to leave, and they left. She tried not to resent it.

"Papa Stefan," her father said to her. "He didn't feel well enough to come in, but he had planned a family reception."

She could not imagine Papa Stefan anything but well; he had been white-haired even in her childhood, but vigorous, riding and working alongside his sons and grandchildren. Things had changed, then. She had known they would, eventually, but—it was hard to feel the same gravity, breathe the same air, recognize the same smells, and think of change. The buildings they drove past, the substantial stone blocks that housed stores and banks and offices, were the same she had always known.

Outside the city, the grasslands surged up to the mountains, as always. Esmay looked out the window, relaxing into that familiar view. The Black Teeth, between which dark spires lay the legendary lair of the Great Wyrm. As a child, she'd believed the dragon stories were about her own world; she had believed the lair was stuffed with dragon's treasure. She'd been bitterly disappointed to find out that the Great Wyrm was the code name of the rebel alliance that had (so legend went) massacred the original owner of Altiplano and all his family. A school field trip to the "lair" showed it to be a perfectly ordinary bunker built into the cliff on one side of a canyon.

South of the Black Teeth were other peaks of the Romilo Escarpment, lesser only by contrast to the Teeth. Esmay squinted across the kilometers of shimmering light, looking for the gap in the line, the grassy embayment of her family's estancia. There—the trees marked it out, the long lines of formal plantings along the road and the drives.

The car slowed, pulling off the road. Her father leaned closer. "I don't know if you still observe," he said. "But it's customary, when someone returns from a long journey . . . and anyway, I'm going to light a candle."

Esmay felt the heat rise to her face. Bad enough to forget, but to have her father suspect she'd forgotten was worse. "I, too," she said. She clambered out of the car, stiff and feeling even more awkward than stiffness would explain. She hadn't thought of the ceremonies since she left home; she wasn't sure she remembered the words.

The shrine, built into the estancia gate wall, had a row of fresh flower wreaths laid out below the niche. She could smell the faint sweet scent of the wreaths, and the stronger aroma of the great trees that loomed above. Even as an imaginative child, Esmay had never been able to see any meaning in the blurred shape of the statue in the niche. She had once been unwise enough to say it looked like a melted blob. She had never said it again, but she'd thought it often enough. Now, she saw with fresh eyes, and it still looked like a grayish, shiny melted blob, taller than it was wide. Around its base, the candle cups were clean as always, the little white candles in a box to one side.

Her father took one, set it in the green glass cup, and lit it. Esmay took another, lit it from her father's flame, and got it into a cup without burning her fingers. Her father said nothing, and neither did she; they stood side by side, watching the flames writhe in the breeze. Then he plucked a needle from one of the trees, and laid it in the flame. Blue smoke swirled up. Esmay remembered to stoop and find a pebble to lay in the wax of her candle.

Back in the car, with the windows now open to the steady breeze, her father still said nothing. Esmay leaned back, enjoying the many shades of green and gold. The drive, bordered with rows of narrow conifers, ran straight for a kilometer. On the right were the orchards, past blooming now. She could just see knots of green fruit on some limbs . . . on the far side, the first plums should be ripening. On the left, the family polo fields, mown in crisscross patterns . . . someone was out there, stooping, stamping divots back in. Nearer the house, flower gardens burst into riotous color. The car swept around the front, into the wide gravelled space large enough to review a mounted troop. It had been used for that, years back. A broad portico, shaded by tangled vines thick as trees at the root . . . two steps up to the wide double-door . . . home.

Not home now.

Nothing had changed . . . at least on the surface. Her room, with its narrow white bed, its shelves full of old books, its cube racks full of familiar cubes. Her old clothes had been removed, but by the time she came upstairs, someone had unpacked her luggage. She knew, without asking, what would be in each drawer. She undressed, hanging her uniform on the left end of the pole: it would be taken away and cleaned, returned to the right end of the pole. Presently the right end of the pole had two outfits she did not own—someone's suggestion of what to wear to the family dinner. She had to admit they looked more comfortable than anything she had bought off-planet. Down the familiar hall to the big square bathroom, with its two shower stalls and its vast tub . . . after shipboard accommodations, it seemed impossibly large. But just this once . . . she slid the door marker to "long bath" and grinned to herself. She did like long hot baths.

When she came downstairs, in the long cream-colored tunic over soft loose brown slacks, her father and step-mother were waiting. Her stepmother, born elegant, gave an approving nod, which for some reason made Esmay furious. No doubt she had chosen that tunic, had it put in Esmay's closet . . . for a moment Esmay thought of ripping it off and throwing it . . . but R.S.S. officers did not behave like that. And her half-brothers were watching, and others coming into the hall. She smiled at her step-mother, and shook the offered hand.

"Welcome home, Esmaya," her stepmother said. "I hope you will like dinner . . ."

"Of course she will," her father said.

Dinner was in the informal dining hall, its wide windows opening on a tiled courtyard with a pool . . . Esmay could hear the gentle splash of the fountain even over the murmur of voices, the scraping of feet on the tiled floor.

She started toward her old place out of habit, but someone sat there already—a cousin no doubt—and her father was leading her up the table, to sit at Papa Stefan's left hand. Great-grandmother was not at the table; she would be waiting to receive Esmay afterwards, in her own parlor.

"Here she is, at last," her father said.

Papa Stefan had aged; he was thinner, the skin looser over his bones. But his eyes were still sharp; his mouth, even as he smiled at her, still firm.

"Your father tells me you remembered the proper offering for return," he said. "Do you also remember the proper blessing of food?"

Esmay blinked. Once away from Altiplano, she had shed all concern about clean and unclean foods, blessings and

cursings, as happily as she'd shed the traditional under-
garments considered appropriate for a virtuous daughter.
She had not expected this honor . . . as much test as honor,
as everyone knew. Ordinarily only sons and sons of sons
asked blessings on the food at dinner; daughters and
daughters of daughters asked the morning grace at the
breaking of the night's fast, and at the noon meal everyone
held silence.

She looked down the table to see what was on the great
platters . . . it made a difference . . . and was even more
surprised to see the five platters that meant a whole calf
had been butchered in her honor.

She had never heard of a woman speaking at such a
time, but she knew the words.

"Back from the waste . . ." she began, and continued
through the whole, stumbling only momentarily over the
nested clauses where the prayer expected a male speaker
and she had either to speak of herself in the masculine
or change the words. "From father to son it came to me,
and so I send it on . . ." She had not thought about her
own culture in any detailed way after the first year or so
in the Fleet prep schools; she had not noticed how
confining the language really was. Fleet had shocked her
at first, with its assumption of easy relationships between
the sexes, with "sir" used for both men and women. In
Fleet, the important terms for parents distinguished
between gene-parents and life-parents, not between
mothers and fathers. On Altiplano, they had no word for
"parents," and while they knew of modern methods of
reproduction, very few would ever use them.

She finished the blessing, still thinking of the differences,
and Papa Stefan sighed. Esmay glanced at him; his eyes
twinkled.

"You didn't forget . . . you always had a good memory,
Esmaya." He nodded. The servants stepped forward; the
great platters were shifted to the sideboards for carving,
while bowls of soup were offered.

Fleet food had been good enough, but this was the food
of her childhood. The thick blue bowl with the creamy

corn soup, garnished with green and red . . . Esmay's stomach rumbled at the familiar aroma. The spoon she lifted had her family's crest on it; it fit her fingers as if it had grown there.

The first salad followed the corn soup, and by then the meat had been sliced and layered on blue platters swirled with white. Esmay accepted three slices, a mound of the little yellow potatoes that were a family specialty, a scoopful of carrots. It was worth the long wait to have food like this.

Around her, the family carried on soft-voiced conversations; she didn't listen. Right now all she wanted was the food, the food she had not let herself realize she missed. Puffy rolls that could have floated up into the sky as clouds . . . butter molded into the shapes of heraldic beasts. She remembered those molds, hanging in a row in the kitchen. She remembered the rolls, too—no use letting them get cold, when they were dry and tasteless. They deserved to be soaked in new butter or drenched in honey.

When she came up for air, no one seemed to be paying attention to her anyway. They had finished eating; servants were taking the plates away.

"It's a matter of pride," Papa Stefan was saying to her cousin Luci. "Esmaya would not fail in anything that touched the family honor." Esmay blinked; Papa Stefan's notion of family honor had wildernesses no one had ever explored fully. She hoped he wasn't hatching up one of his plots with her assigned the role of heroine.

Luci, the age Esmay had been when she left, looked much as Esmay remembered herself. Tall, gangling, soft brown hair pulled back severely, with escaping wisps that ruined the intended effect, clothes that were obviously intended for a special occasion, but looked rumpled and dowdy instead. Luci looked up, met Esmay's eyes, and flushed. That made her look sulky as well as unkempt.

"Hi, Luci," Esmay said. She had already greeted Papa Stefan and the elders; the cousins were far down the list of obligatory greetings. She wanted to say something helpful, but after ten years she had no idea what Luci's enthusiasms were—and a very clear memory of how embarrassing it was when elders assumed you still liked the dolls you'd played with at five or seven.

Papa Stefan grinned at her and patted Luci's arm. "Esmaya, you will not know that Luci is the best polo player in her class."

"I'm not that good," Luci muttered. Her ears looked even redder.

"You probably are," Esmay said. "I'm sure you're better than I am." She had never seen the point of milling about chasing a ball on horseback. A horse was mobility, a way to get off by herself, into places vehicles couldn't go, faster than anyone could follow on foot. "Are you playing on the school team, or the family team?"

"Both," Papa Stefan said. "We're looking for championships this year."

"If we're lucky," Luci said. "And speaking of that, I wanted to ask about that mare Olin showed me."

"Ask Esmay. Her father bought a string for her to put out on the grant, and that mare was one of them."

A flash of anger from Luci's eyes; Esmay was startled both by the gift of horses, and her cousin's unexpected reaction.

"I didn't know about that," Esmay said. "He hadn't mentioned anything." She looked at Luci. "If there's one you wanted in particular, I'm sure—"

"Never mind," Luci said, standing up. "I wouldn't want to deprive the returning hero of her loot." She tried to say it lightly, but the underlying bitterness cut through.

"Luci!" Papa Stefan glared, but Luci was already out the door. She didn't reappear that evening. No one commented, but they were already drifting from the table . . . she remembered from her own adolescence that such a thing would not be spoken of in company. She did not envy Luci the rough side of Sanni's tongue that would no doubt work her over in private very shortly.

CHAPTER FIVE

After dinner, Esmay went to the private apartment where her great-grandmother waited. Ten years ago, the old lady had still lived apart, refusing to inhabit the main house because of some quarrel that no one would explain. Esmay had tried to wheedle it out of her, unsuccessfully. She had not been the kind of great-grandmother who encouraged the sharing of secrets; Esmay had been scared of her, of the sharp glance that could silence even Papa Stefan. Ten years had thinned the silver hair, and dimmed the once-bright eyes.

"Welcome, Esmaya." The voice was unchanged, the voice of a matriarch who expected reverence from all her kin. "Are you well?"

"Yes, of course."

"And they feed you decently?"

"Yes . . . but I was glad to taste our food again."

"Of course. The stomach cannot be easy when the heart is uncertain." Great-grandmother belonged to the last generation which adhered almost universally to the old prohibitions and requirements. Immigrants and trade, the usual means of fraying the edges of cultures, had brought changes that seemed great to her, though to Esmay hardly significant compared to Altiplano's difference from the cosmopolitan casualness of Fleet. "I do not approve of your gallivanting around the galaxy, but you have brought us honor, and for that I am pleased."

"Thank you," Esmay said.

"Considering your disadvantages, you have done very well."

Disadvantages? What disadvantages? Esmay wondered if the old woman's mind was slipping a bit after all.

"I suppose it means your father was right, though I am loathe to agree, even now."

Esmay had no idea what Great-grandmother was talking about. The old lady changed topics abruptly, as she always had. "I hope you will choose to remain, Esmay. Your father has chosen for you the reward of bloodstock and land; you would not be as a beggar among us—" That was a dig; she had complained, just before she left, that she had nothing of her own, that she might as well be a poor beggar living here on sufferance. Great-grandmother's memory had not slipped at all.

"I had hoped you might forget those rash words," she said. "I was very young."

"But not untruthful, Esmaya; the young speak the truth they see, however limited it is, and you were always a truthful child." That had some emphasis she could not interpret. "You saw no future here; you saw it among the stars. Now that you have seen them, I hope you can find one here."

"I . . . have been happy there," Esmay said.

"You could be happy here," the old lady said, shifting in her robe. "It is not the same; you are an adult, and a hero."

Esmay did not want to distress her, but across the impulse to comfort came the same impulse to honesty which had led to that earlier confrontation. "This is my home," she said, "but I don't think I can stay here. Not always . . . not for ever."

"Your father was an idiot," her great-grandmother said, on the trail of some other thought. "Now go away and let me rest. No, I'm not angry. I love you dearly, as I always did, and when you go I will miss you extremely. Come back tomorrow."

"Yes, Great-grandmother," said Esmay meekly.

Later that evening, in the great library, she found herself comfortably ensconced in a vast leather chair, with her father, Berthol, and Papa Stefan. They started with the questions she'd expected, about her experiences in Fleet. To her surprise, she found herself enjoying it . . . they asked intelligent questions, applied their own military experience to the answer. She found herself relaxing, talking about things she had never expected to discuss with her male relatives.

"That reminds me," she said finally, after explaining how Fleet handled the investigation of the mutiny. "Someone told me that Altiplano has a reputation for being Ageist—opposed to rejuvenation. That's not so, is it?"

Her father and uncle looked at each other, then her father spoke. "Not exactly against rejuvenation, Esmaya. But . . . many people here see it as bringing more problems to us than it could solve."

"I suppose you mean population growth . . ."

"Partly. Altiplano's primarily an agricultural economy, as you know. Not only is this world suited to it, but we have all those Lifehearts and Old Believers. We attract immigrants who want to live on the land. Rapid population growth—or slow growth long continued—would start encroaching on the land. But—consider what it means to a military organization, for a start."

"Your most experienced personnel wouldn't get too old for service," Esmay said. "You . . . Uncle Berthol . . ."

"Generals are two a credit . . . but of course, the most experienced you have—the fellow who can always cobble up a repair for your landcruiser or your artillery—will stay useful and perhaps even pick up more expertise. Experience counts, and with rejuvenation you can accumulate more experience to learn from. That's the positive. The negative?"

Esmay felt that she was back in school, being forced to perform in front of the class. "Longer lives for the seniors mean fewer slots for juniors to be promoted into," she said. "It would slow down career advancement."

"It would stop it in its tracks," her father said soberly.

"I don't see why."

"Because it's repeatable now. The rejuvenated general—to start at the top—will be there forever. Oh, there'll still be some slots for promotion—someone will die of an accident, or in a war. But that's not many. Your Fleet will become the weapon of an expansionist Familias Regnant empire—"

"No!"

"It has to, Esmay. If rejuvenation gets going—"

"It's already widespread; we know that," Papa Stefan said. "They've had the new procedure forty years or more now, and they've tried it on a lot of people. Remember your biology classes, girl: if the population expands, it must find new resources or die. Changes in population are governed by birth rate and death rate: lower the death rate, as rejuvenation does, and you've got an increase in population.

"But the Familias isn't expansionist."

"Huh." Berthol snorted and hitched himself sideways in his chair. "The Familias didn't announce a grand campaign, no, but if you look at the borders, these last thirty years . . . a nibble here, a nibble there. The terraforming and colonization of planets which had been written off as unsuitable. Peaceful, cooperative annexation of half a dozen little systems."

"They asked for Fleet protection," Esmay said.

"So they did." Her father gave Berthol a glance that said *Be quiet* as clearly as words. "But our point is, that if the population of Familias worlds continues to increase, because the old are being rejuvenated—and if the population of Fleet continues to increase for the same reason—then this pressure can move them toward expanding."

"I don't think they will," Esmay said.

"Why do you think your captain went over to the Black Scratch?"

Esmay squirmed. "I don't know. Money? Power?"

"Rejuvenation?" her father asked. "A long life and prosperity? Because, you know, a long life *is* prosperity."

"I don't see that," Esmay said, thinking of her great-grandmother, whose long life was now coming to an end.

"A long *young* life. You see, that's the other thing that bothers me about rejuvenation. Longevity rewards prudence above all . . . if you live long enough, and are prudent, you will prosper. All you have to do is avoid risk."

Esmay thought she saw where he was going, but preferred not to risk charging ahead. Not with this canny old soldier. "So?" she asked.

"So . . . prudence is not high on the list of military virtues. It is one, sure enough, but . . . where are you going to get soldiers who will risk their lives, if avoidance of risk can confer immortality? Not the immortality of the Believers, who expect to get it after they die, but immortality in this life."

"Rejuvenation may work in a civilian society," Berthol said. "But we think it can cause nothing but trouble in the military. Even if you could retain all your best experienced men, you would soon be out of the routine of training recruits—and the population you served would be out of the routine of providing them.

"Which means," he went on, "that a military organization with anything but mud between the ears is going to see that it must limit the use of rejuvenation . . . or plan on a constant expansion. And at some point it's going to run into a culture of younglings, a culture which doesn't use rejuvenation, and is bolder, more aggressive." He had never been able to resist belaboring a point.

"It sounds like the old argument between the religious and the nonreligious," Esmay said. "If immortality of the soul is real, then what matters most is the prudent life, to make sure the soul qualifies for immortality . . ."

"Yes, but all the religions we know of which offer that prize also define such prudence in more stringent terms. They require active virtues which discipline the believer and curtail his or her selfishness. Some even demand the opposite of prudence—recklessness of life in the service of their deity. This makes good soldiers; it's why religious wars are so much harder to end than others."

"And here," Esmay said, to preempt Berthol, "you see rejuvenation rewarding—encouraging—merely practical prudence, pure selfishness?"

"Yes." Her father frowned. "There will no doubt be good people rejuvenated . . ." Esmay noted the assumption that good people would not be selfish. It was a curious assumption for a man who was himself rich and powerful . . . but of course he didn't define himself as selfish. He had never had to be selfish, in his own terms, to have his least wish satisfied. "But even they will, over several rejuvenations, realize how much more good they can do alive, in control of their assets, than dead. It's easy to lie to yourself, to convince yourself that you can do more good with more power." He was staring blankly at the books; was this self-assessment?

"And that's not even considering the dependency created by reliance on rejuvenation," Berthol said. "Unless you have control of the process, adulteration—"

"As happened recently—" her father said.

"I can see that," Esmay said, cutting off the obvious; she was not in the mood for a longer lecture from Berthol.

"Good," said her father. "So when they offer you rejuvenation, Esmaya, what will you do?"

For that she had no answer; she had never even considered the question before. Her father shifted the topic to a reprise of the ceremony, and soon she excused herself and went to bed.

The next morning, waking in her own bed in her own room, with sunlight bright on the walls, she was surprised by a sense of peace. She had suffered enough bad dreams in this bed; she had been half-afraid the nightmares would recur. Perhaps coming home had completed some sort of necessary ritual, and they were forever banished.

With that thought, she hurried down to breakfast, where her stepmother offered the morning grace, and then out into the cool gold of a spring morning. Past the kitchen gardens, the chicken runs where every hen seemed to be clucking her readiness to lay eggs, and every rooster crowed defiance at the others. She had heard them faintly through her window on the front side of the house; here they were deafening, so that she was not tempted to slow and look at them.

The great stables smelled as always of horses and oats and hay, pungencies that Esmay found comforting after all these years. There had been a time when she resented them, back when she, like all the children, had been expected to muck out her own pony's stall. Unlike some of the others, she had never enjoyed riding enough to make the work worthwhile. Later, when a horse became her escape route into the mountains, she was old enough that she no longer had the daily chores to do anyway.

Now she walked down the stone-flagged aisle, the great arches opening to her left into one of the exercise yards. On her right, rows of stalls with the dark narrow heads of horses peering out. A groom came out of a tackroom at the sound of her steps.

"Yes, dama?" He looked confused; Esmay identified herself and his face relaxed.

"I was wondering—my cousin Luci mentioned a mare she'd looked at—that Olin showed her—?"

"Ah—the Vasecsi daughter. Down here, dama, if you'll follow me. Excellent bloodlines, that one, and has done very well in training so far. That is why the General chose her for your foundation herd."

Outside the mare's stall, a twist of blue and silver; Esmay looked down the row and saw more such twists. This was her herd, picked by her father, and although she could exchange them, it would shame him. But to make a gift of one mare, to Luci—that would be acceptable. She hoped.

"Here, dama." The mare had her rump to the door, but when the groom clucked she swung round. Esmay recognized the qualities for which her father had chosen the horse: the good legs and feet, the depth of heart-girth, the strong back and hindquarters, the long limber neck and well-bred head. Solid dark brown, just lighter than black— "You would like to see her move?" the groom said, reaching for the halter that hung beside the stall.

"Yes, thank you," Esmay said. She might as well. The groom led the mare out of the stall, across the aisle, and out into the courtyard. There, in the open ring, the groom put the mare through her paces, which accorded with her conformation. A long, low walk, a sweeping trot and long level canter. This was a horse to cover the ground, mile after mile, and yet she would be handy as well. A good mare. If only Esmay cared particularly—

"I'm sorry I was rude," Luci said, from the arches. Her face was in shadow; her voice sounded as if she'd been crying. "She's a lovely mare, and you deserve her."

Esmay walked nearer; Luci had been crying. "Not really," she said quietly. "I'm sure you heard all about my regrettable attitude towards horses back when I left."

"I inherited your trail horse," Luci said without answering the comment. She said it as if Esmay might be angry about it. Esmay had not thought about old—Red, had that been his name?—in years.

"Good," Esmay said.

"You don't mind?" Luci sounded surprised.

"Why should I mind? I left home; I couldn't expect the horse to go unused."

"They didn't let anyone ride him for a year," Luci said.

"So they thought I might flunk out and come back?" Esmay said. It didn't surprise her, but she was glad she hadn't known that.

"Of course not," Luci said, too quickly. "It's just—"

"Of course they did," Esmay said. "But I didn't fail, and I didn't come back. I'm glad you got that horse . . . you seem to have inherited the family gift."

"I can't believe you really haven't—"

"I can't believe anyone really wants to stay on one planet," Esmay said. "Even when it feels right."

"But it's not crowded," Luci said, flinging out one arm. "There's so much *space* . . . you can ride for hours . . ."

Esmay felt the familiar tension in her shoulders. Yes, she could ride for hours and never come to a border she need worry about . . . but she could not eat a meal without wondering if some old family grievance were about to explode. She turned to Luci, whose eyes kept following the mare.

"Luci, would you do me a favor?"

"I suppose." No eagerness, but why would there be?

"Take the mare." Esmay almost laughed at the shock

on Luci's face. She repeated it. "Take the mare. You want her. I don't. I'll square it with Papa Stefan, and with Father."

"I—I can't." But naked desire glowed from her face, a wild happiness afraid to admit itself.

"You can. If that's my mare, I can do what I want with her, and what I want to do is give her away, because I'm going back to Fleet . . . and that mare deserves an owner who will train her, ride her, breed her." An owner who cared about her; every living thing deserved to be cared about.

"But your herd—"

Esmay shook her head. "I don't need a herd. It's enough to know I have my little valley to come home to . . . what would I do with a herd?"

"You're serious." Luci was sober again, beginning to believe it would happen, that Esmay was serious, and that different.

"I'm serious. She's yours. Play polo on her, race her, breed her, whatever . . . she's yours. Not mine."

"I don't understand you . . . but . . . I do want her." Shy, sounding younger than she was.

"Of course you do," Esmay said, and felt a century older, at least. Embarrassment hit then—had she seemed this young to Commander Serrano, to everyone who had a decade or more on her? Probably. "Listen—let's go for a ride. I'll need to get back in shape if I'm going to visit the valley." She couldn't yet say "my valley" even to Luci.

"You could ride her—if you wanted," Luci said. Esmay could hear the struggle in her voice; she was trying hard to be fair, to return generosity for generosity.

"Heavens, no. I need one of the school horses, something solid and dependable . . . I don't get any riding in Fleet."

Grooms tacked up the horses, and they rode out toward the front fields, between the rows of fruit trees. Esmay watched Luci on the mare . . . Luci rode as if her spine were rooted into the horse's spine, as if they were one being. Esmay, on a stolid gelding with gray around its eyes and muzzle, felt her hip joints creaking as she trotted. But what was her father going to say? Surely he had not expected her to manage a herd from light-years away? Had he expected to manage them for her? As Luci cantered the mare in circles around Esmay, she decided to go the whole way.

"Luci—what are you planning to do?"

"Win a championship," said Luci, grinning. "With this mare—"

"In the long run," Esmay said. "Strategy, cousin."

"Oh." Luci halted the mare, and sat silently a moment, obviously wondering how much to tell her older cousin. *Is she safe* was written on her face as if with a marker.

"I have a reason for asking," Esmay said.

"Well . . . I was going to try for the vet course at the Poly, though Mother wants me to study 'something more appropriate' at the University. I know there's no chance of getting on the estate staff here, but if I qualified, I might somewhere else."

"I suspected as much." Esmay meant it benignly, but Luci flared up.

"I'm not just dreaming—"

"I know that. Get the hump out of your back. You're serious, just as I was serious . . . and nobody believed me, either. That's why I had the idea—"

"What idea?"

Esmay nudged her horse, and it ambled over to Luci's mare. The mare twitched her ears but otherwise stood still. Esmay lowered her voice. "As you know, my father gave me a herd. The last thing I need is a herd, but if I try to give it back, he'll be hurt and I'll hear about it forever."

Luci's face relaxed; she almost grinned. "So?"

"So I need someone to manage my herd. Someone who will make sure that the mares go to the right stallions . . . that the foals get the right training, and are actually put on the market—" Family horses almost never went to market. "—And so forth," Esmay said. "I would expect to compensate the manager, of course. The eye of the master fattens the herd . . . and I will be far away, for a very long time."

"You're thinking of me?" Luci breathed. "It's too much—the mare, and—"

"I like the way you handle her," Esmay said. "It's how I'd want my horses handled, if I wanted horses at all . . . and since I have them, that's what I'd like. You could save up the money for school—I know from experience that it impresses them if you fund your own escape. And you'd get the experience."

"I'll do it," Luci said, grinning. Despite herself, Esmay thought back to the previous night's conversation. Here was someone for whom prudence could never swamp enthusiasm.

"You didn't ask what I'm paying," Esmay said. "You should always find that out first . . . what it's going to cost, and what you're going to get."

"It doesn't matter," Luci said. "It's the chance—"

"It matters," Esmay said, and surprised herself with the harshness of her voice; the horse under her shifted uneasily. "Chances aren't what they seem." Then, at the look on Luci's face, she stopped herself. Why was she being negative, when she had just been admiring Luci's impetuosity? "Sorry. Here's what I want from you—a fair accounting of costs and income. Midsummer—that should give you time to write it up after the foal crop arrives."

"But how much—" Now Luci looked worried.

"You didn't ask before. I'll decide later. Maybe tomorrow." Esmay nudged her mount, and started off toward the distant line of trees beyond the canter track; her cousin followed.

She had forgotten about the old man at the reception until a servant announced him after lunch, when she had lingered in the kitchen over a second piece of rednut pie smothered in real cream.

"Retired soldier Sebastian Coron, dama, requests a few moments of your time."

Seb Coron . . . of course she would see him. She wiped the last of the pie from her mouth, and went out to the hall, where he stood at ease, watching one of the younger cousins practice the piano with Sanni standing by, counting the time.

"Reminds me of you, Esmay," he said when she came forward to shake his hand.

"It reminds me of hours of misery," Esmay said, smiling. "The untalented and unrhythmic should never be forced to go beyond learning a few scales . . . once we've admitted how hard it is, we should be let off."

"Well, you know, it's in the old law." It was, though Esmay had never understood why every child, with or without ability or interest, should be forced through ten years of musical training on a minimum of four instruments. They didn't make all children learn soldiering.

"Come on in the sitting room," Esmay said, leading him to the front room where women of the family usually received guests. Her stepmother had redone it again, but the bright floral-patterned covers on the chairs and long padded benches were in a traditional print. This one had more orange and yellow, and less red and pink, than Esmay remembered. "Would you like tea? Or something to drink?" Without waiting for an answer, she rang; she knew that with his arrival the kitchen staff would have started preparing the tray with his favorites, whatever they were.

She settled him in one of the wide low chairs, with the tray at his side, and herself chose a seat to his left, the heart-side, to show her awareness of the family bond.

Old Sebastian twinkled at her. "You have done us proud," he said. "And it's all over for you, the bad times, eh?"

Esmay blinked. How could he think that, when she was still in Fleet? She had to expect other combat in the future; surely he realized that. Perhaps he meant the recent trouble.

"I certainly hope I never have to go through a court-martial again," she said. "Or the mutiny that led to it."

"You did well, though. That's not exactly what I meant, though I'm sure it was unpleasant enough. But no more old nightmares?"

Esmay stiffened. How did he know about her nightmares? Had her father confided to this man? She certainly wasn't about to tell him about them. "I'm doing all right," she said.

"Good," he said. He picked up his glass, and sipped. "Ah, this is good. You know, even when I was still active, your father never stinted the good stuff when I came here. Of course, we both understood it was special, not something to be talked about."

"What?" Esmay said, without much curiosity.

"Your father, he didn't want me to talk about it, and I could see his point. You'd had that fever, and nearly died. He wasn't sure what you remembered, and what was the fever dreams."

Esmay fought her body to stillness. She wanted to shiver; she wanted to gag; she wanted to run away. She had done all those, in past times, without success. "It was the dreams," she said. "Just the fever, they said, something I'd caught when I ran away." She managed a dry laugh. "I can't even remember where I thought I was going, let alone where I got to." She did remember a nightmare train ride, fragments of something else she tried not to think about.

She did not know what tiny movement—a flicker of eyelid, a tension in the muscles along his jaw—but she *knew* at once that he knew something. Knew something that she did not, which he longed to convey and felt he must conceal. Her scalp prickled. Did she want to know, and if she did, could she get him to tell her?

"Well, you went to find your father . . . that was simple. Your mother had died, and you wanted him, and he was right there in the midst of a nasty little territorial dispute. That was when the Borlist branch of the Old Believers had decided to pull out of the regional planning web, and take over the upper rift valley."

Esmay knew about that miscalled dispute: the Califer Uprising had been a civil war, small but intense.

"No one realized you could read that well, let alone that you could read a map . . . you hopped on your pony, with a week's food, and set off—"

"On a *pony*?" She could hardly imagine that; she had

never liked riding that much. She'd have expected her young self to sneak a ride on a truck bound for town.

Seb looked embarrassed—she couldn't imagine why—and scratched at his neck. "Back then you rode like a tick on a cowdog, and just as happy. You were hardly ever off your pony, until your mother died, and they were happy enough to see you back on it. Until you disappeared."

She couldn't remember that—couldn't remember a time when she would have chosen to spend all those hours on a horse. What she remembered was how much she hated it, the lessons and the sore muscles and all the work of picking out hoofs and grooming and mucking out a stall. Could this be true, that an illness had wiped out not only her pleasure in horses, but all memory of a time when she had enjoyed them?

"I guess you'd planned pretty well," he went on, "because they couldn't pick up your traces anywhere. No one thought of what you'd really done; they thought you'd gotten lost, or gone up in the mountains and had an accident. And no one ever knew the whole story, because you didn't make a lot of sense when we found you."

"The fever," said Esmay. She was sweating now; she could feel it, like a sick slime all over.

"That's what your father said." Sebastian had said it before; now his voice echoed with her memory, and her new adult ability to interpret nuances of expression compared the two versions and found hidden disbelief.

"My father said . . . ?" Esmay said, carefully neutral, not looking at his face. Not directly, anyway; she could see the pulse in his throat.

"You'd forgotten it all, with the fever, and all for the better, he said. Don't bring it up, he said. Well, I guess you know by now it wasn't *all* a dream . . . I suppose those Fleet psychnannies dug it out and helped you deal with it, eh?"

She was frozen; she was simmering in her own terror. Cold and hot at once, closer than she wanted to some terrible truth, and yet not able to move away. She could feel his gaze on her head, and knew if she looked up she would not be able to hide her terror and confusion. Instead, she busied her hands among the little dishes of breads and condiments, pouring the tea, handing over a delicate cup and saucer with the spray-pattern touched with silver . . . she could hardly believe her hands were so steady.

"Not that I could have argued with your father, of course. Under the circumstances."

Under the circumstances Esmay could cheerfully have wrung his neck, but she knew that wouldn't work.

"It was not only my duty to him as my commander, but . . . he was your father. He knew best. Only I did wonder sometimes if you remembered something from *before* the fever. If perhaps that was what changed you . . . ."

"Well, my mother had died." Esmay got that out past her tight throat. Her voice, too, was steady as her hands. How could that be, with terror shaking the roots of her mind? "And I was sick so long—"

"If you'd been my daughter, I think I'd have told you. It helps the trainees to talk things through after a bad engagement."

"My father thought differently," Esmay said. Dust was no dryer than her mouth; she felt drought-cracks opening in her mind, bottomless mouths to trap her . . .

"Yes. Well, anyway, I'm glad you had the chance to deal with it in the end. But it must've been hard when you had that traitor captain to deal with, that second betrayal—" The almost musing tone of his voice sharpened. "Esmaya! Is something wrong? I'm sorry, I didn't mean—"

"It would be most helpful if you could simply tell me the story from your point of view," Esmay managed to say; her voice was thickening now, the dust compressing into angular blocks of rock-hard clay. "Remember, I had only my own somewhat fragmentary memories to go on, and the psychnannies found them somewhat inadequate." The psychnannies would have found them inadequate, if they'd found them at all, but they hadn't. They had assumed that anyone with her background would have had any such problems dealt with earlier. And she, convinced by her family's insistence that everything in the nightmares was just fever dreams, had been afraid to let them know she had problems. She'd been afraid of being labeled crazy or unstable, unfit for duty . . . rejected, to come home a failure. Was this why her family had assumed she'd fail, even to the point of keeping her trail horse unassigned?

"Perhaps you should ask your father," Coron said doubtfully.

"I suspect he would be displeased at having his judgment questioned," Esmay said with all sincerity. "Even by the Fleet's psychiatric specialists." Coron nodded. "It would be a help, if you wouldn't mind."

"If you're sure," Coron said. She had to meet his eyes a moment; she had to endure the worry in them, the tightness of the lines around his eyes, the furrowed brow. "It's not a pleasant matter—but of course you know that already."

Nausea bucked in her gut, sending sour signals to her mouth. *Not yet,* she begged it. *Not until I know.* "I'm sure," she said.

It had been a time of riot and civil disorder, when a single small child, if determined and sure of herself, could travel by pony and then by rail some thousand kilometers. "You'd always been good at explaining yourself," Coron said. "You could come up with a story the moment you were caught out. I suppose that's why no one really noticed you—you spun some yarn about being sent to an auntie or grandmother, and since you didn't act scared or confused, and you had enough money, they let you on the trains."

All this was supposition; they had not been able to trace her path between the time she left the pony—they never found it, but in those days it might well have ended up in someone's stew pot—and the last part of her journey, the train she'd taken right into disaster.

"The last despatches home had given your father's station as Buhollow Barracks, and that's where the train would have gone. But in the meantime the rebels had overrun the eastern end of the county, putting everything they had into an assault aimed at the big arms depot at Bute Bagin. The force at Buhollow Barracks was too small to hold them, so your father had rolled aside to hook around and cut them off from the rear, while the Tenth Cav moved up from Cavender to hit them in the flank."

"I remember that," Esmay said. She remembered it from the records, not from real memory. The rebels had counted on her father's reputation which had never included leaving a plum like Buhollow unprotected . . . they had planned to immobilize his forces there with part of their army, while the rest went on to Bute Bagin and the supplies there. Later, his decision to abandon Buhollow and trap the rebel army would be taught as an example of tactical brilliance. He had done what he could for the town. The civilian population of Buhollow fled ahead of the rebels; they had been told which way to go. Most of them survived.

But Esmay, crammed in amongst refugees from earlier fighting, had ridden the train two stops too far. Both sides had mined the railroad; although the official reports said a rebel mine had blown the low bridge over the Sinets Canal just as the locomotive passed, Esmay had never been sure. Would any government admit its own mines had blown up its own train?

She did remember the enormous jolt that slammed the carriage crooked. They had been going slowly; she had been stuffed between a fat woman with a crying baby and a skinny older boy who kept poking her ribs. The jolt rocked the carriage, but didn't knock it over. Others weren't so lucky. She could just recall jumping down from the step—a big jump for her at that age—and following the woman and her baby for no reason other than that the woman was a mother. The skinny boy had poked her once more then turned away to follow someone else. Streams of frightened people scurried away from the train, away from the blowing smoke and screams at the front end of the train.

She had lost track of direction; she had forgotten, for

the moment, which way she was supposed to go. She had followed the woman and baby . . . and they had been following others . . . and then her legs were too tired, and she stopped.

"There was a little village the locals called Greer's Crossing," Coron went on. "Not even one klick from the train track, where the shipping canal turned. You must've gone there with others from the train wreck."

"And that's when the rebels came through," Esmay said.

"That's when the war came through." Coron paused; she heard the faint slurp as he sipped his tea. She glanced up to meet a gaze that no longer twinkled. "It wasn't just the rebels, as you know only too well."

I do? she thought.

"It was right about there the rebels realized that they were being herded into a trap. Say what you like about Chia Valantos, he had a tactical brain between his ears."

Esmay made a noise intended to indicate agreement.

"And maybe he had good scouts—I don't know. Anyway, the rebels had been on the old road, because they had some heavy vehicles, and so they had to go through the village, to get across on the bridge. They were making a mess of the village, because the people around there had never been supporters. I suppose they thought the people from the train had something to do with the loyalists . . ."

The old memories forced themselves up, lumping under her calm surface; she could feel her face changing and struggled to keep the muscles still. Her legs had begun to hurt, after the hours on the train, the crash, the fall . . . the woman, even with a baby, had longer legs and took longer steps. She had fallen behind, and by the time she got to the village it was gone. Already the roofs had collapsed; what walls remained were broken and cantways. Smoke blew across streets littered with stones and trash and tree limbs and piles of old clothes. It was noisy; she could not classify the noises except that they scared her. They were too loud; they sounded angry, and tangled in her mind with her father's voice scolding her. She wasn't supposed to be so close to whatever made those noises.

Blinded by stinging smoke, she had stumbled over one of the heaps of old clothes, and only then recognized it as a person. A corpse, her adult mind corrected. The child she had been had thought it a silly place for someone to go to sleep, a grown woman, and she had shaken the slack heavy arm, trying to wake an adult to help her find her way. She had not seen death before, not human death—she had not been allowed to see her mother, because of the fever—and it took her a long time to realize that the woman with no face would never pick her up and soothe her and promise that everything would be all right soon.

She had looked around, blinking against the stinging in her eyes that was not all smoke, and saw the other piles of clothes, the other people, the dead . . . and the dying, whose cries she could now recognize. Even across the years, she remembered that the first thought she could recognize was an apology: I'm sorry—I didn't mean to . . . Even now, she knew this was both necessary and futile. It had not been her fault—she had not caused the war—but she was there, and so far untouched, and for that, if nothing else, she must apologize.

That day, she had stumbled along the broken lane, falling again and again, crying without realizing it, until her legs gave out and she huddled into the corner of a wall, where someone's garden had once held bright flowers. The noise rose and fell, shadowy figures moving through the smoke, some wearing one color and some another. Most, she knew later, must have been the terrified passengers on the train; some were rebels. Later—later they all wore the same uniform, the uniform she knew, the one her father and uncles wore.

But she didn't remember. She couldn't remember, not all of it. She had remembered, and they'd said it was dreams.

"It'd have been better, I always thought, if they'd told you," Sebastian said. "At least when you got old enough. Bein' as the man was dead, and couldn't hurt anyone again, least of all you."

She did not want to hear this. She did not want to remember this . . . no, she *could* not. Fever dreams, she thought. Only fever dreams.

"Bad enough for it to happen at all, no matter who did it. The rape of a child—sickening. But to have it one of ours—"

She fixed on the one thing she could stand to know. "I . . . didn't know he was dead."

"Well, your father couldn't tell you that without bringing up the rest of it, could he? He hoped you'd forget the whole thing . . . or think it was just a fever dream."

He'd said it was a fever dream; he'd said it was over now, that she'd always be safe . . . he'd said he wasn't angry at her. Yet his anger had hovered around her, a vast cloud, dangerous, blinding her mind as the smoke had blinded her eyes.

"You're . . . sure?"

"That the bastard died? Oh yes . . . I have no doubt at all."

The invisible mechanisms whirled, paused, slid into place with a final inaudible crunch. "You killed him?"

"It was that or your father's career. Officers can't just kill their men, even animals who rape children. And to wait, to charge him—that'd have brought you into it, and none of us wanted that. Better for me to do it, and take my lumps . . . not that there was anything worse than a stiff chewing out, at the end of it. Mitigating circumstances."

Or extenuating . . . her mind dove eagerly into that momentary tangle, reminding her that extenuation and mitigation were, although similar, applied to different ends of the judicial process, as it were.

"I'm glad to know that," Esmay said, for something to say.

"I always said you should be told," he said. Then he looked embarrassed. "Not that I talked about it, you understand. I said it to myself, I mean. It was no use arguing with your father. And after all, you were his daughter."

"Don't worry about it," Esmay said. She was finding

it hard to pay attention; she felt the room drifting slowly away, on a slow spiral to the left.

"And you're sure you got it all sorted out, all but him being dead, I mean? They helped you in the R.S.S.?"

Esmay tried to drag her mind back to the topic, from which it wanted to shy away. "I'm fine," she said. "Don't worry about it."

"No . . . I was real surprised, you know, when you wanted to go off-planet and join them. Figured you'd had enough combat for any one life . . . but I guess it's your blood coming out, eh?"

How was she going to get rid of him, politely and discreetly? She could hardly tell him to go away, she had a headache. Suizas did not treat guests that way. But she needed—how she needed—some hours alone.

"Esmaya?" Esmay looked up. Her half-brother Germond grinned shyly at her. "Father said would you come to the conservatory, please?" He turned to Coron. "If you can excuse her, sir?"

"Of course. It's your family's turn now—Esmaya, thank you for your time." He bowed, very formal again at the end, and withdrew.

CHAPTER SIX

Esmay turned to Germond, now fifteen, all ears and nose and big feet. "What—did Father want?"

"He's in the conservatory with Uncle Berthol . . . he said you'd be getting tired of listening to old soldiers' tales, for one thing, and for another he wanted to ask you more about Fleet."

Her mouth was dry; she could not think. "Tell him . . . tell him Seb's gone, and I'll be out in a few minutes. I've gone upstairs to . . . to freshen up." For once, the impenetrable assumptions of Altiplano society worked in her favor. No male would question her need to be alone for a few minutes with an array of plumbing fixtures. Nor would they rush her.

She went up the stairs by instinct; she was not seeing the brass rails holding the carpet snug to the risers, the scuffs on the steps themselves. Her body knew how to get up the stairs, around the corners, where to find the switches that gave her absolute privacy.

She leaned against the wall, turned on the cold-water tap, and put her hands into it. She wasn't sure why. She wasn't sure of anything, including the passage of time. The water cut off automatically, just as it would aboard ship, and she nudged the controls again. Abruptly she threw up; the curdled remains of lunch slopped into the clean swirl of water and disappeared down the drain with it. Her stomach heaved again, then settled uneasily. She cupped her hand under the faucet, and drank a handful of the cold, sweet water. Her stomach lurched, but steadied. She had never been prone to nausea. Not even then, not even when the pain was so bad she'd been sure she was being torn apart. The real pain, not the imagined pain induced by fever dreams.

In the mirror, she looked like a stranger—a gaunt old woman with flyaway dark hair, face streaked with tears and vomit. This would never do. Methodically, Esmay took a towel from the rack, wet it, and cleaned her face and hands. She rubbed her face hard with the dry end of the towel, until the blood returned and the greenish tinge of nausea disappeared under a healthy pink. She attacked her hair with damp hands, flattening the loose strands, then dried her hands. The water stopped again, and this time she didn't turn it back on. She folded the damp towel, and hung it on the used rack.

The woman in the mirror now looked more familiar. Esmay forced a smile, and it looked more natural on that face than it felt on her own. She should put on something, she thought, looking to see if she'd spotted her shirt. A few drops showed, dark against the pale fawn. She would change. She would change into someone else . . . her mind stumbled over something in the smoke that was all she could see.

Still navigating by habit, she unlocked the door, and returned to her own room. By the time she'd taken off the shirt, she knew she'd have to change from the skin out. She did that as quickly as she could, taking what lay on top in her drawers, and glancing at herself only long enough to be sure the wide collar lay flat and untwisted around her neck. The pallor had gone; she looked like Esmay Suiza again.

But was she? Was Esmay Suiza a real person? Could you build a real person on a foundation of lies? She fought her way through the choking dark clouds in her mind, trying to cling to what she remembered, what Seb Coron had told her, to any logic that could connect them.

When the smoke-cloud in her mind cleared, the first thing she recognized was smug relief: she had been *right*. She had known the truth; she had made no mistakes. Her adult mind intruded: except for the stupidity of leaving home in the first place, the idiocy of a child trying to travel cross-country in the midst of a civil war. She batted that critical voice down. She had been a child; children were,

by definition, ignorant of some things. In the essentials—
in recognizing what she had seen, in telling the truth about
what happened—she had been right.

Rage followed that moment of delight. She had been
right, and they had lied to her. They had told her she was
mistaken—that she was confused by the fever . . . or was
there even a fever? She had started to call up the household medical records before her critical voice pointed out
that of course the records would show such an illness, such
a hospitalization. It could have been fabricated, all of it—
how would she know? And to whom did she want to prove
it?

To everyone, at that moment. She wanted to drag the
truth before her father, her uncle, even Papa Stefan. She
wanted to grab them by the neck, force them to see what
she had seen, feel what she had felt, admit that she had
in fact endured what she had endured.

But they already knew. Exhaustion followed exhilaration
just as it followed fever; she could feel the familiar languor
in her veins, dragging her down to immobility, to acquie-
scence. They knew, and yet they had lied to her.

She could keep her own secret, and let them think
theirs safe, run away again as she had run before. They
would be comfortable still, indulged by her complicity.

Or she could confront them.

She looked again in the mirror. That was the person
she would become, if she became an admiral like Heris
Serrano's aunt. The diffidence, the uncertainty, that had
mocked her so often had burned away in the last hour.
She did not yet feel what she saw in that face, but she
trusted the eyes that blazed out at her.

Would he still be in the conservatory? How long had
this taken? The clock surprised her; she had been upstairs
only half a local hour. She headed for the conservatory,
this time with all senses fully awake. It might have been
the first time she came down the stairs . . . she felt the
slight give in the sixth from the bottom, noticed a loose
tack on the railing side of the carpet, spotted a nick in
the railing itself. Every sight, every smell, every sound.

Her father and Berthol were stooped over a tray of bedding plants with one of the gardeners. Her new clarity of vision noticed every detail of the plants, the notched petals of fire-orange and sun-yellow, the lace-cut leaves. The gardener's dirt-blackened fingernails where his hands were splayed out on the potting table. The red flush along the sides of her uncle's neck. White lines in the skin of her father's face, where he had squinted against the sun so long that the creases had not tanned. A loose thread on the button of Berthol's sleeve button.

Her foot scraped on the tile floor because she let it; her father looked up.

"Esmaya . . . come see the new hybrids. I think they'll do very well in the front urns . . . I hope old Sebastian didn't wear you out."

"He didn't," Esmay said. "In fact, I found him quite interesting." Her voice sounded perfectly calm, perfectly reasonable, to her, but her father started.

"Is something wrong, Esmay?"

"I need to talk to you, Father," she said, still calm. "Perhaps in your study?"

"Something serious?" he asked, not moving. Rage surged through her.

"Only if you consider a matter of family honor serious," she said. The gardener's hands jerked; the plants shivered. The gardener reached for the box of planters, and he murmured something. Her father lifted his chin, and the man grabbed the box and scuttled away, out the back door of the conservatory.

"Do you want me to leave?" her uncle asked, as if he were sure she would say no.

"Please," she said, this time testing her own power to put a sting in it. He flinched, his eyes shifting to her father, then back to her.

"Esmay, what . . . ?"

"You will know soon enough," Esmay said. "But I would prefer to speak to Father alone, just now."

Berthol flushed, but turned away; he did not quite slam the door going out.

"Well, Esmaya? There was no need to be rude." But her father's voice had no power in it, and she heard an undertone of fear. The little muscles around his eyes and nose were tense; the contrast between his tanned skin and the untanned creases had almost disappeared. If he'd been a horse, his ears would have been flat and his tail switching nervously. He should be able to put the sum together: she wondered if he would.

She came toward him, running her hand through the fronds of one of the sweetheart palms; it still tickled. "I talked to Seb Coron—or rather, he talked . . . and I found it most interesting."

"Oh?" He was going to brazen it out.

"You lied to me . . . you said it was all a dream, that it didn't happen . . ."

For a moment, she thought he would try to pretend he didn't understand, but then a quick wash of color rose to his cheeks and drained again.

"We did it for you, Esmaya." That was what she'd expected to hear.

"No. Not for me. For the family, maybe, but not for me." Her voice did not waver, which surprised her a little. She had decided to keep going even if her voice broke, even if she cried in front of him, which she had not done in years. Why should he be protected from her tears?

"For more than you, I admit." He looked at her from under those bushy brows, gray now. "For the others—it was better that one child suffer that confusion—"

"Confusion? You call that *confusion*?" Her body ached with remembered pain, the specific pains that had specific causes. She had tried to scream; she had tried to fight him off; she had even tried to bite. The strong adult hands, hardened by war, had held her down easily; bruising her.

"No, not the injuries, but not being sure what had happened—you couldn't tell us who, Esmaya; you didn't really see him. And they said you would forget . . ."

She felt her lips pulling back from her teeth; she saw in her father's expression what hers had become. "I saw him," she said. "I don't know his name, but I saw him."

He shook his head. "You couldn't give us any details at the time," he said. "You were exhausted, terrified—you probably didn't even see his face. You've been in combat now as an adult; you know how confusing it is—"

He doubted. He dared to doubt, even now, her knowledge. A bright ribbon of images from *Despite* rippled through her mind. Confusing? Perhaps, in terms of organizing information to relate in court, but she could see the faces of those she had killed, and those who had tried to kill her. She always would.

"Show me the regimental roster," she said, her voice choked with rage. "Show me, and I'll point him out."

"You can't possibly—after all these years—"

"Sebastian says he killed him—that means you know who it is. If I can point him out, that should prove to you that I do remember." *That you were wrong, and I was right.* Why it mattered so much to prove this was not a question Esmay wanted to examine. Proving a general wrong was professional suicide and military stupidity. But . . .

"You can't possibly," her father said again, but this time with no strength. He led the way to his study without another word; Esmay followed, forcing herself not to strike him down from behind. He moved to the console, and stabbed at the controls. Esmay noticed that his fingers were shaking; she felt a calm satisfaction. Then he stepped back, and she came forward to look.

The faces came up, six to a screen. She stared at them, one part of her mind sure that she would know, and another sure that she wouldn't. Had her father even called up the right year? He wanted her to fail, that was clear enough. He might have cheated—but she could not believe that of him, even now.

Suizas did not lie . . . and he was her father.

He had lied before, *because* he was her father. She tore her mind away from that dilemma and stared at the screen.

She did not recognize most of the faces at all. She had no reason to; she had not been to Buhollow Barracks after her father was posted there. She found a few faces vaguely familiar, but unthreatening. They would have been men who had served with her father before, even among the household guard at the estancia. Among them, a much younger Sebastian Coron, whom she recognized instantly . . . so her memory was clear in some details that far back.

She could hear her father's breathing, as she scrolled through the list. She did not look at him. It was hard enough to focus on the screen, to breathe through the tightness in her throat. Screen after screen . . . she heard her father shift in his chair, but he did not interrupt. Someone came to the door; she heard the rustle of clothing, but did not look up. Her father must have gestured, for without a word she heard the rustle of clothing retreat, and the gentle thud of the door as it shut.

Through the entire enlisted ranks, and she had not found that face her mind refused to show her. Doubts chilled her. The face she remembered had been contorted with whatever emotion makes men rape children . . . she might never find it among these solemn, almost expressionless faces in the catalog. It must be here . . . surely Coron would have told her if it had been someone in another unit, or an officer.

Or would he? She made herself keep going, to the officer ranks. There at the head was her father, no gray in his hair, his mouth one long firm line. Beneath, in descending order, the . . . her breath caught. Yes. Her heart fluttered then raced thunderously in her chest, spurred by the old fear. He stared out of the page, sleek and handsome, the honey-colored hair swept back . . . she remembered it darker, matted with sweat and dirt. But 'no doubt at all, not one.

She searched his face for clues to his choices . . . for some mark of depravity. Nothing. Regular features, clear gray eyes—coloring not that common on Altiplano, but much prized. The little button of an honor graduate, the braid on his epaulet that declared him an eldest son, of whom more was expected. His mouth was set in a straight line, a conscious copy of her father's . . . it looked no crueler. His name . . . she knew his name. She knew his family. She had danced with his younger brothers, at the Harvest Games, the year before she left Altiplano for the stars.

Her mouth was too dry to speak. She struggled to swallow, to clear her tongue. She had struggled then, too. Finally she got out a word: "This." She laid her finger on the image, surprised at the steadiness of her hand; her finger didn't tremble at all.

Her father got up; she could hear him coming up behind her and fought not to flinch away. He grunted first, as if someone had slugged him in the belly. "Gods! You *did*—how did you—?"

Anger released her tongue. "I told you. I remember."

"Esmaya . . ." It was a groan, a plea, and his hand on her hair was another. She slid aside from it, pushing herself away from the console, scrambling out of the chair.

"I didn't know his name," she said. Amazingly, it was easy to keep her tone even, her words crisp. "I was too young to have been introduced, even if he'd been at our house before. I couldn't tell you his name, or give the kind of description that an adult might have been able to give. But I *knew*. You did not show me the rolls then, did you?"

Her father's face, when she looked, might have been carven in bleached wood; it looked dry and stiff, unnatural. Was that her vision, or his reality? Her gaze wandered away, around the room, just noticing the familiar things before moving on to something else. In her mind, more and more of the certainties shifted, as if stone walls had been only scenery painted on movable screens. What did she really know about herself, about her past? What could she rely on?

Against this chaos the past years in Fleet stood firm: she knew what had happened there. From her first day in the prep school to the last day of the court-martial, she knew exactly what she had done, and who had done what to her. She had created that world for herself; she could trust it. Admiral Vida Serrano, an easy match for her father, had never lied to her . . . had never screened anyone else, at her expense.

Whatever she had had to suppress, to limit, in herself in order to make this haven was expendable. She didn't need to find the part of herself that had loved to ride, or paint, or play antique instruments . . . she needed to keep herself safe, and she had managed that quite well. She could give up Altiplano; she had already done it.

"Esmaya . . . I'm sorry." He probably was, she let herself think, but it didn't matter. He was sorry too late and too little. "If—*since* you remember, you probably need therapy."

"Therapy *here*?" That got out before she could control the emotion in it, the scorn and anger. "Here, where the therapists told me it was all my imagination, all fever dreams?"

"I'm sorry," he said, but this time with an edge of irritation. She knew that tone; he could apologize, but that was supposed to be the end of it. She was supposed to accept that apology and let it go. Not this time. Not again. "I—we—made a mistake, Esmaya. We can't change that now; it's past. I can't possibly convince you how badly I feel about it—that it was a mistake—but there were reasons. I asked advice . . ."

"Don't," she said harshly. "Don't make excuses. I'm not stupid; I can see what you would like to call the realities. He—" she could not bring herself to dirty her mouth with the name. "He was an officer, the son of a friend; there was a civil war in progress; you could not risk a feud—" Memory reminded her that the young man's father had commanded a sizable force himself. Not merely a feud, but potentially a lost war. Her military training argued that a child's pain—even her pain— weighed less than an entire campaign. But the child she had been, the child whose pain still shaped her reactions, the child whose witness had been denied, refused that easy answer. She had not been the only victim—and for the victims, no victories sufficed . . . the victories were not for them, did not help them. Yet defeat promised only more of the same. She squeezed her eyes shut, trying to force back all the feelings that wanted to escape, shut them back into the darkness. "It did not take rejuvenation to make you *prudent*," she said, throwing at him the only new weapon she had.

A short silence, during which her father's breathing was almost as harsh as hers had been that bitter day.

"You need help, Esmaya," her father said, finally. His voice was almost back to normal, warm and steady; the general in command of himself, a lifetime's habit. She wanted to relax into the promise of fatherly love and protection.

She dared not. "Probably I do," she said. "But not here. Not now." Not with the father who had betrayed her.

"You won't come back," he said. He had never been stupid, only selfish. That wasn't entirely fair, but neither was he. Now he looked at her, as straight a look as he might have given a commander he respected. "You won't come back again, will you?"

She couldn't imagine coming back, but she wasn't quite ready for that negative commitment. "I don't know. Probably not, but—you might as well know . . . I've worked out a deal with Luci for the herd."

He nodded. "Good. I shouldn't have done that, but . . . I suppose I was still hoping you'd come home for good, especially when they treated you like that."

And you treated me better? hovered on her lips but did not quite emerge. Her father seemed to hear it anyway.

"I understand," he said. He didn't, but she wasn't going to argue, not now. Now she wanted to get away, far away, and have some time alone. She suspected she would have to spend some time with Fleet psychnannies in the end, but for now . . . "Please, Esmaya," he said. "Get help in your Fleet, if you won't accept it here."

"I'm going to ride out to the valley," she said, ignoring that. He had no right to tell her what to do about the wound he'd inflicted. "Just for a day. Tomorrow. I don't want company."

"I understand," he said again.

"No surveillance," she said, meeting his gaze squarely. He blinked first.

"No surveillance," he agreed. "But if you stay overnight, please let us know."

"Of course," she said, her voice relaxing even as his had. They were alike in ways she had never noticed; even in her anger she suddenly felt the urge to tell him about the mutiny, knowing that he would not find her actions surprising, inexplicable, as the Familias officers had.

She walked out into the afternoon, feeling nothing but a great light emptiness, as if she were a seed pod at summer's end, ready to blow away on the first autumn stormwind. Across the gravel drive, crunching under her feet. Between the beds of flowers whose color hurt her eyes. Across the sunlit fields beyond, where shadows shifted and moved and called her name, but she did not answer.

She came back when the sun fell behind the distant mountains, tired in ways that had nothing to do with walking however far she'd walked, and went into the dim entrance hall, where the smell of food and clatter of dishes stopped her short.

"Dama?" Esmay whirled, but it was one of the servants, offering a tray with a cup and a folded note. She shook her head to the cup of tea, took the note, and went upstairs. No one followed, no one intruded. She laid the note on her bed, and went down the hall to the bathroom.

The note, as she'd half expected, was from her great-grandmother. *Your father told me I am now free to talk to you. Come see me.* She put it on the shelf above the clothes pole and thought about it. She had always assumed that her father obeyed his grandmother, as she obeyed her grandfather; though men and women had different roles, elders always ruled. She had thought so, anyway, imagining the chain of authority coming down, link by link, from eldest to youngest through all the generations.

Had her great-grandmother really known the truth and *not* told her? How had her father gained so much power?

She lay back on the bed, and as the hours passed she could not find the strength to move, to get up and bathe or change her clothes or even turn away from the square of sky she could see darkening from blue to gray to the star-spangled midnight. It was all she could do to blink her eyes when they burned from staring at the window; it was all she could do to breathe.

In the first light of dawn, she struggled up, stiff and miserable. How many mornings she had wakened stiff and miserable, hoping to see no one on the way to the baths, on the way out . . . and here she was again, supposedly a hero—she would have laughed at the thought if she could—once more alone at the top of her father's house, once more awake and miserable after a sleepless night.

She told herself, firmly, in the tone she thought Admiral Serrano would use, to get a grip on herself. A deep breath of the morning air, sweet-scented with the nightblooming flowers on the house wall. She made it to the bathroom, showered, brushed her teeth. In her room she dressed in riding clothes; when she came down the stairs she heard the familiar clatter in the kitchen where the cooks were already at work. If she put her head in, hoping for a taste of the first baking, they'd want to talk to her. She went on, past the kitchen, to the storeroom. Inside on the right, if the custom hadn't changed, was a stone jar of trail bread. Anyone could grab a handful, if headed out to do early chores.

The stable, busy as always by daylight . . . the grooms and their helpers scurrying from stall to stall, buckets clattering. She went to the stable office, where she found her name at the top of the list of the day's riders. Her father had done that, probably the night before, and she felt no gratitude. In another hand, someone had written in a horse's name, Sam.

"Dama?" One of the grooms. "When you're ready, dama."

"I'm ready," Esmay said through a dry throat. She ought to have taken a water bottle too, but she didn't want to go back for it. The groom went ahead of her, down the aisle of that barn and into another and out again into the small training ring, where a bored brown horse leaned its chin on the rail where it was tied. A trail saddle, slicker tied neatly behind the cantle, saddlebags, water bottle . . . her father must have specified that, too. She hadn't needed to take the trail bread. A trail bridle, easy to unclip the bit so the horse could graze, a long lead-line now clipped into the hitching rail's permanent loops.

The groom offered his linked hands, and she mounted; he unclipped the lead and handed her the end to tuck into the saddle ring. "He is good, but not too fast," the groom said, and opened the gate into the upper pastures.

She turned the horse's head onto the trail that would, hours later, lead to her valley. Eventually her stiff body relaxed into the rhythm of its walk, and she made herself look around. Morning light lit the recesses of the mountains on her right, and the vast rolling pastures that spread from their foot as far east as she could see.

She could remember riding out here from childhood. She had always taken a deep breath, going out the gate, because it meant freedom. Thousands of hectares, dozens of trails, hidden wooded hollows even in this open grazing land, and all the intricate topography of the mountains . . . no one could find her, once she was out of sight of the house. Or so she'd thought.

She took the deep breath, and it caught in her throat. Anger sat on one shoulder, and grief on the other; the stink of old lies filled her nose and she could not think of anything else. She had lived through the assault itself— she had, thanks to Seb Coron, outlived the assailant. But she had not outlived the effects . . . worst of all effects, the lies.

The horse ambled on, carrying her along as time did, mere passage without change . . . without the right change . . . without healing. She could ride forever—the horse slowed, and she looked up to find they'd come to a fork in the trail; she legged it to the right—and it would not help. Nothing would help. Nothing *could* help. Nothing on Altiplano, at least.

At the second fork, she turned right again. It was stupid, going to the valley when she felt like this, and yet it had helped before. At other bad times in her life, she had gone there and found peace, at least for awhile. She rode on, seeing little, hearing little. It hurt so much. It hurt beyond hurting, to the point where pain became a white fog, as the physical pain had been then.

She argued with herself, part of her defending her family even now. It wasn't true they had done nothing: the man was dead. *But that was Seb Coron, doing it for her father, not her father doing it for her.* And what if Coron had lied about that? It wasn't true that her father hadn't cared: he'd done what he thought would help. *But it hadn't helped, and he hadn't changed his mind. He, whose rule had been "If one thing doesn't work, try another."*

She rode beside the creek now, but its spring-full rushing made only a white noise she found annoying. It was too loud. In the shade of the trees, she felt cold; in the sun she felt scorched. The horse sighed, and pulled a little toward the water. She halted it, clambered off feeling every stiff muscle, and led it down to drink. It laid its lips on the water and sucked; she could see the gulps rising up its gullet. She waited until it was finished, until it lifted its head and gave her a look and then tried to stray off toward some buttonweed twigs. She didn't want to climb back on, but she had to.

She walked instead, leading the horse, until her legs felt better. By the sun, it was late morning. She didn't really want to go on to the valley but where else could she go? Someone would ask, knowing where she always went . . . she pulled herself back into the saddle, and rode on.

The valley was smaller than she remembered, and she could feel nothing for it. The pines, the poplars, the creek, the meadow. She looked around it, trying to feel something . . . it was hers, it would always be hers . . . but all she felt was pain and emptiness. She slid off the horse and took the bit out of its mouth. She could walk around and let it graze for an hour before heading back. She remembered to loosen the girth, then took down a water bottle and drank. Her body wanted food, but her mind did not; she made it halfway through the lunch the cooks had packed for her before her mind won the battle, and she threw up what she'd eaten.

She felt faint, then, and sat on the cold ground with her head down on her knees; the horse snatched at the grass nearby, the ripping and chewing of grass punctuating her thoughts. What could she do? Emptiness behind her, emptiness before her.

In the middle of that emptiness, those few vivid moments when she had done something right, and saved someone else. Heris Serrano. Vida Serrano. What would they say now, if they knew all this? Would it explain what the admiral had wanted explained? Would it change anything? Or would it be worse, far worse, to let them know what had happened to her? She already had black marks against her; she had known from childhood that nothing in a military career is ever completely forgotten or forgiven. If she became not only the colorless, ordinary young officer from a backwoods planet, who just happened to do the right thing once and save a Serrano neck . . . if she admitted that she was damaged, fractured, prone to nightmares . . . that had to put her in more jeopardy. That had to risk being thrown out, sent home . . . except she had no home. Not this valley, not anywhere.

When her head cleared a little, she made herself drink again, and eat the other half of lunch. This time it stayed down. It tasted like dust and wood, but it stayed down.

She was home well before dark, handing over the dry, cool horse to the groom with thanks. Her stepmother hovered in the hall; Esmay nodded politely.

"I rode too far," she said. "I need a long bath, and bed."

"Could I send up a tray?" her stepmother asked. It was not her stepmother's fault. It had never been her stepmother's fault; she wasn't sure her stepmother even knew. If her father had kept it such a secret, perhaps she didn't know even now.

"Thank you," Esmay said. "Soup and bread would be fine—I'm just too tired."

She was able to get herself in and out of the bath, and she ate the food on the tray when it came. She put the tray back out in the hall, and lay on the bed. She could just see the corner of her great-grandmother's note on its shelf. She didn't want to see it; she didn't want to see anything.

The next morning was marginally better. Luci, who clearly knew nothing, wanted her to come watch a schooling session with the brown mare. Esmay could think of no polite way out of it, and partway through the session came out of herself far enough to notice that the problem with the canter depart was Luci's failure to keep her outside hip in place. Luci accepted this with good grace, and offered a tube of liniment for Esmay's obvious stiffness. They went in to lunch together.

In the afternoon, her conscience would not let her avoid her great-grandmother any longer.

"You are very angry with me," her great-grandmother said, not looking up from her embroidery. She had to use a thick lens and a special light, but she worked on it every day, Luci had said.

"I am angry," Esmay said. "Mostly with him, I think." Meaning her father, which surely her great-grandmother knew.

"I am still angry with him," her great-grandmother said. "But I'm too old to put much energy into the anger. It's very tiring, anger, so I ration it. A sharp word a day, perhaps."

Esmay suspected humor at her expense, but the old woman's face had a soft vulnerability that she'd never noticed before.

"I will say I was wrong, Esmaya. It was how I was brought up, but it was still wrong of me. Wrong not to tell you, and wrong to leave you as I did."

"I forgive you," Esmay said quickly. The old woman looked at her.

"Don't do that. Don't lie to me, of all people. Lies added to lies never make truth. You don't forgive me—you can't forgive me that fast."

"I don't . . . hate you."

"Don't hate your father, either. Be angry with him, yes: he has hurt you and lied to you, and anger is appropriate. You need not forgive him too soon, any more than you forgive me. But don't hate, because it is not natural to you, and it will destroy you."

"I'm going away, as soon as I can," Esmay said. "And I'm not coming back."

"I know." Again, a sense of vulnerability, but not intended to sway her decision. Her chin firmed. "Luci told me about the herd. You are right, and I will argue for Luci when the time comes."

"Thank you," Esmay said. It was all she could say; she kissed the old woman and went away.

The days crept by, then the weeks. She counted them off; she would not cause a scandal by moving to the city for the rest of her leave, but she could not help watching the calendar. Her resolve had hardened: she would go, and never return. She would find someone—not Luci, who had no feel for it, but someone else—to become the valley's guardian. Nothing here meant anything to her now but pain and sorrow; the very food tasted bad in her mouth. She and her father had spoken each day of other things; she had been amazed at both of them, the way they could evade any mention of or reference to that disastrous afternoon. Her stepmother took her shopping in the city; she allowed herself to be draped in suitable clothes; she packed them into her duffel to take along.

Then it was the last week . . . the last five days . . . the last four. She woke one morning stabbed by the sorrow that she had been *in* her valley, but she had not *seen* it. She had to go one more time; she had to try to salvage something, some real memory that was also a good memory, from her childhood. She had been riding almost every day, just to keep Luci company, so if there was a horse free, she could go now, today.

For the dama, there was always a horse free. A trail horse? Of course, dama, and the saddle, and the bridle.

And might the groom suggest that this horse accepted hobbles well? Very good. She went back into the kitchen, and collected a lunch. She felt, if not happy, at least positive . . . the pull of Fleet, she thought, the knowledge that in just a few days she would be back in her new home, forever.

The valley opened before her, magical again, as it had been in her childhood . . . . as she would remember it in the moment of her death. It hardly deserved the name of "valley," although when Esmay had first seen it, she'd been so young it seemed large. Now she could see that what she remembered was merely a saucer in the side of the mountain, a grassy glade in which a small pool trickled away in a murmuring stream that would become a rushing noisy stream only further down. On one side were the dark pines, secretive, rising from rocky ledges, and facing them were the white-boled poplars with their dancing leaves. In this brief mountain spring, the new grass was spangled with pink and yellow and white, the wind-flowers and snowflowers . . . a few weeks later, the tall scarlet and blue lupines would bloom, but now all the flowers lay close to the ground.

Esmay leaned back in the saddle and took in a deep breath. She wanted to breathe in and in, filling herself with the resinous scent of pine, the crisp scent of mint and grass, the sweetness of the flowers, the tang of poplar and even the sour rank smell of the lush weeds near the water. She could feel tears rising, and she clamped down on her emotions. Instead of crying, she dismounted, and led her horse forward to drink from the pool. Then she removed the saddlebags, and slung them over her shoulder. She led the horse to the fallen pine—still there after all these years—and unsaddled it; she put the saddle over the leaning trunk, then hobbled the horse before removing the bridle.

The horse worked its way back out into the sunshine, in the meadow grass, where it set to grazing. Esmay settled herself on the convenient rock she had placed years before, and leaned back against the saddle. She unbuckled the left saddlebag and took out the meat-filled pasties Veronica had packed. She would have five hours of peace here, before she had to start back.

She could hardly believe it was hers now. She belonged to it, to this chill rock with its multicolored lichens, to the trees and the grass, to the mountain itself . . . but by law and custom, as their saying went, it was now hers. By custom and law she could bar anyone from trespassing here . . . she could fence it, shield it, build a house here that no one ever entered but herself.

It had been her dearest dream, once. A little cabin, one or two rooms, all to herself, with no memories in it, here in this golden place. She had been a child then; in her daydream, food had appeared on the table without any effort of hers. Breakfast had been . . . had been cereal with cream and honey. Someone else, some invisible magical person, had washed the sticky bowl. She had always been out for lunch, usually perched on a rock high above, watching the sky. Dinner, in those dreams, had been fish from the stream, sweet-fleshed mountain trout, lightly fried.

Not this stream; it was too small, but downstream a few kilometers. She had fished there, the time she camped here for a week: reality, not dreams, by then, the summer she was eleven. The fish were as tasty as she'd imagined, but the hike back and forth had convinced her that she would have to find another food source.

Papa Stefan had been furious; so had her father, when he came back from the situation in Kharfra (there was always a Situation in Kharfra). Her stepmother had panicked, convinced that Esmay had killed herself . . . remembering that unsavory row, Esmay felt herself knotting up, the cold of the stone striking deep. She pushed herself off the rock and walked out into the sun, stretching out her arms to it.

Even at eleven she had known she would never kill herself, no matter what. Had Arris ever told her father? Probably not. She would have been afraid to introduce any more tension, any more difficulty, between father and daughter. Poor Arris, Esmay thought, closing her eyes against the sun as she lifted her face to it. She had been six years too late with her sympathy, six years too late with her shock and horror. Now she could understand how futile Arris must have felt, with a stepdaughter so awkward, so independent.

Esmay walked down the slope to the open grass. She crouched, putting a hand to the ground. It was cool—only on the hottest midsummer day would the ground feel warm up here—but not as cold as the rock. She let herself down onto the grass, and leaned back with her hands clasped behind her head. Above, the morning sky burned blue, the exact blue that felt right, that made her happiest. She had never found that blue on another planet. Under her shoulders and back, the land upheld her with just enough pressure.

"You're not making it easy," she said to the glade. Here and now, she could not imagine leaving Altiplano forever, giving this up forever. The horse, a few rods away, waggled an ear at her but went on munching.

She stretched out on her side, and looked at the flowers, reminding herself of their names. Some were original terraforming rootstock, and others had been developed here, for this particular world, from Terran gene lines. Pink, yellow, white, a few of the tiny blue-violet starry ones she had privately named wish-stars. She had had private names for all of them really, taken from the plant names in the old stories, whether or not they were really related. Campion and rosemary and primrose sounded pretty, so she used them; harebell sounded silly to her, so she didn't. She touched them now with a fingertip, renaming them: pink rosemary, yellow campion, crisp white primroses. It was her valley, these were her flowers, and she could give them her names. Forever.

She looked over at the horse. It was grazing steadily, not so much as an earflick to indicate any danger. She leaned her head back on her arm again. She could feel the warmth of the sun where it touched her, and the coolness of the shadows. She felt herself relaxing, as she had not relaxed since she arrived—or for how long before?— and let her eyelids sag shut. She rolled her face into the fragrant grass to get the annoying sun off her eyelids . . .

And woke with a jerk and a cry as a shadow stooped over her. Even as she lunged up, she recognized the horse. It snorted and plunged away, fighting the hobbles, frightened because she was.

It had only wanted a treat, she told herself. Her heart was racing; she felt sick to her stomach. The horse had settled uneasily a short distance away, watching her with pricked ears.

"You scared me," Esmay said to the horse. It blew a long rattling sigh at her, meaning Me, too. "It was your shadow," Esmay said. "Sorry." She looked around. She had slept at least an hour, more likely two, and she could feel the heat of sunburn on her ear. She had worn a hat . . . but not when she lay down. Idiot.

When her heart slowed, she felt better, rested. Lunch, her stomach reminded her. She walked back to the rock, shaking the kinks out of legs and arms, and then took her hat and the lunch sack back into the sun. Now she was ready for that meat pasty, and the horse would enjoy the apple.

After lunch, she walked down by the stream, and let her mind loose again. She had come home, and found the truth, and it had not killed her. She didn't like it—it hurt, and she knew it would continue to hurt—but she had survived the first terrifying hours as she had survived the initial assault in childhood. She felt shaky, but not in danger of dissolution.

Was she ready to give this up, this lovely valley that had helped her cling to sanity so often? The stream chuckled and splashed at her feet; she knelt and put her hand into its icy flow. She loved this sound, the smell of the pungent herbs on its bank, the feel of icy water on her hands and face when she knelt to drink. She loved the heavy *tonk* of stone on stone when she stood on the uneven one that rocked back and forth.

She did not have to decide now. She had years . . . if she stayed in Fleet, if she qualified for rejuvenation, she had many, many years. Long after her father died, long after everyone who had betrayed her died, she could come home to this valley, still young enough to enjoy it. She could build her cabin and live here in peace. It would not have to hurt to return; she could avoid that pain just by persisting.

Against this vision rose the vivid, eager face of her cousin Luci, Luci willing to risk struggle, conflict, pain . . . the opposite of prudence. But Luci had not suffered what she had suffered. Tears burned in her eyes again. If she gained her peaceful valley at the end by simply outlasting those who had betrayed her . . . Luci would be old, perhaps dead . . . because how many normal lifetimes would she live, before she had earned retirement and the peace of her valley?

She would like to have Luci for a friend as well as a business partner, Luci who now looked up to her, as she could not recall anyone in the family looking up to her before.

"It's not fair," she said to the trees and the slopes and the gurgling water. An icy breeze slid down the creek bed and chilled her. Stupid complaint; life was not about fairness. "He *lied* to me!" she screamed suddenly. The horse threw up its head, ears pointed at her; somewhere upstream jays squalled and battered their way through thickset twigs.

Then it was quiet again. The horse still watched her with the suspicion of the edible for the eater, but the jays had flown away, their scolding voices diminishing. The water gurgled as before; the breeze failed and came again like the breath of some vast being larger than mountains. Esmay felt her rage draining away with it, not really gone but its immediate pressure eased.

She spent another hour wandering around the glade, drifting in and out of moods like the clouds drifting in and out of sight above the slopes. Sweet memories of her childhood trips—of learning to climb on the boulders at the foot of the cliff, of the time she found a rare fire-tailed salamander under the ledge of the creek's largest pool—swept over and under the other memories, the bad ones. She thought about climbing the cliff again, but she had not brought any climbing gear, and her legs were already stiff and sore from riding.

Finally, as the afternoon shadows began to climb the boulders, she caught and saddled the horse again. She found herself wondering if her father had told Papa Stefan . . . or only Great-grandmother. She wanted to be furious with Great-grandmother for not overruling her father, but she had used up her store of anger on her father. And besides—when she'd come back from the hospital, her great-grandmother had not been in the house at all. Was that *why* she had moved away—or been sent away?

"I am still an idiot child," she said to the horse, as she unlooped the hobbles and prepared to mount. The horse eyed her and flicked an ear. "Yes, and I scared you out of your wits, didn't I? You're not used to that kind of behavior from Suizas."

She rode down the shadowy trail beside the stream deep in thought. How many of the family knew the truth, or had known it? Whom, besides Luci, could she trust?

The upper pastures, when she came to them, were still in sunlight, out of the shadow of the mountains. Far away to the south, she saw a drift of cattle moving slowly. In the distance, the buildings of the estancia were nested in green trees like little toys, bright-painted. For some reason she felt a rush of joy; it passed through her to the horse, which broke into a trot. She didn't feel her stiffness; without realizing she was going to, she legged the horse into a canter, and then let it extend into a gallop. Wind burned in her face; her hair streamed back; she could feel each separate tug on her scalp and the power of the galloping animal beneath her lifted her beyond fear or anger.

She walked the last mile in, as she had been trained to do, and grinned at Luci who was just coming in from polo practice when they met in the lane.

"A good ride?" asked Luci. "Was that you we saw galloping in the upper fields?"

"Yes," Esmay said. "I think I've remembered how to ride."

Luci looked worried, and Esmay laughed.

"The deal is good, Luci—I'm going back to Fleet. But I'd forgotten how much fun it can be."

"You . . . haven't seemed very happy."

"No. I haven't been, but I will be. My place is out there, as yours is here."

They rode in together; Esmay did not have to say more, because Luci was ready to talk for hours about the brown mare's talents and her own ambitions.

CHAPTER SEVEN

The team from Special Materials Analysis came off the commercial line at Comus along with all the other passengers, some hundred and thirty. Here, in the interior of the Familias, the customs checks were perfunctory. A glance at the ID, a glance at the luggage . . . their matching briefcases, matching duffels, all with the company logo.

"Consultants, eh?" said the customs inspector, clearly proud of his guess.

"That's right." Gori smiled at the man, that friendly open smile which was just a bit too memorable sometimes. Arhos wondered if he should have let Gori come—but Gori was the best with such devices, faster by thirty seconds than anyone else. He would edge their profit up on the Fleet contract, too—thirty seconds a hundred times a day was fifty minutes off the top.

"What a life," the customs man said. "Wish I could be a consultant—" He passed them through.

"They always think it's glamorous," Losa grumbled, audibly enough. "If they had to be on the road all the time, hear the complaints at home—"

"You didn't have to marry that loser," Pratt said. This was an old script, one they could improvise around for an hour.

"He's not a loser, he's just . . . sensitive."

"Artists," Gori said. "I don't know why intelligent women always fall for losers who claim they're creative—"

Losa huffed, something she did well. "He's not a loser! He's sold three works—"

"In how long?" asked Gori.

"Stop it," Arhos said, as any manager would. "It's not important—Gori, let her alone. She's right; people think

112

our job is glamorous, and if they knew what it's really like, on the road all the time, working long hours for people who are already angry they had to hire us, they'd know better. But no more personal problems on this trip, all right? We're going to be stuck out here long enough without making it seem longer."

"All right," Gori said, with a sidelong look at Losa.

"I need to stop in here," Losa said, ducking into a ladies' without looking at Gori at all. Arhos glared at Gori, who shrugged. Pratt shook his head. The two junior women, technicians newly hired from a large firm which hadn't offered them enough challenge, glanced at each other, and made a tentative move toward the ladies'.

"Go on," Arhos said. "We've got enough time."

"She's the sensitive one," Pratt said, continuing the argument even without Losa.

"Stop it. It doesn't help, and we can't run her life." The rest of the team caught up with them, and formed a clot in the passage until Losa and the other women reappeared. Then, not speaking, they moved on to the gate that divided Fleet space from civilian space. Here, instead of a bored civilian customs inspector, they faced a cluster of alert, edgy, military guards.

"Arhos Asperson, Special Materials Analysis Consulting," Arhos said, handing over his ID case. "And this is the contract—" A data cube, embossed with Fleet's own insignia on one side, and an elaborate marbled etching on the others. It had taken them two years to develop a duplicate of Fleet's equipment, so that they could fabricate their own cubes rather than having to steal and reprogram them. Then they'd gotten this perfectly legitimate contract, and hadn't needed to use their fake.

"Yes, sir," the first guard said. "And how many in your group?"

"Seven," Arhos said. He stood aside, while the second guard collected everyone's ID cases. He would have worried, on Sierra Station, even with a real Fleet cube . . . though they had used the faked Fleet cubes before, and faked ID before, Fleet was unusually alert, thanks to the repercussions from Xavier. Here, he expected no trouble—and in fact the cube reader had already accepted, then spat out, the fake cube.

"All clear, sir," the guard said. "We'll have to check all the luggage, of course."

"Of course." He handed over his own duffel and briefcase. Standard civilian electronics: datapads, cube reader, cubes, portable computers in all sizes from pocket to briefing, communications access sets, data probe wands . . .

"You can't use this shipboard, sir," the guard said, holding up the comm access set and the data wand.

"No, I understand. Last time out, your people provided a shielded locker."

"We can do that, sir," the guard said, with obvious relief. Inexperienced consultants sometimes insisted that they would not give up any of their equipment . . . they got no more contracts. The other guard, Arhos noticed, was calling someone in Fleet territory, and soon a lowly pivot appeared with a luggage truck and a lockable container for the restricted electronics.

"You don't have to lock it up now," the guard said. "If you want to place calls from the Fleet areas, that's permissible from any blue-coded booth. But before boarding—"

"We understand," Arhos said. He knew there would be another search before they boarded.

The Fleet area of Comus Station had its own eating places, its own bars, its own entertainment and shopping outlets and even public-rental sleeping. They had plenty of time before their ship left.

"What exactly is your area of expertise, Dr. Asperson?"

Arhos allowed his mouth to quirk up at one corner, restrained amusement at the naivete of the question. "My degrees are in logical systems and substrate analysis."

The young officer blinked. " . . . Substrate?"

"Classified, I'm afraid," Arhos said, with a little dip of the head to take the edge off.

"Lieutenant, I believe you have duties forward," said the lieutenant commander at the head of the table.

"Oh . . . of course, sir." He scurried out.

"I'm sorry," the lieutenant commander said. He wore no name tag; none of the officers aboard such a small ship wore them. "Please forgive us—we're not usually carrying civilians—"

"Of course," Arhos said. "But you understand our situation—?"

"Certainly. Only—I didn't recognize your firm's name."

"Subcontractors," Gori said, grinning. "You know how it is—we used to work for the big firms, one and another of us, and then we struck out on our own. Got our first jobs as sub-subs, and now we're all the way up to subcontractors."

"It must be hard, going out on your own after working for a big company," the officer said. Arhos thought he was buying the whole story.

"It has been," Arhos said. "But we're past wondering how we're going to pay the rent."

"I imagine you are," the officer said, with a knowing smile for the quality of the clothes they wore, the expensive cases they carried.

"Not that it's easy profit," Arhos said, putting in the earnest emphasis that impressed the military so well. "We're working harder than we used to—but it's for ourselves. And you, of course."

"Of course."

At Sierra Station, they had no customs to pass, nothing but a long walk down one arm of the station and out another. An escort, ostensibly to ensure that they didn't get lost; civilians did not wander the Fleet sections of stations—especially stations this near the borders—without an escort. In the comfortable ease of someone who had not intended mischief anyway, the team ambled along, chatting aimlessly about the food they'd had, and the food they hoped to have.

Koskiusko's docking bay was actually a shuttle bay. Here, Arhos handed the contract cube to the ranking guard, who fed it into a cube reader.

"I'll call over, sir, but it'll be at least two hours before a shuttle comes in. The little pod's halfway over with an arriving officer, and the shuttle's already loaded with cargo—no room for you, and it's down at Orange 17 anyway."

"No problem. Is there someplace to get a drink, meanwhile?"

"Not really—there's a food machine just down the corridor there, between the toilets, but nothing really good."

"Nothing edible" grumbled another guard. "Station food service's supposed to replace those snacks before they turn green but—"

"We could call in for something," the first guard said. "They deliver from civ-side, but there's a fee—"

"That would be great," Arhos said. "The ship we came in on was skewed five hours off Station time by the last jump, and I for one would enjoy something. And if it's near a break for you—"

"No, thank you, sir. Here's the order list . . ."

"Ever been aboard a DSR before?" asked the bright-eyed young man who escorted them from the docking bay.

"No . . . main station yards, a couple of cruisers, but no DSR."

"Let me get you a shipchip," the youngster said. He touched a control panel, entering a sequence so fast that Arhos couldn't figure out the placement of sensors on the unmarked surface. Something bleeped, and tiny disks rattled into a bin below the panel.

Arhos looked at his and wondered how to activate it.

"Voice," the young man said promptly. "It'll project a route from your position to the location you name—for the low-security areas, that is. If you need access to the high-security areas, you'll have to get it reset. That'll be in ship admin, which it'll guide you to. I mean, I will, that's where you're going first, but any other time—"

"Thank you," Arhos said. Behind him, the rest of the team murmured appropriate thanks as well.

They were passed from desk to desk in the admin bay, collecting ship's ID tags, access cards for a variety of spaces, and a new set of shipchips. Then someone came to fetch them to the admin offices of the 14th Heavy Maintenance Yard.

"We don't have slideways, but we do have lift tubes," they were told. "Don't try to hitch a ride on the robo-carts—they're programmed to stop if they sense extra mass."

They spent the first several days looking over the inventory, and discussing their plan with the senior technician, a balding master chief named Furlow.

"I think Headquarters has its nose up its tail again," Furlow said at the first meeting. "Rekeying *all* the weapons guidance codes? That assumes the people doing the job are competent and loyal." He gave Arhos a sideways look. "Not that I'm saying you aren't, but it's too big a job to go without hitches."

"You're probably right," Arhos said. "But I'm not going to pass up a contract . . . it's how we make a living."

"Yes, well . . ." A heavy sigh. "I know you've got clearances from transcendent deities or something, but on my watch, these weapons are my responsibility and I'll have one of my people with you."

"Of course," Arhos said. "We don't want any misunderstandings either. This is the protocol we were sent— I'm assuming you have the other part—"

"Yes, sir, I do." The chief took Arhos's version and peered at it. "Scuzzing waste of time, but it'll work. How long did *you* tell 'em it'd take?"

"Five minutes per weapon, an hour to retool between types. That's what it took on the racks they mocked up for us to bid on." Arhos allowed himself to smile. "We were one minute faster than the next fastest on each, and a solid ten minutes faster in retooling. Then when they had us work on a patrol craft, we were able to work that fast even in tight situations. We weren't told what your inventory was, of course. We're just supposed to do it until it's done.

Then when the other ships return from deployment, we'll do theirs as well."

"I imagine," the chief said, "that there weren't many people that wanted to spend a standard year or more out here in Sector 14."

"Not that many," Arhos admitted. "Fleet had a lot of contracts to hand out for this work, and most of 'em were either bigger, smaller, or in more popular places. We happened to fit the profile for this one—and we performed well in the test series."

"Umph." The chief didn't look any happier, but at least seemed slightly less hostile. "Well, you have your work cut out. We store the weaponry for all of Sector 14. There's no rear supply depot out here, because of security concerns—Sierra Station gets a fair bit of civilian traffic, and we know some of it's Bloodhorde agents."

"We'd better get started, then, hadn't we?"

The chief still didn't move. "It's not going to be that easy. This thing is big, but not big enough to hold inventory like that in convenient arrays. Weapons and guidance systems are stored separately, and since the guidance systems are compact, we've squirreled them away wherever they'd fit. It's not anything like the way you worked on that patrol ship. At least we have an automated system. Let me show you some video." He ran his hand over the control panel on his desk, and a display came up on the wall. "That's one of the inventory bays in which guidance systems are stored." Racks rose from the deck to the overhead, the familiar pattern of automated inventory systems controls along the vertical rails. "Because the guidance systems are small, and most of the time we're not restocking the warships, we fit them in by size, not by type."

"So we're going to have to go through there and pull them out one at a time?"

"Not quite that bad. One rack at a time, though. This bay, right now, has . . ." The chief flicked another control that brought up a display on his desk. "Eight thousand two hundred sixty-four ASAC-32 modules. But they're on at least eight different stacks, and I'd bet that someone has moved at least a few of them when restocking other goods, and hasn't bothered to update the file."

"Won't your automated system do that?"

"So-so." The chief wobbled his hand in the age-old gesture. "High-security items have a tracer that sounds off if they're removed from that hold, but not if they're moved a few meters. We'd have spent all our time rekeying the tracers—we're always having to move things in and out."

"So you know they're in there, and you probably know where most of them are, but . . ."

"But not all. Which is why it's a stupid idea, thought up by someone who's never seen a big repair inventory." The chief grinned. "I hope they're paying you a daily allowance, and not by piece, or you'll be here forever and earn nothing."

Arhos wasn't sure that prospect would bother the chief, but it certainly bothered him. He had worried that the job wouldn't take long enough—that he'd have to stretch it out—that they wouldn't need to wander over enough of the ship to find the self-destruct. Instead . . . they would be here far too long, and although they'd have wide access they might be too busy to use it.

"I wonder if someone leaked this problem to Burrahn, Hing & Co., and that's why they didn't bid on this job," he said, and watched the chief's face. No flicker, but . . . but someone had to have leaked it. Damn the Bloodhorde! "At least we are getting a per diem . . . but it's going to be a bitch."

Arhos eyed his partners and gave a meaningful glance at the gray cylinder on the table between them. Fleet would expect them to disable the simpler scans of their compartment; Arhos had not concealed the device. Now he turned it on. Telltales blinked hotly: it had detected signals it could not fog. He'd expected that. Right now, it was important for Fleet to think its more delicate scans worked here. What lay concealed within the familiar cylinder, under the Morin Co. seal, was for later use, and more private conversations. His partners would know that, and would interpret what he said in the light of the caution now necessary.

"We have a problem," Arhos began, when the team had assembled. Quickly he repeated the chief's explanation of the way weapons guidance systems were stored on *Koski-usko.* "It's going to take a lot longer than we thought. It might be better to start with the weapons on the warships, since they're in the arrays we know—"

"But our contract states that we should begin with the DSR," Losa said, playing up beautifully.

"Yes, but they didn't tell us the whole story. With this arrangement, there'll be a lot of dead time—we'll be waiting around while they figure out where some of the weapons are. I'm considering whether to discuss a restructuring of the whole job." It would be difficult, with a signed contract; he would have to prove that Fleet had not provided necessary information. He wasn't sure he could trust that Chief Furlow to give evidence, if it came to that.

"A suggestion . . ." Gori said.

"Go ahead."

"Why not split the team, and send some of 'em over to the larger warships? That way, the manhours lost in dead time won't be as great."

"Possibly . . . in fact, that's a good idea. We won't have to worry about them . . ." Noticing anything, he didn't say, but Gori's upward twitch of eyebrow meant he'd understood exactly what Arhos didn't say.

"We don't look like whiners, we get the job done faster . . . and we're here to show that our top people cope with the unexpected." Losa sounded enthusiastic; her eyes sparkled. Arhos thought it over, liking the idea better every moment. The one thing they'd worried about was having one of their own people notice something. Yet the Fleet contract had required a larger team. This way—this way he got rid of those bright, inquisitive minds, in a way that could cast no suspicion on the partners.

"Good, then. I'll speak to the admiral's office. If we're

sending people off, we need to do that before we leave Sierra."

From Altiplano to Comus Station, Esmay traveled by civilian carrier, a regularly scheduled passenger ship. In the thirty days of her leave, other news had come to dominate the screens. No one seemed to recognize her in her civilian clothes, for which she was grateful. She divided her time between her own quarters and the ship's palatial fitness equipment. It felt odd to be aboard a ship and have no duties, but she was not about to call attention to herself by hanging around the crew looking wistful. Better to sweat on the exercise machines, and then cool off in the pool. She was vaguely aware that some of the other passengers who regularly used the fitness equipment might have wanted to chat, but swimming steady laps made that difficult. In her quarters, she worked her way through one teaching cube after another, everything in the ship's library that seemed relevant.

At Comus, she chose to walk the distance from the liner's docking bay to Fleetgate rather than taking a slideway. She needed to do a bit of shopping; she wanted to replace every bit of clothing she'd brought from Altiplano. It was wasteful, she admitted, to throw away perfectly good garments . . . but she wanted nothing to connect her to her past. When she found a Space Relief outlet store, she emptied her cases, and then handed over the cases, all but her Fleet duffel.

She needed little, really. A few comfortable things for lounging, one good dress outfit. She found all that in the first store she entered, picking the things hastily. It didn't really matter what she wore when she was off-duty. She was eager to get back to Fleet territory. When she arrived at the Fleetgate, the sentry's cheerful "Welcome home, Lieutenant!" sent her mood up three notches.

Esmay found her new assignment posted to her private mail when she checked in. She had expected a tour on Comus itself—else why send her out here in the first place?—but her orders directed her to Sierra Station, there to take up her duties with the Fourteenth Heavy Mainten-ance Yard aboard the *Koskiusko*. She'd never heard of that ship; when she looked it up in the Table of Ships, she discovered that it was a DSR, a deepspace repair ship, part of the second-wave deployment out of Sierra Station.

Someone must be seriously annoyed with her. Repair ships were huge, ungainly, complicated, and totally unglamorous. Worse, DSR ships were a logistics nightmare, the natural and lawful prey of every inspector general: it was impossible to keep them in perfect order, up to nominal inventory, because they were always losing parts to some other vessel. Legitimately, but inevitably, the paperwork lagged reality.

For this, among other reasons, very few people—except the specialists who actually did the repairs on other vessels—wanted assignment to a DSR. Young officers considered such an assignment proof that someone was down on them; Esmay followed the herd in this, if nothing else, and took it as evidence that exoneration by the official court hadn't convinced someone of her innocence. She looked up the next available transfer to Sierra Station. Because she had arrived on Comus almost 24 hours before her leave was up, she could just catch a Fleet supply run to Sierra . . . and she had no good excuse not to catch it, since her duty status went active the moment she logged on to pick up her orders.

Esmay checked—the supply ship had space available, and she had two hours to report aboard. A bored clerk stamped and validated her original and amended orders, updated her hardcopy ID and her files. She dashed in and out of the tiny PX to pick up her new insignia—the clerk told her that her promotion to lieutenant had come through while she was on leave—and get a *Koskiusko* shiptag for her duffel. That wasn't required, since she hadn't signed aboard, but her duffel was more likely to arrive there if it had a shiptag than a name-and-number. When she got to the docking bay for the supply ship, she found herself in a queue with half a dozen other Fleet personnel making a transfer. No one stared at her; no one seemed to know who she was or care. Most of the talk was about a parpaun match played recently between the crews of two ships in dock—apparently someone had kicked all three of the possible goals in one play—but Esmay had never really understood parpaun. Why two balls? Why three differently colored goals? Why—she often thought to herself, but would not say—bother? Now she was glad to hear the others full of enthusiasm for something that banal, and she hoped that her moment of fame had already vanished.

The supply ship was hauling parts that would resupply *Koskiusko*; its exec had noticed her orders, and put her to work checking the inventory. Sixteen days of counting impellers, gaskets, lengths of tubing, fasteners of all kinds, tubes of adhesive, updates to repair manuals (both hardcopy and cubes). . . . Esmay decided that someone at Headquarters *really* hated her.

She was good at this kind of thing; she didn't find it difficult to keep her concentration. On the fourth day, she noticed that of the 562 boxes supposed to contain 85mm star-slot fasteners with threads of pitch 1/10 and interval 3mm, one was labeled for 85mm star-slot fasteners with threads of pitch 1/12 and interval 4mm instead. Two days later she found three leaky tubes of adhesive, which had glued themselves to neighboring tubes in a container; it was clear from the discoloration of the labels that they had been flawed from the beginning; she noted that. She could see why this was necessary—someone would find the errors and better now than in the midst of an emergency repair—but it wasn't the glamorous sort of job she'd thought of when she had dreamed of leaving Altiplano. Either time she'd left Altiplano.

She wondered if she'd spend her entire time aboard *Koskiusko* doing the same thing. That would make a very long two years. She didn't want notoriety, exactly, but she would like something more interesting than bean-counting.

In her off-shift, she listened to the sports fans, hoping for a change in topic, but they seemed to have no other interests. Apparently, they had all played on a parpaun team at one time or another, and after they'd rehashed the recent match they were happy to tell each other in detail about every match they'd played. Esmay listened long enough to understand at last what the rules were, and why two balls (each team had its own ball, and scores could be made with the opponent's ball only on the third, "neutral" goal. It still seemed an unreasonably complex game, and as boring as any other for nonplayers to listen to.

She finally gave up and started reading the supply ship's tech support cubes. Inventory control, principles and practice. The design of automated inventory systems. Even an article on "static munitions recognition systems"—which she couldn't imagine needing—was better than the eighty-eighth rehash of a game she hadn't seen and didn't care about anyway. She was sure she'd never come face to face with a Barasci V-845 mine or its nastier cousin, the Smettig Series G, but she stared at the display until she was sure she would know them again if she were unlucky enough to see one.

Sierra Station served both Fleet and civilian interests, but Fleet predominated. Two long arms docked only military vessels; Esmay watched the names scroll past on the ward-room screen. *Pachyderm*, the oldest active cruiser, and Fleet's largest. *Plenitude, Savage,* and *Vengeance*, cruisers much like Heris Serrano's *Vigilance. Plenitude* had a star by its name—it was the flagship of some combat group. A gaggle of patrol craft: *Consummate, Pterophil, Singularity, Autarch, Rascal, Runagate, Vixen, Despite . . . Despite?* What was *Despite* doing here?

Esmay felt cold all over. She had left that very lucky (in one way) and unlucky (in another) ship almost the full length of Familias space away . . . she had not expected to see *Despite* again unless she was transferred to its sector. Why had they moved it at all? And why, of all places, *here*?

She didn't want to know. She didn't want to see that ship again; the memory of victory could not erase the memory of what had gone before, that bloody mutiny, and the mistakes she had made later.

She shook that off. She couldn't afford to be upset by it, and it was unlikely she'd have anything to do with *Despite* and her new captain.

Koskiusko, the screen read, blinking now because she had put a tracer on the name. She noted the concourse and docking number in her personal compad. One corner of the screen turned yellow, then flashed their arrival dock number in blue. Esmay referred to the station map . . . *Koskiusko* was out at the far end of the longest arm, but she could get there without going past *Despite*.

When she made it to the gate area, a pair of Fleet security personnel checked her orders again. To her surprise, they made no move to open the access hatch. "It'll be a few minutes, Lieutenant," one of them said. He had sergeant's stripes on his uniform, and his unit patch read Sierra Station, not *Koskiusko*. Esmay noticed that nowhere on the deck of the gate area were the traditional stripes defining ship space from station space. "They've sent a pod but it's not here yet."

"A pod?"

"DSRs don't actually dock at stations." The tone was carefully respectful, though Esmay had the feeling she had just asked a stupid question. "They're too big—the relative masses would play hob with each other's artificial gravity." A pause, then a neutral, "Would you like to see *Koskiusko*, Lieutenant?"

"Yes," Esmay said. She'd already shown she was ignorant; she might as well learn what she could.

"Here, then." Up on the gate display came a blurry view of something large; the view sharpened, leaped nearer, and finally stabilized as the biggest and most unlikely excuse for a ship Esmay had ever seen. It looked like the unfortunate mating of an office building with a bulk-cargo tank and some sort of clamshell array. "Those funny-looking things are on the main repair bays," the sergeant said helpfully. "They've got 'em open now, testing. As you can see, an escort can fit all the way in, and even most patrols . . . then the ports swing down . . ."

That opening was the size of an escort? Esmay revised

her assumptions about size upward steeply. Not just an office building, but—she realized that the array of lights beyond a rounded bulge was another "office building." It looked nothing like the DSR stats she'd seen at the Academy six years before. The two DSRs they'd been shown designs of had been built like clusters of grapes, with a single cylindrical repair bay running through the cluster. When she said that, the sergeant grinned.

"*Koskiusko* wasn't commissioned then," the sergeant said. "She's new—and she's not the same as she was, either. Here—I'll show you a design plot."

This came up in the three standard views, plus an angled one similar to that Esmay had seen. In design, the DSR still looked like several disparate (but large) components had been squashed together. Five blunt arms ran out from a central core: that was the "office building" part. Two adjacent arms had the clamshell arrangements on them. Behind those trailed great oblong shapes labeled "drive test cradle." The arm adjacent to neither "main repair bay" had the tanklike object—larger, Esmay realized, than any tank she'd seen—stuck on its end like a bulbous nose. Without the tank, it would have looked like an orbital station specialized for some industrial process.

"What is that tank?" she asked, fascinated by this impossible oddity.

"Dunno, sir. That was added about three years ago, maybe two years after she was commissioned. Ah—here's your pod." The display blinked out, then reappeared as a status line; Esmay heard the clunk as the pod docked, then the whistling of an airlock cycling. Finally the status light turned green, and the sergeant opened the hatch. "Good luck, sir. Hope you enjoy your tour."

Esmay found the pod unsettling. It had no artificial gravity; she had to strap into the passenger racks and hang there facing a ring of ports. The pilot wore an EVA suit; his helmet hung on a drop-ring just above him, suggesting that the EVA suit was more sense than worry. Through the pod's wide ports she could see entirely too much of Sierra Station and its docked vessels, barnacles on a floating wheel. Station navigation beacons and standing lights played over them, glittering from the faceted hulls of pressurized bulk cargo tanks, gleaming from brightly colored commercial liners, and scarcely revealing the matte-dark hulls of Fleet vessels, except for pricks of light reflected from shield and weapons fittings. Beyond, a starfield with no planets distinguishable. Sierra System had them, but not out here, where the station served primarily outsystem transport. Sudden acceleration bumped Esmay against the rack, and then ceased; her stomach lagged behind, then lurched forward.

"Bag's on the overhead, if you need it," the pilot said. Esmay gulped and kept her last meal firmly in place. "We're over there—" The pod pilot nodded to the forward port. A tangle of lights that diverged as they came nearer. Suddenly a glare as a searchlight from one arm flared across another, revealing the hull surface to be lumpy and dark . . . and big. Esmay could not get used to the scale.

"Passenger pod docking access is near the hub," the pilot said. "That gives passengers the easiest access to personnel lifts and most admin offices. Cargo shuttles and special cargo pods dock near the inventory bays for the specific cargo. Minimizes interior traffic." He leaned forward and prodded the control panel; deceleration shoved Esmay against the straps. Closer . . . closer . . . she glanced up to the overhead port, and saw the vast bulk of the DSR blocking out most of the starfield—then all of it.

Exiting the pod into the passenger bay, Esmay stepped across the red stripes that signaled where the ship formally began (something that had no relation to its architecture) and saluted the colors painted on the opposite bulkhead.

"Ah . . . Lieutenant Suiza." The sergeant at the dock entry looked back and forth from her ID to her face several times. "Uh . . . welcome home, sir. The captain left word he wanted to see you when you came aboard . . . shall I call ahead?"

Esmay had thought she'd have time to put her duffel away first, but captains had their perks. "Thank you," she said. "Can you tell me my bunk assignment?"

"Yes, sir. You've got number 14 in the junior officers section of T-2, 'cross ship from where we are now. This is the base of T-4. Do you want someone to take your duffel down?"

She didn't want anyone messing with her things. "No, thanks. I'll just stick it in a temp locker for now."

"It's no trouble, Lieutenant. The temp lockers are out of your way to the captain's office anyway . . ."

She also didn't want to start with a reputation for being difficult. "Thanks, then." She handed over the duffel, and accepted the sergeant's directions to the captain's office . . . turn left out that hatch, take the second lift up five levels to Deck Nine, then left out of the lift and follow the signs.

The wide curving corridor matched the size of the ship; it belonged on an orbital station, not a warship. Esmay passed the first bank of lift tubes; the signs made it clear she was on Deck Four, which on an ordinary ship would be Main, not that any ordinary ship would have signs. At the second bank of tubes, she stepped in and watched the numbers flash by. Eighteen decks . . . what could they find to put on eighteen decks?

She stepped out of the lift tube on Deck Nine. Here the wide curving corridor that went around the core had the gray tile she associated with Main Deck in ordinary ships. Across from the lift tube openings a corridor led away, she supposed down one of the arms . . . T-5, said the sign on the overhead. A clerk sat at a desk in an open bay to one side. Esmay introduced herself.

"Ah. Lieutenant Suiza. Yes, sir, the captain wanted to see you right away. Captain Vladis Julian Hakin, sir. Just let me buzz the captain . . ." Esmay could not hear any signal, but the clerk nodded. "Go along in, sir. Third on your left."

This captain had had a wooden door substituted for the standard steel hatch; this was not unusual. It was somewhat unusual for it to be closed when a visitor had been announced. Esmay knocked.

"Come in," came a growl from the other side. She

opened the door and entered, to find herself facing the top of a gray head. The captain's office had been carpeted in deep green, and paneled in wood veneer. The Familias seal hung on the bulkhead behind the captain's desk on one side, and a framed copy of some document—probably his commission, though she couldn't see it—on the other.

"Ah . . . Lieutenant Suiza." That seemed to be the greeting of the day. In Captain Hakin's tone of voice, it sounded more like a curse than a greeting. "I hear they consider you quite the hero on Altiplano." Definitely a curse. The distinction between *on Altiplano* and *here in the real world* might have been printed in red with less emphasis.

"Local interest, sir," Esmay said. "That's all."

"I'm glad you realize that," Captain Hakin said. He looked up suddenly, as if hoping to catch her in some incriminating expression. Esmay met his gaze calmly; she had expected repercussions from the awards ceremony, that was only natural. His glance flicked down to her uniform, where the silver and gold ribbon was *not* on the row allotted to non-Fleet decorations. By law, she was entitled to wear major awards from any political system within the Familias Regnant; by custom, no one did unless on a diplomatic assignment where failure to wear a locally awarded decoration might insult the giver. Junior officers, in particular, wore no personal awards except when in full dress uniform. So Esmay had the S&S, the ships-and-service ribbons appropriate to her past service, including the two decorations awarded *Despite*'s crew for the recent engagement—and, incongruously, the Ship Efficiency Award won under the late Captain Hearne. Traitor Hearne might have been, but her ship had topped the sector in the IG's inspection.

"Yes, sir," Esmay said, when his gaze flicked back to hers.

"Some captains would be concerned about a junior officer who had been involved in a mutiny, no matter how . . . er . . . warranted the action was later shown to be."

"I'm sure that's true, sir," Esmay said, unruffled. She had dealt with this sort of thing all her life. "There must be some officers who remain concerned even after a court has considered the matter in detail. I can assure the captain that I will not overreact to such concern, if anyone expresses it."

Hakin stared. What had he thought, that she'd turn red and bluster, trying to justify herself? She had stood before a court; she had been exonerated of all charges; she need do nothing but live out her innocence.

"You seem very sure of yourself, Lieutenant," Hakin said finally. "How do you know that I am not one of those so concerned?"

Idiot, thought Esmay. His determination to prick her had overcome his good sense. No answer she could give would entirely ease the tension he had created. She chose bluntness. "Is the captain concerned?"

A long sigh, through pursed lips. "About many things, Lieutenant, of which your potential for mutiny is only one minute particle. I have been assured, by those who are supposed to know, that the public reports of your court-martial were in fact accurate . . . that there is no suspicion of your having conspired to mutiny ahead of your captain's treacherous act." He waited; Esmay could think of nothing helpful to say, and kept quiet. "I shall expect your loyalty, Lieutenant."

"Yes, sir," Esmay said. That she could do.

"And have you no corresponding concern that your next captain might also be a traitor? That I might be in the pay of some enemy?"

She had not let herself think about that; the effort pushed her response into exclamation. "No, sir! Captain Hearne must have been an aberration—"

"And the others as well? You're happier than I, if you can believe that, Lieutenant."

Now what was he getting at?

"We've had investigators all over every ship in the Fleet—and that's reassuring only to those who think the investigators can't be bent. A mess of trouble that Serrano woman caused."

Esmay opened her mouth to defend Heris Serrano, and realized it would do no good. If Hakin seriously believed that Serrano had "caused trouble" by unmasking traitors and saving the Familias from invasion, she couldn't change his mind. She could only ruin her own reputation.

"Not that she isn't a brilliant commander," Hakin went on, as if she had said something. "I suppose Fleet must count itself lucky to have her back on active status . . . if we do get into a war." He looked at Esmay again. "I'm told Admiral Vida Serrano is pleased with you . . . I suppose she would be, since you saved her niece's neck."

That, too, was unanswerable. Esmay wished he would get to the point, if his point was not merely to needle her, trying to get some sort of reaction.

"I hope you don't have a swelled head from all the attention, Lieutenant. Or some kind of psychological trauma from the strain of the court-martial, which I've been warned is sometimes the case, even with a favorable verdict." From his expression, he would want some kind of answer this time.

"No, sir." Esmay said.

"Good. I'm sure you're aware that this is a time of crisis for both the Fleet and the Familias. No one knows quite what to expect . . . except that on this ship, I expect everyone to attend to duty. Is that clear?"

"Yes, sir."

"Very good, Lieutenant; I'll see you from time to time as the mess rotations come around." He dismissed her with a nod, and Esmay went out trying to suppress a resentment that she knew would do her no good. No one lasted long in any service with a "why me?" attitude; she wasn't to blame for the things held against her, but what was new about that? In the history of the universe, Papa Stefan had taught them all, life was unfair more often than not . . . life wasn't about *fair*. What it was about had filled more than one evening with explosive argument . . . Esmay tried not to think about it more than necessary.

She handed her order chip to the clerk in the front office. "What's my duty assignment, do you know?" He glanced at it and shook his head. "That's the 14th Heavy Maintenance Yard, Lieutenant: Admiral Dossignal's command. You'll need to report to his Admin section . . . here—" He sketched out a route on her compad. "Just keep going clockwise around the core, and you'll come to it at the base of T-3."

"Is the bridge on this deck?" asked Esmay, gesturing to the color-coded deck tiles.

"No, sir. The bridge is up on 17; this ship's too big for the usual color-codes. There is a system, but it's not standard. We call this command deck because all the commands have their headquarters units here. That's just for convenience, really; it cuts down the transit time." Esmay could imagine that in a ship this size any hand-carried message could take awhile to arrive. She had never been on a ship where the captain's office and the bridge were not near each other.

On her way around the core, she passed another obvious headquarters, this one with a neat sign informing her that it was the Sector 14 Training Command, Admiral Livadhi commanding. Underneath were smaller signs: SENIOR TECHNICAL SCHOOLS ADMIN OFFICE, SENIOR TECHNICAL SCHOOLS ASSESSMENT, SUPPORT SYSTEMS. She walked on, past the base of another wing, this one labeled T-2. That was where she would be living, but she didn't have time to explore it now. On and on . . . and there ahead she saw a large banner proclaiming *Fourteenth Heavy Maintenance Yard: The Scrap Will Rise Again.* Below that, smaller signs directed the ignorant to the administrative offices. There, a bright-eyed pivot-major sent her directly to the admiral's chief of staff, Commander Atarin. He greeted Esmay's appearance in a matter-of-fact way she found reassuring. He had already read her report on the inventory aboard the supply ship, and seemed far more interested in that than her past.

"We've been trying to nail our supplier on these leaky adhesive tubes for a couple of years," he said. "But we couldn't prove that the supplies were damaged before we got here. I'm glad old Scorry—the XO on that supply ship—thought of having you go over the stock on your way here. We may finally get some leverage on them."

"Yes, sir."

"How much experience do you have with inventory control?"

"None, sir," Esmay said. Her record cube, she knew, was on the XO's desk, but he might not have had time to look at it.

"I'm impressed, then, especially that you caught those fasteners. Most people give up after fifty or sixty items. Or assume the computer will catch it. It's supposed to, of course—there's supposed to be automatic labeling, right from the manufacturing machinery. Zero-error, they keep claiming. Never have *seen* zero errors, though." He grinned at her. "Of course, it could be someone from the I.G.'s office, putting little tests in our path, to see if we're alert."

That possibility hadn't occurred to Esmay, though sabotage had. But he hadn't been on *Despite*.

"Of course, it could also be enemy action," he said. She hoped he hadn't seen that on her face. "But I'd rather believe in stupidity than malice." He looked down at his desk display. "Now let's see . . . your last duty was on a patrol craft—your emphasis on your last few cruises was scan technology. Frankly, we have plenty of scan tech experts aboard now, all more experienced than you in the field. It would do you good to branch out, get some expertise in other ship systems—" He looked up as if expecting her to disagree.

"Fine, sir," Esmay said. She hoped it was fine. She knew she needed to learn about other systems, but was he just determined to keep her away from scan, because scan was political?

"Good." He smiled again, and nodded. "I expect most of you juniors think DSR is a bad assignment, but you'll discover that there's no better way to learn what really keeps ships operational. No ordinary ship deals with as many problems as we do, from hull to electronics. If you take advantage of it, this tour can teach you a lot."

Esmay relaxed. She recognized someone happily astride

his favorite hobby horse. "Yes, sir," she said, and wondered if he would go on.

"Personally, I think every officer should have a tour on a DSR. Then we wouldn't have people coming up with bright ideas—even installing bright ideas—that they should know wouldn't work." He reined himself in with a visible effort. "Well. I'm going to assign you to H&A first—Hull and Architecture, that is. You'll find it a lot more complicated than your basic course at the academy."

"I expect so, sir," Esmay said.

"You'll be working with Major Pitak; she's on Deck Eight, portside main, aft third of T-4 . . . you can ask someone from there. Had time to stow your gear yet?"

"No, sir."

"Mmm. Well, technically you're not on duty until tomorrow, but—"

"I'll go see Major Pitak, sir."

"Good. Now, the admiral will want to meet you, but he's tied up right now in a meeting, and I don't expect he'll be free until tomorrow or the next day. Check back with me, and I'll set it up. You might want to take a look at the command structure here—it's more complex than you'd find in most assignments."

"Yes, sir."

Not only the command structure was complex, Esmay discovered. She headed clockwise from T-3, where the 14th Heavy Maintenance had its administrative offices, to T-4, sure that she had now caught on to the *Koskiusko's* peculiar structure. At the hub end of T-4, she found an array of personnel and cargo transport tubes, and took the personnel lift down to the eighth deck. There she faced an axial passage wide enough for three horsemen abreast, and plunged into it, looking for the third crosswise passage. She passed one administrative office after another, each occupied by busy clerks: Communications Systems, Weapons Systems, Remote Imaging Systems . . . but nothing labeled Hull and Architecture. Finally she stopped and asked.

"Hull and Architecture? That's on the portside main

passage, sir. You'll have to go back to hub and clockwise
to it—"

Esmay suspected a joke at her expense. "Surely there
are cross-passages?"

A quickly-suppressed laugh. "No, sir . . . T-4 has one
of the main repair bays . . . nothing goes straight across
at this level, from Deck Three up to Deck Fifteen."

She had forgotten the repair bays. She felt annoyed with
herself and the clerk both. "Oh yes. Sorry."

"No problem, sir. It takes awhile for anyone to get used
to this place. Just take this passage back, turn left—" The
civilian term seemed right for something this size, Esmay
realized. "Then look for the P-designations on the bulkheads. That's portside main—if you keep going, you'll get
to portside secondary, which you don't want. Hull and
Architecture is about as far down portside main as we are
down starboard, so . . ."

So she had given herself a lot more walk than she
wanted. "Thank you," she said, with what courtesy she
could muster past her annoyance. This ship shouldn't need
any fitness equipment, if everyone got lost occasionally.

Although she felt the length of the hike in her legs,
she had no more trouble finding Pitak's office. The portside
main passage was easy enough, and at the third passage
aft she found a pivot who directed her the rest of the way.

Major Pitak wasn't in that office. The pivot had said
something about "the major's on a bit about something"
but Esmay didn't know what that meant. She glanced up
and down the passage. Crewmen moving along as if they
knew what they were doing, and no major. She thought
of going to look, and decided not to play that game. She
would simply park here until Pitak came back.

She glanced around. On the bulkhead facing the
entrance was a display of metal pieces. Esmay wondered
what it was, and moved closer to read the label below.
COMMON WELDING ERRORS it said. Esmay could see the
big lopsided blob at the one joint, and the failure of
another blob to cover the joint . . . but what was wrong
with the rest of them?

"So you're my new assistant," someone said behind her. Esmay turned around. Major Pitak looked like her name sounded: a short, angular woman with a narrow face that reminded Esmay uneasily of a mule.

"Sir," Esmay said. Pitak scowled at her.

"And no background at all in naval architecture or heavy engineering, I notice."

"No, sir."

"Do you at least have *some* background in construction of anything? Even a chicken house?" It was clear that Pitak was furious about something; Esmay hoped it wasn't her own presence.

"Not unless helping put a roof back on a stable after a windstorm counts," Esmay said.

Pitak glared a moment longer, then softened. "No . . . it doesn't. Someone must be mad at both of us, Lieutenant. Sector HQ stole three of my best H&A specialists, promoted my assistant off this ship, and left me short . . . and now they've sent you, whatever your background is."

"Scan, mostly," Esmay said.

"If I were religious, I would consign their sorry tails to some strenuous afterlife," Major Pitak said. The corner of her mouth twitched. "Blast it. I never can stay mad long enough to singe them properly, and they know it. All right, Lieutenant, let's see what you do know. Whatever it is, it's not enough, but at least you haven't done anything stupid yet."

"I've hardly had time, sir," Esmay said. She was beginning to like the major, against all expectation.

"There's a naive statement," Pitak said. She had moved to her desk, where she yanked at a drawer without effect. "I've been sent idiots who managed to screw up before I'd met them." Another yank, this one hard enough to shift the desk itself. "For instance, this drawer . . . it never has worked right since your predecessor times two thought it would be clever to rekey the lock. We still don't know what he did, but none of the command wands work on it, nor does anything else but brute force and profanity." Without changing expression, Pitak launched a blistering stream of the latter at the drawer, which finally yielded with a squawk.

Esmay wanted to ask why anyone would use such a pesky drawer—why not clean it out and leave it empty?—but this was not the time. She watched Pitak rummage through the contents, coming up with a couple of data cubes.

"You probably wonder why I put anything in here," Pitak said. "Frankly so do I, but there's little enough secured storage down here—not with all the specialists we have aboard, people who know all the tricks of every security device since the latch. They sent some background on you, but I haven't looked at it yet, which I hope you won't hold against me."

"No, sir."

"For pity's sake, Lieutenant, loosen up. Find a seat somewhere. Let's see here . . ." She inserted the cube in a cube reader as Esmay looked around for something to sit on. Every horizontal surface was crusted in clutter; the two chairs had piles of hardcopy that looked like inventory lists. Pitak glanced up. "Just shove some of that onto the floor. Danton was supposed to clean it up yesterday, but he's in sickbay with some crud he caught . . . I think we'd do better to let them brew their nasty chemicals on board; they always get sick ashore."

Esmay set a pile of paper carefully on the floor, and sat down. Pitak was scowling at the cube reader's display.

"Well. For a mutineer and a hero, you're awfully quiet, Lieutenant Suiza. Trying to cover your tracks?"

Esmay couldn't think of anything to say.

"Hmm. The strong, silent type. Not mine, as you've already discovered. Planetary militia family . . . ye gods, one of *those* Suizas!" Esmay hadn't had that reaction from anyone in Fleet before; she could feel her eyebrows going up. Pitak stared at her. "Do they *know?*"

"I'm not sure what you mean, sir."

A disgusted look, which Esmay felt she deserved. "Don't play your games with me, Lieutenant Suiza. I mean, does

Fleet understand that 'planetary militia' is an under-statement when applied to the Suiza family of Altiplano?"

"I had assumed they did," Esmay said cautiously. "At least, when I applied, there was a background check, and surely they found out."

"You're a careful pup," Pitak said. "I noticed that 'had'—what do you think now?"

"Uh . . . most don't realize it, but I presume someone must." Esmay wanted to know how Pitak knew—surely she wasn't from Altiplano herself. Esmay had thought she was the first.

"I see." Pitak scrolled through the cube contents; Esmay presumed it was a precis of her record. "Interesting place, Altiplano, but I wouldn't want to live there. Ah—at least you were on the science branch at the Academy . . . interesting. You didn't take the usual courses for someone going command track. What did you think, technical?"

"Yes, sir."

"And then you end up the most junior officer ever to command a patrol vessel in combat—and win. I'll bet someone's looking into your background again. Well, I'll tell you what, Lieutenant—the most important thing you can do right now is learn your way around this ship, because when I have something for you to do, I don't want you to spend an hour finding out where it is. So—next three days, while we're docked, go everywhere and see everything and be ready for an orientation exam when you come back. That's 0800 on the 27th—clear?"

"Yes, sir," Esmay said. Curiosity burned away the last shreds of her caution. "If the major doesn't mind—how did you know about Altiplano?"

"Good for you," Pitak said, grinning now. She had a strange grin, in that narrow face, all teeth somewhat bigger than seemed possible to fit in it. "I was wondering if you'd get up the nerve to ask. Met a fellow one time I thought of hitching up with, back when I was a jig and things weren't going too well. Spent a leave on Altiplano, with his family. Heard all about the Suizas and their relations, and the local politics, but the whole time he was extolling the beauties of those big rolling plains and snow-capped mountains, I was wishing for a nice tight spaceship. Especially after a gallop over the plains in a rainstorm— I was sure I'd be fried by lightning, and I was so sore I couldn't walk for days. I suppose you ride?"

"When I have to," Esmay said. This was not the time to mention her own herd, which she hadn't wanted anyway. "It's—expected, riding. But I chose space."

"My kind of woman. Now—get out of here and start learning where things are. I warn you, my exams are no joke. Here—this is what you need." She tossed over a data cube. "That and good legs."

"Thank you, sir," Esmay said.

"0800 on the 27th."

"Yes, sir." Esmay paused, but the major didn't look up. She retraced her way back to the hub corridors, then looked up her assigned quarters and figured out a route to that compartment. T-2 should be back the way she'd come, counterclockwise . . . then up the personnel lift, and . . . she paid close attention to the axial passage designation, even though T-2 wasn't split by a repair bay . . . somewhere around here. . . .

CHAPTER EIGHT

Her compartment was small, but her own—lieutenants had that bit of privacy. Her duffel was waiting on the bunk, its seals unbroken. She stowed her gear in the locker, activated the status board, and confirmed her identity to the computer's flat-voiced inquiry. On a bulkhead a colored plan explained the officer housing arrangement. T-2 was configured for personnel housing: decks of enlisted bunking, broken into large bays for most, with two- or four-person compartments for the most senior. An entire deck for junior officers, with ensigns in ten-man bays, jigs in two-person compartments, and lieutenants in separate compartments, ranging outward by seniority. Above her was a deck of billeting for field grade officers, and above that a deck for the flag officers; she blinked at the number of admirals aboard.

Messing was in the same wing: two levels of food storage, kitchens, and dining halls. Exercise rooms, gyms, pools, even team sports space—she groaned at the thought of more parpaun enthusiasts—and on the top decks, open gardens. Gardens? Some space stations had gardens, but no Fleet vessel she'd ever been on. She thanked whatever beneficent deities had not assigned her to Environmental; it must be unbelievably difficult on a ship like this.

She looked around her compartment again. She hadn't minded ensign bunking, when she'd been that junior. Some automatic device in her brain kept the worst dreams away when she was sleeping in a public space. Lack of privacy when awake had rarely bothered her either; she had not had much free time to miss it. Now . . . now she would have to hope that the nightmares didn't wake her neighbors on either side. Her conscience pointed out that

she could always go to Medical and request help from
the psychs; she ignored it.

She had no messages waiting; she was not expected
anywhere in particular. Which meant she could take a
look at Pitak's assignment on the cube, if she could find
a cube reader free. The console informed her that she
had her own cube reader . . . it took her a moment to
find it; she had never seen one in the fully-stowed
position. Most people left them half-open at least, for
the next user.

The cube contained what looked like ordinary ship
schematics. Not ordinary, exactly—this ship wasn't ordinary—but nothing she couldn't have pulled off the general
user base and displayed on her own console. Esmay called
up the schematics on the console to check that.

Not quite the same. Passages that went through on one
schematic dead-ended in the other . . . lifts were in slightly
different places. Esmay scowled at the display. Was the
major trying to play her for a fool, or was the ship's own
database wrong? If so, why?

She looked for the nearest non-match, which was back
on T-3, where a cross-corridor on Deck Three that the
ship's database said ran through "Forming Workshop 2-B"
ended on Pitak's data cube before reaching the workshop;
according to her data, "forming workshop 2-B" couldn't be
reached except by a detour around "Die Storage."

Only one way to find out. She glanced at the time . . . she
could get up there and back to her assigned mess in T-2
before the next meal.

Back to the hub end of T-2, then clockwise to the base
of T-3 . . . she was getting the hang of this. She located
the personnel lift tube beside a cluster of four labeled
CARGO ONLY.

The personnel lift light changed to green, and Esmay
punched in. When the second light came on, she stepped
in and felt a quick double lurch of her innards before she
came to rest at the hatch eight decks down. Waiting there
was another lieutenant, male, with a couple of ensigns in
tow.

"I don't know you," the lieutenant said, as she stepped out. "Are you assigned here?"

"Just aboard, sir," Esmay said, hoping she didn't have the bug-eyed look that usually followed a short hop on the lift tube. "Esmay Suiza, assigned to Hull and Architecture . . ."

"Oh, yes." He extended a hand; he had a good handshake. "Tai Golonifer. Short for something horrible and familial, don't ask. I heard you were coming; I'm with 14th Maintenance staff. Are you busy at the moment?"

What was this? "I'm assigned to Major Pitak," Esmay said, intentionally oblique.

"You're busy," Golonifer said, as if there were no doubt. "I'm not surprised she's already got you running all over the ship. But meet these two—also newbies—Ensigns Anson and Partrade." The two ensigns returned Esmay's handshakes—Anson had a chilly, damp palm, and Partrade's felt as if he'd lined it with saddle leather. "See you at mess," Golonifer said. "Come on, guys, down the tube we go."

Esmay turned away and looked around her. She needed the starboard main axial passage for T-3. On this deck, the corridor was wide enough to drive a small truck through, and the inlaid guidelines for transport carts, along with marked pedestrian lanes on either side, suggested that small trucks did in fact drive it, at speed.

A soft rushing . . . she glanced back and saw a flatbed carrier loaded with canisters rolling smoothly along the guideline, its red sensor blinking like a mad red eye. Five meters from her, its automatic warning bleated three times . . . then it was past. Ahead, Esmay saw it slow and swing into a large hatch on the outboard side. When she got to the hatch and looked in, she saw a long robotic arm plucking canisters off the carrier and placing them on racks. Someone in the compartment yelled—she couldn't hear clearly—and the arm stopped in mid-move, with one canister in its pincers.

She couldn't stand there all day—she would have the rest of her tour to figure out what was going on in there. She set off again. The first cross-passage was double the width of the one she was using, with warning lights as well as mirrors at the corners. Esmay glanced at the mirrors, even though the lights were green. Far down the inboard side something large and lumpy with flashing yellow lights sat motionless, with little dark figures swarming over it . . . she blinked, startled again at the distances inside this ship.

Esmay almost missed the second cross-corridor; a dark slit opened on either side, barely one pedestrian wide, and lit only by wide-spaced lights. Again she stopped and peered at it. On a cramped escort, this might be a normal width—but it didn't fit with the others she'd seen. The third aft was the most normal so far, if anything about this ship was normal. Three could have walked abreast, if they didn't mind banging hands now and then. Evenly spaced hatches opened off it on either side. The fourth aft was much like it . . . a passage that might have been on any ship, save for its length. The fifth, the one she'd come to see . . . she turned inboard.

Forming Workshop A was right where both Pitak's cube and the ship's own schematics said it should be. Esmay wasn't sure what a forming workshop was, but she could tell that it was important. Guide lines for robotic carts streaked the floor, curving into one hatch after another. Through the open hatches she could see long arrays of equipment that meant nothing to her: cylinders and inverted cones, racks of nozzles mounted overhead on tracks, great blank-faced cubes with warning logos on them.

Ahead of her, the passage ended in a sealed hatch. Esmay glanced again at her notes. The ship's computer evidently thought this passage continued . . . and perhaps it did, past the obstruction. NO ADMITTANCE WITHOUT AUTHORIZATION in yellow on red . . . and Esmay suspected that some of the little gleaming knobs on the hatch seal were actually video sensors.

She retraced her way to the longitudinal passage, and followed the indirect path suggested by Pitak's cube. It took longer than she'd expected . . . she kept being surprised at the size, and annoyed with herself for still being surprised. But she found Forming Workshop B where Pitak's cube said it would be, and on this side the obstruction looked like an ordinary hatch with the label DIE STORAGE.

A soft tone rang through the ship, and she glanced at her handcomp. Almost late—she would have to hurry, and she was on the other side of the ship from territory she was already thinking of as home. She didn't bother to compare Pitak's data with the ship's own this time; she jogged forward on the portside main passage, back around the hub passage, popped into the first passenger tube, and fetched up at her assigned mess only just ahead of the gong.

Here she found that lieutenants were expected to head a table of jigs and ensigns. She had met none of them yet. They introduced themselves politely and she tried to sort out names and faces. She said little, listening to them and hoping to find out something to make them memorable. The light-haired ensign on the left had a scrape on his left hand; surely by the time it healed she'd have another reason to know him. The jigs seemed a bit stiff, as if they were afraid of her. They must have heard about the court-martial, but was that all?

"Lieutenant Suiza, did you really meet Admiral Serrano?" That was an ensign, not the blond one but a thin dark young man with green eyes. Custis, his nametag said.

"Yes, I did," Esmay said. Ensign Custis opened his mouth to say more, but the blond ensign elbowed him visibly and he shut it again. A brief silence followed, during which Esmay ate steadily. Out of the corner of her eye, she could see Custis glancing at her from time to time. Finally he got his courage up again.

"You know her grandson's aboard . . . Barin Serrano . . ."

"Toby!" That was the blond, disapproving. Esmay didn't rise to that bait, but she did wonder if coincidence or Serrano influence had anything to do with a young Serrano's assignment.

"If you'd eat without talking, you wouldn't get your foot in your mouth," said one of the jigs further down the table.

Esmay looked up in time to see a Look pass from that jig to another one. Great. Something mysterious which would, no doubt, end up on her shoulders.

She put her fork down; her appetite had disappeared. "Admiral Serrano's a very interesting person," she said. That was always safe . . . she hoped. From the startled looks of the two jigs, perhaps it wasn't. "Not that it wasn't an alarming   uation." Now everyone was looking at her. A year ago, she might have felt her face flushing, but the publicity around the court-martial had taken care of that. She smiled around the table. "Any of you ever serve with Admiral Serrano?"

"No, sir," said the senior jig. "But she's a Serrano, and they're all pretty much alike." His tone tried for superior, that of the one with secret knowledge, but its very smugness defeated its intent. Esmay knew exactly what he didn't know. For the first time she realized she could enjoy this.

"I don't think I'd put it that way," she said, leaning forward a little. "Frankly, having served under both of them—" She had served under Admiral Serrano only remotely, and briefly, but this was no time for precision on that point. "Admiral *Vida* Serrano, that is, and Commander *Heris* Serrano . . ." Thus reminding everyone that a lineup of all the admirals and commanders Serrano would take up a fair length of deck. "I thought them quite individual. Nor is the difference all seniority." Let them make what they could of that.

"But isn't Commander Serrano—Heris Serrano that is— the admiral's niece?"

Esmay let her eyebrows go up at this appalling lack of manners. "What, precisely, are you suggesting?"

"Well . . . you know, they all stick together. Being related so close, I mean."

Esmay had not imagined that kind of prejudice aimed at anyone but Fleet outsiders like herself, those who had enlisted from some planet. The Serranos were Fleet royalty, one of the fourteen private military forces that had combined into the Regular Space Service of the Familias

Regnant. Through the white rage she felt, her mind reacted as if pricked, correlating remarks made months ago, even years ago, as early as her second term in the Fleet prep school. She had always ignored them, labeled them pique or envy or momentary annoyance. If those people had been serious . . . if there were serious resentment of the Serranos—and possibly some of the other First Fourteen—someone should know. She should know, and she should not lose her temper and shove this brash youngster's face in the stew.

Her temper bucked, like one of the green colts in training, and she rode it down, hoping her eyes showed none of the strain.

"I think with a little more experience you won't either think or say things like that, Jig Callison," Esmay said in the mildest tone she could manage. Callison turned red, and looked down. Someone snickered; she didn't spot who.

Conversation, naturally, died, and she pretended to eat the rest of her dinner. When the senior lieutenant tapped on his glass for attention, Esmay felt more relief than curiosity. She found it hard to keep her attention on the announcements of who had the duty, and almost missed her introduction. She stood, off-balance mentally if not physically, and nodded to the faces that seemed only pale and dark blurs.

After the meal, she left for her quarters as soon as she could. She was annoyed with herself for her immediate prickly response to the mention of the Serrano name. And why was she so blurry? Usually she could focus on new people without much trouble.

When she thought about it, she realized that she had actually run about thirty standard hours without sleep. Her transport ship had come in on its own schedule, skewed a full shift and a half from the *Koskiusko*. Shiplag . . . luckily she never had much trouble with it. One night's sleep seemed to rearrange her internal timer . . . but right now she wanted that sleep badly. She wasn't on the watch schedule yet, so she set her personal timer to allow ten hours.

Her compartment filtered out most of the noises . . .

she could just hear the bass thump of someone's music cube, DUM-da-DUM-DUM, over and over. She didn't like it, but it wouldn't keep her awake. She logged off the status board, and stretched out on her bunk. She had just time to wonder if she would have nightmares when she fell asleep.

Beside her, Peli leaned out to toss a gasser into the passage. A blue line traced the air just above his head and he jerked back. Esmay pressed the filters snugly into her nostrils and peered through the helmet visor. When the smoke obscured normal vision, her helmet sensors gave her a wiggly false-color view of the corridor. She snaked out into it, hoping that whoever'd been shooting at them didn't have a similar helmet. They thought they'd gotten to the locker before the traitors, but none of the juniors knew how many helmets were supposed to be in that locker.

Ahead, someone braced into an angle of a hatch, weapon at ready. Esmay couldn't see the features, but she could hear, with the clarity provided by the helmet external pickups, the words "Get this bunch of little fuckers, and we'll have only Dovir to worry about—"

She braced her own weapon and fired. The wiggly pink-and-green image blew apart; something wet and warm splashed her arm. She ignored it. Through the dense stinging fog, she slithered on, attention focussed on the helmet's input . . . aware that behind her Peli and the others followed, that somewhere Major Dovir still led the few other loyalist officers. . . .

The fog lifted in ragged wisps . . . ahead she could see the scorched lines on the bulkheads . . . she did not look at the deck except when she had to, when she would have fallen over the obstructions . . . but even so she saw them. Heaps of old clothes, dirty and stained, scattered here and there . . . she would not think of it now, she would not, later was soon enough. . . .

She woke in a sweat, heart pounding. Later. Later was now, when she was safe. She turned on her bed light, and lay staring at the overhead. They had not been heaps of clothes; she had known it even then. Her father had been all too right—warfare was ugly, no matter where. Guts and blood and flesh stank the same in a spaceship as in the aftermath of a street riot. And she herself had added to that stench, that ugliness. She and the other juniors had fought their way up the ship, onto the bridge, where Dovir, mortally wounded, held the command chair after Hearne was dead. Dovir, his guts slipping out of his hands, had given her that one glazed look . . . his voice, struggling for control, as he gave his last orders. . . .

She blinked, trying not to cry. She had cried; it didn't do any good. She felt slimy all over, the sweat cold and slick now, the bedclothes damp and tangled around her. It reminded her of her aunt's description of menopause, waking up sweaty and then having cold chills. Or something like that. She forced her mind back to this place and time. Thinking about home wouldn't help her at all.

According to the chronometer, she had slept a solid seven hours. She could try for another short nap . . . but experience suggested that she wouldn't really sleep. Better would be a shower—it was late third shift on this ship—and an early start on the working day.

No one was in the big shower room; she let the hot water warm her and wash away the fear-stink. As she came back down the passage, she heard someone's alarm go off. Not hers—she had carefully shut hers off. Then, from down the passage, another alarm. She made it into her compartment before those alarms stopped, and when she emerged, it was to find two bleary-eyed ensigns on their way to the showers, and a jig leaning on the bulkhead folding down the top flap of his uniform boot.

"Sir!" they all said, coming to more or less upright posture. Esmay nodded, feeling the momentary glow of virtue that accompanies an early rising, clean teeth, and the evidence that one's associates are still half-asleep.

She did not let herself dwell on that. She had work to do—not only learning the ship, as Major Pitak had said, but figuring out why the major's data cube and the ship's records were so different. All that day, except for hurried meals, Esmay mapped the real ship against two dissimilar records. Major Pitak's data cube was right except once, far in the bow end of T-1, Deck Thirteen, when neither fit the reality. A hatch had disappeared completely, replaced by a bulkhead painted in garish stripes. As Esmay stood there, wondering what the pattern meant, a bald senior chief bustled out of the nearest cross-passage, and hurried toward her.

"What are you—oh, excuse me, sir. Can I help you find something?"

Esmay had not missed the tension . . . something was clearly going on. But it was not yet her job to find it. She smiled instead. "I'm Lieutenant Suiza," she said. "Major Pitak told me to familiarize myself with the entire ship by 0800 on the 27th, and I thought there was a hatch up here to the electronics warehouse facility."

"Oh . . . Major Pitak," the man said. Evidently Major Pitak was well known outside her own bailiwick. "Well, sir, the ship's database hasn't caught up to renovations. The electronics warehouse access is up that way." He pointed. "I'll be glad to show you."

"Thanks," Esmay said. As they turned away, she said "This bulkhead pattern—is it something they didn't teach us, or—?"

A red flush went up the back of his neck. "It's—probably unique to DSR ships, Lieutenant. They're so big, you see . . . the captain's permitted some nonreg markings to keep newbies oriented."

"I see," Esmay said. "Very sensible—I've gotten lost several times already."

The red flush receded; she could hear relaxation in his voice. "Most people do, Lieutenant. That pattern just lets people know that what the ship's schematics show isn't there any more—they haven't gone the wrong way, exactly, but the way's changed."

Something about the intonation of that almost put a capital letter on "way." Esmay stowed that slight emphasis for later consideration, and followed the chief outboard, then forward again, to a hatch clearly labeled ELECTRONICS

WAREHOUSE FACILITY. Under that official label was another.

CHECK OUT WITH DUTY CHIEF
BEFORE YOU REMOVE ANY PARTS:
THIS MEANS YOU!

Esmay thanked her guide, and went in. It looked like any storage facility she'd seen, as large as most on major bases. Racks of containers labeled with part numbers; bins with the most commonly needed parts piled loosely. A jig she had not yet met came out from a warren of racks.

"Sher, is that you—oh, sorry, sir." Esmay went through her explanation again, introducing herself to Jig Forrest. He seemed eager enough to show her the whole warehouse.

"I just wondered—my ship schematic showed a different entrance."

"Before my time," he said. "I know—I got lost trying to find this place when they sent me up from the 14th. We share this warehouse with Training—those technical schools people are always needing more parts in the lab. That's why they moved this warehouse. I don't think they update the ship's schematics often enough, especially since this is a DSR—it's important for us to know where we are. But you know how it is, Lieutenant: no one asks jigs for their opinion."

Esmay grinned. "I do indeed. And I suspect, new as my extra bar is, that no one asks lieutenants their opinion either." At least not until the middle of a mutiny, when everyone else was dead. But this fresh-faced young man with the coppery hair hadn't been through that.

"You must be with Major Pitak," he said now, and at her expression laughed again. "She always sends her new juniors out to find impossible corners of the ship. I've never been in H&A, for which I thank whatever gods govern the assignments."

"At least I know where this is now," Esmay said. "And I'd better get back to my list."

She was glad for the years of open-country navigation on the estancia . . . she had no problem retracing her route down and aft, and arrived in the junior officers' section in plenty of time to freshen up before taking her assigned table at mess. Now that she was wide awake, she found it easier to engage them in conversation.

Callison, the senior jig, had a graduate degree in environmental engineering. Partrade, the junior jig, worked in administration—a specialty still called paper-pushing, though relatively little of it was on paper. The five ensigns at her table included one in Hull and Architecture, two in Weapons Systems, and one each in Medical Support and Data Systems.

Esmay wondered if any of them had served aboard a ship in combat, but didn't like to ask. She had spooked them enough the previous night. Partrade brought the topic up without her having to ask.

"Was the Xavier action your only experience in combat, Lieutenant Suiza?"

Esmay managed not to choke on her peas. "Yes, it was." End of sentence.

"I've never even served on a warship," Partrade went on, with a glance around. "I don't think anyone at this table has. They put me in Maintenance Administration right away, and I've been on the *Kos* for five solid years."

"I was on *Checkmate*," one of the ensigns said. "But we never did anything but patrol."

"Be grateful," said Esmay, before she could stop herself. Now they all stared at her. She hated this. She felt too young and too old at the same time.

"If the lieutenant doesn't want to talk about it, don't push her." That from the lieutenant at the next table, whom Esmay now remembered was the one she'd met outside the lift tube. "Dinner's not the time for gory stories anyway." He winked at Esmay. She grinned in spite of herself.

"He's right," she said to her table. "It's not a fit topic at the table." Or among strangers, she realized. Now she understood why the veterans tended to cluster apart to tell their tales, why they had fallen silent when she and other juniors had tried to overhear them. "Any of the rest of you have any experience?" She was surprised to hear in her own voice the same slight emphasis to the word which she had heard from more senior, and experienced officers. Their heads shook. "Well," she said. "Then we won't be tempted to bring up things like that at dinner." Her smile would, she hoped, take the sting out of that. "Now . . . Zintner, you're in H&A. Was that your intent at the Academy?"

"Yes, sir." Zintner, who must have stood on tiptoe to make the minimum height requirement, almost sparkled in her seat. "My family's been in shipbuilding forever—a long time anyway. I wanted to work on military hulls . . . that's where the good new stuff is."

"And this is your first assignment?"

"Yes, sir. It's great. You've met Major Pitak—she knows so much—and we get to work on everything, once we're out with the wave."

"Mmm. My background's scan technology, so I don't know much about H&A. I expect you'll be teaching me a lot."

"Me, sir? I doubt it—the major's got me working on a technical manual right now. She'll probably tell Master Chief Sivars to take you on."

Direct contradiction was rude, but the ensign looked too bouncy to have intended any rudeness. She was simply full of what she was doing. Esmay understood that. She turned to the jigs. Callison was pleasantly willing to discuss the less disgusting processes that kept the ship's crew alive, and had amusing anecdotes of the sorts of things that went wrong. It had not occurred to Esmay that a few insect egg cases caught in the mud in someone's hiking boots could hatch and cause serious problems, but apparently they had, on another ship. That story led Partrade to regale them with a story about the time an unnamed junior lieutenant transposed a few numbers and caused a massive overdraft of his ship's account . . . everyone had been bumped up ten grades, so the whole ship was crewed—according to the computer—by officers, and the captain outranked the sector commander.

One of the many differences from home that Esmay savored was this . . . that they could talk about their assignments at dinner. On Altiplano, nothing related to one's work could be discussed at dinner, even if all at the table were working together. She found that unnatural . . . here, a flurry of shop talk would unwind naturally into other topics.

"Are you ready for my exam?" Major Pitak asked when she reported.

"Yes, sir," Esmay said. "But I do have a question."

"Go ahead."

"Why doesn't the ship's schematics agree with reality—or with the schematics on your cube?"

"Excellent. How many discrepancies did you find?"

Esmay blinked. She hadn't expected that reaction. She began to describe the discrepancies, starting at the bow and working aft. Pitak listened without comment. When she had finished, Pitak made a note on her pad.

"I believe you found them all. Good work. You asked why we have discrepancies, and that's not a question I can answer. I suspect it's the new AI subroutines, which actively protect data considered especially important. A software glitch, in other words, though we can't seem to convince the Fleet systems designers that it's a problem. They take the view that architecture, once launched, shouldn't change . . . which is probably true for most hulls."

Esmay thought that over. "So you create new data cubes individually when you change architecture."

"Right. We can actually change the main system for a time—usually an hour or so before it 'heals' itself and repairs what it thinks is a data injury."

"But there were two places where your data cube didn't match the reality."

Pitak grinned at her. "I gave you an old data cube, Lieutenant—to see if you'd really check things out. The stupid ones come back all confused, complaining that they can't find their way by ship schematics. The clever ones check out one or two locations, then come back with a list of discrepancies between my cube and the ship schematics. Good, honest officers who aren't afraid of work do what you did—they check *everything*. That's what I want in my section . . . people who skip the details in H&A kill ships, and we're here to save them."

"Yes . . . sir." Esmay thought about that. It was an efficient way of separating lazy and careless from diligent and careful, but she wondered what other tricks Major Pitak had waiting. It would, she thought, be some exam. "Thank you, sir, for explaining."

Pitak looked at her oddly. "Thank you for passing the test, Lieutenant—or hadn't you figured that out yet?"

She hadn't, and now she felt stupid. "No, sir." Stupid, gauche . . . she felt her ears burning and hoped the glow didn't come through her hair.

"A one-track mind, I wonder, or . . . of course you are a dropsquirt." That in a thoughtful voice with no edge to it.

"Dropsquirt?" Esmay hadn't heard that before, though it sounded pejorative.

"Sorry. DSR vessels develop their own local slang . . . almost a local dialect, though we try not to be too impenetrable. It means Personnel of Planetary Origin, the official term . . . someone squirted into deepspace work from a drop—a gravity well. And someone junior, which is when you can really tell the difference. One doesn't expect dropsquirts to get all the nuances of Fleet social structure right away . . . when did you join, Suiza?"

"Prep school, sir." Esmay thought of the years she'd been in a Fleet environment. Two in prep school, four in the Academy, a tour as ensign, and two assignments as jig. If she hadn't caught on by now, would she ever? She'd thought she had—her fitness reports always commented on her quiet, mannerly demeanor. What was she doing wrong, besides getting involved in mutinies?

"Hmm. Technical track, most of the way." Pitak gave her a long look. "You know, Suiza, we technical types have a reputation for being a little dense in some things. Wouldn't surprise me if you are too. That doesn't bother me, and won't cause you as much trouble here as it would on a warship. But since you are not from a Fleet family, you might want to think about opening your sensors to a little wider band. Just a suggestion—not an order."

"Yes, sir," Esmay said. She felt a little dizzy. What was she doing wrong? What was so obvious? She knew she didn't have an accent any more; she had tried so hard . . . but Major Pitak had moved to her process chart.

"To get you up to speed in H&A, you're going to have to take a couple of quick courses. Right now all we have is a minor little plate repair job for an escort—it'll be done before you're through with the tapes, and you'll be more use to us then. How are you with tools? Ever done metal fabrication? Ceramics or plastics molding?"

"No, sir."

"Mmm. All right, then. Take these tapes down to Training, and run through them as many times as it takes. Then come back here, and I'll set you up with some instructors. You've got to know how a process is supposed to be done before you can supervise it."

That made perfect sense, and Esmay had never minded learning new things. "Yes, sir," she said, accepting a thick stack of tapes for the machines.

"We'll probably be out on deployment before you're through with the tapes," Pitak said. "Take what time you need." Then she shook her head. "Sorry—you're naturally thorough—I don't have to warn *you* against rushing through them."

"Sir." Esmay backed out, with very mixed feelings. One side of her mind felt ruffled and itchy; another part felt soothed and confident.

Scheduling sessions in Training took longer than she had expected. The techs in charge of the banks of machines explained. "A DSR needs more specialties than any other kind of ship. And we have to know everything— all the old stuff, and all the new stuff, and anything someone's come up with to make repair easier. Our people are always retraining. The rest of Fleet just thinks it retrains, with its predictable little drills every so many days. But we'll get you in, Lieutenant, don't worry. And Major Pitak knows what the situation is—she's not going to blame you."

Nonetheless, it would be three standard days before Esmay could get a machine, and then only on third shift.

"Do you have anything similar that I could go over on my cube reader?" she asked. The tech ran the tape titles through his scanner.

"Yes, but this is really technical stuff, Lieutenant—what I have on cube is much more basic. The intermediate stuff's all been checked out—in fact, it's overdue."

"I'll take the basic," Esmay said. "A good review for me." She took the cubes, and gave the tech her tapes, to be held for her session. Back in her quarters, she inserted the first cube. An hour later, she was very glad she hadn't been able to get time on the machines right away. The basic level cube was already past her. She sat back, blinking, and realized she'd have to take it in short doses.

Almost lunchtime. She wasn't really hungry, but she did feel stiff and stale. What she wanted was exercise. She changed to shorts and padded shoes, and followed the directions (in this case identical) given by the ship's schematics and Major Pitak's cube to the junior officers' workout area.

Aside from being bigger, it was much like the exercise compartments she'd seen on other ships. Rows of machines for exercising this or that group of muscles, enclosed spaces for pair games played on a small court, a large open space with mats for tumbling and unarmed combat practice. Half a dozen or so junior officers occupied various machines, and two were sparring on the mats. She checked the charts. At this time of the cycle, only a few machines were reserved; she could use almost anything. Esmay avoided the riding simulators, and climbed onto something said to simulate cross-country walking on snow. She had no desire to walk on real snow—she had done that—but it was better than pretending to ride horses by sitting on an arrangement of pistons and levers.

She had just begun to work up her heart rate when someone called her name. She looked around. It was one of the ensigns from her table . . . Custis? No, Dettin, the blond with the scrape, now healed.

"I just wondered if you'd talk to our tactics study group about the Xavier affair," he asked. "Not necessarily your own role, though of course we'd like to hear it, but just how you saw the battle as a whole."

"I didn't see the battle as a whole," Esmay said. "We got there late, as you may have heard."

"Late?" His brow furrowed. Could he really be this ignorant.

"The ship I was on was captained by a—" it was extraordinarily hard to say "traitor" right out loud to a youngster like this. "Captain Hearne left the Xavier system before the battle," she said. She didn't know why she said it that way; she had not cared that much for Captain Hearne. "It was only after the—" *mutiny* was another hard word to say, but this time she got it out. "Only after the mutiny, when all the senior officers had died, that I took the ship back."

She did not expect the look on his face, the expression of someone who has just seen impossible dreams fulfilled. "You—that's like something out of *Silver Stars.*"

"Silver stars?"

"You know—the adventure game series."

Shock knocked out her control. "It was *nothing* like an adventure game!"

He was oblivious. "No, but in the eighth series, when that young lord had to overcome the wicked prince and then lead the ships in battle . . ."

"It's not a game," Esmay said firmly, but with less heat. "People get killed for real."

"I know that," he said, looking annoyed. "But in the game—"

"I'm sorry," Esmay said, "I don't play adventure games." *I only fight wars,* she wanted to say, but didn't.

"But will you talk to our tactics group?"

She thought it over. Perhaps she could make clear the difference between game and reality. "Yes," she said. "But I'll have to check my schedule. When do you meet?"

"Every ten days, but we could move the meeting time if you wanted."

"I'll check," Esmay said. "Now—I've got to finish my set." He went away, and she worked until she felt she'd worked off not only the stiffness of study, but the unreasonable anger she'd felt at being compared to a gaming hero. By the time she'd cooled down again, she began to think whether she should have been quite so quick to agree . . . even if she hadn't agreed to a specific time. Should she talk to a pack of ensigns about the Xavier affair? If she kept her own part to a minimum, and discussed the way Heris Serrano had held off a superior force, surely that could do no harm.

CHAPTER NINE

She was trying to think whom to consult, when she remembered that she needed to make an appointment to meet Admiral Dossignal. Now, while she was working her way through the basic level training cubes, would be an ideal time. She contacted Commander Atarin's clerk, and an hour or so later the message came back that the admiral would see her at 1330. So at 1315, she presented herself at the admiral's office suite, where Commander Atarin happened to be delivering a pile of cubes.

"How's Hull and Architecture, Lieutenant?"

"Very interesting, sir. Major Pitak has me taking some courses, since I had no background."

"Good; she's very thorough. Has she given you the ship test yet?"

"That came first, sir."

"Ah." His eyebrows rose and fell. "Well, you must have passed, or I'd have heard about it. Good for you. How are you getting along in the junior mess? Settling in all right?"

"Fine, sir," Esmay said.

"This ship's so big, none of us can get to know everyone. Sometimes people coming in from smaller craft find that very unsettling. If you have any special interests, you might take a look at the recreational group roster. We encourage people to have acquaintances outside their own work sections—even commands."

"Well, sir, the juniors' tactics discussion group did ask me to speak on the Xavier action."

"Oh? Well, that's not exactly what I had in mind, but it's a start. And they showed some initiative in asking . . . who was it?"

159

"Ensign Dettin, sir."

"Mmm . . . I don't know Dettin. But I'm sure they've all heard something about Xavier, and are curious to know more. I might drop in . . ." Was that a threat, or a warning, or mere interest? "Ah—the admiral's ready."

Admiral Dossignal was a tall man with craggy features and big-knuckled hands that fiddled with things on his desk. Despite this, he seemed more relaxed than Captain Hakin, and considerably more welcoming.

"I've read the notations your Board made in your file, Lieutenant Suiza . . . and though I can understand their concern about your decisions, I do not share them. I have complete confidence in your loyalty to the Familias Regnant."

"Thank you, sir."

"No thanks necessary, Lieutenant. Although we need to smoke out the other traitors we surely have—Garrivay and his cohorts cannot be all of them—we must have trust, or we have no cohesion." He paused, but Esmay found nothing to say. When he resumed, it was in a different tone, less somber. "I understand you and Major Pitak are getting on well . . . and Commander Seveche?"

"I've only met him, sir," Esmay said. The head of Hull and Architecture had spoken to her only briefly; he had seemed even busier than Major Pitak when she saw him.

"I'm sure you've heard this before, but I must say it's unusual to have a lieutenant assigned here without having gone through one of the advanced technical schools first. You may find it necessary to take some courses . . ."

"I'm already signed up for one, sir."

"Good. By your record, you're a quick learner, but heavy maintenance is a lifetime's study." He glanced back at his desk display. "I see you've had recent home planet leave. How did your family react to all the publicity?"

Esmay tried to think of a tactful way to phrase it. "They . . . went overboard, sir."

"Ah? Oh, I suppose you mean the medal?"

Of course it was already in her file; she knew that. "Yes, sir."

"But that was the government, not your family . . . You have . . . a father, stepmother, half-brothers?"

"Yes, sir. Also aunts, uncles, cousins . . . it's a large clan, sir."

"Did they approve of your joining us?" The warm brown eyes sharpened.

"Not . . . entirely, sir. Not at first. Now they do."

"We have no other officers from your planet, you see. The last was some thirty years ago."

"Meluch Zalosi, yes, sir." A Zalosi of the Coarchy, which no longer existed, but had been, at one time, a political force. The Zalosi, though, were servants of the Coarchs. Meluch, the gossip went, had been the illegitimate child of the Tributine Coarch and a Zalosi guard, farmed out to a distant Zalosi relative. He had proven to carry the distinctive feathery brows of the Coarch's line—a dominant trait—and when he qualified for the Fleet entrance exams it had seemed the best solution to everyone. Meluch himself had not been asked; he was a Zalosi, to go where the Coarchy directed.

"I wondered," Admiral Dossignal went on, breaking into her musings, "why so few? Altiplano is, I understand, an agricultural world. We usually get quite a few recruits from ag worlds."

"It's not the usual sort of ag world, sir." Esmay paused, wondering how much to explain. The admiral would have ample data available if he really wanted it.

"And why is that?" he asked. Perhaps he simply wanted her analysis, rather than the raw data.

"No free-birthers," Esmay said succinctly. All the other reasons came back to that: with population growth under control, there were no idle hands to ship offplanet. Immigrants had to agree before they were accepted; if they already had reproduced, they had to agree to pre-emptive sterilization.

"But your family—how many sibs do you have?"

"Two, sir. But they're my father's second wife's, on her permits." She did not mention what he could probably guess, that the birth limits were enforced more strictly on other families. Her father could have sired more children, but he had transferred his remaining permits to Sanni, who wanted them.

"I . . . see. And their attitude towards rejuvenation?"

She hesitated. "I . . . know only my father's view, and my uncle's. They expressed concern about the effect on population stability, although the competitive value of ever-increasing experience would have a positive effect."

"Mmm. So the senior military personnel on Altiplano have not been rejuved?"

"No, sir."

"Did you sense any resentment of the Familias on that basis?"

Esmay felt uncomfortable, but answered with the truth as she saw it. "No, sir, none. Altiplano's an independent; the admiral is no doubt aware that we have no sponsor with a Seat in Council, and Council policy affects us only inasmuch as it affects commercial law."

"There's been some unrest, especially since the revelation about that mess on Patchcock," the admiral said. "There's now a strong political faction opposed to rejuvenation on the grounds that the rich old will exploit the poor unable to afford rejuvenation."

"I don't think anyone on Altiplano feels exploited by the Familias," Esmay said. "Occasionally by each other . . ." More than occasionally, but she didn't see how her limited knowledge of Altiplanan local politics would make the situation clear. She didn't say the first thought that popped into her head, which was that any force trying to exploit Altiplano would have its work cut out for it.

"I'm glad to hear it," the admiral said. "I'll be seeing you from time to time—officers of the 14th get together regularly . . . Commander Atarin will let you know the next event."

"Yes, sir; thank you."

The first thing Esmay did after coming back from her interview with the admiral was pull a diagram of the various commands aboard the DSR. She had thought she understood how the chains of command ran, and who reported to whom about what . . . but several things the admiral had said left her confused.

A few hours later, she was only slightly less confused, but considerably entertained. With very few exceptions—and DSRs were the primary exception—Fleet vessels had a simple command structure, with the captain at the top, and authority descending rank by rank through the officers to the enlisted personnel. An admiral aboard a flagship had no direct authority over the ship's crew: all orders had to flow through the regular captain.

But the size of the newer DSRs had tempted Fleet to treat them as mobile bases. Rather than maintain separate technical schools and laboratory facilities at Sector HQ, staff had decided to put them aboard the *Koskiusko*, which needed most of the equipment anyway. Thus the *Koskiusko* had multiple commands, each headed by an admiral, which were expected to use the same facilities—and even the same experts—for different purposes. If Fleet had wanted to create a venue for massive turf battles, it could have invented no better arrangement.

Esmay found the debris of such battles in the files. The Special Materials Fabrication Facility, for instance: it was supposed to serve the 14th Heavy Maintenance Yard by making all the materials needed to maintain an inventory of structural members. But it also served the Senior Technical Schools, where students learned to make such materials, and the Special Materials Research Lab, where the most inventive materials scientists struggled to develop new materials with exotic properties.

On the first deployment a massive fight developed between the 14th Heavy Maintenance, which wanted a larger inventory of the crystal-bonded structural members for repair, and the other two commands, which insisted that they needed a guaranteed minimum access to the facility to fulfill their missions.

That argument had risen through the various chains of command until the admirals involved were, as Pitak put it, "locked in a room to fight it out until only one emerged victorious." The solution—a compromise reached with all admirals still alive and kicking vigorously—satisfied no one, but its inconvenience suggested that complaint would only make things worse.

Even the traditional division between the ship's crew and its passengers had eroded. Though in theory Captain Hakin had the ultimate authority for the ship's security and functioning, his crew was outnumbered many times by the personnel of the 14th Heavy Maintenance Yard. When a previous Yard commander wanted to run an "outrigger tube" between T-3 and T-4, between the lateral docking bays, he'd done so. Esmay found the furious correspondence launched by the then captain to the admiral then commanding the 14th Heavy Maintenance, and the directive from Sector HQ that the offending tube would be allowed to remain. The captain had been reassigned.

No wonder the ship's architecture didn't match the computer specs, and everyone needed update cubes to keep track of the changes!

Above the ship level, the chain of command looked more like a tree diagram. Captain Hakin's superior was Admiral Gourache, commander of this wave, whose superior was the Sector 14 commandant, Admiral Foxworth. Admiral Dossignal, however, reported directly to the sector commandant; he was responsible for all maintenance functions in the sector. Admiral Livadhi was Training Command's representative in this sector, and not under the sector commander at all: Fleet Headquarters had taken over all training functions sixty years before. Similarly, the medical command had its own separate chain, this time running back to Admiral Surgeon General Boussy, back at Rockhouse.

Her father would never have put up with this mess. On Altiplano, the military medical service was firmly and formally subordinate to the operational command. *Yes, and that's how he was able to conceal your trauma*, her memory prompted. *No one was going to argue with the hero of the war. . . .*

That wasn't fair. She wasn't even sure it had been a military hospital. She wasn't going to think about it anyway. She put the displays away; she understood the command structure well enough now. She could start preparing for her presentation to the discussion group in two days.

The *Koskiusko* had a personnel complement the size of a small city or large orbital station, and the officer list alone was as large as the crew of any normal ship. Esmay knew that, in the intellectual sense, but when she saw the mass of ensigns jamming the lecture hall and crowding the passage outside, numbers became experience.

"You're not all in the tactics discussion group, surely," she said to Ensign Dettin, who had offered to introduce her.

"No, sir. But a lot of others wanted to come—I'll have to shift some of them out, because they're overloading the compartment . . ." She could see that. All the seats had been taken long ago; ensigns were crowded knee to knee in front, and were sitting squashed together in the aisles and in back. They were jamming the passage outside, too.

She watched Dettin trying to shoo them back out, to no avail. She should, she realized, have told someone more senior about this . . . if she'd thought it would be more than a dozen or so ensigns, she would have. Dettin wasn't getting anywhere, and it was her responsibility. She reached for the microphone. "Excuse me," she said. Silence fell, chopping off words in mid-utterance. "How many of you are regular members of the tactics discussion group?"

A few hands went up, about what she'd expected originally.

"This meeting was scheduled for that group," Esmay said. "We can't have a mob scene like this; it's not safe. Those of you who are not members of the discussion group will have to leave, until we're sure we have seating for that group, and then we'll see how many others we can accommodate."

Low mutters of protest, but these were ensigns and she was a full lieutenant now. Squirming awkwardly, those crammed into the aisles began to stand up; those in front waited, perhaps hoping for a reprieve, but Esmay gave them a stern look. Slowly, more awkwardly than necessary, they heaved themselves up and shuffled out. She could hear raised voices from the passage, but first things first. Some of those in seats were now standing; some sat as if glued in place. She hoped those were all discussion group members.

"Ensign Dettin." He looked mildly embarrassed. "Make sure all the discussion group have seats—you know them all, don't you?"

"Yes, sir."

"When they're seated, and if it's agreeable to the others, I don't mind having any spare seats filled. But that's all."

"Sir." He glanced around, his lips moving as he ran down some internal list. "All here but two—they may be outside."

"Go check on them. By name."

He made his way up the crowded aisle and called out into the passage. A knot of ensigns congealed in the opening, and finally two more elbowed their way in. That left seats for another two dozen, Esmay figured. She wished she knew a fair way to allocate those seats, but it was too late for that. More quickly than they'd left, more ensigns came in until all seats were filled.

Dettin introduced her, excitement edging his voice. The lights dimmed, except where she stood. The eager young faces faded into a blur with highlights of eyes and teeth. She had not expected that, but after standing in the glare of flag officers' disapproval, she was not about to crumple in a merely visual spotlight.

She had prepared a display cube with the same information given in court: the geometry of the Xavier system, the disposition of Fleet vessels, available Xavieran and civilian vessels, the number and armament of the invaders. She had been over this so many times, for her counsel and for Board of Inquiry and for the court-martial, that she could have explained in her sleep just how outnumbered Serrano had been even before Hearne defected. When she put up the first display, a faint sigh came from her audience. Breathless silence while she spoke, reciting the familiar sequence. Some of it she knew only by report, and she said that. But the events themselves were so compelling that no one seemed to mind: the Benignity intrusion, the lagging pair of Benignity ships . . . possibly a new tactic, possibly malfunction. No one knew for sure. The successful attack on those ships, the damage to one assault carrier, the effective ambush of the killer-scout sent to form its own ambush. The long and dangerous harrying of the invaders in their course to Xavier, the loss of the space station, the damage to the Xavieran cities.

"Only a scorch, after all," she heard someone mutter. She stopped short; silence returned, thick and tense. She could not see, against the glare of light focussed on her, who had spoken.

"*Only* a scorch . . . someone thinks a scorch is a minor problem? Let me show you video . . ." She switched to that, the former capital of Xavier on one side of the screen, as it had been, a small city of wide streets and low stone buildings, gardens and tree-shaded parks. That was file footage from Fleet databanks; Xavier's own records had all been destroyed.

On the half screen, an uneven field of rubble, the shattered remains of trees, the languid columns of smoke twisting in their own heat, a damage assessment team from Fleet in their protective gear. The video pickup had zoomed in on dead bodies, human and animal. Esmay recognized a dead horse, if no one else did. "All population centers," Esmay said, "were reduced like this. Fire destroyed outlying settlements, as well as millions of hectares of pasture and farm crops. A 'scorch' is intended to leave the planet barely habitable for the Benignity's own troops, with return to agricultural production in three to five years. That doesn't leave much for the people who live there."

"But weren't they all killed?" someone asked.

"No, thanks to the foresight of Commander Serrano and their own government. Most of the population survived in remote regions—they have caves, I heard—but their economic base is gone. It will take a generation or two just to recover what they lost." She could imagine the sequence; Altiplano had suffered similar damage during the Succession Wars when their Founder had died. The years of hunger, while they reestablished their agricultural base. The years after that when just enough to eat was no longer enough. As distant as they were, they could not expect much help from the rest of the Familias, once some new crisis caught public attention.

Silence again, this time with a different flavor.

"Let's begin with the situation as it first appeared to Commander Serrano." Esmay changed displays, to show the Xavier system again. "Xavier had been troubled by periodic incursions over the past few years, that appeared to be independent raiders of some sort. These had threatened the orbital station, and in fact had damaged it on more than one occasion. Xavier's defense consisted of outmoded, under-supported Demoiselle-class ships, of which only one was really space-worthy by the present. The others had been cannibalized for parts to keep that one working. Xavier is off regular passenger service, and ships out its agricultural products—mostly large-animal semen, ova, and frozen embryos—aboard locally-owned private vessels. Nearly all its mining production is used locally, for building up the infrastructure."

Esmay had not known any of this until she read Heris Serrano's brief—concise, but hardly brief in the usual terms—to the admiral. She had found it easy to follow, because Altiplano and Xavier had many similarities.

"The government enlisted Commander Serrano, then acting as a civilian captain of a private yacht—but a very well-armed one—in defense against just such a raider. As you might expect—" she allowed herself a brief smile "—the unsuspecting raider didn't have a chance."

"How big was it?" came from the back of the room.

"According to scan reports at the time, it was an Aethar's World raider—" Esmay flashed the hull specifications on the display. "Commander Serrano anticipated its attack course, and was able to surprise it."

"But that wasn't the whole battle, was it? One lousy little raider?"

"No, of course not." Esmay changed displays again, to show the location of Xavier relative to Benignity and Familias territory. "Commander Serrano's scan techs noticed another ship in system, which appeared to be an observer . . . she suspected that the raider's attack was merely a probe for a larger invasion force. She transmitted that concern to the nearest Fleet headquarters."

"And got a bunch of traitors," came a mutter from midway back.

"Not a 'bunch,' " Esmay said. "Most of the officers and crew of all three ships were loyal, or things would have turned out very differently. Fleet dispatched a small force, under the command of Dekan Garrivay. Two patrol ships, one cruiser. The captains of all three ships were prepared to cooperate with the Benignity, but that is not true of others."

"Exactly how many traitors were there, and how do we know they were all discovered?"

"I don't know the answer to either question," Esmay said. "Some died fairly quickly—it's impossible to determine their alliance. And it's possible—though unlikely—that some traitors did not reveal themselves during the fighting on each ship. The last estimate I saw was that five to ten percent of each crew was actually traitorous—that includes both officers and enlisted."

She watched the sideways looks, as the young officers estimated how many of the people in the room that would be.

"Naturally, most of them were in fairly senior, critical posts. Five traitorous ensigns wouldn't do the enemy as much good as one captain and the senior scan tech. The problem for the Benignity, as I understand it, is that the sort of thing they planned at Xavier required their long-standing agents to identify themselves to each other—a very risky affair. This need to confer was their undoing."

Esmay skipped rapidly past the still-classified methods by which Koutsoudas had overheard the conspirators in the midst of their plotting.

"Commander Serrano had to prevent Garrivay from destroying Xavier's orbital station, and she needed those ships to defend from the expected invasion. That meant she had to relieve Garrivay and the other traitorous captain of their commands, identify any other traitors, and rally the loyal crews."

"Well, but she's Admiral Serrano's niece," someone said. "She could just say so—"

Esmay almost grinned. Had she ever been that naive, even before she went into Fleet?

"Commander Serrano, remember, was operating as a civilian, whose resignation from Fleet had been highly publicized. There is some evidence that Commander Garrivay worried about what she might do, especially the influence she might have on the Xavieran government. He was trying to discredit her there. But consider: you are a civilian—at least apparently civilian—and you are on a space station where two Fleet vessels are docked. Another one is on picket at a distance. How are you going to gain access to the docked ships? We don't let civilians just wander in. And once in, how are you going to convince an ignorant crew that their captain is a traitor, and you should be allowed to take over? Would you, for instance, readily believe that your captain was a traitor, just because someone told you so?"

She saw comprehension of the difficulties on most faces.

"I didn't," she said, fighting down the tension of that confession. "All I knew of the situation—as a jig on *Despite*, under Kiansa Hearne—was that we were on patrol, while the rest of the group was docked. I knew nothing about an invasion; we thought we had come to Xavier to babysit some paranoid colonists who had panicked over a perfectly ordinary random raid. A lot of us were annoyed that we'd missed the chance to compete in the annual Sector war games . . . we felt our gunnery was outstanding."

"But surely you suspected—"

Esmay snorted. "Suspected? Listen—my real concern was stuff disappearing out of personnel lockers. Minor theft. I didn't worry about the captain . . . the captain was the captain, doing her job of commanding the ship. I was a mere jig, doing my assigned job, which was servicing the automatic internal scanners and trying to find out who was getting into the lockers, and how. When the . . . mutiny started on *Despite*, I was so surprised I nearly got shot before I caught on." She waited for the nervous giggles to die down.

"Yeah—like that. It was ridiculous . . . I couldn't believe it. Nor could most of us. That's why conspirators are always a step ahead of the people who get real work done . . . they can count on that surprise."

"But how *did* Serrano get command?" someone asked.

"I can only tell you what I heard," Esmay said. "Apparently, she and some of her former crew got aboard by some ruse, asked to talk to Garrivay in his office. By good fortune—or perhaps she had some way of knowing—some of the other conspirators were there. She and her crew . . . killed them."

"Right away? You mean they didn't try to talk them out of it?"

Esmay let that lie in a stillness that was as scornful as her own. When the stirring began, she ended it by speaking. "When someone has determined on treason—is commanding a ship, and planning to deliver helpless civilians to the enemy—I doubt any moral homilies would change his mind. Commander Serrano made a command decision; she eliminated the most senior conspirators as quickly as possible. Even then it wasn't easy."

Esmay put up new displays. "Now—Captain Hearne took *Despite*—with me, and the rest of the crew—quickly out of Xavier system. Our exec was also involved, but the next junior officer was both loyal, and on the bridge to hear Commander Serrano's transmission to Captain Hearne, requesting her return to station and her assistance in defending Xavier. He actually began the mutiny, appealing to the bridge crew . . ." She stopped, flooded in memories of the next few hours. The contradictory orders on the ship's internal communications, the total confusion, the time it took—which now seemed inexplicable—for the loyalists to realize that a mutiny was necessary, and that they'd have to use deadly force on their crewmates.

"From the tactical point of view," she said, forcing all that back down, "Commander Serrano faced a very difficult task. The Benignity force arrived almost simultaneously with her assumption of command. Had she waited even a few more hours, it would have been impossible. The Benignity force—" Esmay outlined its specifications, reminding her audience of the usual tactics used by Benignity strike forces. Now, describing decisions and actions she had not personally witnessed, she found it easier to be calm and logical. This ship here, these over there, expected and unexpected choices of maneuver . . . results, neatly tabulated without reference to the people whose lives had just been changed forever.

All too soon, she had to come back to her own experience. She skipped over the internal battle for control of *Despite*. She had relived that too many times for the court to do it again, for these callow youngsters. But they needed to know how the battle ended, including the mistakes she had made.

"We came in too fast," she said, displaying yet another visual. "My concern was that we might arrive too late, and I assumed that any insertion barrage would be sufficiently dispersed. As you know, calculation of real elapsed time in multiple FTL hops is difficult at best—but the error is usually negative, not positive. As it happened, we made it through insertion safely, and skip-jumped to here—" she pointed. "Without dumping enough residual vee. We were short-crewed, with some damage to the nav computers, so I couldn't get a quick solution to a microjump that would have allowed the right angular motion. So . . . we blew past Xavier, and in that interim *Paradox* took fatal damage." More than eighteen hundred dead. Her fault. War left no margin for mistakes. She remembered the desperate scramble on the bridge of her ship, the bridge crew fighting to get control, to get a jump solution that would let them get back in time to do some good.

"We got a jump solution," she said, leaving out the rest of it, that instant when she had to accept it, with the risk, or not. The risk had been substantial—the confidence interval on that very unorthodox jump was broad enough that they could have gone right into Xavier itself. "And we came out of jump with a clear shot up the rear of the Benignity command cruiser." And a vector that gave them only one chance for that shot. The crew that had resented losing a chance to become the Sector gunnery champions had made their shot in the narrow window . . . and then had managed to reposition *Despite* in a stable orbit.

"The Board of Inquiry," Esmay said, "did not approve of the means, though they liked the results." She didn't want to discuss that; she hurried on to show how the Xavieran defenses had contributed: the suicidal use of phase cannon on a shuttle, the improvised mines, little *Grogon's* few telling shots, the yacht's astonishing defeat of the killer-ship.

"Only because they weren't expected," Esmay pointed out. "The Benignity ship intended ambush—post-battle analysis picked up enough transmissions to know that—and simply didn't know the yacht was there. When it shut down active systems to lie low for several hours, it was an easy target."

"What difference would it have made if *Despite* had also been in the Xavier system the whole time?"

An intelligent question, but difficult. "By the ship stats, it would have improved the odds ratio only about fifteen percent. To my own knowledge, *Despite* had the best weapons performance in the Sector: whatever Hearne's failings, she demanded and got quick and accurate fire from her crew. But if it had stayed, it would have been a known quantity, and Commander Serrano's force would still have been outnumbered and outgunned. I haven't seen any of the senior analysts' reports, but my own guess is that its contribution throughout the long battle would have been less than its effectiveness as an unexpected opponent at the end. That is, however, only my guess—it does not change the fact that the lack of another hull severely limited Commander Serrano's choices of action—and that its absence was the result of treason."

Silence, attentive and almost breathless. Esmay waited. Finally someone shifted, a very audible rasp of clothing against the seat cushions, and that broke their immobility. Ensign Dettin clambered up to take the podium, and thank her for her talk. Hands rose for more questions, but Esmay caught sight of senior rank in the rear. When had they come in? She hadn't noticed . . . but certainly no ensign guarding the door from other ensigns would refuse entry to the handful of majors and lieutenant commanders gathered there.

Dettin saw them, finally, and stopped short in his closing remarks. "Uh . . . sir . . . ?"

Commander Atarin, Esmay finally recognized as he moved out of the dimness back there and into the light. "I presume you'd be willing to give the same briefing to senior officers?"

A shiver of apprehension ran down her backbone. She couldn't tell if he was angry, or amused; she didn't know whether to apologize or explain. Both were bad ideas, her family heritage reminded her. "Of course, sir." She choked back the automatic qualifiers: if she wasn't really qualified, why was she showing off to the ensigns?

"If I could have a word . . ." he murmured, his glance raking the ensigns, who immediately began scrambling from their seats to leave by the other entrance.

"Of course, sir." Esmay retrieved her display cube from the projector, and came down from the dais. Major Pitak was not one of the officers there, and she didn't recognize any of the others besides Atarin. They gazed at the departing ensigns with the kind of neutral expression which she interpreted as trouble on the half-shell and bubbling from the broiler. Atarin said nothing more until the ensigns had gone.

"Very clearly explained, I thought," he said then. Esmay did not relax; from his tone he might have been discussing a textbook, and she wasn't sure whether she was being considered the textbook's author or its topic. "I was impressed with your analysis of your own errors."

Textbook case of junior officer putting feet clumsily in mouth, then.

"Just how badly was that nav computer damaged?"

A factual question she could answer. "It had taken direct fire—we'd replaced components from storage, but we couldn't get the microjump functions within 80 percent of normal function."

One of the other officers spoke up. "Couldn't you have used components from the weapons board? There's duplication in some of that, if I recall. "

"Yes, sir, there is. But we didn't want to risk having any delay in target acquisition or getting a firing solution."

"Umm. So you were skip-jumping with a faulty system . . . a bit risky, wasn't it?"

Esmay could think of no real answer but a shrug; one did not offer shrugs. "Somewhat risky, yes sir." It had been terrifying at the time, as the confidence intervals broadened and she had had to feel her way from one jump to the next. Instinct, she had been well taught, made a lousy guide to navigation in space.

"When I read the Board of Inquiry report," Atarin said, "I didn't notice that they acknowledged the difficulty with the nav computer. I presume you mentioned it."

"It was in the record, sir," Esmay said. She had not dwelt on the difficulties it presented; it would have been whining, making excuses.

"Yes. Well, Lieutenant Suiza, I think you'd better expect an invitation to the senior tactics discussion group. I quite realize that you aren't a senior analyst—but I doubt we can resist having a firsthand account of so . . . striking . . . an engagement."

"Yes, sir."

"And you might want to check the orientation of your illustration eight . . . I think you've got the axes rotated ninety degrees . . . unless there was a reason for that."

"Yes, sir."

With a nod, Atarin led the other officers out. Esmay

felt like falling into one of the seats and shaking for a half hour, but Dettin was peeking in at her, obviously hoping to chat.

✧   ✧   ✧

"So you don't think she's rousing the ensigns to any sort of . . . undesirable activity?"

"No, sir. You know how ensigns are: they'll go after anyone with real experience to talk about. They love gory stories, and that's what they were hoping for. Instead, she gave them a perfectly straightforward account, as unexciting as possible, of an innately thrilling engagement. Absolutely no self-puffery at all, and no attempt to romanticize Commander Serrano, either. I've invited her to address the senior tactics discussion group—she'll get more intelligent questions there, but I suspect she'll answer them as well."

"I don't want to make her into some sort of hero," Admiral Dossignal said. "It will rile our touchy captain. Too much attention—"

"Sir, with all due respect, she *is* a hero. She has not sought attention; from her record she never did. But she saved Serrano's ship—and Xavier—and we can't pretend it didn't happen. Letting her discuss it in professional terms is the best way to ensure that it doesn't become an unprofessional topic."

"I suppose. When is she speaking? I'd like to be there."

"The meeting after next. We have that continuing education required lecture next time."

✧   ✧   ✧

When Esmay reported to duty the next day, Major Pitak said, "I hear you had an interesting evening. How does it feel to have an overflow audience? Ever thought of being an entertainer?"

The nightmares that had kept her awake most of the night put an edge in Esmay's voice. "I wish they hadn't asked me!" Pitak's eyebrows rose. "Sorry," Esmay said. "I just . . . would rather put it behind me."

Pitak grinned sourly. "Oh, it's behind you, all right— just as a thruster's behind a pod, pushing it ever onward.

Face it, Suiza, you're not going to be an anonymous member of the pack ever again."

Just like my father, Esmay thought. She couldn't think of anything to say.

"Listen to me," Pitak said. "You don't have to convince me that you're not a glory-hound. I doubt anyone who's ever served with you or commanded you thinks you're a glory-hound. But it's like anything else—if you stand in the rain, you get wet, and if you do something spectacular, you get noticed. Face it: Deal with it. And by the way, did you finish with that cube on hull specs of mine-sweepers?"

"Yes, sir," Esmay said, handing it over, and hoping the topic had turned for good.

"I hear you're on the schedule for the senior tactics discussion group," Pitak said. Esmay managed not to sigh or groan. "If you've got any data on the hull damage to Serrano's ship, I'd like to hear about it. Also the Benignity assault carrier that blew in orbit . . . mines, I think it was . . . it would be helpful to know a little more about that. The mines and the hull both. I realize you weren't in the system for long afterwards, but perhaps . . ."

"Yes, sir."

"Not that it's tactics proper, but data inform tactics, or should. I expect Commander Serrano made use of everything she knew about H&A."

Forewarned by this exchange, Esmay was not surprised to be buttonholed by other senior officers in the days that followed. Each suggested particular areas she might want to cover in her talk, pertaining to that officer's specialty. She delved into the ship's databanks in every spare moment, trying to find answers, and anticipate other questions. Amazing how connected everything was . . . she had known the obvious for years, how the relative mass of Benignity and Fleet ships governed their chosen modes of action, but she'd never noticed how every detail, every subsystem, served the same aims.

Even recruitment policy, which she had not really thought of as related to tactics at all. If you threw massive ships in large numbers into an offensive war, seeking conquest, you expected heavy losses . . . and needed large numbers of troops, both space and surface. Widespread conscription, especially from the long-conquered worlds, met that need for loyal soldiers. Recent conquests supplied a conscripted civilian work force for low-level, labor-intensive industries. A force primarily defensive, like the Familias Regular Space Service, manning smaller ships with more bells and whistles, preserved its civilian economic base by not removing too many young workers into the military. Hence hereditary military families who did not directly enter the political hierarchy.

Fascinating, once she thought about it this way. She couldn't help thinking what widespread rejuvenation would do to this structure, stable over the past hundred or more years. Then she surprised herself when she anticipated the next set of hull specs on Benignity killer-escorts . . . on their choice of hull thickness for assault carriers. How had she known? Her father's brusque *You're a Suiza!* overrode the automatic thought that she must have seen it before somewhere, she couldn't possibly be smart enough to guess right.

By the time of her second presentation, she felt stuffed with new knowledge barely digested. She'd checked her illustrative displays (yes, number eight had been rotated ninety degrees from the standard references) and assembled what she hoped were enough background references.

CHAPTER TEN

"Looks like you came prepared," Major Pitak said, as Esmay lugged her carryall of cubes and printouts into the assigned conference room. This was a large hall in the Technical Schools wing, T-1, its raked seating curved around a small stage.

"I hope so, sir," Esmay said. She could think of two dozen more cubes she might need, if someone asked one of the less likely questions. She had come early, hoping for a few minutes alone to set up, but Pitak, Commander Seveche, and Commander Atarin were already there. Her chain of command, she realized.

"Would you like any help with your displays?" Atarin asked. "The remote changer in this room hangs up sometimes."

"That would be helpful, yes, sir. The first are all set up on this cube—" she held it out. "But I've got additional visuals if the group asks particular questions."

"Fine, then. I've asked Ensign Serrano to make himself available—I'll call him in."

Serrano. She hadn't met him yet, and after what she'd said at dinner, no one had gossiped more about him in her presence. She hadn't wanted to seek him out. What could she have said? *I saved your aunt's life; your grandmother talked to me; let's be friends?* No. But she had been curious.

Her first thought when he walked in was that he had the look of a Serrano: dark, compact, springy in motion, someone whose entire ancestry was spangled with stars, someone whose family expected their offspring to become admirals, or at least in contention. Her second was that he seemed impossibly young to bear the weight of such ambition. If he had not worn ensign's insignia, she'd have guessed him to be about sixteen, and in the prep school.

She had known there were young Serranos, of course, even before she got to the *Koskiusko*. They could not be hatched out full-grown as officers of some intermediate grade. They had to be born, and grow, like anyone else. But she had never seen it happen, and the discovery of a young Serrano—younger than she was—disturbed her.

"Lieutenant Suiza, this is Ensign Serrano." The glint in his dark eyes looked very familiar.

"Sir," he said formally, and twitched as if he would have bowed in other circumstances. "I'm supposed to keep your displays straightened out." Generations of command had seeped into his voice, but it was still expressive.

"Very well," Esmay said. She handed over the cube with her main displays, and rummaged in the carryall. "That one's got the displays that I know I'll need—and here, this is the outline. They're in order, but in case someone wants to see a previous display, these are the numbers I'll be calling for. Now these—" she gave him another three cubes, "—these have illustrations I might need if someone brings up particular points. I'm afraid you'll have to use the cube index . . . I didn't know I'd have any assistance, so there's no hardcopy listing. I'll tell you which cube, and then the index code."

"Fine, sir. I can handle that." She had no doubt he could.

Other officers were arriving, greeting each other. Ensign Serrano took her cubes and went off somewhere—Esmay hoped to a projection booth—while she organized the rest of her references. The room filled, but arriving officers left a little group of seats in front as if they'd had stars painted on them. In a way, they did . . . the admirals and the captain came in together, chatting amiably. Admiral Dossignal nodded at her; he seemed even taller next to Captain Hakin. On the captain's other side, Admiral Livadhi fiddled with his chair controls, and Admiral Uppanos, commander of the branch hospital, leaned toward his own aide with some comment. Atarin stood to introduce Esmay; with the admirals' arrival, the meeting started.

Esmay began with the same background material. No one made comments, at least not that she could hear. All her displays projected right-side-up and correctly oriented . . . she had checked them repeatedly, but she'd had a nagging fear. This time, her recent research in mind, she added what she had learned about the Benignity's methods, about the implications of Fleet protocols. Heads nodded; she recognized an alert interest far beyond the ensigns' hunger for exciting stories.

When the questions began, she found herself exhilarated by the quality of thought they implied. These were people who saw the connections she had only just found, who had been looking for them, who were hungry for more data, more insights. She answered as best she could, referencing everything she said. They nodded, and asked more questions. She called for visuals, trusting that the Serrano ensign would get the right ones in the right order. He did, as if he were reading her mind.

"So the yacht didn't actually get involved in the battle? Aside from that one killer-escort?"

"No, sir. I have only secondhand knowledge of this, but it's my understanding that the yacht had only minimal shields. It had been used primarily to suggest the presence of other armed vessels, and would not have fired if the Benignity vessel hadn't put itself in such a perfect situation."

"It can only have confused them briefly," a lieutenant commander mused from near the back. "If they had accurate scans, the mass data would show—"

"But I wanted to ask about that ore-carrier," someone else interrupted. "Why did Serrano have it leave the . . . what was it? Zalbod?"

"It's my understanding that she didn't, sir. The miners themselves decided to join in—"

"And it shouldn't have got that far, not with the specs you've shown. How did they get it moving so fast?"

Esmay had no answer for that, but someone else in Drive & Maneuver did. A brisk debate began between members of the D&M unit . . . Esmay had never been attracted to the theory and practice of space-drive design, but she could follow much of what they said. If this equipment could be reconfigured it would give a 32 percent increase in effective acceleration. . . .

"They'd still arrive too late to do any good, but that's within the performance you're reporting. I wonder which of them thought it up . . ."

"*If* that's what they did," another D&M officer said. "For all we know, they cooked up something unique."

Esmay snorted, surprising herself and startling them all into staring at her. "Sorry, sir," she said. "Fact is, they cooked up a considerable brew, and I heard about the aftermath." Scuttlebutt said that Lord Thornbuckle's daughter had been dumped naked in a two-man rock-hopper pod . . . supposedly undamaged . . . and the pod jettisoned by mistake into the weapons-crowded space between the ore-carrier and Xavier. Esmay doubted it was an accident . . . but the girl had survived.

Brows raised, the officer said, "I wonder . . . if they added a chemical rocket component . . . that might have given them a bit of extra push."

The talk went on. They wanted to know every detail of the damage to *Despite* from the mutiny: what weapons had been used, and what bulkheads had been damaged? What about fires? What about controls, the environmental system failsafes, the computers? The admirals, who had sat quietly listening to the questions of their subordinates, started asking questions of their own.

Esmay found herself saying "I'm sorry, sir, I don't know that," more often than she liked. She had not had time to examine the spalling caused by projectile hand weapons . . . to assess the effect of sonics on plumbing connections . . .

"Forensics . . ." she started to say once, and stopped short at their expressions.

"Forensics cares about evidence of wrongdoing," Major Pitak said, as if that were a moral flaw. "They don't know diddly about materials . . . they come asking *us* what it means if something's lost a millimeter of its surface."

"That's not entirely fair," another officer said. "There's that little fellow in the lab back on Sturry . . . I've gone to him a few times asking about wiring problems."

"But in general—"

"In general yes. Now, Lieutenant, did you happen to notice whether the bulkhead damage you mentioned in the crew compartments caused any longitudinal variation in artificial gravity readings?"

She had not. She hadn't noticed a lot of things, in the middle of the battle, but no one was scolding her. They were galloping on, like headstrong horses, from one person's curiosity to another's. Arguments erupted, subsided, and began again with new questions.

Esmay wondered how long it would go on. She was exhausted; she was sure they had run over the scheduled meeting time—not that anyone was going to tell the captain and senior officers to vacate the place. Finally Atarin stood, and the conversation died.

"We're running late; we need to wrap this up. Lieutenant, I think I speak for all of us when I say that this was a fascinating presentation—a very competent briefing. You must have done a lot of background work."

"Thank you, sir."

"It's rare to find a young officer so aware of the way things fit together."

"Sir, several other officers asked questions ahead of time, which sent me in the right directions."

"Even so. A good job, and we thank you." The others nodded; Esmay was sure the expressions held genuine respect. She wondered why it surprised her—why her surprise made her feel faintly guilty. The admirals and the captain left first, then the others trailed away, still talking among themselves. Finally they were all gone, the last of them trailing out the door. Esmay sagged.

"That was impressive, Lieutenant," Ensign Serrano said as he handed her the stack of cubes. "And you kept track of which display went with which question."

"And you handled them perfectly," Esmay said. "It can't have been easy, when I had to skip from one cube to another."

"Not that difficult—you managed to slide in those volume numbers every time. You certainly surprised them."

"Them?"

"Your audience. Shouldn't have—they had recordings of the talk you gave the juniors. This was just fleshed out, the grown-up version."

Was this impertinence? Or genuine admiration? Esmay wasn't sure. "Thanks," she said, and turned away. She would worry about it tomorrow, when Major Pitak would no doubt keep her busy enough that she wouldn't really have time. The young Serrano gave her a cheerful nod before taking himself off somewhere.

The next morning, Major Pitak said, "You know, there are still people who think that mutiny must've been planned ahead."

Esmay managed not to gulp. "Even now?"

"Yes. They argue that if Hearne knew she was going to turn traitor, she'd have her supporters in key positions, and it would have been impossible to take the ship without doing critical damage."

"Oh." Esmay could think of nothing further to say. If after all the investigation and the courts-martial, they wanted to believe that, she didn't think she could talk them out of it.

"Fleet's in a difficult situation right now . . . what with the government in transition, and all these scandals . . . I don't suppose you'd heard much about Lepescu." Pitak was looking at her desk display, a lack of eye contact that Esmay realized must be intentional.

"A few rumors."

"Well. It was more than rumors—that is, I know someone who knew . . . more than she wanted. Admiral Lepescu liked war and hunting . . . for the same reasons."

"Oh?"

"He got to kill people." Pitak's voice was cold. "He hunted people, that is, and your Commander Serrano caught him at it, and shot him. A result that suits me, but not everyone."

"Was he a Benignity agent?"

Pitak looked surprised. "Not that anyone noticed. I've never heard *that* rumor. Why?"

"Well . . . I heard that Commander Garrivay—who had the command of—"

"Yes, yes, the force sent to Xavier. I don't forget that quickly, Suiza!"

"Sorry, sir. Anyway, I heard he had served under Lepescu. And Garrivay *was* a Benignity agent . . . or at least a traitor in their pay."

"Mmm. Keep in mind that there are officers on this ship who served under Lepescu some time back. Far enough back not to be caught by Serrano, but . . . that might not be a healthy thing to speculate about, whether he was an agent or not."

"No, sir. Anyway, he's dead, so it doesn't matter." The moment it was out of her mouth she wished she hadn't said it; the look on Pitak's face was eloquent. It mattered, if only to the dead, and given Pitak's expression it mattered to some of the living too. It probably mattered to Heris Serrano. "Sorry," she said, feeling the hot flush on her face. "That was stupid . . ."

"Um. Just watch yourself, Lieutenant."

"Sir."

Since she didn't have another public appearance to get ready for, she headed for the gym when she came offshift. She'd missed out on her regular exercise.

The gym was crowded at this hour, but almost at once one of the machines came vacant, and the jig who'd been leaning against the bulkhead waiting waved her on. "Go on, Lieutenant. I'd really rather have one of the horsebots."

Esmay climbed onto the machine and set it for her usual workout. She had been aware of quiet competition to have the machine next to hers in the exercise room, the eagerness to invite her onto wallball teams despite her indifferent play, the little favors offered casually. She supposed it would go away in time, when people forgot about her so-called fame. She had never had really close friends in Fleet, and she didn't expect to acquire any now. Her mind hung on that thought. Why shouldn't she have friends? If people liked her, and they seemed to . . . .

It was only her transient fame. It had nothing to do with her real self.

Could she be sure?

She worked harder, until she was breathless and sweating and all thought of friends had vanished in the struggle for breath and strength.

At dinner, she listened to the chatter at her table with a mind uncluttered by worry about a coming presentation. Ensign Zintner's enthusiasm for Hull & Architecture reminded her of Luci's uncomplicated enthusiasm for stock breeding. She could like Zintner. She glanced around the mess hall, and found another female lieutenant watching her. It made her feel itchy, and she looked back at her plate. The hard workout had damped her appetite; she would be hungry in three hours, but not now.

On her way out, two other lieutenants stopped her. "If you don't have duty tonight, would you like to come watch a show with us?" They had asked before, but she had been preparing for the discussion group presentation. Now she had no excuse ready. She agreed to come, expecting to slip away after a few minutes.

Instead, she found herself locked into a row of others, with someone leaning over the back of her seat to speak to her. When the show started, she had that much peace, but as soon as it was over, she found herself the center of attraction.

It was ludicrous. It could not be real liking, real interest. It was only her notoriety. She hated herself for enjoying it, even the small amount that she did enjoy. She shouldn't like it; the only legitimate way for an Altiplano woman to be the center of attention was as matriarch of a family. Her great-grandmother would scold . . . her great-grandmother was light years away, if she was still alive.

Esmay shivered, and someone said "Are you all right . . . Esmay?" She looked over. A lieutenant . . . Kartin Doublos . . . so the use of her first name was not familiarity, but the normal usage between those of the same rank off duty.

"I'm fine," she said. "I just thought of my great-grandmother." He looked puzzled, but shrugged it off.

Over the next weeks, she noticed that the interest in her, the competition for her attention, did not slack off. It puzzled her. What could they hope to gain? What were they trying to prove?

Tickling at the edge of her mind were all the things Admiral Serrano had said . . . that legal counsel had said . . . and her father . . . and Major Pitak. She pushed them aside. She could not cope with a demand to break out of the comfortable safe niche she had created for herself. She would crawl back into it, pull it around her, an inviolable shield.

The nightmares came oftener, further proof that she was not, could not be, the person these others seemed determined to see. Not every night, but especially after those times when someone had talked her into a game, a show, some recreation which had—as far as she could tell—no connection with the content of either set of dreams. She started running a noise generator in her compartment, hoping it would cover any sound she made. No one had complained, but when she woke, heart pounding, at 0300, she was always afraid she had cried out in real life the way she had in the dream.

The dreams tangled, the helpless child caught in a war she did not understand merging abruptly into the terrified young officer belly-down on a bloody deck, firing into the haze.

She considered going to Medical. She would have to, if it affected her performance. So far it had not, that she could tell. Pitak seemed pleased with her progress; she got along fine with Master Chief Sivars, whose massive frame was so unlike Seb Coron's that she was startled only occasionally by the same kind of attitude.

*   *   *

"And how is Lieutenant Suiza shaping, Major?" Commander Seveche asked, at the quarterly review.

"Very well, of course." Pitak looked down at the record cube she held. "She's worked hard to get herself up to speed, though she has no background in heavy engineering and she'll never be the technical help that Bascock was."

"She shouldn't be technical track at all," Seveche said. "That presentation to the senior tactical came out of a command-track mind."

"She asked for technical," Admiral Dossignal said, but with the quirk in the corner of his mouth that his subordinates knew meant he was playing devil's advocate.

"I think it was the colonial background," Seveche said. "I looked up Altiplano's cultural index. Even though she's a general's daughter, they have no tradition of women commanders."

"Of women in the military, period," Dossignal said. "I saw the same report."

"Well, then. And the juniors are around her like bees around honey."

"Which she isn't comfortable with," Pitak said. "She's muttered to me about it, claims not to understand it. If that's honest, and I think it is, she's got no insight into her abilities . . ."

"Which you say aren't technical."

"Well . . ." Pitak considered. "I don't want to overstate it. She's got the brains, and she's applying herself. I can't speak for her qualifications in scan, but she's merely a studious amateur where H&A's concerned. And there's her habit of seeing everything in operational terms."

"Example?"

"Well . . . she's completed the second course in hull design, and I assigned her a report on the modifications necessary to support the new stealth hardware. I was looking for the usual, what I'd have gotten from Ensign Zintner: where to install it based on its need for power, its effect on the center of gravity, and so on. All technical. What she came up with was an analysis of the performance changes in terms of operational capability. I pointed this out, and she blinked twice and said 'Oh—but isn't that what really matters?'"

Seveche and Dossignal laughed. "Yes," said the admiral, "I see what you mean. To her, everything matters because of its use in battle—"

"Which is what's supposed to matter to us," Pitak said. "I know that . . . but I also know that I personally get sidetracked into neat engineering problems, technical bits for the sake of technical bits. She doesn't appear to, and I wonder if she ever did, even in scan."

"I doubt it," Dossignal said. "Because of her record on Xavier, they sent along the entire personnel file. Along with all those ordinary fitness reports, in which she came up bland and colorless and mediocre, there are her Academy ratings. Guess which courses she topped out in?"

"Not tactics and maneuver?"

"No . . . though she was in the top five percent there. Try military history. She wrote a paper analyzing the Braemar Campaign, and was invited to consider an appointment to postgraduate work as a scholar. She turned it down, and applied for technical track instead, where she'd never excelled."

"That's odd," Pitak said, frowning.

"It's more than odd," Dossignal said. "It makes no sense. I can't find anything in the file to show that she was counseled against command track, though I do find the usual comments about non-Fleet family backgrounds down in her prep school files. Yet they assigned her to technical track, purely on the basis of her request and her fairly mediocre scores."

"What were her personal evaluations?"

"What you'd expect for an outsider who wasn't pushing for command track . . . I don't know why we still use those things. If Personnel would ever go back and check officer performance against the predictions of the personal evaluations, they'd have to admit they're useless. She came out midrange in everything except initiative, where she was low-average."

"On which I'd rate her quite high," Pitak said. "She doesn't wait to be told, if she knows what she's doing."

"The question is, what do we do about her?" Dossignal asked. "We've got her for a couple of years, and we can teach her a lot about maintenance . . . but is that the best use of her talents?"

Seveche looked at Atarin and Pitak. "I'd have to say no, sir, it's not. She's a good speaker, a good tactical analyst—she might make a good instructor. Or . . ." His voice trailed away.

"Or the kind of ship commander she was in the Xavier action," Dossignal said. Silence held the group for a moment.

"That's a risky prediction," Atarin muttered.

"True. But—compare her even to officers several ranks ahead of her, in their first combat command. I think we'd agree that she has abilities she has shown only rarely— abilities Fleet needs, if she's really got them and can unlock them. I see that as our task: getting this potentially outstanding young officer to show her stuff."

"But how, sir?" asked Pitak. "I like the girl, truly. But— she's so reserved, even with me, even after this much time. How do we get the lid off?"

"I don't know," Dossignal admitted. "Engineering is my strength, not combat. I know we can't ask Captain Hakin, because he's half-convinced she's a mutineer. But if we all agree that the best use of Lieutenant Suiza is elsewhere, then at least we'll be looking for opportunities to nudge her that way."

Atarin chuckled suddenly. "When I think of all the youngsters who fantasize being heroic ship captains . . . all the untalented children of famous families . . . and here's a shy, inhibited genius who just needs a good kick in the pants—"

"I just hope we can administer that kick in the pants before life does," Pitak said. "However hard we kick her, reality can do worse."

"Amen to that," Dossignal said. He picked up another file. "Now—let's get to the ensigns. Zintner, for instance—"

*   *   *

Esmay had not run into the Serrano ensign for some time; she had seen him occasionally playing wallball or working out with someone on the mats, but he had never approached her. Now, the rotation in table assignments put him at hers. She nodded at him as the others introduced themselves.

"You're in remote sensing, aren't you, Ensign?"

"Yes, sir."

"Your first choice?"

"Actually no." He made a face. "But I had a short-term assignment right out of the Academy, and then I was off-schedule for normal ship rotations."

"It's a wonder," a jig to his right said. "I thought Serranos got whatever they wanted."

The Serrano ensign stiffened for an instant, but then shrugged. "It's a reputation perhaps not quite deserved," he said, in a colorless voice.

"And what's your specialty?" Esmay asked the jig. What was his name? Plecht, or something like that.

"I'm taking an advanced course," the jig said, as if that should impress her. "I'm doing research in low-temperature material fabrication," he said. "But probably nobody would understand it unless they were working in the field."

Esmay considered her options, and decided on blandness. He was making enough of an idiot of himself already. "I'm sure you're very good at what you do," she said, with as little expression as she could manage. It was still too much; two of the ensigns, but not Barin Serrano, snorted and choked on their soup.

On the way out, she got two invitations to come watch the junior officers' parpaun semifinals match.

"No, thank you," she said to each. "I really should spend some time in the gym myself." It was not an excuse; she was still having trouble with nightmares anytime she did not work out to exhaustion. She was sure she would outlast them in time, but for now she was spending a couple of hours a day in the gym.

The parpaun matches had thinned out the gym; Esmay

saw only three others, each engrossed in his or her own
program. She turned on her favorite machine. Someone
had left the display wall on its mirrored setting; she faced
her reflection and automatically looked away from the face.
Her legs, she saw, looked hard and fit. She should probably
do more with her upper body. But what? She didn't feel
like swimming, or using the machines designed for upper-
body-building. What she wanted was a scramble up some
rocks, nothing really hard but movements less regular than
a machine would demand.

"Excuse me, Lieutenant . . ."

Esmay jumped, then was furious with herself for reacting
that way. She looked; it was Ensign Serrano, with what
she privately considered *that look* on his face.

"Yes?" she said.

"I just wondered . . . if the lieutenant . . . would like
a sparring partner."

She stared at him in sheer surprise. It was the last
invitation she'd expected from a Serrano . . . from him.
"Not you!" got out before she could censor it; he flushed
but looked stubborn.

"Not me? Why?"

"I thought you were different," she said.

This time he understood; the flush deepened, and then
he went as pale as a bronze-skinned Serrano could and
pulled himself up angrily. "I don't have to suck up to you.
I have more influence in my family—" He stopped, but
Esmay knew what he would have said—could have said.
With the Serrano Admiralty behind him, he didn't need
her. "I liked you," he said, still angry. "Yes, my cousin
mentioned you, and yes, of course I saw the media
coverage. But that's not why—"

Esmay felt guilty for misjudging him, and perversely
annoyed with him for being the occasion of her misjudg-
ment. "I'm sorry," she said, wishing she felt more gracious
about it. "It was very rude of me."

He stared at her. "You're *apologizing?*"

"Of course." That got out before Esmay could filter it,
the tone as surprised as his and making it clear that in

her world all decent people apologized. "I misinterpreted your actions—"

"But you're—" He stopped short again, clearly rethinking what he had started to say. "It's just—I don't think it needed an apology. Not from a lieutenant to an ensign, even if you did misunderstand my motives."

"But it was an insult," Esmay said, her own temper subsiding. "You had a right to be angry."

"Yes . . . but you making a mistake and me being angry isn't enough for an apology like that."

"Why not?"

"Because—" He looked around; Esmay became aware of unnatural silence, and when she looked saw the other exercisers turning quickly away. "Not here, sir. If you really want to know—"

"I do." While she had a captive informer willing to explain, she wanted to know why, because it had bothered her for years that Fleet officers routinely shrugged off their discourtesies without apology.

"Then—no offense intended—we should go somewhere else."

"For once I wish this was home," Esmay said. "You'd think on a ship this size there'd be someplace quiet to talk that didn't imply things . . ."

"If the lieutenant would consider a suggestion?"

"Go ahead."

"There's always the Wall," he said. "Up in the gardens."

"Gardens don't imply things?" Esmay said, brows rising. They certainly did on Altiplano, where *They're in the garden* meant knowing smirks and raised brows.

"No—the Wall. The climbing wall. Even if you haven't ever climbed a real rock . . ."

"I have," Esmay said. "You mean they have a fake rock wall?"

"Yes, sir. And the parpaun match is on the way."

Esmay grinned, surprising herself. "I always heard Serranos were devious. All right. I'd like to try this fake cliff."

The cliff, when they arrived, was festooned with would-be climbers wearing all the accouterments of their sport.

Esmay stared up at the safety lines swinging from the overhead. "Sorry," Barin said. "I thought they'd be gone by now—it's past the time the climbing club usually finishes, and no one else ever seems to use it."

"Never mind," Esmay said. "They're not paying any attention to us." She examined the cliff closely. The indentations the climbers were using for their feet and hands were molded fiber-ceram, attached to the cliff face with metal clamps. "It looks like fun."

"It is, though I'm not very good at it." Barin peered upward. "But one of my bunkies is an enthusiast, and he's dragged me along a few times. That's how I know when they're *usually* done."

"Come on up . . ." someone yelled from far above.

Esmay fitted her hand into one of the holds. "I don't think so—I don't have any gear, and besides . . . we had a conversation going."

"A conversation or an argument?" Barin asked, then flushed again. "Sorry, sir."

"No offense taken," Esmay said. Around the base of the fake cliff, decorative rocklike forms had been placed to mark off the climbing area from the garden beds. She found a comfortable niche and sat down. "I'm not letting you off, though. If you can explain the protocols of apologies in Fleet, I'll be forever grateful."

"Well, as I said, what you called an insult is not that important . . . I mean, unless you really wanted my friendship, and that's personal. Is it on your world?"

On her world, duels would have been fought, and honor would have been satisfied, for the apologies Fleet never bothered with. Would he think her people barbaric, because they cared? "It's different," Esmay said, thinking how to say it without implying what she really felt about their manners. "We do tend to apologize easily for things . . ."

He nodded. "So that's why Com—some people think of you as tentative."

Esmay ignored the slip, though she wondered which commander. "They do?"

"Yes . . . at least that's what I've heard some people

say. You apologize for things we—sorry, most of the Fleet families—wouldn't, things we just take for granted. So it seems as if you're not sure of what you're doing."

Esmay blinked, thinking back down her years in Fleet, from the prep school on. She had made a lot of mistakes; she had expected to. She had been guided by the family rules: tell the truth, admit your mistakes, don't make the same mistakes twice, apologize promptly and fully for your errors. How could they think that was weakness and uncertainty? It was willingness to learn, willingness to be guided.

"I see," she said slowly, though she still didn't understand. "So . . . when you make a mistake you don't apologize?"

"Not unless it's pretty massive—oh, you say you're sorry, if you step on someone's foot, but you don't make a procedure out of it. Most mistakes—you own up, of course, and take the responsibility, but the apology is understood."

It was not understood, Esmay was sure, nearly as well as an apology properly delivered in plain speech. However, if they chose to be rude about it, she couldn't change that. "Is it offensive?" she asked, intent on mapping the edges of Fleet courtesy.

"Oh no, not offensive. A little bothersome, if someone's always doing it—it makes seniors a bit nervous, because they don't know how sincere it is."

Esmay felt her brows rising. "You have insincere apologies?"

"Of course," he said. Then he took another look at her face. "You don't," he said. Not a question.

"No." Esmay took a long breath. She felt as if she'd ridden out into a dry riverbed and sunk hock-deep in quicksand. She went on, quickly, keeping her voice as unemotional as possible. "In our—on our world, an apology is always part of taking responsibility for errors. It accompanies action taken to redress the wrong and ensure that the error is not repeated." That was almost a quote from the Conventions. "An insincere apology is like any other lie." Serious, she meant, and her mouth tingled at the memory of the hot peppers that had impressed her with the importance of telling the truth, no matter how unpleasant. She had not suspected her father of an insincere apology . . . just one far too late and insufficient.

"Fascinating," he said; by his tone he meant it the right way, real interest and not idle curiosity about the barbarians. "It must be very different, if you didn't know— I mean—"

"I understand what you mean," said Esmay. "It's—a new idea for me, that apologies could get me into trouble."

"Not trouble exactly, but the wrong idea about you."

"Yes. I take your point. Thank you for the information."

"You don't have to thank—" Again that bright-eyed look. "But you do, don't you? Thanking goes with apologizing . . . your world must be terribly formal."

"Not to me," Esmay said. It wasn't formality, it was caring about how others felt, caring how your actions affected them. Formality was Founders' Day dinners, or the awards ceremonies, not one of the twins coming in to apologize for having broken her old blue mug.

"Do we—I mean, do the others born into Fleet—seem rude to you?"

Should she answer that? She couldn't lie, and he had been unexpectedly honest with her. "Sometimes," Esmay said. She forced herself to smile. "I expect that I sometimes seem rude to you—or them."

"Not rude," he said. "Very polite—extremely polite, even formal. Everyone says how nice you are—so nice they couldn't figure out how you could do what you did."

Esmay shivered. Did they really think rudeness went with strength, with the killing way, that someone who said please and thank you and I'm sorry couldn't fight or command in battle? A grim satisfaction flowered briefly: if the Altiplano militia ever came offplanet, Fleet wouldn't know what hit them. *Pride is a blossom of ashes*. The old saying rang in her ears. *Bitter in the mouth, sharp to the nose, stinging to the eyes, and blown away on the first wind from the mountains. Plant no pride, lest you harvest shame*. She almost shook her head to free it from that old voice.

"I'm not sure myself how I did what I did—besides making a great number of unnecessary mistakes."

"Mistakes! You stopped a Benignity invasion—"

"Not by myself."

"Well, no, you weren't out there on your white horse galloping across the stars alone." He sounded as sarcastic as he looked.

This time Esmay took the offensive. "Why do you people use that image so much? The white horse thing, I mean. Yes, we use horses on Altiplano, but where did you get the idea that they're all white?"

"Oh, that's not about *you*," he said. "Nor Altiplano. It's from the Tale of the White Knights, who all rode white horses and spent their time doing great deeds. Didn't you have that in your libraries?"

"Not that I know of," Esmay said. "Our folk tales ran to Brother Ass and the Cactus Patch. Or the Starfolk and the Swimmers of Dawn. The only heroes on horses we know about were the Shining Horde."

He blinked. "You really do come from another culture. I thought everybody had grown up with the White Knights, and I never heard of the Swimmers of Dawn, or Brother Ass. The Shining Horde—that wasn't an ancestor of the Bloodhorde, was it?"

"No." That thought sickened her. "They're just legends; supposedly they were people with strange powers, who could glow in the dark." She glared at the twinkle in his eye. "Without getting too close to atomics," she said firmly.

The climbers, now near the base of the wall, ended that conversation. Esmay went over to see what equipment they used—much like that she'd used at home—and was offered more help than she wanted if only she'd join the climbing club. They would teach her; she could start on the easy end.

"I've scrambled around some boulders," she said.

"Well, you should come join us," one of the climbers said. "We can always use new members and soon you'll be right up there—" he pointed. "It's like nothing else, and this is the only ship I know with a real Wall." He was so clearly entwined in his hobby that Esmay felt no embarrassment; he would have welcomed anyone willing to climb off the flat deck. "Come on—just go up a little, and let me see how you move. Pleeeease?"

Esmay laughed, and started up the wall. She had never done as much climbing as her male cousins, but she had learned how to reach and shift her center of gravity without swinging away from the slope. She made it up a meter or so before losing her grip and slithering back down.

"Good start," the tall climber said. "You'll have to come again . . . I'm Trey Sannin, by the way. If you need climbing gear, there's some in our club lockers."

"Thanks," Esmay said. "I might do that. When's your meeting time?" Sannin told her, then led the other climbers away. "And thank you," she said to Barin. "I'm sorry I misjudged you, and you'll just have to put up with my apology—at least this time."

"Gladly," he said. He had an engaging grin, she noticed, and she felt an impulse to trust him even more than she had already.

That night she slept free of nightmares, and dreamed of climbing the cliffs of home with a dark-haired boy who was not quite Barin Serrano.

CHAPTER ELEVEN

Over the next few decads, Esmay found herself chatting with Barin Serrano even away from the mess hall. They had gone climbing once, with the club, and after a couple of hours of sweating on the Wall, she could not be shy with any of the climbers, let alone Barin. Then they had found themselves in the same corner during one of the officer socials, simply because Ensign Zintner had cornered a tray of the best cookies and they'd spotted her doing it.

Esmay did not let herself notice that the nightmares were not as intense on the evenings she spent with Barin and his friends. Instead, she concentrated on what he could show her about the unofficial customs of Fleet. Gradually, she thought of him less and less as "that nice Serrano boy" and more and more as the kind of friend she had not known she wanted.

In his company, she found herself making other friends. Zintner, whose lifelong background in heavy engineering made her the ideal person to ask for references when Pitak had handed Esmay a problem she couldn't solve. Lieutenant Forrester, who came to the climbing club meetings about half the time, and whose sunny attitude brightened any gathering. She began to realize that not all the people who approached her were interested only in her notoriety.

Once she began to enjoy herself more, she started worrying that she was being too social, neglecting her studies. "I still don't know what I should do to help Major Pitak," she said to Barin one shipnight. She felt guilty about going to the gym to play wallball when she could have been studying. Pitak seemed pleased with her progress, but if a ship needed repair right now, what could she actually *do*?

"You're too hard on yourself," Barin said. "And I know what I'm talking about. Serranos have a reputation for being hard on themselves and each other . . . you're off the scale."

"It's necessary," she said. When had she first discovered that if she had high enough standards, no one else's criticism mattered?

"Not that far," he said. "You're locking down a lot of what you could be, could do, with that kind of control."

She shied away from that. "What I could do, is study."

He punched her arm lightly. "We need you; Alana's not feeling up to a game, and that leaves us short."

"All right." She wanted to cooperate, and it bothered her. Why was she reacting like this, when she was immune to the tall, handsome Forrester, who had already asked her what Barin probably never would? She didn't want complications; she wanted simple friendship. That was pleasure enough.

The wallball game turned into a wild melee because most of the players agreed to play a variable-G game. Esmay argued, but was outvoted. "It's more fun," Zintner said, setting the AI control of the variable-G court for random changes. "You'll see."

"Out of black eyes," said Alana, who was refereeing this match. "I won't play VG games, and neither should you, Esmay."

"Be a sport," someone on the other team called. Esmay shrugged, and put on the required helmet and eyeguard.

An hour later, bruised and sweaty, she and the others staggered out to find that they had plenty of spectators.

"Chickens," Zintner said to those watching through the high windows of the court.

"It's easier on you shorties," said the tallest player on the other team. "If all the blood rushes to your head, it doesn't have time to go as fast."

Esmay said nothing; her stomach was still arguing about which way was up, and she was glad she had eaten little for lunch. She refused an invitation to take a cooling swim with the team, and instead showered and changed. By then she was hungry. Outside the showers, she found Barin nursing a swollen elbow.

"You're going to have that checked, aren't you, Ensign?" she said. They had discovered a mutual distaste for medical interventions, and now teased each other about it.

"It's not broken, Lieutenant," he said. "I believe surgery won't be necessary."

"Good—then perhaps you'll join me for a snack?"

"I think I could just about manage to get my hand to my mouth," he said, grinning. "It was Lieutenant Forrester's fault, anyway. He went for my shot, and got his knee in the way of my elbow."

Esmay tried to work that out—in a variable-G game, a lunge could turn into an unplanned dive and end in a floating rebound—and gave up.

As they ate, she brought up her past experience with his family for the first time. "I served on the same ship as Heris Serrano, back when I was an ensign. She was a good officer—I was in awe of her. When she got in that trouble, I was so angry . . . and I didn't know what I could do to help, if anything. Nothing, as it turned out."

"I met her just one time," he said. "My grandmother had told me about her—not everything, of course, only what was legal. She sent me with a message; she wanted to use only family as couriers. We weren't sure which of us would find her, and I was the lucky one." From the tone, Esmay wasn't sure he thought it was lucky.

"Didn't you like her?"

"Like her!" That, too, had a tone she couldn't read. Then, less explosively, "It's not a matter of *liking*. It's— I'm used to Serranos; I'm one myself. We tend to have this effect on people. We're always being accused of being arrogant, even when we aren't. But she was . . . more like Grandmother than any of the others." He smiled, then. "She bought me dinner. She was in a white rage when I first showed up, and then she bought me dinner, a really expensive one, and—well, everyone knows what she did at Xavier."

"But you ended up friends with her?"

"I doubt it." Now he looked down at his plate. "I doubt she's friends with any Serrano now, though I hear she's speaking to her parents again."

"She wasn't?"

"No. It's all kind of tangled . . . according to Grandmother she thought they would help her when Lepescu threatened her—and they didn't—and then she resigned. That's when Grandmother told everyone to leave her alone."

"But I thought she was just on covert ops then."

"That too, but I don't know when—or what was going on. Grandmother says it's none of my business and to keep my nose out of it and my mouth shut."

Esmay could imagine that, and wondered that he broke the prohibition even this much. She had prohibitions of her own that she had no intention of breaking, just because she'd found a new friend.

"I met her, of course, after Xavier, but only briefly," Esmay said. In the dark times before the trial, when she had been sure she'd be thrown out of Fleet, the memory of the respect in those dark eyes had steadied her. She would like to have deserved that look more often. "There were legal reasons for keeping us apart, they said." Then she turned the topic to something less dangerous.

A few days later, Barin asked her about Altiplano, and she found herself describing the rolling grassy plains, the mountain scarps, her family's estancia, the old stone-built city, even the stained glass she had liked so much as a child.

"Who's your Seat in Council?" Barin asked.

"Nobody. We have no direct representation."

"Why?"

"The Founder died. The Family we served. Supposedly, half the militia died along with the Family. There are those who say otherwise, that the reason no one from Altiplano has a Seat in Council is that it was a mutiny."

"What does your grandmother say?"

"My *grandmother*?" Why should he think her grandmother's words had any weight . . . oh, of course, because *his* grandmother was Admiral Serrano. "Papa Stefan says it's a ridiculous lie, and Altiplano should have a Seat or maybe four." At his look, she found herself explaining. "On Altiplano, we're not like Fleet . . . even if we're military. Men and women don't usually do the same things . . . not as life work, that is. Most of the military, and all the senior commanders, are men. Women run the estancias, and most of the government agencies that aren't directly concerned with the military."

"That's odd," Barin said. "Why?"

She hated to think about it, let alone talk about it. "It's all old stuff," she said dismissively. "And anyway, that's just Altiplano."

"Is that why you left? Your father was a—a sector commander, you said?—and you couldn't be in the military?"

Now she was sweating; she could feel the prickle on the back of her neck. "Not exactly. Look—I don't want to talk about it."

He spread his hands. "Fine—I never asked, you never got upset, we can just talk about my relatives again if that's all right."

She nodded, stabbing her fork into food she barely saw, and he began a story about his cousin Esser, who had been consistently nasty during long vacations. She didn't know if it was true; she knew it didn't matter. He was being polite; she was the occasion for more politeness, and that in itself was humiliating.

That night the nightmares recurred, as bad as the worst she'd had. She woke gasping from the battle for *Despite* only to find herself in the body of that terrified child, helpless to beat off her assailant . . . and from that relived the worst of the time in hospital. Dream after dream, all fire and smoke and pain, and voices telling her nothing was wrong even as she burned and writhed in pain. Finally she quit trying to sleep, and turned the light on in her compartment. This had to stop. She had to stop it. She had to get sane, somehow.

The obvious move presented itself, and she batted it

away. She had enough bad marks on her record, with the
Board of Inquiry and the court-martial and then that
ridiculous award from Altiplano . . . let her get a psych
note in her record and she'd never get what she wanted.

And what was that? The question had never presented
itself so clearly before, and in that bleak night she looked
at it straight on. She wanted . . . she would have said safety,
awhile ago. The safety Fleet could give her from her past.
But the man was dead, the lie exposed . . . she was safe,
in that way. What did she really want?

Fragments popped into her mind, as brief and bright
as the fragments of traumatic memory. The moment on
the bridge of *Despite* when she had given the order to
go back to Xavier system . . . the moment when she'd
given the order to fire, and the great enemy cruiser had
gone up. The respect she'd seen on the faces of those
at her briefing, when even the admirals—even the captain,
in spite of himself—had admired the way she presented
the material. Even the admiration of the juniors, which
she half-hated herself for enjoying. The friendships she
was beginning to have, fragile as young plants in spring.

She wanted that: those moments, and more of them.
Herself in charge, doing the right things. Using the talents
she had shown herself were hers. Recognition of her peers;
friendships. Life itself.

The critical side of her mind pointed out tartly that she
was unlikely to have many such moments as a technical
specialist, unless she made a habit of serving on ships with
traitorous or incompetent captains. She wasn't as good at
the technical bits as others; she studied hard, she achieved
competence . . . but not brilliance.

You're too hard on yourself. She was not hard enough
on herself. Life could always be harder; it was necessary
to be hard first. *You're locking down what you could be.*
What did he think she could be, that Serrano ensign? He
was only a boy—*a Serrano boy*, her critical self reminded
her. So . . . he thought she wasn't using all her talents.
If he knew anything. If, if, if . . .

She could hardly apply for command track now, this

many years into technical. She didn't even want command track. Did she? She had hated combat, from the first moment of the mutiny through to that last lucky shot that burst the enemy cruiser like a ripe seedpod. She pushed down the memory of the feeling that had accompanied the fear, the sick disgust with the waste of it . . . that feeling entirely too seductive to be reliable.

Who knew what they felt at such times anyway? Perhaps she could go into teaching—she knew she was good at presenting complex material. That history instructor had even suggested it. Why had she fled from that offer into the most unsuitable specialty? Her mind thrashed around like a fish on a hook, unable to escape the painful reality that she had trapped herself stupidly, blindly. Like a fish indeed . . . she, who was meant to swim free. But where?

The next morning, she was tired enough that Major Pitak noticed.

"Late night, Suiza?"

"Just some bad dreams, Major." She made it as dismissive as she could without rudeness. Pitak held her gaze a long moment.

"Lots of people have post-combat dreams, you know. No one will think less of you if you talk them over with someone in Medical."

"I'll be all right," she said quickly. "Sir." Pitak kept looking, and Esmay felt herself flushing. "If it gets worse, sir, I'll keep your advice in mind."

"Good," Pitak said. Then, just as Esmay relaxed, she spoke again. "If you don't mind telling me, what made you choose technical instead of command track?"

Esmay's breath shortened. She hadn't expected to face that question here. "I—didn't think I would be good at command."

"In what way?"

She scrambled to think of something. "Well, I—I'm not from a Fleet family. There's a natural feel."

"You honestly never wanted to take command of a unit until you ended up with *Despite*?"

"No, I . . . when I was a child, of course I daydreamed. My family's military; we have hero tales enough. But what I really wanted was space itself. When I got to the prep school, there were others so much better suited . . ."

"Your initial leadership scores were quite high."

"I think they gave me some slack for being planet-born," Esmay said. She had explained it to herself that way for years, as the leadership scores dropped bit by bit. Until Xavier System, until the mutiny.

"You're not really a technical-track mind, Suiza. You work hard, you're smart enough, but that's not where your real talent is. Those briefings you gave the tactical discussion groups, that paper you wrote for me . . . that's not the way a tech specialist thinks."

"I'm trying to learn . . ."

"I never said you weren't trying." From the tone, Pitak could have intended the other meaning; she sounded almost annoyed. "But think of it this way: would your family try to make a draft horse out of a polo pony?"

For some reason the attempt to put the problem in her culture's terms made her stubborn; she could almost sense her body changing, long dark legs and hard hooves sinking into mud, leaning backwards, resisting. "If they needed a load hauled, and the pony was there . . ." Then, before Pitak exploded, she went on. "I see your point, sir, but I never thought of myself as . . . as a pony mismatched to a load."

"I wonder what you *did* expect," Pitak said, half to herself.

"A place to work," Esmay said. "Away from Altiplano." It was the most honest thing she could say, at that point, without getting into things she never intended to discuss with anyone, ever.

Pitak almost glared. "Young woman, this Fleet is not 'a place to work away from home.'"

"I didn't mean just a job—"

"I should hope not. Dammit, Suiza, you come so close . . . and then you say something like that."

"Sorry, sir."

"And then you apologize. Suiza, I don't know how you

did what you did at Xavier, but you had better figure it out, because *that* is where your talent lies. And either you use your abilities or they rot. Is that clear?"

"Yes, sir." Clear as mud in a cattle-trampled stock tank. She had the uneasy feeling that Barin wouldn't be able to explain this one, in part because she would be too embarrassed to ask.

❖   ❖   ❖

"I put the bug in her ear," Pitak said to Commander Seveche.

"And?"

"And then I nearly lost my temper and pounded her. I do not understand that young woman. She's like two different people, or maybe three. Gives you the impression of immense capacity, real character, and then suddenly flows away like water down a drain. It's not like anything I've seen before, and I thought I'd seen every variety of strangeness that got past the psychnannies. She's all there . . . and then she isn't. I tried to get her to go talk to Med about her combat experience, and she shied off as if I'd threatened her with hard vacuum."

"We aren't the first commanders she's puzzled," Seveche reminded her. "That's why it was such a surprise . . ."

"One good thing is she's coming out of her shell with some of the other juniors," Pitak said. "She and that Serrano ensign and some others."

"The young Serrano? I'm not sure that's a good idea. There were two Serranos at Xavier."

Pitak shrugged. "I don't see a problem. This one is too young; those were much her seniors. Besides, they're not plotting; they're climbing the Wall and playing team games together occasionally. My thought was that maybe the Serrano arrogance would get through her shell, whatever it is, and release that natural command ability."

"Maybe. She's not seeing just him, you say?"

"No. I hear about it mostly from young Zintner, who plays wallball with them. She says Suiza hates variable-G games but is a good sport. I haven't asked, but she's told me that two or three young men are pursuing Suiza, without much success. 'Not really a cold fish when you get to know her, but reserved,' is what Zintner said."

Seveche sighed. "She must be hiding something; they always are, the juniors, even when they think they're not."

"And we aren't?" Pitak said.

"We are, but we know we are. The advantages of maturity: we know where our bodies are buried, and we know that anything buried can be exhumed. Usually at the wrong moment."

"But Suiza?"

"Let her be for a bit; see if she gets somewhere on her own, now that you've planted the idea. We've agreed she's not stupid. She'll be here a couple of years, anyway, and if she hasn't unstuck herself by the end of the next review period we'll try again. If, as we said before, life doesn't give her the necessary kick in the pants."

✧　　　✧　　　✧

Esmay stared at her work, feeling resentful. She knew that was an unsuitable feeling for any junior officer . . . unproductive, not useful, even if justified. In this case it wasn't even justified. She liked Major Pitak and trusted in her honesty; if Pitak said she didn't have a technical mind, then she didn't have a technical mind. She tried to ignore the self-pitying self that wanted to whine about all the hours of study, the diligence, the self-sacrifice . . .

"Stupid!" she said aloud, startling herself and Master Chief Sivars, who had come in to bring something to Major Pitak. "Sorry," Esmay said, and felt her face heat. "I was thinking about something else."

"That's all right, Lieutenant," he said, in the indulgent voice of the very senior NCO to the very junior officer he tolerates out of misguided affection. Or so it seemed to Esmay, making her even more resentful.

"Chief, how can you tell which junior personnel are going to have a knack for technical stuff?"

He gave her a look that clearly said this wasn't her business, or his, but then leaned back against the bulkhead and answered. "Some of 'em come in with such a genius for it you don't have the slightest doubt. I remember a pivot, six or seven years ago, straight out of basic, who had blown the top off the placement exams. Well, we'd had high-scorers before . . . but this kid couldn't touch something without making it work better. In two days, we knew what we had; in a decad, we were just holding our breath hoping he wouldn't get crosswise of anyone important, because he did have a way of speaking his mind." He grinned at the memory. "That was before we were on *Kos*, you understand; she was under construction, and we were working out of Sierra Station. Major Pitak was a lieutenant then, same as you are now, except she was herself, if you know what I mean. Well, this kid snapped back at her one day, and she went the color of bad polyglue. Then she blinked, and looked at me, and said the kid was right, and walked out. Told me something about both of 'em, though of course I had to give the kid what-for, for sassing an officer. It wasn't really sass; he just knew what he knew, and didn't bother to hide it."

"And the ones that aren't quite that good?"

"Well . . . I can tell the ones that'll work hard, of course. That always helps. Anyone with enough smarts to pass the placement exams can learn enough to be useful if they work at it steadily, the way you've done. But nothing replaces the knack, the feel . . . I can't explain it, Lieutenant. Either they have a feel for the material, or they don't. Some of 'em have it real narrow . . . they may be technical geniuses in scan, say, and useless for anything else. Others have a knack for a lot of things in the technical area—they can work almost any system."

"Are you ever wrong?" Esmay asked.

He chewed his lip. "Sometimes . . . but usually it's not to do with their talent. I've missed other things about them, things that interfered. I remember a sergeant minor, transferred in from Sector 11, with scores off the chart. That was odd in itself—why would another sector let him go, if he was so good? But we were short-handed, like we always seem to be, and he was awfully good."

"So what was wrong with him?"

"Pure meanness. Turned out he got his kicks making

trouble: on his own crew, in barracks, everywhere. Set people against each other, skinned the truth to the bone but always in ways that he could explain as not really lies. Nothing he did was against regulations . . . he was careful about that . . . but by halfway through his tour we'd have done anything to get rid of him. I would, anyway. I'd just been promoted to master chief; I wanted my section to run smoothly and here he was stirring things up. We finally got rid of him, but it wasn't easy." By the tone, he did not want to explain how, and Esmay didn't ask. "Then there was a kid who was smart enough when he could keep his mind on the job, but he was always in emotional hot water over something. Or rather, somebody. We finally got him to Medical and they had some treatment, but then he wanted to transfer. I heard later he was doing fine over in Sector 8." He gave Esmay a smile as he pushed himself up and started out. "Just keep plugging away, Lieutenant; you're doing fine."

So even he knew she wasn't that good at this. Esmay resisted the childish urge to throw something at that broad back.

At dinner that evening, she said less than usual, listening to the chat at her table. The self-proclaimed genius of special materials research wasn't talking either; he had the abstracted expression of someone trying to solve problems in his head. Barin Serrano was describing his attempt to recalibrate a gravscan in which, as he put it, "someone had been tap dancing on the connections." He sounded happy enough, and the jig at the far end, talking about her current love affair, sounded even happier.

Perhaps it was only lack of sleep that made her want to crawl under the table. She had had nightmares all night, and a confusing and disappointing talk with her commander; of course she felt down. She didn't eat dessert, and decided to go to bed early.

✧   ✧   ✧

"Found it," Arhos said. "It's a good tricky one, too."

"Not too different from what we were told, I hope," said Losa.

"No . . . but apparently the captain's a bit paranoid, moves it around from time to time. And checks out the circuitry periodically, to make sure it works."

"So we have to fix it with a built-in test circuit to fake the test?"

"Yes. I've got the details . . . amazing how some of these people will talk if they think you sympathize with their problems. There's a petty-light who's convinced the captain is down on him because of a practical joke actually concocted by someone else . . . he was so anxious to convince me how unfair and unreasonable Hakin is, that he practically handed me the whole mechanism on a chip."

"So when can we do it?"

"The captain tested it two days ago. He's using some schedule of his own devising, but he's never yet tested it within five days of a previous test. So if we do the main part tomorrow, that should give us a few days to test the test, as it were."

"I hope this is all right," Losa said, frowning. "I mean— we're stuck on this ship now, and we can't pretend we don't know what it's for . . ."

"I can," Arhos said. "In anticipation of immortality, I can pretend any number of impossible things."

"But if the Bloodhorde shows up . . ."

"Here? Where our very efficient escorts will chase them into the arms of the neighboring cruisers? I refuse to worry; there's nothing we can do. As far as I'm concerned, there's a dangerously paranoid captain on this ship, who might at any time see a dust spot on a vidscan and decide it's an enemy fleet—and then decide it's his duty to blow us all away. While I'm on this ship I *particularly* want that device out of his control, lest I lose my chance at a long happy life because of some knotheaded captain's mental quirk."

"You're not happy about it either," Losa said with satisfaction.

"Yes, I am."

"No . . . every time you get flowery like that it means

you have doubts. Serious doubts. I think we ought to put the controls in our own hands."

Arhos considered. "Not a bad idea, that. If nothing else, it will keep you satisfied. Gori?"

"I like it. What time tomorrow?"

"Well—the easiest access will be through the inventory bay on Deck Ten, the one across from T-4. And there are weapons components in that bay."

"How fortunate," Losa said.

"Especially since the computer indicates they're located in exactly the right place . . ."

"You fiddled, Arhos."

He grinned. "What use to have the ability, if no use is made of it? It's true that I . . . transposed some numbers in the database, but . . . it was in a good cause."

"I hope so," Losa said soberly. "I do hope so."

With their most advanced equipment, they were able to locate and fox the scan which supposedly kept anyone from tampering with the device. It took a day or so to create the blind loops they'd insert while they worked. Another day or so to create a convincing errand in that bay again.

Then they were in, and the device in its casing looked just as they'd expected.

"The tricky bit," Arhos said, but he didn't sound worried. Rapidly the case came open, the controls yielded to their intrusion, the codes changed . . . and the telltales stayed a friendly green.

"Might as well run the test," Gori said.

"Might as well—we've got ten minutes." Arhos nodded to Losa, who pricked her intercept into the captain's control line and then inserted a two-layer code. The telltales changed, in sequence, from green to yellow. She inserted another code, and they went back to green.

"Lovely," Gori said. "I really do like it when we're right the first time."

"If we *were* right," Losa murmured.

Arhos grinned. "Three rejuvs, Lo. Three, first-class, guaranteed with the best drugs. We were right." He finished cleaning up, putting everything back as they'd found it, even to the tiny piece of metal filing that just happened to have lain a half a centimeter in from the right front corner of the case. "We're going to live forever," he said, backing out, wiping the deck behind him. "Forever, and be very, very rich."

That night they brought out one of their treats from home, and toasted each other. For the benefit of the ship's scan, they congratulated themselves on their progress so far in getting the weapons rekeyed. It made a delicious joke. Arhos sank into sleep and dreamed of the future, when he would be so rich, and so well known, that he'd never have to take a Bloodhorde contract again.

CHAPTER TWELVE

Esmay was asleep, having a different dream for once, when the alarm bleeped, bringing her upright even before she woke. All down the passage she could hear voices; her heart stammered and she felt cold sweat break out. But even as she dressed, the nature of the emergency became clear: ships coming in for repair. Not a mutiny. Not combat. Not—she told herself firmly—as bad. For her.

Even as she dressed and scampered along the passage and up ladders to her section, she felt the gut-twisting lurch of a ship overpowering its way through a jump point. Fear crawled back up her spine, vertebra by vertebra. DSRs were not built for racing and jumping; DSRs moved at the leisurely pace appropriate to their mass and internal architecture. She understood now, after the time in Hull & Architecture, why it wasn't a matter of adding more power—what the trade-offs were, in making *Koskiusko* so big and so massive. What had happened? Where were they going? And more important, were they fleeing with trouble on their tail, or running toward it?

Hull & Architecture, like every other section, swarmed like a kicked anthill. In the departmental briefing room, Commander Seveche was putting a cube in the display. "Ah . . . Suiza. Hook up your compad, this is going to be interesting." Esmay plugged in her compad, and made sure it was set to record the display directly. Most of H&A was in the room when Seveche started his briefing; the rest straggled in within a few minutes.

"This is what we know—and we all know that it will be worse. *Wraith* is a patrol ship, commissioned ten years ago, out of the Dalverie Yards—one of the SLP Series 30 hulls—" A couple of low groans, which Esmay now understood. The SLP Series 30 had well earned the nickname "slippery," meaning its architecture lent itself to unauthorized and possibly damaging revisions. "She's been in combat against the Bloodhorde, and despite their technological inferiority, they managed to wipe most of her scan systems and then bludgeon her with heavy explosive. There was shield failure of the starboard arc, forward of frame 19—" Esmay now knew exactly where frame 19 was on that class and series. "—with resulting damage to the forward weapons pods, and a hull breach here—" Seveche's pointer circled the intersection of frame 19 with truss 7.

"And she's coming *in*?" Someone less inhibited than Esmay had voiced her surprise exactly.

"She was lucky," Seveche said. "They knocked out her scans, but not the scans of her hunting partners. *Sting* and *Justice* were in the system, and they blindsided the Bloodhorde ships, drove them off. *Wraith* had heavy casualties of course, but they were able to patch things up enough to make it through one jump point. They couldn't manage two: the hull patch was leaking again, and they had nothing more to use on it. So—as you all no doubt felt—we're jumping out to meet them."

No one said it this time, but the tense faces around Esmay revealed their thoughts. DSRs stayed well behind any line of war for a very good reason . . . they couldn't fight, maneuver, or get away. If they were attacked . . .

"I did remind our captain that old *Kos* isn't an escort," Seveche said wryly. "But we should be fine. Half our protection jumped ahead of us, and the rest with us. We'll have *Sting* and *Justice* as well. And it looks like all the experimental stuff on *Justice* worked."

"How long do we have?" asked Pitak.

"We expect to come into the same system in—" Seveche looked at the chronometer. "Seventy-eight hours and eighteen minutes. We'll be making a series of fast-insertion jumps, coming out of the last at a slow relative vee; they'll tow *Wraith* out to us."

Seveche went on with the briefing. "We won't know more about the hull damage until we come out of the last jump: we're pushing this ship to its max, and not hanging around anywhere to pick up messages. For all we know, *Wraith* won't make it until we arrive."

By the time *Koskiusko* came out of its last jump, Esmay had been all over the ship on errands for Major Pitak. "Don't be insulted, but you still don't know enough to be really useful—and I need someone to keep up with all the other departments. Ship's comm is overloaded, or will be."

Esmay didn't feel insulted at all. She was quite willing to check with Inventory Control on the stock of fasteners, star-slot, 85mm, pitch 1/10, interval 3mm (she patted the boxes with a proprietary hand—those were *her* fasteners), to ask the chief in Weapons Systems for an estimate of the damage that *Wraith* might have suffered from its own weaponry exploding when the hull breached, to crawl around the depths of the storage hold full of structural members checking each one with instruments that should detect any dangerous deformities. Everything had been checked before, and would be checked again, but she understood the need. Mistakes happen. The wrong color uniform gets on the person with the . . . no, she didn't have time to think of that.

She had avoided Medical, in the superstitious belief that any wandering psychnanny would see in her face that she had terrible secrets, and she'd be out on a psych discharge before she could argue. But in the last hours before they closed with *Wraith*, Pitak sent her there, to coordinate the search and rescue with what was known about the hull and its problems.

Medical occupied a large chunk of T-5, with onboard operating suites, decontamination suites, regen tanks, neural-assisted-growth tanks, isolation chambers for exotic infectious diseases, diagnostic labs . . . the equivalent of a sector hospital. Esmay found it in the same state of bustle as her own department, and was passed from one desk to another until she located Trauma Response.

Esmay handed Pitak's cube of data—updated since the downjump by direct transmission from *Wraith*—to the lieutenant in charge of the extrication and trauma transport teams.

"Hang around until I'm sure we understand all this," he said, stuffing the cube into a reader. The display came up on the wall; the others milling around settled to look at it. "Forward hull breach—that'll mean decompression injuries in the nearest compartments beyond the breach—" In the breach itself, it meant deaths, the responsibility of Personnel Salvage, not Extrication and Transport.

"Looks like truss failure here—" he pointed. "We'll have to cut our way around that. Lieutenant, what'll happen if we cut here and here?" He pointed. Esmay, briefed by Major Pitak, pointed to alternative cuts, already on the cube display in green. He scowled. "That'll just barely give clearance for our suits—we don't want to snag on anything—and we'll have casualties coming out . . . we need more room than this. We've told H&A before—we need a solid two-meter clearance . . . why can't we make this cut?" He pointed again at his first choice.

Esmay thought she knew, but this was a job for someone with seniority. "I'll get Major Pitak for you," she said.

"Do that."

Esmay found Pitak deep in one of the holds stocked with H&A gear, and patched her through to the E&T commander . . . then backed off as the air heated up around her. She'd never actually heard Pitak swear before, but on this occasion the major left curlicue trails of smoke down the bulkheads. After the first explosion, she settled into explanation.

"—And if you want several dozen *more* casualties and a lot of sharp-edged ejecta floating around, then you go on and cut to your heart's content—"

"Dammit, Major—"

As abruptly as a mule's kick, the major calmed. "Now—what do you need for your suits? I'll get you space, just tell me—"

"Two meters."

"Mmph. All right. I'll send Suiza back with a new plan that'll give you two meters—round section or square?"

"Uh . . . square would be nice, but round will do. If it were only one it wouldn't matter, but—"

"Yes, well, if the Bloodhorde were recruits on a first mission, *Wraith* wouldn't be full of holes. I'll get back to you." Pitak turned on Esmay. "And why are you looking so surprised? Didn't know I could turn the air blue, or didn't think I could calm down? Either way, it looks bad . . . don't just stare at me, Lieutenant, you're making me nervous."

"Sorry, sir," Esmay said.

"Two stinking meters they want. Greedy pigs. I suppose they can't be sure what they'll find in there, and they need space—but they certainly can't cut that one. If I lend them a structural tech to do the cutting, that shorts me on the main job—but it might save some lives and shouldn't cost any. All right—here's what you tell them." She rattled off a series of contingent plans, and sent Esmay back to the medical deck. Esmay wanted to ask why she didn't just call them on the com, but this was no time to ask Pitak anything.

Eight hours before the last jump point, Esmay and all but essential crew went down for a forced rest period, augmented by soporifics in the compartments. Esmay understood the reason for this—exhausted, twitchy people would make unnecessary mistakes—but she hated knowing that her calm repose had been created chemically. What if something happened and those awake forgot—or had no time—to turn on the antidote sprays?

She was still worrying at that when she woke, feeling rested and alert, to the soft chime of the downshift alarm. It had worked, as usual . . . but she didn't have to like it.

The *Koskiusko* had emerged at near-zero relative vee to the system it entered, the safest way to dump something of its mass out of jumpspace. Before Esmay could get back to Pitak's office in H&A, word had come down that *Wraith*'s tow was within twenty thousand kilometers. That made not only a bull's-eye, but a potential disaster. "An error of considerably less than a tenth of a percent in exit vee, and we'd have romped right into her and her damn-fool escorts," Pitak growled. "But it does mean we can get to work quickly. Might save a few survivors in the forward compartments."

Tightbeam comlinks were already up; realtime data poured into *Koskiusko's* communications shack, to be decoded and routed to the relevant departments. Esmay spent the first hour or so watching the H&A data, and sending it on to the subspecialists. Then Pitak found another job for her. "Troll the stuff they're sending Drives and Maneuver, and Special Materials. You're good at picking up connections—someone upstairs may have misrouted something we need."

Pitak herself had a model of the SLP Series 30 hull set up in both virtual and wireframe floor versions in the briefing room. Around it clustered the senior H&A engineers, making changes to reflect the peculiarities of *Wraith* as the data streamed in. Esmay looked up often to peek at the progress. She had seen plenty of computer 3-D displays of ship hulls, but never the scaled-down wireframe that now occupied a five-meter length of the floor. It looked like fun—though the empty space along one forward flank had nothing to do with fun.

She wondered if it was safe to set up for repair so close to the jump point exit lane. What if someone else came through? That wasn't her problem; she shook her head to clear that worry away and went back to scanning the topics routed to SpecMat. There—*that* was her concern, a request to schedule the fabrication of four twenty-meter crystal fibers. She checked the origin . . . if it wasn't someone in H&A, Pitak wanted to know. And it wasn't— it was a damage assessment specialist aboard *Wraith*, who wanted them to replace some communications lines. She called Pitak.

"Aha! Good for you. No, dears, you don't get to pick your own priorities," Pitak said. She flagged the item, then sent it on to Commander Seveche's stack. "They always want to, though," she said, grinning at Esmay. "They think they're helping us, figuring out what they need, when they don't realize the sequencing problem. We can't start anything in the SpecMat until we know everything we need at the structural level. If we get the sausage busy working on things we don't need yet, so it can't do what we need immediately, then either we lose that job or sit around like ducks on a pond until it's done."

"What will come first?" Esmay asked, since Pitak didn't seem in a hurry to get back to the floor model.

"After assessment and evacuation, we have to clear away the old damage—there's always something you can't see until you get the skin off and expose at least ten meters you think is undamaged. I don't care what they say about diagnostic equipment, nothing beats cutting into a carcass to find out what the bones look like. Anything this badly damaged requires rebuilding from the main structure on out, just as if it were new. It's harder, because we do try to save some of the old . . . we save time and material, but it's not as efficient as building it whole. My guess is that the first things we'll want out of SpecMat are much longer crystals, grown in clusters and resin-bonded in the zero-G compartment. These will be stabilizing scaffolds for the real repair later. Then we'll want the big framing members . . . and it can take weeks to do those. No one's yet figured out how to grow the long ones and the ring ones in the same batch. Meanwhile, the die-and-mold sections can be working on little stuff like hatch frames and hatches. But the communications linear crystals come much later."

"I . . . see." Esmay felt she understood much better why Pitak had her doing this apparently unimportant job. She knew a lot more about hulls than she had, but this matter of sequencing repairs had never occurred to her. It made sense, now she thought of it.

"How'd you like a little adventure?" Pitak asked.

"Adventure?"

"I need someone to do a visual survey of the hull breach, and everyone I've got is busy. You'd need EVA gear— go over with the first teams, carry a vidcam and transmitter, and record everything for me."

"Yes, sir." Esmay wasn't sure if she was more excited or scared.

"It'll be about six hours, they think, when they're in position."

Esmay had never done EVA since the Academy—and that was from a training shuttle hanging just a kilometer from a large station, in sight of a habitable planet. Out here, even the local star was far away, hardly a disk at all and giving minimal light. *Koskiusko's* brilliant lights flooded the near flank of the *Wraith*, casting sharp black shadows. Esmay tried not to think of the nothing around her, and the way her stomach wanted to crawl out her ears, and looked instead at the damaged ship. She hadn't seen the outside of a ship with her own eyes, rather than vidscan . . . and it was instructive.

Like most Familias warships, *Wraith* had a long rounded profile that could have been confused with airstreaming— but was instead the result of a compromise of engineering constraints. Shield technology dictated the smooth curves: the most efficient hull shape for maximum shield efficiency was spherical. But spherical ships had not proven themselves in battle; it had been impossible to mount drives— either insystem or FTL—to provide the kind of reliable maneuverability needed. The only spherical ships now in service were large commercial freight haulers, where the gain in interior volume and ease of shielding from normal space debris was worth the decreased maneuverability.

So a patrol craft like *Wraith* had a more ovoid shape, giving it a distinct longitudinal axis. Forward, its bow should have been a blunt rounded end, only slightly pointier than the stern. What Esmay saw instead was a crumpled mess, the shiny glint of fused and melted skin where it should have been (as the undamaged hull was) matte black. Aft, the smooth curves of the drive pods appeared to have suffered no damage, though she'd heard that Drives and Maneuver were worried about the effect of jumping with an unbalanced hull.

She dared a look over her shoulder, even though that

twist made her swivel around the safety line like a child's toy. *Koskiusko*'s vast bulk blocked out the stars well beyond the banks of searchlights that held the patrol craft in their gaze. She wasn't even sure where the working lights on its exterior became stars against the dark.

Someone punched her shoulder. Right. Get on with the job. She pulled herself along, taking no more sight-seeing looks. *Wraith*'s damaged hull inched closer. Now she could see the pale tracks of fragments—of the weapons or the hull itself she didn't know—against the dark normal hull coating beyond. The entry gaped, jagged and unwelcoming. Something whispered against her suit helmet, and she jerked to a halt. A firm tap on her shoulder sent her on. In a moment her brain caught up and she realized it must be minute ejecta from the breached hull: probably ice crystals from the continuing air leak the crew had not been able to seal completely.

She hit the red section of line: only ten meters from the attachment. Ahead of her, someone had already clipped on the first of the branch lines that would frame the working web. But this was Esmay's station for now. She locked the slide on her safety line, clipped on the secondary stabilizing line that would confine her rotation to one plane, and waved the others past.

With the vidscan recorder aimed at the hole and the work going on, she could avoid thinking about where she was. Major Pitak wanted details—more details—even more details. "Don't rush," she'd said. "Take your time—stay at the ten-meter line until you're sure you've shown me everything you can from there. You won't be in the way of the scaffolding crews, but you will be able to see a lot. Every detail can help us. Everything."

So Esmay hung in her harness and worked the recorder's eye along the edge of the hull breach. Everything? Fine, she would spend a few minutes on those pale tracks, on the way the hull peeled back *there* to expose a twisted truss, on the odd bulge forward of the breach. By the time she'd filled half a cube from that location, the scaffolding crew had placed the major grid lines that would define the location of specific damage sites. Esmay signaled her intention to the chief, received permission, and clipped on to one of the cross-lines.

Really, she thought, it wasn't that bad out here. Once the stomach adapted to zero gravity, it was kind of fun, scooting along the line with only an occasional tug . . . a red tie bumped her hand, and she grabbed. Her arm yanked at her shoulder, and she spun dizzily, cursing herself for forgetting that she was supposed to move *slowly*. When she got herself straightened out again, someone's helmet visor was turned her way; she could imagine what they thought. Another dumbass lieutenant learns about inertia. She would have apologized, except that they weren't supposed to use the suit radios unless it was a real emergency.

She was now on the opposite side of the hull breach, nearer the bow. From this angle, she could see into the hole better—or the searchlights had found a better angle. She forced herself to look in . . . but she didn't recognize any bodies. The mess inside all looked mechanical, like a child's toy that had been stepped on. Twisted, broken, shattered . . . all the words she knew for destruction. Slowly, recording, she made sense of it. The forward bulge came from a separation of the forward framing members— they had sprung, like an old-fashioned barrel-ring, under concussive force, and the shattered truss had gone with them.

Pitak would want to know how far forward the bulge extended. It could be mapped from *Koskiusko*, if no one was using the near-scan . . . but someone would be. Esmay looked at the bulge and wished she could ask the major. If she could get on the other side of it with the recorder . . . but there was no scaffolding line there. She thought of asking the scaffolding chief to string one for her, and thought again. They were far too busy to do favors for one curious lieutenant. No, she would either string one herself, or not. Not didn't sound like a good option. She had four additional lines slung to her own suit, just as all the scaffolding crew had . . . so it was only a matter of setting the hooks.

She left the big vidscan behind, without admitting to herself the reason. She didn't intend to come loose and drift away; it was just good sense to leave the vidscan where it would be easily found. The one built into her helmet would do well enough for this short excursion. She clipped the end of one of her long lines into the ten-meter safety ring, then edged along the scaffolding line to the hull itself. Her short safety line slid along the scaffolding line on its ring. The scaffolding line was anchored with a double pin-and-patch. She ran her long line through the ring that attached there, which took longer than simply clipping in, but was more secure.

She put a boot on the hull and tested. Nothing. She had halfway hoped that *Wraith's* internal artificial gravity would give some adhesion, but it might not even be functioning. She could put short-stick patches on her boots, or she could just go on . . . it would be easier to go on, and she could always put the patches on if she couldn't make progress.

She fished a stickpatch out of her toolband with her right hand, positioned it on the end of her gloved middle finger and gave the slightest push with her left hand. She slid to the end of her safety line, slowly. Reaching out cautiously, she touched the stickpatch to the hull; it adhered just as it was supposed to. Now she could stick a pin to the patch . . . she hoped. She left her right hand on the stickpatch, and fumbled for a pin. There it was. When she reached over slowly, her safety line tugged at her waist. She had definitely gone as far as she could go with that on. She got the pin stuck to the stickpatch with its own quick-setting backing, then opened a connecting ring, locked her long line into it, and clipped the ring into the pin's opening.

The next move had a certain finality—when she unhooked her safety line from the scaffolding cable, she was depending on her own ability to set patches and pins. Caution reminded her that she was not a specialist in EVA work . . . that she would not have the right reactions if something went wrong. Esmay grinned at caution, alone inside her helmet. She had listened to caution and what good had it done her? First they thought she was dull, and then they thought she was a wild radical.

It wasn't that different from climbing the rocks at the head of her valley, or the exercise wall in the *Kos*. Reach, place a stickpatch, a pin, clip into the pin, move past that protection to the next. Twenty pins along, and she was beyond the bulge of damage . . . though the bow shield outlet access points, which should have been smooth glossy nubs protruding a few centimeters from the hull surface, were instead jagged-edged holes. Esmay turned up the light on her helmet vidscan to examine them more closely. Something glinted, ahead of her. More debris—and surely Major Pitak would want a picture of it. She placed another pin, clipped in carefully and finger-walked herself nearer.

Then tried to push herself back, and made a move violent enough to fling her off the hull, to hit the end of her line. She tried to swim herself into a position where she could see, where she wouldn't be flung back into the hull . . . what if there were *two* of them?

Was she even sure of what it was? And even if it was, it could be the *Wraith*'s own weapons, by chance stuck to its own hull by . . . by some reaction Esmay couldn't begin to understand. She forced herself to breathe slowly. Mine. It was a mine, exactly like the ones in the handbooks of enemy weaponry she'd been looking at in the supply ship on the way to Sierra Station.

Meanwhile, she reeled herself in, hand over hand, coming in too fast to her last clip; she bumped the hull with bruising force, and would have bounced free except that she grabbed the pin and outward line in one hand and the inward line with the other and let her arms take the strain. Now she wished she had stickpatches on her boots—it seemed she hung there a very long time, bouncing back and forth. Finally the oscillations died down. With great care, she reached inward for the next clip, then unclipped from that pin. Twenty . . . twenty-two . . . twenty-seven pins in all, each requiring slow, careful movement to pass. She thought several times of using her suit comunit—but was that mine an emergency now? If no one else approached it before she warned them—and the scaffolding crew was still setting up their workspaces in the hull breach.

When she made it back to the scaffolding cable and clipped on her safety line, she felt it must have taken a half-shift at least. But her chronometer didn't agree. Barely an hour had passed. She retrieved the big vidscan, and looked around for the scaffolding chief. She couldn't go back to the *Koskiusko* without warning someone here. She spotted him at last, and edged from line to line until she could tap his shoulder, and then the message board he carried. His helmet nodded. Quickly, Esmay drew a clumsy sketch of the bow—the bulge, then the location of the mine. MINE she printed in careful letters.

He shook his head. Esmay nodded. He pointed to the big vidscan and drew a question mark. She had to shake her head, and point to the scan lens in her helmet. FOLLOW he signed, and led her along the scaffolding to a com nexus. While she was gone, they'd strung a direct line from ship to ship, and passed a wire into *Wraith*, so that the ships could talk without unshielded transmission. Esmay and the scaffolding chief both hooked their suits to the nexus.

"What do you mean, mine?" the chief asked. "And what were you doing that far up the bow, anyway? Your safety line isn't that long."

"You saw the bulge of damaged frame," Esmay said. "I went to scan it for Major Pitak. I put out stickpatch pins and clipped in. And when I got beyond the bulge, I was scanning damaged shield nodes . . . turned up my suit scan lights . . . and there it was."

"A mine, you say." He sounded unconvinced.

"It looks like the illustrations in the handbooks. Not one of ours, either. A Smettig Series G, is what it looked like to me."

"What kind of fuse, did you see that?"

"No." She didn't want to say it, but she couldn't leave it at that. "I tried to jump back and . . . lost contact with the hull."

"So . . . you don't have full documentation?"

"No." She didn't even know how much of the mine her scan had picked up. How long had she looked at it before panicking?

"If it is a mine . . ." He sighed, the exasperated sigh of someone who does not want one more complication in a day already stuffed with complications. "Well . . . hell. I see you have to report it, and if it *is* a mine we'll have to do something . . ." His voice trailed off, someone who didn't know what to do next. He looked at her, and her intention to say anything vanished. She was an officer; it was her job to make decisions. This is what came of ignoring caution, she thought bitterly, as she tried to think who to report this to, aboard *Koskiusko*. The simple answer was Major Pitak, but an enemy mine stuck aboard a ship under repair wasn't simple.

Pitak's reaction, when Esmay finally got her on the other end of the connection, was hardly reassuring. "You think you saw a mine . . . an enemy mine." Flat, almost monotone. "And you may or may not have gotten it on the vid . . . ?"

"Yes, sir. I . . . pushed off too hard. I was afraid . . ."

"I should hope so." That with more energy. "You know, Suiza, you do have an instinct for drama. An enemy mine. Not everyone would think of that."

"Think?" She wasn't sure if she heard scorn or genuine amusement in the major's voice. Or something else.

"Thinking is good, Suiza. Now the first thing you do, is tell the chief to get his crew the hell away from *Wraith*. Then you get your sorry tail back out there and get some decent vidscan of this putative mine. I hope you have enough air . . ."

"Uh . . . yes, sir," Esmay said, after a quick glance at her gauges.

"That's reassuring." A long pause, during which Esmay wondered if she was supposed to cut the connection and go. But Pitak wasn't quite through. "Now I'll go tell our captain to tell *Wraith*'s captain that a totally inexperienced junior officer on her first real EVA thinks she saw an enemy mine stuck to his ship and while she didn't get any good pictures the first time, she is now taking pictures which, if the mine doesn't blow her up, may show us whether she's right. And give us a clue how to do something about it."

"Yes, sir."

"That did not require an acknowledgement, Suiza. Can you think of any mistake you haven't made yet?"

"I didn't set it off," Esmay said, before she could stop herself. A harsh bark of laughter came over the com.

"All right, Suiza . . . send the crew home and go bring me some decent pictures. I'll see what I can do to scare up a bomb squad."

The scaffolding chief was quite willing to take the orders of a junior officer; he scarcely bothered to utter a ritual grumble. Esmay didn't wait for the crew to leave. She fished out stickpatches for her boots, checking twice to be sure she had the kind that would not adhere permanently. She didn't want to be stuck there like an ornament. Then she used one of her safety lines and extra clips to sling the big vidscan on her back.

This time the trip was easier, with the pins already in place, and the grip of her boots on Wraith's hull. She could walk part of the way between the pins, paying out line to herself from the clip before . . . it was easy to see, from this position, that she had not laid a straight course in the first place. She had angled across the bulge, rather than taking the shorter route straight forward. She didn't look at anything but the pins, the clips, the line itself, until she was almost at the twentieth pin. Then light flooded over her from behind, washing out the fainter light from her helmet, and she missed the pin. When she turned to look, her helmet visor darkened automatically; she could see that one of Koskiusko's big lights had turned away from the hull breach to search along the bows. Evidently Major Pitak had reached the captain. . . .

She reached again for the pin, and clipped into it safely. In the brighter light, the edges of the shattered shield nodes cast jagged shadows that striped the hull's dull black.

Things looked different now . . . she couldn't see the mine, but it had to be close. Another pin, and another, and another . . .

EEEEERRRRP! Esmay jerked to a halt, and slammed her feet into the hull. The whiny, irritable, noise demanded her attention. A light flashed red in front of her . . . emergency . . . oh. She leaned her chin on the comunit switch.

"Don't move," a voice said in her ear. "Look down, knee level, 10 o'clock . . . but don't move." Esmay looked down, half her gaze cut off by the helmet. Something . . . something *moved.* Something small, perhaps the size of her ungloved fist, dark and glossy, rising on a thin wire stalk that gleamed in the searchlight . . . she wanted to tip her head and see where it was coming from, though she knew without seeing. "Just don't move," the voice said again. "With any luck it will think you're part of the ship."

Just as she opened her mouth to ask, the voice added, "And don't talk. We don't know what its sensor characteristics are."

The little black ovoid on its wire—the programmable sensor pod of a smart mine—rose higher . . . she could see it clearly now, and presumably it could see her. Sweat sprang out on her whole body at once; it tickled abominably as it rolled down her ribs, down her belly . . . she wanted to scratch. Not as bad as she wanted to run.

She was part of the ship. She was a . . . an automatic repair mechanism. Turned off at the moment, nonfunctional . . . she tried not to breathe as the sensor swayed nearer, sweeping in a conical pattern dictated by the stiffness of its wire stalk and the vibrations induced at its source. She had been in scan herself; she knew what such a small package might contain. It could already have matched her thermal profile to that of "human in EVA suit" if that was part of its programming. It could have recorded her skeletal density, her respiratory rate, even her eye color.

And if it had done all that, she was already dead, she just hadn't been killed yet.

The little pod on its stalk continued to revolve . . . but it was lower again. She didn't know what that meant. Would a smart mine bother to retract its sensor array before blowing up? She could barely see it now, above the sight rim of her helmet. Then it was below her vision . . . she was not tempted to bend over and look more closely.

"Sorry, Lieutenant," came the voice in her ear again. "Our searchlight brought your shadow up past its threshold. But you were dead right—it's definitely a mine, and definitely an enemy weapon."

Dead right . . . she didn't like that at all.

"We've got a hazardous equipment assessment team on the way," the voice went on. "Just don't move."

She had no intention of moving; she wasn't sure she would ever be able to move again. A few moments later, the tremors began, behind her knees; she struggled to control them. How sensitive was the sensor pod? Which little twitch might set it off? Reason suggested that she'd been moving more before, and it hadn't reacted . . . but reason had no control over her hindbrain, where panic danced its jig on her spine.

She was very bored with being that scared by the time the voice spoke again.

"You put down a good line, Lieutenant. Don't move . . . we're at the next pin, we can see you clearly."

She wanted to turn and see them, see something friendly, even if that was the last thing she saw . . . but she did not move.

"We're afraid if we douse the spotlight, that'll trigger another search sequence, and we don't know how it's programmed."

The voice didn't have to say more; she remembered that some mines were set to go after a specific number of searches had been triggered, even if they didn't find anything. She might have triggered an earlier search, when she first flung herself away from the thing.

"If we're lucky, it's looking for a match to something specific, which we don't resemble, but . . ."

She wished the voice would shut up now . . . what if

the mine reacted to minute vibrations carried through someone's suit? Even hers. Surely they had someone watching it . . . surely they had a plan. . . .

"*Wraith's* given us an update on what's beyond the hull breach—they're evacuating personnel now." A pause; she tried not to think. Then, "How's your suit air? Give me a one-letter answer: A for ample, S for short, C for critical, then a number for minutes remaining."

Esmay looked, and was startled to see how far down the gauge had gone. "S," she said. "Sixteen."

"I'd call that critical, myself," the voice said. "Here's what we'll do. Someone's going to come up behind you, trying to match your profile and cast the same shadow, and pop on an external reserve. Don't move. He'll do all the hooking up from his end."

"Yes, sir," Esmay said. Her eyes had locked onto the air gauge; the number flicked down to fifteen, and it was definitely in the red zone.

"Breathe slowly," the voice said. "You're not doing any work; you may have longer than that."

Fear burns oxygen. She remembered that, along with other pithy sayings. It was amazingly hard to breathe slowly because you needed to save oxygen . . . she tried thinking of other things. Would she feel the vibration of the person coming up behind her? Would the mine's sensor pod notice it? That kind of thought didn't help her take slow breaths. She tried to send her mind back to her valley, that favorite and reliable relaxation exercise, but when the gauge flicked to fourteen, she gasped anyway. Don't gasp. Don't look at the gauge. It will either go down to zero, or it won't.

She did not feel the vibration; what she felt first was a tiny push that made her sway forward. She stiffened against it. Then something tapped the back of her helmet, and a new voice spoke in her ear.

"Doin' good, Suiza. Just don't wiggle . . . while I . . . get this tank attached . . ." Random bumps and prods, which she tried to resist so that she wouldn't move enough to trigger the pod's notice. She eyed her oxygen gauge. Nine. Had she really been standing there waiting more than six minutes? Apparently so. The gauge flicked down again, to eight. She could hear clicks and squeaks from her suit as her unseen rescuer tried to hook up the auxiliary tank with the least possible movement.

"Gauge?" asked the voice.

She looked. Now it read seven. "Seven," she said.

"Damn," said the voice. "It's supposed to—oh." She didn't know what that "oh" meant, and it infuriated her. How dare they mean whatever "oh" meant? An irritating scritch, repeated over and over, as she tried not to watch the gauge. It seemed a long time, but it hadn't flicked down to six when the indicator whipped over to the green section.

"Gauge?" asked the voice again.

"Green," Esmay said.

"Number," the voice said, with a bite of disapproval.

Esmay swallowed the "uh" she wanted to make and blinked to focus on the number. "One four seven."

"Good. Now I'm going to hook into your telemetry—you've been out more than your suit's rated for—"

Another set of scritches; Esmay didn't care. She was breathing; she would not run out of oxygen.

"Your internal temp's low," the voice said. "Turn up your suit heater."

She complied, and warmth rose from her bootsoles. The tremor she'd been fighting to control eased—had it been only cold, and not panic after all? She wanted to believe that, but the sour smell of her sweat denied it.

CHAPTER THIRTEEN

"We have a problem, Suiza," said the voice in her ear. Esmay thought they could have said something more helpful. She knew they had a problem—*she* had a problem. "If that's the only mine, if it blows it will probably damage only those forward compartments, which as far as anyone knows are empty anyway. And you, of course."

No comment seemed necessary.

"We haven't spotted any other mines—but we can't figure out why there's only one. If there is only one."

Did they expect her to figure it out?

"It's not like the Bloodhorde, but there's no doubt that the ships that attacked *were* Bloodhorde ships. Came right in for the kill—*Wraith* got unequivocal scan data—and then broke off when *Sting* and *Justice* closed and started raking them."

Esmay wondered about that. By rumor, if a Bloodhorde group closed with prospect of a kill, it would not break off just to avoid contact with another ship. Unless its ships were having trouble . . . she wished she could see the scan data herself. Not likely, if the mine blew. But . . . she dared a transmission. "Were they close enough to plant the mine by hand?" she asked.

"Don't transmit," the voice said. "If it hears you—"

"You wanted to know why," she said. "Is *Wraith*'s scan tech available?"

"Wait."

She could imagine the scene in *Koskiusko*'s communications shack—perhaps Major Pitak was there; certainly the captain was. A different voice came with a tiny physical tap on her EVA suit. "You're going to upset 'em, Lieutenant." That voice sounded amused; she wasn't

sure what it meant. She shrugged enough to move the
shoulders of the suit; a chuckle came through the link.
"You got an idea, huh? Good for you. I can't figure out
why that thing hasn't blown us both—but I'm willing to
live with that." Another chuckle. Esmay felt her own stiff
face relaxing into a grin.

"Suiza, just in case you've got an idea, we've patched
you through to the *Wraith* senior scan tech. Just try to
keep your transmissions short, do you understand?"

"Yes, sir. Did the Bloodhorde ships come close enough
for an EVA team to plant the mine by hand, or by pod?"

. A pause. Then yet another voice. "Uh . . . yes . . . I
suppose. We were trying to rotate, because of the damage
to the starboard shields and hull. They got pretty close . . ."

Esmay wanted to yell "NUMBERS, dammit!" but she
could hear a roar in the background that might be the
scan tech's supervisor saying the same thing, for the next
transmission gave her the figures she wanted. Close enough
indeed; her mind raced through the equations for both
EVA and pod movement . . . yes. "How soon after that
did the Bloodhorde ships pull away?"

"As soon as *Sting* and *Justice* came back," the tech said.
Esmay waited, confident in that background bellow. Sure
enough, the tech came back on with the precise interval.
Esmay felt as if someone had run a current down her
spine. Maybe they'd spotted the Fleet ships before they
were fired on, or maybe they hadn't. They'd planted a
smart mine, programmed for a specific task, and then
they'd gone away, leaving *Wraith* damaged but not killed.
And why?

What did the Bloodhorde expect to happen next? A
damaged Familias military vessel would not be abandoned,
so they couldn't have hoped to capture it—in fact, if they
had, why mine it? Damaged Familias vessels . . . went
to repair facilities. Either dockyards, in this case too far
away for a cripple like *Wraith* to reach, or the mobile
dockyards called DSRs . . . *Koskiusko*. What would the
Bloodhorde know about DSRs? Whatever was in the public
domain, certainly—and Esmay knew that the public knew

DSRs were capable of taking the smaller Fleet ships into the DSR's vast central repair bay.

That made sense. She thought it all through, then transmitted it. "The Bloodhorde chose a small ship to disable, planted a smart mine, then withdrew, so that *Wraith* would lead the way to a DSR. The mine's programmed to go off when *Wraith* enters the repair dock—disabling the DSR. It's not strong enough to destroy it, but it would probably be unable to make jump—"

"Certainly unable to make jump," came Pitak's voice in her ear.

"And thus would be immobilized for attack." Esmay paused, but no one said anything. "Either they followed *Wraith* and her escort to this system, or the mine will also have a homing module to lead them here. They want the DSR, almost certainly for capture, since they could have covered *Wraith* with enough mines to blow the whole DSR if they'd wanted."

Another long pause, during which the contact hissed gently in her ear. Then: "It makes sense. Never thought the Bloodhorde were that sneaky . . . and what they want a DSR for, unless they've got significant battle damage somewhere . . ."

Esmay rode the wave of her confident intuition. "They lack technical skills they need; they don't have a military-grade shipyard. They want a DSR to upgrade their entire space effort. In one blow they get manufacturing facilities, parts, and expert technicians. Given a DSR, they could upgrade any of their ships to Fleet equivalency—or quickly learn to manufacture their own cruisers."

The long hiss that followed conveyed both horror and respect. "Of course," someone said softly.

"Which means," Esmay said, "that this thing won't go off until the parameters match whatever they think the inside of a repair bay looks like, or until someone tries to remove it. It doesn't know it's been detected until we try to do something about it." Relief weakened her knees; she leaned back against the unseen person behind her.

"Which means we can walk away and it won't blow—as long as we don't put *Wraith* in the repair bay."

"Not so fast," said Pitak, over a gabble of other voices. "You still need to get good scan on it."

"Not active," Esmay said. "But yes, I can do vidscan." Without waiting for orders or permission, she moved, leaning over to aim at it. There it was, the blunt-ended cylindrical shape, the little sensor pod on its wire now retracted to form a knob on the cylinder. She could pick out a serial number, and one of the swirling shapes that meant something in the language of Aethar's World. Probably something rude; the outside of Bloodhorde ships were usually decorated with slogans intended to shock and frighten their neighbors.

She patched the vidscan signal to her headset, and waited for Pitak to say they had enough data. Finally she heard, "That's enough—now the guy behind you is going to withdraw—" A final tap on her shoulder, and then she saw the shadow cast by *Koskiusko*'s light waver as he left. The smart mine's sensor pod didn't move. Curious, but welcome. She waited a little longer, watching her oxygen display count the seconds and minutes, then lifted one stickpatched boot from the hull. The sensor pod stirred, rotating on its wire stalk.

"The sensor pod's moving a bit," Esmay said. "How about dousing the light while I get loose."

"We were afraid the change might trigger something," the voice said.

"If it's programmed for repair bays," Esmay said, "then light will activate the matching program, but dark will turn it off."

The light behind her vanished, and with it the crisp shadow she'd cast. She turned up the sensitivity of her helmet scan, and just made out the mine . . . the sensor pod did not move. Slowly, she folded herself up as much as the EVA suit allowed, so that she could grip her safety line close to the pin and kick the other boot free. No movement from the sensor pod. Slowly, she worked herself hand by hand backwards, around the curve of the hull, until she was out of sight of the mine. Then she stuck her boots onto the hull and walked back to the line connecting *Wraith* to *Koskiusko*. There the specialists of the bomb squad waited for her, in the strange bulky suits she had seen only in training cubes.

"Suiza, come back to *Koskiusko*," she heard.

"Yes, sir." She wanted to know what the bomb squad was going to do about the mine; now that she was here, she might as well stay. But the voice in her ear had left her no options. And she'd need another auxiliary tank to stay out longer.

"Good job, Lieutenant," said one of the bomb squad. "Glad you figured out it was safe for me to come back."

"Me, too," Esmay said, then hooked herself to the transfer line and pushed away.

By the time she had clambered out of her EVA suit, she felt like collapsing in a heap on the deck. The undersuit clung to her nastily; she hated having to stand around in it while the chief in charge of suits examined and checked off the condition of the one she turned in. After one glance, she ignored the big mirror at the end of the bay; her hair looked like dirty felt glued to her head.

Showered and properly dressed once more, she headed to the compartment number waiting in her message bin. T-1, Deck 9, number 30 . . . that was in the administrative area of the Senior Technical Schools, down the passage from Admiral Livadhi's office.

The conference, when she got there, consisted of Captain Hakin, Admiral Dossignal, Admiral Livadhi, Commander Seveche and Major Pitak from Hull and Architecture, and two lieutenant commanders she did not know. One wore the insignia of the 14th Heavy Maintenance, with the collar flashes of weapons systems; the other, also with weapons collar marks, wore the armband of ship's crew. The captain spoke first.

"Well, Lieutenant . . . glad your guess about the mine's programming turned out to be right. At least as far as you were concerned."

"Me, too, sir." Esmay hoped the edge in the captain's voice had as much to do with the situation as with her.

"I don't suppose you've had time to figure out how we're going to evacuate *Wraith* and repair her without triggering the mine's recognition program?"

"No, sir." He was definitely displeased with her; that frosty glare could mean nothing else.

"What I'd like to know is how much time delay is built into that program," said Commander Seveche, after a quick glance at Dossignal. "Would they have sent it open-ended, or would they have built in a hard delay, for just this situation?"

Eyes shifted to Esmay but she had nothing to say. Shrugging was inadvisable in the midst of that much brass, so she simply didn't say anything.

"Do we have any Bloodhorde analysts aboard?" asked Dossignal, looking at Admiral Livadhi.

"Not really, Sy. They pulled the best for some sort of policy/strategic planning thing back at Rockhouse, and the next best is on the flagship with Admiral Gourache. I've got an instructor for the tactics course, but his specialty is Benignity history. He's hitting the databanks . . ."

"Abandoning *Wraith* is not an option," the captain said. "The admiral's made it clear that we're not to give the Bloodhorde any chance at advanced technology, and even stripped, that hull has too many goodies to let fall into the hands of the Bloodhorde, or even a random pirate. If she can't be repaired well enough to get her back to safety—"

"She can be," Admiral Dossignal said. "This is exactly the kind of damage we're equipped to repair. The only question is how to do it safely, without risking the integrity of *this* ship." He glanced at Commander Seveche, who took over.

"We have to repair that hull breach, and reset the engines, or she won't make jump again . . . and that means working all around that mine, even if we don't stick her into the repair bay. I'd like to hear from the weapons experts."

The captain nodded, and the crew weapons officer spoke. "Given the kind of mine, there are several approaches we can use, depending on the amount of damage tolerable on *Wraith* . . ."

"*Wraith*'s already got enough damage—" Pitak sounded outraged. Dossignal held up his hand and she subsided.

"We realize you want to minimize any further damage, but there's a trade-off between speed and safety here. We can get the remnants of *Wraith* in to repair faster if some additional damage is acceptable; if not, we're looking at a long period of preparation in an already damaged ship—dangerous time, for both the workers and both ships—to attempt something which may not be possible."

"Explain what procedures you might use," the captain said.

"Ideally, we'd detach the mine, enfold it in a foam-mold casing, and set it off at a safe distance. However, we—Lt. Commander Wyche and I—believe that there's considerable risk of detonating the mine if we try to detach it. So the next best thing is a foam bed both interior—behind the hull where it's attached—and on the exterior. Here the problem is how much of the interior needs to be foamed. And that homing signal we suspect, though that depends on which kind it is."

"How long before you can set it off?"

"That depends on what H&A tells us." He turned to Commander Seveche. "Will we need to foambed the interior as well? How much additional damage would such a mine cause?" With a gesture, Seveche passed the question to Pitak.

Pitak scowled; Esmay recognized thought in progress. "There's already so much damage forward—we're going to have to replace most of the structure anyway. On the other hand, it's stretching our resources, especially if we expect an attack. Do you think it's an aimed charge, or just a straightforward blow-em-up?"

He shook his head. "If they went to the trouble of hand-placing this thing, I'd bet on a directed charge, probably with substantial penetrating power. It's definitely a hull-cracker."

Someone down the table stirred. "But if they wanted to disable the DSR, wouldn't the charge be directed outwards?"

"Not necessarily," Pitak said. "An explosion of that magnitude, in the repair bay, could be expected to damage sensitive equipment—certainly enough to keep us from withdrawing *Wraith* and closing the bay." She paused, and no one interrupted. "Sorry, but I think you'd better foambed the interior, at least these compartments—" She called up a display, and highlighted some of the forward compartments. "If we can possibly save these: seventeen A, eighteen A and B, and twenty-three A, it'll save us considerable time on the repairs."

"Then—with the precautions we need to protect personnel—we're talking ninety-six hours to foambed those compartments and the exterior—"

"Why the exterior?" asked someone else.

"Because we don't want pieces flying around hitting us," Pitak said. "Or the rest of *Wraith*."

"And I'll need additional squads," he said. "The more people, the faster it'll go. As long as they're not working in close, it should be safe enough."

"Unless it has a fixed delay of some kind—"

"Unless stars sprout horns . . . sure, that'd kill us all, but there's no way to know but go."

"Very well, Commander," the captain said. "I presume damage control would have personnel trained to spray a foam bed?"

"Yes, sir."

Captain Hakin turned to his exec. "Make sure he gets what he needs. Major Pitak, can H&A do anything to expedite this?"

Pitak nodded. "Yes, sir. With the captain's permission, I have construction crews standing by to widen access to the compartments that must be foamed; they've been clearing debris already—"

"I thought we pulled everyone out," the captain said.

"We did, sir, but when tactical analysis concluded that the mine had its programming set for our internal bay, I sent them back over."

"Very well. Keep me informed." With that, the captain rose; everyone stood as he left. Pitak beckoned to Esmay.

"Lieutenant, you're not ready to direct a crew in this kind of situation; I want you to hold down the office—be my communications link. I'm going over myself."

"Yes, sir."

Pitak started down the passage; Esmay followed.

"You'll be in charge of expediting the transfer of materials and tools as we need them. I've set up a model in my office, but it'll need modification—they always do. Keep in mind the limited staging area on *Wraith*. We don't want things backing up there."

The model lasted only about an hour, then Pitak was calling in changes, and Esmay thought of nothing but her assignment. She relayed requests for tools, for materials, for personnel. Several glitches required intervention from above; she sicced Commander Seveche's office on the stubborn senior chief in the Technical Schools who didn't see why an instructor in weapons systems should dismiss a class and go help deal with the mine. He'd argued that the 14th was supposed to have its own bomb disposal squad . . . but polite requests through appropriate channels soon produced a cheerful woman with one prosthetic hand and her custom EVA suit slung on her back. Esmay directed her to the right EVA hatch, and went back to work.

She would like to have watched the work on *Wraith*; she knew only vaguely what a "foam bed" was, and what it was supposed to accomplish. But Pitak's construction teams had found more casualties in the forward compartments, most dead and the rest unconscious.

"The artificial gravity failed up here, along with the communications lines—some shrapnel, probably, sliced them like a hot knife. It's a wonder any of 'em are alive, and I don't know how many will survive—they look pretty bad. But they're all out now, so you can send over the next load of stuff as soon as they're logged clear of the lanes."

Esmay looked at the cluttered screen that now

represented everything between *Koskiusko* and *Wraith*. A query to the scan supervisor tagged the medical evac pod on her screen; when it was out of the way, she put a priority tag on the shipment Pitak had asked for, and talked to the sergeant minor in T-3 responsible for sending it off.

She was concentrating so hard on keeping up with Pitak's requests that she jumped when the sergeant at the other console said "Wow!" and then "Good thing they foamed it . . ."

"The mine?" she asked, when she got her breath back.

"Yeah. Want a replay?"

She couldn't resist; he transferred the replay to her console. *Wraith*'s hull breach no longer faced *Koskiusko*; she could just see the edge of it. That meant the mine was out of line of sight; the viewpoint shifted. Now, where she remembered the mine should be, there was an irregular grayish blob strongly side-lit by *Koskiusko*'s floods.

"They took this from a pod," the sergeant said. "Relayed on tightbeam . . . they had several out there watching."

This view closed in, until she could see that the blob looked like whipped cream or icing piped into a slumpy cylinder. As she watched, another blob of foam appeared, rising then slipping sideways to seal off the end of the cylinder.

"They foamed all the compartments inboard," the sergeant said. "And foamed a cylinder around it, aiming it away from us . . . then finally put a lobe over the top. That's when . . ."

It blew; the blob of the foam bed burst apart, and something shot out the top, away from *Wraith*.

"All the ejecta went the right way," the sergeant said. "Good design. Reports are that very little blew in the interior. All they have to do now is get all that foam back out, and we can do that in the big bay."

"I don't understand how it works," Esmay said. "I thought if you confined an explosion, that only made it worse."

The sergeant shrugged. "I don't really understand it

either, but I had a buddy back in Sector 10 who was in their bomb squad. He said you had a choice—you could try to aim it somewhere, and let all that energy escape in a direction that didn't bother you, or you could put enough padding around it to absorb the force."

"But the foam bed blew apart—"

"Well, maybe it needed to be thicker . . . but it was thick enough to aim the ejecta in a direction that doesn't bother us. Notice where it's going?"

"Away from *Kos* is all I know or care," Esmay said.

"Toward the jump point exit," the sergeant said, grinning. "We can always hope some fool Bloodhorde ship comes roaring in here and gets a mouthful of its own bullet."

"Suiza!" That was Pitak, wanting to know if she could find someone to go into inventory and get the lights and limbs of the idiot who insisted they didn't have any more temporary hull curtains in stock and would have to wait until more were fabricated. "I know what I've used," Pitak said. "And I know what I put into stock, and what was on the inventory when we left Sierra Station. There ought to be sixteen more of 'em, and I want 'em two hours ago."

✦   ✦   ✦

"Lots of blood," said the nanny at the forward triage station.

"At least they're breathing." The extrication team rolled the slack shape in blood-soaked uniform off the board and onto a gurney with practiced skill, then reached for the next. "They're all unconscious; we did a quick-scan of the first two and found blood levels of slow-oxy . . . probably someone popped the emergency supply when the hull blew."

"So you don't have a survey?"

"No—if they aren't missing limbs, we're just bringing them out with all due precautions." All due precautions to preserve whatever spinal cord integrity was left.

"Number?"

"Thirty or so, I think. I'm not sure yet. We're just now getting access to the most forward compartments."

The extrication team turned away, heading back for another load.

Esmay watched as *Wraith*'s damaged bow edged into the repair bay. It was easy to forget how large that bay was, empty, but the ship gave a reference for the eye.

"Suiza!" That bellow had to be Pitak. "Quit looking at the view, and give me a readout."

"Yes, sir." Esmay glanced at her board. Pitak's concern was the change in center of gravity as *Wraith* entered *Koskiusko*'s artificial gravity field. Rapid changes could stress the internal structure of *Koskiusko* beyond safe limits. "Is *Wraith*'s artificial gravity on in any part of the ship?"

"No, it's not."

"There's a torque force developing in the contralateral midsections . . . only 5.4 dynes right now, but it's increasing in a linear relationship to the mass of *Wraith* within *Kos*'s field."

"That's expected . . . not desirable, but expected. Transfer a plot of that to my screen and to Power."

"Yes, sir." Esmay locked in the curve, keyed for the transfers, and continued to watch her board. Her gaze kept twitching upward to the view of *Wraith*'s approach, but she yanked it back each time. The strain she'd noticed dipped below the curve; she called Pitak. "It's dropped below line—"

"Good. That means Power is compensating. But watch for that bulge ahead of the damage—that's something we can't really model for the field generator."

Centimeter by centimeter, *Wraith* edged in. When the mooring lines were secured, warning bells rang throughout the DSR. "Cradles shifting in T-minus 15 minutes. Cradles shifting—"

Esmay transferred her final readouts to Major Pitak and Power, then withdrew to a monitoring station behind the double red lines. Only a few essential personnel would ride the cradles during shift.

"I hate to think what that mine would have done to

the cradle mechanisms," someone said behind her. She glanced back. Barin Serrano, his dark brows lowered.

"It's taken care of," she said. She wondered what he was doing there; his assignment, in scan, wasn't needed at the moment.

"Lieutenant Bondal sent me down here to see if Major Pitak had decided where to put the new RSV units," he said, anticipating her question.

"She hasn't told me—but I'll check for you. Have you heard anything about Bloodhorde ships coming in?"

"No . . . and I'm sure I would have, because . . . well, anyway, I would have. But I do know that *Sting* and *Justice* have jumped out."

"Why?"

"They delivered *Wraith* . . . and they're supposed to be patrolling out wherever they were. Maybe they thought they'd spot anyone following *Wraith's* trail in."

✧   ✧   ✧

Gar-sig (Packleader) Vokrais woke to the bustle of a medical ward; when he turned his head, he saw his pack-second Hoch staring back at him.

"What happened?" he asked, in his best Familias Standard.

"Effing sleepy gas," Hoch said. "We got hauled in as casualties . . . I don't think this is the same ship."

They lay, listening to the chatter around them.

"We're on the DSR," Hoch said finally, with a wolfish grin. "Right inside."

"All two of us," Vokrais said. He lifted his head cautiously since no one seemed to be paying any attention to him. He was wearing a clean pale blue shift of some crinkled fabric, and all up and down the rows of beds were the rest of his assault team dressed the same way. Most of them, anyway. He counted only twenty-five of the original thirty, and Tharjold wasn't there—their technical expert, the one who knew most about Familias technology. Nor Kerai, nor Sij . . . his mind ticked off the missing, and consigned them to either of the two possible eternal destinations. The rest were there, all butt-naked in hospital gowns . . . but all awake now, staring at him in wild surmise.

Before he had time to worry about how he was going to get his team clothed and out of medical, a heavyset man with a scowl worthy of a Bloodhorde senior sergeant bustled down the aisle between the beds.

"All right, sleepyheads," he said. "You're awake, and none of you got worse than a dose of trank. Come with me—I'll get you clean clothes and put you to work . . . we'll need your help to get *Wraith* repaired."

"Our IDs?" Hoch asked. He sounded half-strangled, but it was probably just his attempt to control his accent.

"I've got 'em—already passed on the stats to Supply, so you'll have something close to fitting."

Vokrais rolled out of bed, surprised to find that he wasn't at all dizzy. The others followed; he saw arms twitch as the automatic habit of saluting conflicted with awareness of their position. Their guide didn't notice; he was scowling at a list in his hand.

"Santini?"

Vokrais scrabbled through his memory of the alien vocabulary, and finally remembered that the nametag on the uniform he'd stolen had been something like that, in their misbegotten tongue. "Uh . . . yes, sir?" Someone sniggered, three beds down, to hear him say "sir" to a Familias enemy. Someone would feel the lash for that later.

"Wake UP, Santini. Listen—says here you were a specialist in ventilation?"

"Sir," Vokrais said, wondering which of several meanings he knew for that word mattered here. Ventilation? As in, artificial breathing? As in, perforating?

"That's good—I'll send you over to Support Systems as soon as you've got your gear. Oh, and Camajo?" Silence again. Vokrais prayed to the Heart-Render that someone would have the sense to say something.

After too many heartbeats, Hoch coughed—an obviously fake cough, to Vokrais's ear—and said, "Yes, sir?"

"I guess you're all still a bit dazed—they told me to give you another hour, but we need help now. Camajo, you'll report to Major Pitak, in H&A. Now, let's see . . . Bradinton?"

This time, the others caught on quicker, and someone said "Yes, sir," almost brightly. Vokrais wondered if the others remembered the names on the uniforms they'd stripped from dead men, or if they were just answering blind. It probably didn't matter. Supposedly the Familias ships had a fancy way of figuring out who was really one of their own, but so far he hadn't seen any sign of it.

Eventually all of them had answered to their new names—names which felt uncomfortable even held so lightly, names with no family chant behind them. For a moment Vokrais wondered if the strangers had families . . . if those families had chants of their own . . . but this was not the right kind of thought for the belly of an enemy ship. He pushed it away, and it fell off his mind like a landsman off the deck of a dragonship in rough seas. Instead he thought of the battle to come, the hot blood of enemies that would soak his clothes, not cold and clammy this time but properly steaming. He had not minded stripping the dead and putting on their blood-soaked uniforms . . . not after the rituals of the Blooding . . . but it had been distasteful to feel it already cold.

His pack followed him through the enemy ship; he could feel their amusement even as his own bubbled just beneath the surface. The enemy . . . more like prey than enemy, like sheep leading a wolf into the fold in the mistaken notion that it was a sheepdog. Even as he accepted a folded pile of clothes, he was sure that his pack could have taken this ship bare naked, with only their blood-hunger. Instead . . . he dressed quickly, carefully not meeting anyone's eyes. He had worn Familias clothing before, in his years as a spy . . . the soft cloth, the angled fastenings, felt almost as familiar as his own.

The lack of weapons didn't. He missed the familiar pressure of needler and stunner, knocknab and gutstab. Familias troops carried weapons only into battle . . . and DSRs didn't fight.

The helpful enemy had leapfrogged them over the first

two phases of the plan, handing them the chance to disperse throughout the ship. With any luck at all—and the gods definitely seemed to be loading luck upon them—no one from *Wraith* would notice that the men wearing the uniforms of shipmates were not shipmates at all.

Vokrais followed the route displayed on the palm-sized mapcom, sure that he could deal with whatever he found when he arrived.

"No, I'm not going to send anyone from *Wraith* back over there—not after they've been knocked out for a week or so with sleepygas. Their cogs won't be meshing for another two shifts, and we don't want accidents." Vokrais heard the end of that and wondered whether feigning mental illness would do anything useful. Probably not. They might send him back to the medical area, where he could end up in bed with no pants on. Better to seem dutiful but slightly confused—the confusion at least was honest enough.

Familias technology impressed him as it had before—so much of it, and it worked so well. No familiar stench of sweat and gutbreath. Clean air emerged from one grille, and vanished into another; the lights never flickered; the artificial gravity felt as solid as a planet. The little communications device and the data wand he'd been given were smaller and worked better than their analogs on the Bloodhorde ships.

This was what they had come for, after all. The technology they had not been able to buy or steal or (last and least efficient ploy) invent. Bigger ships, better ships, ships that could take on Familias and Compassionate Hand cruisers and win. The technicians to keep the technology working . . . Vokrais eyed the others around him. They didn't look like much, but he had somewhat overcome the prejudice of his upbringing; he knew that smart minds could hide in bodies of all shapes. But hardly one in fifty looked like any kind of warrior.

Meanwhile . . . meanwhile his pack was dispersed throughout the DSR, very handily. Probably several supervisors would decide, as his had, to assign them simple duties. Eventually a meal would come, and they'd have access to eating utensils, so easily converted to effective hand weapons.

An hour . . . two. Vokrais worked on, willing enough to sort parts, package them in trays, stack them on automatic carriers. There was no hurry; they had gained time by being put to sleep and admitted as casualties, an irony he hoped to be able to share at the victory feast with his commander. Once he caught a glimpse of another pack member, carrying something he didn't recognize; for an instant their gazes crossed, then the other man looked away. Yes. Huge as this ship might be, they would locate one another, and their plan would work. And the longer they had to explore it, to learn its capabilities, the easier to slit its guts open when the time came.

✦   ✦   ✦

Esmay glanced up as a shadow crossed her screen. CAMAJO, the nametag said, clipped to a uniform that fit its wearer like a new saddle . . . technically fitting, but uneasy in some way. The insignia of a petty-light had been applied recently, and not quite straight, to his sleeve.

"I was told to report here," the man said. "To Major . . . Major Pitak." His eyes roved the compartment as if scanning it for hidden weapons; his glance at Esmay had been dismissive. Her skin prickled. He reminded her of something— someone—her mind, suddenly alert, scrabbled frantically in memory to figure out what. She looked back at the screen before she answered.

"She's in with Commander Seveche. Are you from *Wraith*?" She couldn't imagine anyone from *Koskiusko* giving her quite that look. It wasn't the "you're not really Fleet are you?" look, or the "you're that kid who commanded *Despite*, aren't you?" look, or any of the others she'd have recognized.

"Yes . . . sir." The pause snagged her attention away from the screen graphics again. "We were . . . in the forward compartment . . . the sleepygas . . ."

"You're lucky to be alive," Esmay said, instantly forgiving

the man's odd behavior. If he'd been through all that, he could still be affected by the drug. "We've got *Wraith* in now; work's already started. You can wait here for Major Pitak, or at Commander Seveche's office."

"Where's Commander Seveche's office?" the man asked. The shipchip in his pocket bleeped, and he peered cross-eyed at a space between him and Esmay. She knew what that meant—the shipchip was projecting a route.

"Just follow your shipchip," she said. He turned, without the proper acknowledgement; Esmay started to say something, but . . . he had been gassed, and might be still a bit hazy. Something wasn't quite right . . .

"Petty-light . . ." she said. He stopped in mid-stride, then turned jerkily. Something not right at all. His eyes were not the eyes of someone dazed by drugs . . . his eyes had a bright gleam half-hidden behind lowered lids.

"Yes . . . Lieutenant?"

She could not define what was wrong . . . it was not anything so positive as disrespect, which she had experienced often enough. Respect and disrespect occurred in a relationship, a connection. Here she felt no connection at all, as if Petty-light Camajo were not Fleet at all, but a civilian.

"When you do see Major Pitak, tell her that the simulations for fabrication have arrived from SpecMat."

"The simulations have arrived . . . yes . . . m . . . sir." Camajo turned, moving more decisively than someone fogged on sleepygas, and was gone before Esmay could say more. She scowled at the screen. *Yes . . . m . . . sir?* What had he been about to say?

She felt uneasy. Had *Wraith* had traitors on its crew? Was that why it had suffered such damage? Why was Camajo alive, uninjured, after such a hull breach between him and the rest of the ship?

This was ridiculous. She had not noticed anything amiss in *Despite*, had not recognized that any of the traitors were traitors. She had not been uneasy this way then. Perhaps that experience had made her paranoid, willing to interpret every discrepancy as ominous. Camajo had been lucky, that was all, and now he was disoriented, on a strange ship with none of his familiar companions.

That didn't work out. The casualties on *Despite*, traitor or loyal, none of them had stumbled over the familiar Fleet greetings and honorifics. With blood in his mouth, as he died, Chief Major Barscott had answered "Yes, sir . . ." to Esmay. How many of the survivors in those forward compartments had been lucky? How lucky? And was it luck?

Camajo's eyes . . . his gaze . . . reminded her of her father's soldiers. Groundpounders' eyes . . . commandos' eyes . . . roving, assessing, looking for the weaknesses in a position, thinking how to take over . . . Take over what?

Scolding herself, Esmay flicked to the next screen, but her mind wandered anyway. In the civil wars—she called it that now, though to her family it was still the Califer Uprising—both sides had tried infiltrating the others' defensive positions with troops wearing stolen uniforms, using stolen ID. It had worked a few times, even though both knew it was possible. She'd never heard of such a thing happening in Fleet. Ships weren't infiltrated by individuals . . . they were attacked by ships. Very rarely in Fleet history were attempts at hostile boarding mentioned; battle zones were too dangerous for EVA maneuvers. Pirates sometimes boarded individual commercial vessels . . . but that wasn't the military. It would take . . . it would take a single badly damaged Fleet ship, one that could not detect the movement of individuals in EVA gear . . . a hull breach that let them in . . . a way to get the right uniforms . . . no. She was being silly.

Major Pitak came in while she was still arguing with herself. "That Camajo fellow from *Wraith* must be still half-tranked," she said, dropping a half-dozen cubes onto her desk. "I couldn't get out of him *which* simulations were in . . . sent him on down to E-12; they can use him for a runner if nothing else. Can't cause much trouble that way."

Esmay lost her argument with prudence. "Major, I was wondering about a security breach . . ."

"Security breach! What are you talking about?"

"Camajo. I'm not sure, but . . . something wasn't right."

"He'd been out for a week; that scrambles anyone's brain. How could he be a security breach?"

"He just didn't react the way he should," Esmay said. "The way he looked at me—it wasn't a tranked-out sort of expression."

Pitak looked at her, alert. "You've been through one mutiny; if it hasn't made you paranoid, maybe you would notice something wrong. So you think he might be a traitor, like Hearne and Garrivay?"

"No, sir. I was thinking . . . what if someone infiltrated *Wraith*. Through the hull breach maybe. Couldn't Bloodhorde troops have gotten in there, before *Wraith* jumped out?"

"You mean like boarding a watership in a pirate story? Nobody does that, Suiza, not in real life in deep space. Even pirates send people over in pods. Besides, how would they survive through jump?"

"Well . . . there were survivors in the forward compartments."

"But those were *Wraith* crew, in *Wraith* uniforms, with their names on the crew list. I was there myself, Suiza. I didn't see anything that looked like Bloodhorde commandos, just wounded who'd been knocked out by sleepygas to conserve oxygen."

"You're sure?"

Pitak looked at her with a combination of exhaustion and irritation. "Unless you're suggesting that the Bloodhorde cleverly dressed their soldiers in our uniforms— uniforms that just happened to have the right ID patterns in the cloth, and the right nametags on the pockets—and wounded them, drenched them in their own blood, then left them there to jump in a damaged ship—?"

"I suppose they really were wounded?"

Pitak snorted. "I'm no medic—how would I know? They were unconscious and covered with blood, wearing our uniform. What more do you want?"

It was a silly question, but Esmay didn't bother to point that out. The itchy feeling between her shoulders wouldn't go away. "Camajo wasn't wounded . . . I think I'll check with sickbay, if you don't mind."

"Snarks in a bucket, Suiza, why don't you keep your mind on your work—or am I not giving you enough? Let Medical worry about the wounded, unless you want to transfer over there—"

"No, sir." Esmay heard in her own voice the stubborn conviction that she was right.

Pitak glared at her. "You're worried about something."

"Yes, sir."

"Spit it out then."

"Sir, I . . . I have a bad feeling—" Pitak snorted and rolled her eyes like a skittish mare; Esmay persisted. "The thing is, sir, if they could get close enough to hand-plant a mine, they could have put some troops aboard."

"Without anyone noticing? That's—"

"Sir, *Wraith* was isolated at the time of the attack; individuals in EVA gear—or even in small pods—wouldn't have shown up on scans by *Justice* and *Sting*; *Wraith's* own scan was badly damaged. The tactical analysis suggested that the Bloodhorde might want to capture a DSR, not just destroy one. I know we don't usually consider the Bloodhorde as having this sort of planning ability, but consider: if they can get a commando team aboard the DSR, they could cause enough disruption to make it easier for a follow-up ship or wave of ships to board and capture it."

"I can see where that might be a plan, Suiza, but I repeat: those wounded wore our uniform. *Our* uniform, with the Fleet recognition code in the weave . . . you think they stole a bale of our cloth and made up uniforms, then stole *Wraith's* personnel list—"

"No, sir." Esmay's mind raced, trying to catch up to her intuition. "Suppose . . . suppose they boarded, forward of the breach, counting on the confusion. Communications to the forward compartments failed, with the damage . . . so whatever they did up there wouldn't be known aft. They could have overpowered any uninjured crew, killed them, put on their uniforms, spaced their own uniforms and the dead—"

"It still sounds like something out of an adventure cube, Suiza, not like real life." Pitak chewed her lip. "Then, on the other hand, the Bloodhorde go for the dramatic. You would argue then that the blood belonged to the real RSS personnel, now dead—and that inside those bloody uniforms, the enemy were unwounded?"

"Yes, sir, unless jump transit did them some harm. Those compartments weren't any too sound, you said."

"No . . ." Pitak glowered at her. "I must say, Suiza, your passion for completeness can be a real pain sometimes. We had enough to do already." She reached for the comm switch. "But I'll check."

For the time it took for Pitak to work her way through the obstacles the medical section put in the way of the merely curious, Esmay tried to settle to her own assignment. The lines and figures blurred on the page . . . she kept seeing in her mind what she had not seen with her own eyes, the dark compartments of *Wraith's* bow section, cluttered with debris and unconscious men and women. Men and women with Camajo's—or whatever his name really was—eyes, the alert eyes of those on a mission. She ran her stylus along a column of figures, trying to force her mind to some useful task.

A change in the tone of Pitak's voice brought her upright, fully alert.

"Oh?" Elaborately casual, that. "Interesting—I helped evacuate some of them, you know, and they were covered with blood—yes. I see. Just the effect of the sleepygas? Are they still in sickbay then?" Her voice sharpened. "When?" Her eyes met Esmay's. "I see."

Esmay waited, as Pitak closed the circuit.

"If you retain this habit of being right, Suiza, you're going to be hated." Esmay said nothing. "They weren't wounded, any of them. Twenty-five males . . . seemed a little dazed and confused when they woke up, and three hours ago they were sent off to various workstations around the ship. Camajo, as we both know, was sent here, to H&A. If they were Bloodhorde . . . that many Bloodhorde loose in our ship could do us real damage . . ."

"Yes, sir."

"And I don't even know where they are. A petty-chief named Barrahide, from Personnel, came and got them. Not somebody from *Wraith*, because all *Wraith* personnel who aren't in sickbay are busy helping our people with damage assessment." As she talked, Pitak was scrolling through the communications tree. "Ah. Here we are. Extension . . . 7762." Another call, but this time Pitak talked as she waited for someone to pick up on the other end. "That's *if* they're Bloodhorde. They might not be. We need someone from *Wraith* . . . or rather, the captain does. But I'll see what Barrahide can tell me."

"Someone might take a look at the communications lines from the forward compartments to the rear in *Wraith* . . . was it explosive damage or were they cut?"

"Good idea, Suiza. You call my chief and tell him to check— Oh, Chief Barrahide? Listen, about those *Wraith* crew you took out of sickbay . . ."

CHAPTER FOURTEEN

Barin tried not to think about Esmay Suiza; he had enough to do, if only he could concentrate on it. Besides, she was two ranks above him; he was a mere boy to her. He told himself that, but he didn't believe it. She respected him; after that first disastrous argument, she had treated him as an equal. He felt himself scowling. This wasn't about respect, exactly. It was about . . . he squirmed, trying to push the thought aside. Planet-born, and higher-ranked . . . he had *no* good reason to be thinking of her that way, and he was. Her soft brown hair made Serrano black look harsh . . . her height made Serrano compactness look stubby. The back of her neck . . . even her elbows . . . he didn't want to feel this, and he did.

Serranos, his mother had said, fall hard when they fall. He had taken that as he took most of the things he was told about his inheritance, with far more than one grain of salt. His mother was not a Serrano; her occasional sarcasms might be envy. His adolescent crushes had been obvious even to him as temporary flares of hormonal activity. He had expected to find someone, if he ever did, in the respectable ranks of Fleet's traditional families. A Livadhi, perhaps. A Damarin—there was one of his year, a sleek green-eyed beauty with the supple Damarin back. If they had been assigned to the same ship . . . but they hadn't been.

This was unsuitable. He knew that. Grandmother would raise those eyebrows. Mother would sigh that sigh. His distant cousin Heris would . . . he didn't want to think about her, either. By rumor she had chosen an unsuitable partner, but he didn't think that would make her sympathetic.

The part of his mind that had not wandered off down this seductive lane prodded him back to alertness. Commander Vorhes would have his head on a platter if he didn't get those scan components out of inventory and down to the repair bay in a hurry. He shook his head at his own folly, and caught an amused glance from another ensign he knew.

"Heads up, Serrano—you hear about the mysterious intruders?"

"Intruders? What intruders?"

"Some casualties off *Wraith* who weren't that badly hurt, so we put 'em to work, and then they disappeared. About that time someone in Hull and Architecture went spacey and started claiming they were Bloodhorde agents or something . . . anyway, nobody can track 'em down, and there's a sort of alert—"

"Nothing official yet?"

"No—" A loud blat-blat-blat interrupted them. "Unless this is it."

It was. "All personnel report to nearest lift tube bay on Decks Seven and Eight for identification confirmation . . . All personnel . . ."

Barin and the others in sight drifted toward the nearest lift tube bay. "This is silly, you know," the other ensign said. "They'll never find anyone in this maze . . . five arms, the core, eighteen decks, all the dead space here and there, let alone the inventory bays . . . it's impossible."

"If it's really a Bloodhorde assault group, they'd better find 'em," Barin said. "Anyway, we've got internal scan in every compartment." He remembered what Esmay had told him about the internal scan evidence used in her trials. "They'd have to know how to disable it to escape detection. Shouldn't be that hard to track 'em, even in a ship this size."

"What could they do, anyway? If we don't find them, they'll just rattle around. It can't be but a few—" The other ensign slowed as the crowd ahead came in sight.

Barin thought of what Esmay had told him about the mutiny and what he'd heard of Heris Serrano's capture of Garrivay's cruiser. "It doesn't take many to create havoc," he said. "If they get command of the bridge . . ." All at once the ship which had seemed too large to be a ship, too safe to be interesting, felt fragile in the immensity of space. He tried to tell himself again that internal scan would find the intruders . . . but there were compartments without full pickup. And the volume of data alone would make it easy to miss significant details. That new AI system which had already glitched on keeping up with changes in the layout . . . could it really handle a job like this?

He joined the line forming in front of a *Koskiusko* crewman wearing Security patches. Ahead of him, others asked the questions he wanted answered, but the answers weren't coming. "Just look in here," they were all told. "Handprints there. You'll feel a prick . . . now move along . . ."

Full ID checks? Barin hadn't been through a full ID check since he entered the Academy. Did they really think someone could fake a retinal scan or handprint pattern? *Could* someone fake all that? He shifted from foot to foot. Behind him the line thickened. It was taking at least a minute to process each person and hand out a new ID tag. He occupied his mind with the obvious calculation . . . a max of sixty people an hour through each checkpoint, and they had only ten checkpoints? It would be hours and hours before they'd confirmed and issued new tags to the whole crew . . .

"Look in here, sir . . . and your hands . . . you'll feel a prick." He blinked from the flash as the machine checked his retinal pattern; he felt a sharp prick as it drew his blood to check against his record. The machine bleeped, and Barin took the bright pink tag they offered. Unlike his old one, it didn't have his picture, just the shiny strip that would allow scan to recognize him as legitimate. Even as he walked off, on his way to inventory for the parts Vorhes had wanted, he saw more security personnel arriving with more screening equipment.

He took the tube up to Deck 13, and gave his request to the master chief who was supervising the automated retrieval system. She did not have one of the new pink ID tags, but nodded toward his.

"I expect the captain'll shut down the automated system soon, and then I can go get my new tags. You're lucky you got here now."

Inside, the noise of the shifting racks was only half as loud as usual. Soon enough, one of the little robocarts slid up to the door with his order; the chief checked it off.

"Do you need transport, sir?"

Barin eyed the load and decided he could manage. "No, thank you."

"Fine, then."

He picked up the packaged components and decided not to take the tube back down . . . he could walk around the core, clockwise with the traffic, then take the ladder up to Deck Twelve and be in the Tech Schools inventory for the other things Vorhes wanted. And he might see something . . . his pulse quickened. If they were intruders, and if they were Bloodhorde, what would they look like? All he knew about the Bloodhorde was that they favored tall blonds.

As he passed the base of T-5, he could see into the ship security bay, which looked like a kicked anthill. Why couldn't he have been in the ship's own crew? He could imagine himself easily as that lieutenant of security, the one scowling at him now as if to wonder what an ensign from the 14th's remote sensing section was doing here. It would be a lot more interesting than his job . . . he wouldn't see any intruders, or any enemy on the outside either. He strode on, wishing hives on the person who'd assigned him to scan on a DSR, instead of something suitable to a Serrano.

The schools inventory, when he got there, was empty. He leaned on the counter, tempted to stick his wand in the console and find out where the parts were that he wanted. It wasn't safe, really . . . if everyone was lined up getting new ID tags, who was making sure the intruders didn't get into someplace like this? Although why they'd want to . . .

He heard footsteps coming, and felt his pulse quicken again. What if it was intruders? He glanced around and saw nothing useful as a weapon . . . but the plump sergeant who puffed into view wore a new pink ID tag.

"Sorry, sir," he said, his cheeks scarlet with exertion. "I had to run up all the ladders . . . they've turned off the lift tubes, just in case, which is ridiculous . . . it only makes more work for the rest of us."

Barin handed over his list. "Perhaps they're concerned that the intruders might cut the power to the lift tubes."

"You don't think they would!" The sergeant paused in the act of entering the access codes.

"I don't know what they'd do," Barin said. "But if someone wanted to cause trouble, that's one way to do it."

"Stupid," the man said, and completed the entry. "Let's see . . . aisle 8, level 2, tray 13. Just a moment, then." The schools inventory had never been automated, and Barin waited while the sergeant found his items and handed them over. Barin signed the terminal and headed back. Should he use the ladders here . . . T-1 was probably less crowded . . . or go on around and straight down in T-3?

He split the decision, dropping to Deck Six, then going around core to T-3 for the final descent to Deck Four.

✧   ✧   ✧

Vokrais had found the place, one of the maintenance shafts for the lift tube clusters, this one at the inboard junction of T-3 and T-2 on Deck Six, on his way to the meal at which he'd picked up the disgustingly dull knife and fork now hidden under his jumpsuit. He'd found Metris again, and passed the word. Metris would pass it on, as he would. How long did they have? His blood sang with excitement, clearing away the dregs of the sleepygas. This was nothing like the usual ship boarding, when they blasted their way in, weapons in hand, to take swift control of some fat, lazy trader. This was a real challenge.

He wondered if anyone had noticed their weapons and equipment, back on *Wraith*. They'd found the mine—that was common gossip, which they were glad to tell a presumed *Wraith* crewman.

"Would have blown you to hell and back," someone had said to him. "If our people hadn't found it and foamed it down."

But had they foamed the inner compartments too? If so, his favorite knives and tools might be safely embedded in the foam, and he could retrieve them later. It had been his grandfather's battle knife too . . . he wanted it back.

They needed weapons. He knew he could take any two or three of these effete technicians barehanded, but there were thousands of them. His whole team together could kill dozens, but it would not be enough. Somewhere on this monster ship were weapons of all sorts, hand weapons and ship weapons, ammunition, powerpacks . . . everything. He just had to find it.

His supposed supervisor wasn't watching him closely; he walked off casually in the direction of the dumps . . . no, they called them "heads" for reasons he'd never figured out. He was willing to call any of these fools shithead, but it still seemed an odd name for the receptacle. He felt eyes on him, and glanced back to see his supervisor, looking annoyed. The man shrugged as Vokrais went on through the door.

Inside were three others, a man and two women. Vokrais eyed the women. The Bloodhorde hired some female mercenaries, but they fought in all-female units. That was the natural way, otherwise men would think of nothing but rut, day in and day out. He was thinking of it now, as the tall redhaired one was washing her hands. She looked into the mirror, met his gaze, and scowled at him. Scowl all you wish, Vokrais thought. You will be tossed on my spear before morning. Or another one would; it didn't really matter.

When they left, he explored the echoing space with its seamless hard floor, its shiny walls. He found two other doors; one opened into a storage closet, and one into a different corridor. He tested the top of the closet—he could get out that way, if he had to—but chose to walk out the other door as if he had come in that way. Here he would have no pesky supervisor watching his every move. He tried to remember where his pack-second had been sent, and thought of using the data wand.

He pushed it into one of the dataports, and flicked through the controls coding queries.

"Need some help?" someone asked at his elbow. Vokrais managed not to strike, but his move was sudden enough that the man—older, gray-haired—stepped back, startled.

"Sorry," he muttered. "Timing still off . . ." and he gestured to his ID tag, which had the *Wraith* shipcode on it.

"Oh—I thought perhaps you were lost or something. That's a slow-stream dataport; if you want a quick answer to anything, there's a fast-stream down there."

"I would like to find the other survivors," Vokrais said. He struggled to remember the names on the uniform tags. "Camajo, Bremerton . . ."

"Ah . . . you know their numbers?"

No, he didn't know their mythical numbers that went with their mythical names. He shook his head, not trusting his voice.

"A search on *Wraith* should get 'em," the man said, and put his own wand into a port a few meters away. Vokrais noticed that this one had a double ring around it, blue and green. The one he had been using had a double band of yellow and green. "Here you are," the man said then. "I'll transfer it to yours . . ." He reached for Vokrais's data wand, then snugged it next to his for a moment, and handed the wand back.

"Thanks," Vokrais remembered to say; the man nodded and strode off. He looked at the display options, and walked down the corridor as if thinking, looking at the names and duty assignments coming up. Would that man remember him? Report him? Would anyone be expected to know about the color codings on the dataports? He'd felt smug that he'd recognized a dataport at all.

Hoch was indeed in Hull and Architecture, in wing T-3 and on Deck Four. Vokrais considered the distance and cursed to himself. What misbegotten brain-dead fool of an engineer had designed this ship . . . it made no sense.

A space station with an oversized drive, that's what it was, not a ship at all. He was wasting too much time hunting people, but he could hardly get on the shipspeaker (surely they had a shipspeaker) and call.

He spotted another of his people lounging along looking the picture of a lazy incompetent, and signaled him. Sramet wandered over, and Vokrais told him where to meet, and that he would find Hoch. "And don't slouch like that," he said, as he finished. "At least look like you're on business." Sramet nodded, and put on the character of earnest, hardworking dullness as if he had pulled a mask over his head.

And that was another thing lost in *Wraith* . . . not only their technical expert and their weapons, but their tools, and their special gear that included disguises and camouflage.

Hoch, when he found him, was being chewed out by one of the Familias NCOs, who finished a scathing description of his abilities with a couple of ethnic slurs aimed at his presumed planet of origin. "And you can take your sorry tail back to Commander Atarin's clerk, and explain that Petty-major Dorian won't have you on the crew, is that clear?"

Hoch caught Vokrais's eye, but his expression of sullen incompetence did not change. "Yes, sir," he said, in a strangled voice.

"Get on with it, then." The NCO, suppressed fury in every line of his body, stalked off down the passage. Hoch looked straight at Vokrais, this time with the expression of his mind: he would kill that one, when he found him again.

"We have a place," Vokrais said, as they walked back the other way. He gave the location, then said, "I need to find more—only two others so far . . . this thing is too big."

"I'll go too . . . do you know where they are?"

Vokrais was able to repeat the trick, as he thought it, of mating his data wand with Hoch's to transfer the list of personnel locations. "We're going to be discovered soon," he said. "I can feel it. We don't fit in with these . . . people."

"Slaves," Hoch said, in their tongue, and Vokrais looked at him sharply.

"Careful. We still have to do it."

"In my sleep, packleader." That in a lower voice still, but still in their tongue.

"Soon, then," said Vokrais, in the Familias. "Make one sweep clockwise—they all seem to go clockwise on the big passage around the core—and then meet. I want to make one trip as far upship as I can get before they realize we're aboard."

"Why should they? They're half-asleep, sheep ready for shearing."

"Go, packbrother," Vokrais said. Hoch's eyes gleamed, and his arm twitched; he moved off to the left. Vokrais went across to the nearest cluster of lift/drop tubes and shot upward. He had enjoyed the swift ride many times on his visits to Familias space stations; the Bloodhorde had sufficient trouble with the technology of gravity control that they used lift tubes rarely, never for such distances. He didn't suppose it would take him all the way to the top, but there it was: Deck Seventeen.

He stepped out into the same wide curving corridor, here less busy than down on Deck Four. He walked along briskly, as if he knew where he was going. A bored guard stood at an opening that might lead to the bridge, on the core side; Vokrais didn't try to look in. His shoulders itched; he knew he was being watched. He walked on, most of the way around the core, surprised to find no other lift tube clusters, as there had been on the lower decks. Did only one set come this far? He didn't want to go back past the first guard, like someone who had lost his way.

He came to another guarded opening. Here the guard looked more alert, eyes shifting back and forth. Vokrais could see the bulge of lift tubes ahead, but before that was a wide opening into T-2 . . . it had the label above . . . and he remembered that the dining hall had also been in T-2. He looked in and almost stumbled in amazement. The place was full of plants, green plants.

He turned in through the door as if this was what he'd intended all along, and felt the guard's attention drop from him like a heavy load. Beneath his feet, something that almost felt like soil cushioned his steps; on either side were the plants, from ankle to waist-high, some with colorful flowers on them. He ambled along a path, seeing no one. Paths met the one he was on, diverged, wound around taller plants that made screens so that he could not tell how large this place was.

Water pricked his face; when he looked up, he could see a foggy halo around the lights far overhead. The path ended abruptly in a waist-high wall of fake stone—he felt it, and was sure it was molded. A path ran beside the wall to rustic fake-stone steps to his left. Below . . . below was more garden, and one enormous tree rising up past him to end fifteen meters over his head. Behind it, a rough-looking gray wall with patches of blurred white, on which someone was splayed out as if for sacrifice: arms wide, legs stretched apart. As he watched, someone laughed, far below, and the figure heaved upward, lost its grip, and fell.

Vokrais watched the fall, waiting for the satisfying thunk, but instead the climber jerked to a halt in midair, and hung swinging. Now he could see the thin line, looped far above and coming back to the hand of someone standing beside the wall.

He started down the steps. Were the Fleet planners finally schooling their troops in hostile boarding techniques? But if so, why not have them in the gear they'd need? Why practice in thin short pants and little raglike shirts?

From the garden on Deck 16, he ran down one of the sets of stairs—stairs in stairwells, as in a building, not ladders as in a real ship—to Deck 14, then went out on the main curved passage again to catch the drop tube down to Deck 6. He could have used the access shaft itself, checking it out as he came, but he was eager to see how many people Hoch had collected.

When he came through the hatch, he saw nothing at

first, which was what he expected to see. Above and below, the shaft seemed empty, a smudged gray tube with a spiral ladder curling around bundled cables and pipes in the middle. Vokrais grinned, noting where lights had burnt out in helpful places, and whistled a few notes.

His pack reappeared, one after another moving out of the shadows, out of hatches that opened into other access tunnels, out of whatever cover they'd found. One by one they came up or down the ladder to cluster near him. One, three, four, six, ten . . . plus himself and Hoch. Twelve only, and not enough. He scowled at Hoch.

"Is this all?"

"No . . . but all who could come safely right now. Three more coming, when they can slip away. Sramet saw Pilan and Vrodik, but couldn't speak to them long enough. Geller is the only one nobody's seen or reported on."

"Who has weapons?" he asked, pulling out the knife and fork he'd taken.

"They don't carry weapons," Sramet said, sounding disgusted. "Not even the ones with Weapons Systems patches."

Two others had stolen dinner knives; Brolt had already started to sharpen his to a stabbing point.

"The contractors?"

"They're here," Hoch said. "But we haven't contacted them yet."

"So we don't know about the mechanism." Vokrais thought a moment. "It would be better to find out for ourselves, without asking them. I don't trust them." His distrust had brought them all here; he had argued, successfully, that even if the scum were honest, they might panic and undo the job once they realized their own necks were in danger. Later his plan had expanded; if they were quick enough, his warband would have the entire glory to themselves, the richest capture in the history of the Bloodhorde.

"We could take them . . . we could make *sure* they did it right."

Vokrais grinned. "We do need a few hostages."

"They won't care—" Hoch said. The Bloodhorde didn't.

Anyone careless enough to get caught was worthless; even if he escaped later, he wouldn't be trusted again for a long time.

"Familias is different. Besides, we need some of their technical tricks. We're supposed to know how to do things we don't understand." They nodded; they'd all found that out in only the few hours. Astounding that a warship crew, even down to the fewest of stripes, would be expected to understand all the gadgetry . . . but so it had proved. Only the fact that they'd been gassed, and assumed to have residual problems from that, had kept them from being discovered simply by their ignorance. "If we get one of the right family, it'll slow 'em down. They'll stop to think about it; they'll try a rescue. Then we get more."

"So you want us to pick certain needles out of a stack of thousands?"

"If they come handy. Here—shove that wand into the 'port and let's get a crew list." It was a blue-and-green ringed port, he noticed. Hoch put his wand in, and information appeared in little glowing letters, projected on the air itself.

At first, the long list of names meant nothing. Then Vokrais remembered the Familias habit of putting organizational charts on the system, and figured out the right code to ask for. "We want someone in scan, so they can tell us how to disable their miserable systems without blowing them away," Hoch said.

"The question is, do we want someone on the ship's crew, someone from the schools division, or the heavy maintenance division?"

"Heavy maintenance," Vokrais decided. "From what I heard, they've made all sorts of modifications to the original ship's architecture . . . the crew may not know about it, but those in maintenance will."

In a few minutes, they had a list of personnel assigned to Remote Sensing, 14th Heavy Maintenance Yard. "Commander Vorhes," Vokrais muttered. "That won't work—he'll be surrounded by people all the time. Lieutenant Bondal . . . Ensign Serrano . . ." He looked up, grinning.

"Serrano. Wasn't that the bitch who caused us trouble at Xavier?"

"And an important Fleet family. Even though he's only an ensign, that'll make them take notice."

"If he knows enough," Hoch said. "He's only an ensign. The lieutenant I found in Hull and Architecture isn't an expert . . . the junior officers can be sent here for short runs."

"If he doesn't know enough, we can snatch another from scan—the family connection alone will be useful."

"Hostage or vengeance?"

"Well . . . we tell *them* it's a hostage." Another low chuckle; they understood that. This Serrano cub would go back to his family—if he did—toothless and tamed, a warning not to interfere with Bloodhorde nobles. "Now—have you all used the mapping function on these things?"

Heads shook, and Vokrais glared at them. They'd come for the technology; they should be learning to use it. The data wands weren't difficult. He put his own in the port this time, telling them about the fast and slow ports as if he'd known all along. Then he switched to the open display, and the ship graphics glowed before them.

"We need a higher access probe to find everything we want," he said. "So we need to kill someone in ship security—with lots of stripes—and use theirs. But here you can see . . ." He pointed out the bridge, the secondary command center tucked in between the two FTL drives, the medical decks and the ship security offices on T-5. "They'll have weapons in security—even these sheep must run amok sometimes—and if we knock out their security personnel, we've eliminated resistance." All that counted, all that knew how to fight in any organized way. "In medical, they'll have more of that sleepygas, and the antidotes—"

"Eye for eye," murmured Hoch, grinning. Bloodhorde tradition, to return insults as exactly as possible, before the final bloodletting.

The loud blat-blat-blat of some alarm made them all look around. Then the muffled voice that must be a transmitted announcement. Hoch stuck his data wand back in the 'port, this time choosing the faster display, which only the user could see.

"They caught on," he said after a moment. "They're pulling everyone in for identification checks, full-scale . . . whatever that means." Vokrais was impressed. After that sloppy beginning, he'd expected to have days to wander around unnoticed before being found out. But this was better. He grinned at his pack.

"They know something's wrong, but they don't know where we are. It'll take them awhile to do the checks and issue new ID tags. Hours, probably. In the meantime, they won't even know how many of us there are. Vanter, Pormuk—" These were not their Fleet names, but their own. "You'll get us new tags. Try to dispose of the bodies where it'll take awhile to find them. Get the data wands, too. If you see any more of our people, sweep them up. Hoch, take two—three if you must—and get those contractors; we need to know where the self-destruct is, and be sure the captain can't use it. The rest of you, come with me. We need weapons, especially as we're short-handed right now."

"We come back here . . . ?"

"No. They have gardens on this ship, if you can believe it. Maybe more than one, but at the top of T-2, Decks 16 and 17. Lots of places to hide, and many ways in and out. There's a big tree—you can't mistake it—and an assault wall."

"If we're seen . . . ?"

"Capture or kill, and don't capture more than you can handle on the move. They know they've got trouble; we'll show them how much." Low growls answered him; they liked this much better than pretending to be softbellied Fleet techs. "Go."

✧   ✧   ✧

Captain Hakin, wearing his own new ID tag, looked as grim as expected when he met with the other senior officers aboard. He had called them to the officers' lounge nearest the bridge, where officers just going off or coming on duty met informally. Now the room was guarded by security personnel, their wary eyes watching everyone in sight.

"The *Wraith* crew members who came aboard as casualties from the forward compartments have not appeared for ID checks," he said. "We have forwarded what little videoscan we have to Captain Seska aboard *Wraith*, and he is sure that at least eight of those were never his personnel. He is showing every image to his remaining crew, to check on the ones he said he wasn't sure of. But we must assume that all twenty-five *Wraith* casualties who were not injured, and who were sent to work assignments by Chief Barrahide, are actually impostors. We do not know where they came from; I understand that Lieutenant Suiza had a notion that they might be Bloodhorde intruders. If so, this ship is in even more peril than we thought."

"Any sign of a Bloodhorde ship?" asked Admiral Dossignal.

"No, Admiral. However, the situation with regard to our escort is . . . tenuous."

"Tenuous?" asked Admiral Livadhi.

"Yes . . . *Sting* and *Justice*, as the admiral recalls, were assigned to patrol the same area as *Wraith*. Their captains insisted on returning to that patrol area, arguing that they could then guard the exit jump point there if the Bloodhorde tried to use it. That made sense, before we knew about the mine on *Wraith*; they'd been long gone by the time we suspected that intruders had come aboard."

"And our present escort?"

"Is useless if the intruders gain control of this ship— they could destroy *Koskiusko*, of course, if they were ordered to do so, but who is to give the order? I have made it clear to both captains that they should do precisely this, if they think the ship has been captured, but they have not yet agreed. Captain Plethys said he did not feel certain he could know that the ship had been irrevocably lost, even if he could not make positive identification of an officer on the crew list on a comlink. He argued that communications capacity might be interdicted by the intruders without their actually gaining control—"

"Which is quite possible," Admiral Livadhi put in.

"Quite so. In fact, any type of signal which I tried to imagine could, in theory, be interdicted by the intruders before they gained control. Captain Martin agreed with Captain Plethys, and added that he did not wish to be responsible for the considerable destruction of life and materiel, even if the intruders did appear to control this ship. He argued that the rest of the wave will no doubt return to guard us, and offered his ship to go and explain the situation. I insisted that he stay, but I'm not sure he will."

"You think he'll desert us in the face of enemy attack? That's treason!"

"There are no enemy ships on scan," Livadhi pointed out, hands steepled. "And he knows he can do nothing about the intruders already aboard. He probably thinks that will clear him with a Board."

"Not if I'm around to argue it," Dossignal growled.

"I agree . . . but if I remember Captain Martin, and I believe this is the same Arlen Martin I once attempted to teach Military Justice to, he's got a mind like an eel. Twisting and slithering away is his nature. I never did understand why he was given a ship."

"So you think he'll go," Captain Hakin said.

"Probably. Certainly, if his scan techs can locate an enemy ship at a distance where he thinks we can't . . . and then he'll claim he didn't know it was there. He doesn't make mistakes, you see."

Hakin looked even grimmer. "Then, sirs, I'm faced with a dilemma which you have probably already anticipated . . . when do I throw the switch?"

"The switch?"

Hakin sighed. "The admiral will recall that this ship, unlike vessels intended for combat, carries a self-destruct device and my orders are unequivocal. If I believe that the *Koskiusko* is in imminent danger of capture by a hostile force, I am to prevent such capture and appropriation by

the enemy . . . by destroying the ship and—if necessary—
her entire complement of personnel."

"But . . . are you *serious*?"

"Quite." Hakin looked ten years older at the word.
"We've talked about how useful this ship would be to the
Bloodhorde—their own private shipyard capable of
manufacturing two or three fully-armed cruisers just with
the materiel in inventory, and with resupply of the most
basic type, capable of building a battle group. Right now
it's full of the very people who know how to use it—some
of whom, faced with torture or death, would cooperate
with the Bloodhorde, at least long enough to train
replacements."

"Nobody would—!" began Livadhi.

"Begging the admiral's pardon, but no military organization in the history of man has had zero failure rate in
any system, including the human system. The recent action
at Xavier—and for that matter Captain Martin—shows that
Fleet is no exception. Besides, even if every person now
aboard this vessel chose death, the Bloodhorde can hire
civilians from all over the galaxy to operate what they can't
figure out."

"But surely—we're not at that point yet. There are only
a few Bloodhorde aboard; security will no doubt pick them
up in a few hours—"

"The point at which I *should* push the button is before
the Bloodhorde have a chance to prevent it working. Do
you think they haven't assumed such a device exists? Do
you think they're not looking for it right now, disarming
it if they've found it? They don't want to lose this ship
any more than we do—but the only way I can ensure that
we don't lose it is to destroy it."

Dossignal looked at him compassionately. "You're right,
Captain, that's a tough decision. Are you asking for
advice?"

Hakin grimaced. "It's my decision . . . my responsibility
. . . but I'll be glad to hear your ideas on choosing the
right time. Only realize that I know the right time must
be too soon rather than too late."

"How do you test the device integrity?" asked Livadhi. "And what's your normal test cycle?"

"It's tested weekly, by partially arming the device—it has its own control board, with the usual sensor array and so on. I have a vidscan of it, so I can see the attached status lights, and I also have scan that reports whether the circuits are functioning correctly."

"So . . . have you tested it since the intruders came aboard?"

"Not yet. My concern, though, is that even if it tests out now, they could find and disable it at any time."

"You've put a guard on it?"

"Yes . . . but as you know we need security personnel in other areas, including searching for the intruders. They might overpower the guard."

"Still, that should give you some warning. If the guard doesn't report . . . if the vidscan changes. You *can* test the system while the guard is there, can't you?"

"Yeees . . ."

"Would you like a witness to the test?"

"Yes, I would."

"Then my suggestion is that you test it now—immediately. And my second suggestion is that you jump back out of this system, which would make it harder for the Bloodhorde group we expect to find us."

"And for our ships as well," Captain Hakin said.

"Yes, that's true. But avoiding a Bloodhorde assault group seems more important at this juncture . . . I'm convinced that with over 25,000 loyal personnel on board, we can deal with the intruders—be they Bloodhorde commandos or any other hostile group—as long they aren't reinforced by outside forces."

"Very well." Hakin spoke to the guard at the door, and led them across to the bridge.

CHAPTER FIFTEEN

"The Captain asketh, and the Admiral respondeth," said Lieutenant Bondal, staring at his status board.

"Sir?" Barin pulled himself away from another daydream, this one of himself rescuing Esmay Suiza from faceless Bloodhorde goons.

"All that vidscan that's supposed to be watching every square centimeter of this ship . . . which in theory could find the intruders?"

"Mmm?"

"Isn't there, or isn't working, and the captain has quite reasonably asked the 14th to come to his aid. So we—you and I, for example—replace, install . . . and somehow I suspect the intruders, whoever they are, will manage to undo what we did, right after us."

"I hope not," Barin said. "Why doesn't the captain seal off the different wings? He could do that, couldn't he?"

"He could blow us all to glory if he wanted to, or turn off the artificial gravity, or . . . I don't know why he's done what he's done, or why he'll do what he's doing, and it's not my problem. Scan is my problem." He sighed, heavily, and began to make notes. "I know you went to inventory only an hour or so ago, Ensign, but you'll have to go back."

"It's what ensigns are for," Barin said cheerfully. "That's what you said yesterday: scutwork, gofering . . ."

"And making smart remarks. Yes, well, you're on your way to a successful career as an ensign, laddy-o."

Barin winced dramatically. Lieutenant Bondal had a freakish sense of humor, but was easy to work with if he thought it was appreciated. And he knew his business, which made the teasing worthwhile.

Traffic in the corridors was down except for the line still backed up at the ID station. Barin flashed his pink pass at the guard before entering the lift tube. It was like being back at school, where you'd had to have a hall slip to use the toilet. He decided not to make that remark to the grim-faced guard watching him. In the aftermath of the shipwide identification verifications, Barin understood why the automatic inventory racks had been disabled. With hostiles aboard, the captain didn't want anyone confused by the sudden shift of a rack . . . if it shifted now, they'd know it was enemy action. Still, that made retrieving a component stored on the second-to-top rack, at the rear, a time-consuming procedure. He looked up, checking the rack numbers. Yes, 58GD4 was up there, and what he needed should be on it. He looked at the maintenance ladder with its warning signs and tangle of safety harness . . . DANGER: VIBRATION FROM MOVING RACKS. CLIP IN BEFORE USING. But the racks wouldn't be moving, and putting on the harness would slow him down. On the other hand, he'd look pretty stupid if he slipped for some reason and broke an arm. Lieutenant Bondal would be furious; they were shorthanded already, what with the intruder scare.

Sighing, he got himself into the harness. It felt awkward; he was three-quarters sure he didn't need it. The safety clip fit around a rod beside the ladder steps, but had to be unclipped and reclipped every five or six rungs. He glanced around; he hoped no one was watching his clumsy caution. Up the first level, then the second. It was annoying to stop and unclip and clip every single time, even though he was getting faster at it. Somewhere across the compartment, he heard a clang and a muffled curse. His heart raced a moment, then quieted. It had to be a crewmate; the last reported sighting of the hostiles had been two decks down and over on the starboard side . . . a kilometer away, and only five minutes before. Should he call out and identify himself? Probably.

"Yo," he said. A distant voice replied with an indistinct bellow that seemed to be a familiar grade and name, with a questioning intonation on the end. He heard the rhythmic sound of footsteps coming nearer.

"—You all right?"

"Fine," Barin said, from his perch now eight racks off the deck. He could see a brown head moving along an aisle, a familiar uniform, though the angle was wrong to see insignia. "Up here," he said.

The person looked up, and grinned. "See you. You hear me trip over the vent hatch someone left undogged?"

"Vent hatch undogged?" Barin didn't like the sound of that. "Where?"

"Back there." Closer now, the man pointed back toward the compartment entrance. Barin saw by his stripes that he was a sergeant minor. "Inboard ventilation access hatch . . . probably some idiot guardsman went through looking for the bad guys and forgot to close it behind him."

"We can hope," muttered Barin. He felt cold, and he wasn't sure why. He glanced around. The inventory racks ran up to the overhead, fifteen meters from the deck, divided by aisles and cross-aisles usually humming with robotic carriers. He couldn't see far in any direction but along that one aisle. The racks he climbed beside were a half-meter high, but the ones across from him were a full meter . . . some full, and some partly empty. Plenty of room for someone to hide, even in the half-meter racks.

"What were you looking for?" he asked the other man.

"57GD11, code number 3362F-3B," the other said promptly. "Scrubber port covers. Should be around here somewhere."

"I'm on 58GD4," Barin said. "If that's any help." He watched as the other man peered at one rack after another.

"Ah—here it is." The other man started up the ladder of a stack two down from Barin without putting on the harness. Barin started to say something to him, but shrugged. He hadn't needed his own harness so far. He turned back to his own ladder; he had a long way to go.

By the time he was up ten more levels, he was breathing hard. A vertical fifteen meters wasn't like the short 3-meter ladders he was used to. The climbing wall was only ten meters. Still . . . he was over halfway. He looked up; the remaining racks seemed to loom over him. He glanced around for the other climber.

No sign of him. Had he found his items and gone away? Barin leaned out against the safety belt, trying to see . . . nothing. When he looked down, nothing but deck showing in the aisle. Odd. He'd have expected the other man to say something when he left. Barin shrugged, finally, and climbed up another rack level, reaching up over his head to clip in the safety line.

As his eyes came level with the rack edge, he had just time to think "How odd" before the cold round muzzle of a riot gun prodded him under the chin. It looked exactly like the ones that ship security carried.

"Don't move." The voice had no expression. Barin stiffened for a moment he would later realize was critical, and then someone grabbed his ankles. He arched back, trying to kick loose; the barrel of the gun slammed into the side of his head hard enough to stun. He struggled, but now something had caught his safety harness and pulled him hard against the ladder—his feet—then his arms—and finally another blow to the head that dropped him into a dark hole where he was only vaguely aware of being dragged off the ladder and onto the chill metal mesh of the inventory rack.

He felt too many things to sort out easily. His feet, bumping over some surface with regular obstructions. His shoulders, painfully cramped from the traction on his arms. His head throbbed, with occasional flashes of brighter pain that left ghostly spikes across his vision. Other things hurt too—his ribs, his left hip, his wrists—but *where was he?*

He tried to ask this, but choked on the gag in his mouth. Something soft—cloth or another soft material, that he could not spit out, though he tried. The part of his brain that could think suggested caution . . . waiting to see what happened . . . but between the choking and the dark his body's instincts opted for action. He flared his nostrils, trying to suck in more air, and twisted as hard as he could. Someone laughed. Blows crashed into him, from all sides; he tried to curl up defensively, but someone yanked his legs out full-length, and the beating didn't stop until he had passed out again.

"You're a Serrano," the voice said.

Barin concentrated on breathing. His nose felt like a pillow-sized mass of pain, and no air went that way; his captors had loosened the gag so he could breathe through his mouth. It had been made clear that this was a privilege they could revoke at any moment. He could barely see through his eyelashes, which seemed to be glued together. When he tried to blink, his eyelids hurt, and his vision didn't clear.

"We don't like Serranos," the voice went on. "But we do recognize your value as a hostage . . . for now."

He wanted to say something scathing, but the noise in his head didn't allow for creative endeavors. He wanted to know where he was, who his captors were, what was happening.

"You might even be valuable enough to let live past the capture of this vessel," the voice said. "It's possible that you'd even make it to Aethar's World . . . a Serrano in the arena would be a profitable attraction."

His remaining intelligence smugly pointed out that these must be Bloodhorde soldiers . . . the hostiles that everyone was searching for . . . and wasn't there something about the arena combats on Aethar's World? Slowly, grudgingly, his memory struggled through the haze of pain and confusion to find the right category and index . . . and offered a precis of what Fleet Intelligence knew about the arena.

Barin threw up, noisily.

"Well, that's one reaction," his captor said, running something cold and metallic up and down his spine. Barin couldn't tell if it was a firearm or the hilt of a knife. "I always look forward to Fight Week. But then I've never been on the sand myself."

"It could be that knock on the head," said another.

"No. He's a Serrano, and I have it on good authority that they are solid granite all the way through."

It was not a good sign that his captors were talking so much. Barin struggled to think what it meant, in all permutations. It meant they felt safe. They must be somewhere they did not expect to be found . . . or overheard, which meant they'd done something to the ship's sensors. The stench of vomit made him gag again; it didn't seem to bother his captors, who kept on chatting, now in a language he didn't understand.

They left the gag loose, which argued that they didn't want him to choke on his vomit if he heaved again. He blinked, and one eye cleared suddenly, giving him a view of uniforms that looked exactly like his own, only cleaner. A *Wraith* ship patch on the arm nearest him, with the stripes of a corporal. He couldn't see the nametag. Another beyond . . . he blinked again, and his other eye came unstuck.

Now he could see that one was watching him closely, cool gray eyes in a broad face. The nametag read Santini; the stripes indicated a pivot-major. The expression said killer, and proud of it.

Barin struggled to regain the moral high ground. He knew what was expected of a Serrano in a tight fix: triumph, despite all odds. Escape, certainly. Capture the bad guys, ideally. All it took was brains, which he had, and courage, and physical fitness—both of which he was supposed to have. His grandmother could do it in her sleep. Any of the great Serranos could.

He didn't feel like a great Serrano. He felt like a boy with no experience, whose nose was at least as big as a parpaun ball, who hurt all over, who was surrounded by big dangerous men who intended to kill him: helpless, that is. He hated feeling helpless, but even that resentment couldn't wake the surge of defiant anger he needed.

Do it anyway, he told himself. If he couldn't feel brave, he could still use his brain. He let his eyelids sag almost shut again. That man was not a pivot-major named Santini, but he had a name . . . and perhaps his companions would use it. He might learn what it was even though he didn't know their language. At least he should be able to figure out the command structure of this group, just by observation.

The man he was watching said something, and Barin felt a sharp tug at his hair. He stifled a groan, and opened his eyes again.

"You don't need to sleep, boy," said the man. His accent was no stronger than others Barin had heard within the Familias, but it had a hard contemptuous edge that even his first Academy instructors had not used. They had not cared if he passed or failed; this man did not care if he lived or died. "You need to learn what you are." A few words in that other tongue—Barin didn't even know what to call the language the Bloodhorde used—and someone behind him laid something cold and hard along the side of his neck.

From behind, another gabble of the strange tongue; the man across from him grinned. Pain exploded in his neck, down his arm; he felt as if it were bursting, as if his fingers had disintegrated into shards of pain flung meters away from him and still hurting. Before he could scream, the filthy gag was back in his mouth. Tears streamed from his eyes; his whole body shuddered. Then it was over.

"That's what you are," the man said. "Entertainment. Keep it in mind." He said something else, and they all stood. Barin was yanked to his unsteady feet, and dragged along with them as they moved off down a passageway he had never seen before. And not a single vidscan pickup in sight.

"Bad news," Major Pitak said as she came in from a briefing. Esmay looked up. "Security's found a body stuffed in a utility closet on Deck 8, T-2, and it was someone who'd had a pink tag. Neck broken, neatly and professionally. Also, they've got a hostage—maybe. Ensign Serrano."

"Barin!" That got out past her guard; she told herself it was no time for silly embarrassments.

"He was sent to get something out of inventory—none of the automated systems are running—and never came back. When his unit went looking for him, they found a harness tucked into the rack he'd have been on, and a smear of blood—as if there'd been more and someone had been careless wiping it up."

"They'd have had to knock him out to take him," Esmay said.

"So you'd think. Commander Jarles and Commander Vorhes are both furious, and nearly got into a flaming row right there at the briefing. Why was he sent alone, and why didn't someone raise the alarm sooner, and so on. The admiral was not happy with them, to put it mildly. The captain . . . I don't even want to discuss. Scuttlebutt has it that he got crosswise of a Serrano twenty-odd years ago. If that kid gets killed aboard his ship, he's going to have the whole family down on him."

"But Bar—Ensign Serrano is surely more important than any feud." Even as she said that, she knew it was wrong. Family was family, but a family would not jeopardize its standing for a single individual. Hers hadn't.

Pitak shrugged. "He's one ensign, on a ship with over 25,000 personnel. The captain can't let concerns about Serrano affect his primary concern: the safety of his ship." Her gaze sharpened. "You've spent some time with him recently, haven't you?"

"Yes, sir."

"Mmm. Something going on there?"

Esmay felt her face heating up. "Not really . . . we're just friends." It sounded as lame and false as it felt. What *had* she been feeling, around Barin? She hadn't done any of the things that regulations prohibited between senior and junior officers in a chain of command, even though they weren't in the same chain of command. But she had . . . if she was honest . . . wanted to do some of those things. If he did. He had never indicated that he did. She forced herself to look Pitak in the eye. "After he helped me at that briefing for the senior tactical discussion group, we talked a few times. I liked him, and he knew a lot of things about Fleet which they never taught us in school."

"I'd noticed some changes," Pitak said, without specifying their nature. "Coaching you, was he?"

"Yes," Esmay said. "Admiral Serrano and others had mentioned that I . . . confused, I think was their term . . . people because of mannerisms which are normal on Altiplano. Barin was able to define what I was doing wrong—"

"I wouldn't say exactly wrong," Pitak murmured.

"And show me what the Fleet customs were."

"I see." Pitak rocked back and forth in her chair for a long moment, staring past Esmay's elbow. "Suiza, everything in your record says you're level-headed and not a troublemaker. But you've never had a partner, that anyone knows about. Have you?"

"No." Direct challenge had gotten the answer out of her before she realized she was giving it. The blush came afterwards. "No, I . . . I just didn't."

"Umm. And you're not on any medication that would explain it. Are you?"

"No, sir."

Pitak sighed heavily. "Suiza, you're ten years too old for this advice, but in some ways, if I didn't know better, I'd think you were ten years younger. So try to take it as well-meant. You're ripe for a fall, and Barin's the only male you've spent more than a work-shift with. Whether you know it or not, you're on the slide now . . ."

"No." That came out in a low whisper. "I won't . . ."

"There's nothing *wrong* with it, Suiza," Pitak said sharply. "You're only a lieutenant; he's an ensign—that's a fairly common level of difference. You're not his commander. The only problem is . . . he's now in enemy hands, and we've got an emergency. I need your brain clear, your emotions steady. No racing off to do useless heroics and try to rescue your lover."

Lover? Her heart pounded; her stomach was doing freefall into her boots. "He's not . . ."

Pitak snorted, so like a lead mare that Esmay was

startled into a grin. "Young woman, whether you have actually been skin to skin or not, he is the first man you've cared about since you were grown. That's clear enough. Admit it, and you'll deal with it better."

Could she admit it? Was it true? She had had those vague wishes, those inchoate fantasies . . . Barin's hands would not be like those other hands. The uniform was different. She dragged herself away from all that, and fought down the flutter in her diaphragm. "I . . . do care . . . a lot . . . what happens to him. I—we hadn't talked about—anything else." She almost said "yet" and saw that Major Pitak had added it without hearing it.

"All right. Now you've faced it, and now you have to face this: you and I have nothing to do with the search for Barin, for the intruders, for anything else. It's our job to get *Wraith* back in service before a Bloodhorde battle group pops out here and blows us all away—or worse, captures us. Whatever happens to Barin Serrano cannot be as bad as the capture of this ship by the enemy. Is that clear?"

"Yes, sir." It was clear, in the part of her mind that was free to think clearly. The word "capture" rang in her mind with the finality of steel on stone. If they did not do their work, they might all be captives . . . and she knew she could not handle that. The vision sparkled in her mind—the quiet, competent, ordinary Lieutenant Suiza going completely and irrevocably crazy, the moment she became a captive again. However much she cared for Barin . . . she could not let that happen.

"Good. I didn't think you'd do anything foolish, but the little I know about Altiplano suggests that you might have triggers set which would push you into some stupid rescue attempt."

"They are going to try one, though, aren't they?" Esmay asked.

"I don't know." Pitak looked away. "The most critical thing is to find the intruders before they do any significant damage. Rescuing one ensign has to be a lower priority. What's really twisting the captain's tail is the fear that they'll disable the self-destruct."

"The self-destruct?"

"Yes. The captain is not about to let us be captured by the Bloodhorde—they could build cruisers with this facility and the expertise of our people. He's told the admirals that he'll blow us up first."

"Good," Esmay said, before she thought. Pitak looked at her oddly.

"Most of us aren't happy about that," Pitak said. "We admit the necessity but . . . you like it?"

"Better than captivity," Esmay said. The tremors were gone; the fear receded.

"Well. You never cease to amaze, Suiza. Since your brain seems to be working well enough, I'll answer some questions you'll no doubt ask in five minutes if I don't. We aren't jumping out of this system, because we can't. I don't know why. It might be that the intruders sabotaged the FTL drive . . . it might be that the fast-sequence jumps we did coming in shook something loose. Drives and Maneuver is on it. I need you to do a search, since you're good at that: if we assume that the fast-sequence jumps caused some structural damage or shift, what would it be?"

"Yes, sir."

"If you come up with anything, buzz me. We've got those *Wraith* structural supports coming over the line, and I need to be there for the installation." She started out the door, and then turned back. "Oh yes: the new procedures are that no one goes anywhere alone, and that includes the head. We know that at least one of the intruders now has a current ID badge—no doubt they'd like more. The captain may decide to firewall the ship, but right now there's not enough security personnel to man the access points. We're supposed to be alert for any strangers, anyone we're not used to seeing around, though on a ship this size that's not much use. I certainly wouldn't know half the instructors over in T-1 by sight, let alone the students." She sighed. "This is going to be a real bitch to implement. Rekeying thousands of IDs every day, and rechecking all personnel they're given to. All of us wearing tagtales, all of us going around in bunches."

"Are we all going to move into open bays for sleeping?"

"I hope not." Pitak scrubbed at her head. "I can't sleep like that anymore; I'm old enough to be wakened by snorers. But it may come to that, though it means leaving a lot of compartments vacant—which can only help the intruders. Anyway, the captain's asked the flags for more personnel for security—and I understand there were words exchanged about that between our admiral and Livadhi. But we've got to get *Wraith* back in action. If, as we suspect, there's a Bloodhorde battle group coming here to pick us off, we'll need every bit of help we can get."

"Is that possible—I mean, you said it would take—"

"Longer than we have. I know. Hull repairs alone should run sixty to seventy days . . . then there's refitting the internal systems, installing the weapons, testing. But there's nothing else to do. Maybe they'll be late—maybe they'll get lost. Maybe our fleet will come back. Or maybe they'll get the self-destruct fixed and we won't have to worry about anything . . . at least those of us who don't believe in an afterlife. Do you? Is that why you think it's a good idea?"

"Not . . . exactly." She didn't believe in the afterlife her great-grandmother had taught her about, where the dead were placed on the level they'd earned like pots of flowers on a stand. But she found it hard to imagine nothingness, an absolute end.

"Mmm." Pitak looked as if she'd like to say something more, but someone called her from the passage and she left without another word. Esmay looked at her screen a moment, and then at the bulkhead. Barin a hostage . . . Barin dead? She could not imagine either of those . . . not Barin, so brimful of energy, so much a Serrano. It was not her assignment. Pitak had warned her. But . . . of all the people on this ship, she was the one who had actually fought on shipboard.

There must be others. Security personnel had experience; that's what they trained for. She wasn't trained. She had no weapons.

She was thinking the wrong things. She wasn't thinking at all. Memory splashed her mind with the images of battle in *Despite* . . . she could imagine that behind the partition between her cubicle and the rest of the offices, someone lurked with a weapon.

Ridiculous. Yet she could not just sit there; she itched to be . . . somewhere, doing . . . something. She scolded herself for letting a brief experience of command turn her head. With a shipful of admirals on down, they weren't going to let a lieutenant in Hull and Architecture do anything but look up statistics in computer files.

Barin had dozed off, but woke when he heard an approaching noise. Help, maybe? Instead it was another of the intruders, with two men and a woman in civilian clothes. Barin knew, in a general way, who they were: civilian technical advisors, experts, contractors hired to do something in weapons systems. He'd never actually met any of them, though he'd seen them in the corridors and lift tubes occasionally. Ordinary middle-aged civilians, he'd thought. Of no interest to him, since they weren't working in his area. Now they stared at him as if he were a monster too. He supposed he looked pretty bad, with his swollen nose and bruised face, but they didn't have to look as if they thought it was all his fault.

"You lied to us," one of the Bloodhorde said. "You were paid to fix this, and you didn't. When we looked, the lights were green."

"But we *did* fix it," said the taller man earnestly. "We fixed it so that it wouldn't work, but the captain would think it did work. That's why all the telltales are green. He could run his system test, and it would come up—"

"They're not green now," his captor said.

"What happened?" The man leaned past his captor to look, and turned an interesting shade of pale green. "You— did you tear those wires out?"

"To make sure it wouldn't work, yes. Because you lied to us."

"But I didn't lie. Now he knows it doesn't work—and he could have a backup—"

"You were supposed to disable all self-destruct devices."

That with a series of shoves that ended when the man bumped into the bulkhead. "You were *paid* to do that!" Another, harder shove; the man staggered. "So if you left one, then you have broken your word to us, and . . . we take that very seriously."

"But—we don't know—we did what you said—" The man looked as if he couldn't quite believe the situation; he kept glancing at Barin and away again.

"Fix it again so that it looks to the captain as if it's working," the Bloodhorde leader said.

"But the captain will know it's been tampered with— fixing it now won't convince him. Someone would have to tell him . . . I could go tell him I could fix it, they know we're experts in weapons systems, and then I could—" The man didn't have time to flinch away before he was dying, the blade deep in his throat and a hard hand squeezing his mouth, stifling his last bubbling scream. Blood spurted, then flowed, then stopped, filling the compartment with the smell of blood so strong it almost covered the stench of death itself.

The woman screamed, a short cry cut off in terror as one of the others slapped her. The killer let the dead man fall, and then wiped his bloody hand across his own mouth, then the woman's. "They don't call us the Bloodhorde for nothing," he said, grinning. With the same knife—and it seemed even worse to Barin that he didn't wipe it clean between the killing and the mutilation—he sliced off the dead man's left ear, bit it hard once, and then tucked it away in his uniform. "Now," he said to the second civilian. "You will fix this so it looks as if it's working."

The second man, shorter and darker-haired than the other, hurried to comply. When he had done, the telltales showed green again.

"That's got it," he said.

"Is this right?" the killer asked the woman.

"Yes . . . yes it is right," she said.

"If you know that, we don't need him," the killer said, and caught the smaller man by the collar, half-choking him. "We'd rather . . . work . . . with you."

"No!" The woman lunged, but one of the others caught her. She tried to fight free, but she had no skill, and no strength to make up its lack. "No, let him—please—"

The killer laughed. "We heard what you said about the Bloodhorde . . . how you taunted our agent."

She turned even whiter.

"You dared to bind him . . ." He twisted the man's collar until the man's face purpled. "You threatened. You had a noose around his neck . . . and now you have a noose around *your* neck. Even barbarians, as you call us, understand poetic justice."

Barin could not look away; there was a fascination in this that disgusted him with himself. The killer twisted . . . twisted . . . and horribly, slowly, the dapper little man about whom Barin knew nothing died, his struggles weaker and weaker until they ceased.

"We pay our debts," the killer said to the woman. "All of them, the ones you know about and the ones you don't. Do we think size is everything? I believe that was your complaint, was it not? Then I believe you should have a chance to experience size in a way suitable to you in particular."

The woman gave Barin a frantic glance, and the killer laughed. "You think he could help you? This boy with a broken nose, that we captured as easily as we took you?"

He had to do something. He couldn't just lie here doing nothing . . . but no matter how he struggled, he couldn't loosen the very efficient bindings they'd taken from ship security. Through all that followed, he struggled, rasping his wrists raw, earning a random cuff now and then from men more amused than concerned with his efforts. The woman struggled too, but it did her no good; one after another they took her, in ways that Barin's inexperience had not imagined. Finally her struggles, her gasps and moans, died away, and she lay still. He couldn't tell if she was dead, or just unconscious. She had been some kind of traitor apparently . . . he had gotten that much from what they'd all said . . . but no one deserved what had happened to her.

One of the men spoke to the other in their language, something Barin could tell was meant as a joke. The one on her pushed himself up, laughing, and then turned to Barin. He grinned even wider.

"The boy's upset," he said. "Maybe she was his girl?"

"Too old," said one of the others. "A nice boy like him wouldn't have a woman like that."

"I'm sure he has a girl somewhere on this ship," the first one said. "We'll have to be sure we find her."

He would have heaved again if he'd had anything left.

"What I don't understand is how they found the self-destruct so fast," Captain Hakin said. "Not that many people know where it is . . ."

"They grabbed those civilian contractors," Admiral Dossignal said.

"But how would they know? They're weapons specialists; they've been busy recalibrating the guidance systems . . . oh."

"If someone suborned the civilians, then they could have disabled the self-destruct—they could have found it while appearing to be working on weapons in inventory. I see . . ."

"What I don't understand is why they were snatched, if they'd already done their job."

"They hadn't," the captain said. "Remember—until an hour ago, all the signals were secure."

"Considering the quality of work they did on the weapons, if they'd done it, I'd expect it to be undetectable," said Commander Wyche. "I'd bet they were snatched simply for their weapons expertise . . . with the data wands the intruders got from the three we know they killed, they'd have high enough access to find that out."

"So now the self-destruct is out of my control." Hakin glared at the admirals. "I should have used it."

"No," Dossignal said. "It was the handiest way, the easiest and least obvious way, for you to have the power of destruction, but it wasn't the only. On this ship, with what we've got in inventory, and the expertise in the 14th alone, we can prevent capture. We will."

"I hope so," the captain said. "I sincerely hope so, because if you don't we are not the only ones who will suffer for it."

"*Wraith* gives us another possibility," Commander Wyche said.

"*Wraith*?"

"She still has a third of her weapons, all in portside mountings. And she still has ample firepower to blow *Kos*. Not from the repair bay—the way she's locked into the cradles, even if she blew herself, there's a 72 percent chance that most of *Kos* would survive. We'd have to reposition her mounts, which would take days. But if we can get her into a position to fire on the core area—"

"She can't maneuver!" said Commander Takkis, head of Drives and Maneuver. "We dismounted the drives when she first came in, and it would take days to remount them. Besides, I have everyone working on the FTL drive for *this* ship."

"I was thinking of the drives test cradle. She doesn't have to maneuver to be slung on there and then towed into position . . . even, if you wish, at the extremity of the lines. The test cradle's own drive would be sufficient, if necessary, to move her into the best firing position for *Kos* . . . or she could get some shots off at the Bloodhorde."

A moment of silence, as they thought it over. Dossignal and Livadhi both nodded. "It could work—certainly, as far as destroying *Kos* is concerned, and quite probably she could do a fair bit of damage to the Bloodhorde ships."

Captain Hakin was nodding too. "If those weapons have not been taken off *Wraith*, and we're absolutely sure they haven't been tampered with, then we've got our fail-safe back . . . as long as they're not depleted taking potshots at the enemy."

"No . . . I can see that there'd have to be strict limits of use, but that should leave enough to do some damage. Especially if we had something else. One of the shuttles, maybe. In the Xavier action, the planetary defense used a couple of shuttles to good effect."

"They used them for mine-laying . . . I don't think that would work here."

"If only we could Trojan-horse them, the way they did to us." Livadhi smiled briefly. "It would be *so* satisfying."

"Get aboard a Bloodhorde ship? I don't see how. Since they do it, they know it can be done—they'd be watching. And our people would be trying a hostile boarding, against resistance."

"I was thinking . . . if we had any native speakers of their language, if we could locate one of these intruders and sweat some recognition codes out of him, then our people could pretend to be their own team coming back."

"Won't work." Admiral Livadhi scowled in surprise at the lieutenant commander two seats down. "Sorry, sir, but—we shouldn't waste time with schemes bound to fail. The Bloodhorde special operations teams—which is what we have aboard—are all members of one lineage. Each team is, I mean. They train together for years, and develop their own distinctive argot. Commander Coston, who went back to Rockhouse recently, had been doing a special study on Bloodhorde special ops. Our people can't imitate a Bloodhorde pack—not without a lot of training we don't have time to give. As well, we have only thirteen people aboard who speak the language with anything like sufficient fluency, and their accents indicate different origins."

"We don't need negativism now, Commander Nors," Livadhi said. "We're at the stage of thinking up possibilities."

"Sorry, sir. Well . . . suppose one of the Bloodhorde ships were close in . . . and empty or nearly empty of its crew. We've developed a fairly good model of a Bloodhorde ship's control systems, working from the commercial models they're built on, and information from scavenge. It wouldn't take long to train our experienced warship crews to use it—or for that matter, import our own scan equipment."

"Just where do you plan to find a close-in Bloodhorde ship with its crew off it?" asked Hakin with some sarcasm. The question hung a moment, as they all considered, then the same idea flickered across several faces. Hakin's turned grim. "No. Absolutely not. I am not going to allow *more* Bloodhorde troops aboard my ship, just for the chance of capturing one of theirs."

"They'd probably like to use one of the repair bays," Dossignal said slowly. "*Wraith's* in one—they know that. The other's empty . . . the best place for a smallish ship to dock, anyway. Full of stuff they want."

"No!" Hakin said, more loudly.

"Do you have any information on Bloodhorde boarding procedures, Commander?" Dossignal asked, ignoring Hakin for the moment.

Nors thought a moment. "All we have is reports from the few civilians who survived a Bloodhorde raid on a large civilian ship. They come in wearing protective gear that functions as both EVA and battle armor . . . they were in that case quite willing to damage the ship they'd captured to gain control of it. None of the civs we talked to could tell one level of weapon from another, but one of them did describe something capable of holing interior bulkheads with one shot. Here, though, we're assuming they want a DSR entire. I expect they'll do as little damage as possible in capturing it . . . but they do have to board."

"Another possibility," said Commander Wyche, "is the weaponry aboard a Bloodhorde ship in a repair bay. Suppose it could be immobilized there. Then its weapons would give us yet another self-destruct capability. They have forward-mounted weapons in every class."

"*If* we were able to get aboard and take control."

"I think we can take that as given, sir. If they just sit there, they aren't accomplishing anything . . . they can't shoot at us without doing the damage they don't want, and besides, they have no reputation for being patient. I think we can count on them coming out, with an intent to take control of key systems."

"Which is why we can't let them do it," Captain Hakin said. "It would take your people some time to get aboard, get control of their ship, and *maybe* be able to use it to defeat their other ships or destroy us . . . and in the meantime, I'd have a shipful of enemy . . . NO."

"So the real problem is getting them off their ship without letting them onto ours," Admiral Livadhi said. He put his fingertips together. "You know . . . there might be a way. If we could shut off the repair bay—that whole wing—"

"We could just take it apart," Admiral Dossignal said.

"Take it apart?" Captain Hakin asked.

"Yes . . . Commander Seveche, review the original construction data and all later modifications . . . there may be a way to cut one of the repair bays loose—unobtrusively, of course—and isolate it from the rest of *Koskiusko*."

In less than an hour, Seveche returned with the data ready to display; he set up the large screen and lit it.

"Here, you see: when they assembled *Kos*, they planned for possible changes by using temporary attachments—"

Hakin turned red. "You mean we've been working in a ship that's not really held together—?"

"No, sir. It is held together, and quite well . . . but it would take only hours, not days, to detach it again. These pressure clamps . . . these connectors here . . ." Seveche pointed to them on the display. "All this can be undone fairly easily. Relatively, I mean. The seal between T-4 and the core cylinder is a large expansion joint of sorts." He switched to another display. "As *Kos* was assembled, before an arm was locked on, the near end of these things were fastened to the core . . . and then the outer end to the arm. As the arms moved in to mate with the core, the corrugations compressed, giving additional safety margin to the join."

"Yes, but—I presume you plan to stretch them out again. Do you really expect them to be sound after all this time?"

"I don't see why not," Seveche said. "We've used the same material over the same span of time, with multiple compressions and extensions, with no failure. Besides, we can have the locks on each side shut. The way the arms are made, there are airlocks on the inner end of each deck."

"I know that, Commander," Hakin said. He sounded

annoyed. "But I'm sure they'll notice that the inner hatches are locked, and then they'll blast them—"

"They won't. We can rig temporary cross-dock access . . . they don't know what it's supposed to look like."

"Then when it detaches, it'll depressurize—"

"Not if someone is there to lock the hatches." Seveche looked to Dossignal for help.

"We're going to take casualties, whatever we do," Dossignal said. "To protect us from capture, you're prepared to destroy the ship and crew. I understand that, and it may be necessary. But I believe we have a chance to save both the ship and much of its crew if we can hold out until Admiral Gourache returns. Denying the enemy the use of a ship—using it ourselves—and using what firepower *Wraith* has left—is the only way I see to do that. I'm sure we'll have volunteers enough for the most hazardous of these hazardous missions."

"We'll have to have someone commanding each section that's freed—with the authority to do what they must, whatever that is. Divided command would be disastrous, and we can't be sure that communications will hold."

"Which means we've got to get those people involved in planning right away—"

"I don't like it," Captain Hakin said. "It's scrabble law: the whole ship is my command, and you're proposing to break off pieces and give them an independent command. Separated, they'll be even easier meat to the invaders—"

"Captain, we're offering a suggestion that gets us both off the hook. *Koskiusko* was assembled from previously independent sections in deep space. You know that. T-4 and T-3 even had names—*Piece* and *Meal* may've been stupid names, but names. They might have been commissioned as ships in their own right, if Fleet had not decided to try for a unified DSR. It's reasonable to maintain that they're both directly under the 14th—"

"You'll have to crew them," Hakin said. "You're not taking any of the crew I need to secure *Kos*."

Was it capitulation? Admiral Dossignal looked at Hakin a long time.

"You know, Vladis, if it's really going to stick in your craw, you can write a report."

"I intend to," Hakin looked even grimmer. "Partly to question your authority to nominate a captain for any vessel in this sector: that's Foxworth's job, or, at the lowest level, Gourache's."

"I see your point. But I'm going to do it anyway, and we can all hash it out with a Board, if not a court, later."

Hakin shook his head. "It won't improve the odds, and it just makes my job harder . . ."

"I don't see how, since we're almost certainly ridding you of most of your intruders, and one of the ships trying to attack you. Now as for crew, we have the uninjured survivors of *Wraith*—"

"Which will be needed to serve *Wraith*'s weapons," Livadhi said.

"Their weapons crews certainly. Since *Wraith* won't be maneuvering, I don't know about their bridge crew. I hate to waste a captain with combat experience aboard a crippled ship. We're not overburdened with such officers."

Commander Atarin spoke up. "Admiral, I have prepared a list of all officers and enlisted aboard with combat experience in the past three years. They're rank-ordered by specialty and performance—not just experience—in combat."

"Good. Let's see . . . oh, my."

"What?" Hakin craned his neck, trying to see.

"We have ample combat-experienced weapons specialists, because the senior weapons technical course is running. Scan . . . not much problem there. We're short environmental systems specialists, but this should be over fast enough that it won't be critical . . . we can have our people in self-contained gear. Communications is also short, but most scan techs are cross-trained in communications and we have plenty of scan techs. What we don't have is ship commanders. Or rather, we have just enough: *Wraith*'s captain for *Wraith*, and Lieutenant Commander Bowry, who's here for a special course, to command the Bloodhorde ship."

"I don't suppose we'd be lucky enough to get more than one of them . . ."

"I doubt it. Why would they bring in more than one ship at a time? If they gifted us with such riches, we'd just have to find someone to take it . . . but that gets us down to fairly junior officers with very little experience of ship command in combat." Dossignal considered telling them who, precisely, but he knew Hakin would have particular objections to Esmay Suiza.

CHAPTER SIXTEEN

Esmay found what might be a possible cause of the failure of the FTL drives, and took that to Major Pitak, who was overseeing the transport of the long crystal bundles from the Special Materials Fabrication Unit to T-3 and *Wraith*. Even bundled, they were more flexible than Esmay had expected, as she watched the special transport teams eased them along the transport track. She had known, intellectually, that all ships had such framing members . . . she had known that they had a lateral flexibility which was essential to the design. But these shivering, wriggling lengths seemed far too frail to trust lives to in deep space.

Pitak gave her a brief glance and turned back to watch. "Ah, Suiza . . . find something?"

"It's only a possibility."

"Good enough. Have you seen these before?" She went on before Esmay could answer. "Wiggly, aren't they?" She sounded pleased.

"More than I thought," Esmay said honestly. Vidscan screens showed the entire route, from the exit port at the end of the SpecMatFab, up over T-1, the core, and down again between T-3 and T-4. "Why didn't they put the repair bays on the same side of the ship as SpecMat? Wouldn't it have been easier to transfer things like that?"

"Yes, but that turned out to be the least important design consideration. If it really interests you, when this crisis is over, you can look it up in the design archives . . . the whole argument is in there." She punched up the view in one screen, and pointed to the bundles. "Now that's a good set. After awhile, you'll be recognizing good strands from bad by the oscillations alone. If we didn't have this other crisis, I'd send you over to SpecMat to watch them during breakoff."

Esmay was just as glad to miss that. She had heard from others about the more spectacular breakoffs, when the test sequences induced more oscillation than a faulty crystal could withstand, and shards flew with a noise that was said to shake reason.

"Let me see what you've got," Pitak said. She looked at the data Esmay had found and frowned. "I don't think this is it. The shearing force isn't enough to unseat the AG generators, and you're suggesting that it was AG instability which caused the drive failure, right?"

"Yes, sir."

"How does it model?"

"They've bumped everyone below department heads off the big computer . . . the little one said it was possible. That's why I brought it."

"Oh. Well, I don't like the modeling program on the little one for anything but pure structural layups. For this sort of thing we need the Mishnazi series . . . but I imagine they're trying to maximize their data analysis. I don't think this is likely enough to ask for the time ourselves." She looked at Esmay. "You should log off and get some sleep while you can—at least a good meal. Have you kept track of who's been to dinner?"

"No, sir, but I can do that as soon as I get back."

"Do that, then, and thanks for this . . . I think it's sabotage, myself, but D&M asked us to consider it."

Esmay nodded and withdrew with her escort, a corporal she'd yanked out of the H&A clerical section when she needed to find Pitak. She hated feeling useless. Of course she should eat; of course she should be making sure that everyone in the section did. But . . . she wanted to do more.

She had just reached Pitak's office and started checking on the whereabouts of all the personnel under her command when the comm beeped at her. It was Pitak.

"Right in the middle of a crisis and they have to short me. Suiza, what have you been doing to get the admirals interested in you?"

"Nothing that I know of," said Esmay.

"Well, you're to report to Admiral Dossignal's office immediately, and the note to me says not to expect you back any time soon. It never fails. I get someone trained to the point where they can do me some good, and the brass taketh away."

"Sorry, Major," Esmay said, before remembering that she wasn't supposed to apologize. She thought of Barin with a pang. Was he still alive? Was he . . . all right?

"Better get going," Pitak said. "And if you have a chance, let me know what's going on. There's an odd feeling in the ship."

"Yes, sir."

In the admiral's outer office, Commander Atarin was watching for her. "Ah—Lieutenant Suiza. Good. We're going directly to a secure meeting room in T-1; our escort will meet us at the lift tube."

"Sir, may I ask—"

"Not until we're there. And don't look alarmed; you aren't in trouble and we don't want to scare anyone."

"Yes, sir."

Two armed pivot-majors, with Security patches, waited by the lift tubes. "Commander, the captain says it would be better to avoid the tubes," one of them said. Esmay saw the sheen of perspiration on his face.

"Something happened?"

"I can't say, sir," the man said. He was breathing a bit too fast.

"Let's go, then." Esmay and Commander Atarin followed as he led them around the core to the base of T-1. The wide passageway was busier than usual, as if others were avoiding the lift tubes and slideways. They had five decks of ladders to climb; when they emerged from the last, Esmay saw another pair of security guards, these with their weapons in hand, outside a secured hatch. A portable ID booth had been set up nearby, and Esmay noticed the heavy gray boxes and cables of a full-strength blanket system positioned along the bulkhead. Whatever this was about, it was being kept as secure as possible from intrusion.

She and Atarin both went through a complete ID check, retinal scans, palmprints, and blood test. Then the guards at the door checked them in.

Inside, the medium-sized conference room was edged with more scan-blanketing equipment; in the center, a cluster of officers leaned over a large table with a 3-D model of *Koskiusko* on it. Esmay already knew Admirals Dossignal and Livadhi by sight, as well as Captain Hakin, but she had not met the lean gray-haired full commander who was introduced as *Wraith's* captain, or his Exec, Lieutenant Commander Frees. Another lieutenant commander named Bowry, who wore no ship patch, but had a collar-pin indicating he was in the Senior Technical Schools for some course. What *was* this?

"Gentlemen." That was Admiral Dossignal, now seating himself at one end of the table. Esmay saw that places had been prepared, with nametags . . . hers near the far end of the table. She sat just as the others did.

"As you know," Dossignal said, even before the last chair slid back into place, "we are in a difficult situation here. In a few minutes, you'll have a chance to review the details of that situation, but the first thing you need to know is that you are all immediately relieved of your former assignments. You are assigned, under my direct command, to a difficult and dangerous mission; this is the first of the meetings you will hold to plan the execution of this mission." He paused, as if for comment, but no one was unwise enough to make any. "You also need to know that Captain Hakin is not in agreement with the aim of this mission, and plans to file a letter of protest. I respect his moral courage in so expressing his disagreement, and his loyalty, which has allowed him to cooperate even under protest."

Esmay glanced at the captain, who went from beet-red to pale in the course of this.

"I take full responsibility," Admiral Dossignal went on, "for what is done here, and its outcome. I have so informed Captain Hakin, and have so stipulated in the official log. Is that clear?"

He waited until everyone had nodded.

"Good. Now: our mission is to capture a Bloodhorde ship, and using that and *Wraith*, successfully defend this ship from capture. You are the officers who will command elements involved in this mission, so you are here to plan it."

"But *Wraith's* crippled," said someone—a lieutenant commander whose name Esmay had already forgotten.

"Correct. *Wraith's* drives are dismounted and she cannot maneuver. But she can be trolled out to the drive test cradle, where her weapons can come to bear on either the Bloodhorde ships or *Koskiusko*, as need requires."

"*Koskiusko* . . ." someone murmured too audibly.

"If capture appears inevitable, *Koskiusko* must be destroyed. Its capability must not fall into Bloodhorde hands—nor must its thousands of skilled technicians."

Esmay felt the heavy silence in the room. She supposed the others had worked through this equation before: the Bloodhorde had never been known to free or exchange prisoners, though a few had been rescued from appalling conditions. Thus a quick death—or relatively quick— would be a mercy compared to slavery on one of the Aethar's World planets. But to contemplate the annihilation of so many of their own . . .

"We believe—*I* believe—that there is a chance to defend this ship and prevent those deaths," Dossignal said. "It's not a good chance, but it is a chance. You are the ones best suited to carry it out. We do not know how much time we have; let's not waste any."

With that the planning session began in earnest. Esmay had never been involved in mission planning before; she said nothing and listened, wondering how she fit into this. Admiral Dossignal outlined his ideas, then assigned officers to specific tasks. "Lieutenant Suiza," he said finally. "Except for the crew of *Wraith*, you have the most recent, and in some ways the most valuable, combat experience."

Esmay could feel them all staring at her; her breath caught. "Sir, the admiral knows I was only—"

He cut her off. "This is no time for humility, Lieutenant. You are the only officer we've got who has actually fought *inside* a ship. And you commanded *Despite*, with remarkable results. I'm not assigning you to command the ship we hope to capture—there's a more senior and more experienced officer—but I am calling on your knowledge of intraship combat."

"Yes, sir."

"At the same time, I think Captain Hakin's security squads would benefit from your expertise . . ." He glanced at the captain, whose face reddened. "We have hostile forces aboard, and we've already taken casualties. Security hasn't located them or prevented the trouble they've caused so far."

"If the admiral wishes," Hakin said, through gritted teeth. "My reservations are on file." He gave Esmay a look of cold distaste.

"Commander Seveche, you will be responsible for the actual detachment of T-4 from the hub. I leave it to you how you're going to keep the necessary preparations from being recognized by the intruders, whom I'm sure are observing what they can."

"Yes, sir. I think some judicious tinkering with the artificial gravity controls could provide an excuse . . ."

"Whatever. If events overtake us before detachment is possible, we need a fallback plan. Along with your other duties, Lieutenant Suiza, I'd like you and Commander Atarin to liaise with *Koskiusko*'s security about that. Commander Jimson, you're to make sure that people get what they need out of inventory, without letting any more personnel be captured."

"We need more security personnel," Captain Hakin said.

"True, Captain. If it would help you, I'm sure that Admiral Livadhi can suggest individuals now enrolled in one of the tech courses who have sufficient background to be useful and have been aboard long enough to know their way around."

"I've had Commander Firin make a list already," Admiral Livadhi said. "We have twenty-eight enlisted personnel with a secondary specialty in ship security, and another thirty-four who have done security work at some time or other within the past ten years. All are currently qualified with shipboard small arms. In addition, we have more personnel in the remote sensing course than Admiral Dossignal thinks will be needed for the rest of this mission. They can improve surveillance . . ."

"I'll be glad of them," the captain said, this time with no resentment in his voice.

"I must emphasize the urgency of the situation," Dossignal said. "We don't know how long before a Bloodhorde battle group arrives—or how many ships it might contain—or how the intruders will affect our efforts. We—" He stopped as someone knocked on the door. The guard there lifted his eyebrows; Dossignal nodded and the guard pulled the door open.

A disheveled security guard looked straight at the captain. "Captain, you're needed on the bridge, urgently. We have a situation."

"Excuse me." Hakin pushed back his chair.

"What kind of situation?" Dossignal asked. The guard looked at the captain who shrugged irritably.

"Tell him, Corporal."

"The emergency oxygen conservation system went off on half a dozen decks of T-5, and knocked out everyone in sickbay and the ship's administrative offices. Two people got out and gave the alarm."

"I'm on my way. You'll excuse me . . ." It was not a question.

"I hadn't thought of that," Dossignal said. "I should have—we haven't had any experience of this sort of thing. Lieutenant Suiza . . . can you tell us . . . what sort of mischief might we expect?"

Esmay gathered her scattered wits. "Sir, they'll try to get weapons, if they don't already have them. With stolen data wands, they can find out where the ship security weapons lockers are, and if they get a data wand keyed for security, it might even give them the access codes. Then they'll try to isolate and immobilize large numbers of the crew, probably by locking them into various compartments. That's what Captain Hearne's allies tried to do to us on

Despite. Here I suppose they'd try to cut off the wings from the core. They'll damage systems that give them effective control of ship operations . . . environmental systems, including ventilation as they did here, hatch controls, communications, scan. I'd expect them to take hostages from critical positions . . . if they've been loose in sickbay, they'll have medical personnel and supplies, including gas exchange equipment, so that we can't use the equivalent trick on them."

"And your response would be—"

Through her mind flashed what she knew about the DSR. "The same tactics would work against them if the captain initiated them. Manually reset the ship's support systems so that each wing is independent for life support, as it was designed, then isolate the wings. They'll be trapped, and outnumbered wherever they are. If they're not in the core section, they won't be able to get to the bridge. If they are in the core section, they won't be able to use the wings for refuge, and ship security can go through the core first, then one wing at a time, until they're located. Ship security will need a different, secure communications system, because we have to assume the present one is already compromised."

"But if we do that, we won't be able to set up for detaching T-4," someone said. "And if the other ships come . . ."

"If we've all been knocked out with sleepygas," Esmay said, "we won't be able to detach T-4 either."

A moment's silence, as the others digested that, and she realized that she had just implied—no, said—that a commander was being stupid.

"Lieutenant Suiza," Dossignal said. "I'm putting you in charge of security for the 14th—specifically, T-3 and T-4. Liaise with regular ship security, but don't wait—do what you think needs doing. Atarin, who've you got for her?"

The door opened again; Captain Hakin interrupted without apology. "They got into Security; they've got the weapons, and gas masks. Riot gas, probably. Maybe more."

Almost as one, heads turned to stare at Esmay, who was still on her feet.

"As I said," Dossignal stood also, and the others scrambled up. "Lieutenant Suiza has been through this before; she correctly anticipated their moves."

"I'm closing off the wings," the captain said, as if Dossignal had not spoken." We'll have to get the support systems isolated, but at least I've ordered the hatches closed, to everything but T-1. I'll give you the new codes, but—"

Outside a confused clatter, followed by soft pops as of something wet being dropped into a deep fryer.

"Captain—!" yelled someone outside. The guard at the door opened it and turned to look out.

Esmay moved before she thought; as the captain started to turn, she tackled him solidly and yelled, "Shut it!" The captain, cursing, writhed and tried to kick her in the head; she released him, rolled to her feet and yanked the guard away from the door, slamming it . . . without taking a breath.

"What—!" began Dossignal, but stopped when the guard sagged to the floor, his face already bluish gray.

The captain sat up, red-faced and furious. "You—" he started to say, then gasped and began wheezing.

"Get him up," Esmay said. "It's heavier than air . . ." If they didn't think to turn off the artificial gravity. If they didn't come right on through the locked door—she took the guard's weapon and used it to smash the internal doorlock control. *Wraith's* captain and exec scrambled to help the captain up and get him to the table.

"Gas, I presume," said Admiral Livadhi in a tone of mild intellectual curiosity.

"The bridge . . ." the captain gasped, struggling for breath.

"After we get out of here," Esmay said. Preferably before the intruders figured out where this compartment's air supply was, and simply poured the gas in that way.

"If we can get out of this compartment, I can suggest a safe—or possibly safe—route away from here," Lieutenant Commander Bowry said. "I've been all over T-1 for the past quarter year."

"The overhead," Esmay said. "Or the deck, but I don't know how to get into it."

"You could just blow a hole in it," said Captain Hakin sourly.

"Waste of ammunition," said *Wraith's* captain, Seska. "We'll go up." He climbed onto the conference table, and pushed aside one of the overhead tiles. "Yep. Just like every other space station, though the one we want is over there—"

It took longer than Esmay wanted to get the entire group up through the hole in the overhead; the captain was still groggy and uncoordinated, and made an awkward bundle to lift. Esmay went last, guarding their rear with her single weapon, though she knew it would be useless if the intruders broke in.

But they wouldn't. She knew that, as if she could read minds. They had isolated the captain and the highest ranking officers, and would let them stew in there as long as they wanted. In the seconds ticking away now, they were wreaking as much havoc as they could. They'd be back at the core, trying to take the bridge, if they hadn't already.

In the dim, unhandy space between the tiles of the overhead and the base of the deck above, she followed the others—Lieutenant Commander Frees, in this instance—and wished she knew more about Lieutenant Commander Bowry. Did he really know a way out of this section? And just how had the wings been sealed off from the core? She supposed it was like the fire drills, but she didn't know for sure.

No time to worry about it. Ahead of her, the others had stopped moving. Esmay squirmed around so that she could look back the way she'd come. There was nothing to see but the smudged track of their passage, where they'd disturbed the dust.

Someone patted her leg, and she turned back; they were moving on again, more slowly. After a minute or two, she realized the leaders were slithering out of the overhead, down into a passage.

When she got close enough, she could hear voices.

"Damn near got us all. And you?" That was Admiral Livadhi, sounding more annoyed than alarmed.

A low murmur she couldn't follow. Frees, in front of her, slid out the gap into helpful arms. Esmay gave a last look back and saw nothing . . . but anyone could follow that track. She turned and dropped through feet first. A couple of enlisted men with Tech Schools patches replaced the overhead panel as she looked up and down the passage.

Some meters in both directions, armed security guards kept watch. One of them had an armor vest and helmet; the other had none. Esmay saw openings into several compartments, but no one moved that way.

"Captain Hakin's still having trouble breathing," Dossignal said. "Does anyone know which gas that was?"

"Probably SR-58," Bowry said. "They'd have the antidote in the hospital, but—" Esmay didn't know anything about the different kinds of volatiles, but from the tone, the captain's life might still be in danger.

"We can't get there."

A shout from the outboard end of the corridor startled them. Quickly, but without panic, they moved into the nearest opening. Esmay flattened against the inner bulkhead, and hoped the security guards had the sense to get out of sight themselves. The footsteps came nearer— more than one person, she thought. They paused outside the opening.

"Admiral Livadhi likes green pea and leek soup," the newcomer announced in a conversational tone.

"Carlton," Livadhi said, grinning. "In here, Major."

The major who came through the opening was festooned with equipment; his brows went up when he caught sight of Esmay and her weapon.

"The admiral might want to put this on," he said, handing over a face filter. "They've been using sleepy-gas . . ."

"They used worse than that," Livadhi said. "Captain Hakin got a faceful; it killed one guard."

"Yes, sir. I have ten filters with me, and Corporal

Jasperson is handing them out to your security detail. Commander Bowry had suggested securing the aid stations and the weapons lockers before he went up to the meeting; we've got enough gear for about fifty. Vests, helmets, comunits, weapons. And the medical supplies."

"Good work. Where'd you stow it?"

"This way, sir." Major Carlton led them down one passage, turned into another; two men helped the captain along. Esmay saw more guards, all with gas masks and some with armor. She wondered where they were going, and why waste time going there instead of breaking out of T-1 now, before they were trapped. But she had a weapon, and she stayed back with the rear guard.

Where they were going, it turned out, was a secure briefing room snugged in among the laboratories of Special Materials Research. "Separate ventilation system, good thick armor all around—it'll take them awhile to get us, long enough to make plans." Admiral Livadhi turned to Carlton. "Any medical personnel in T-1?"

"I've got someone coming who worked in the wing clinic; the only supplies we have are from emergency lockers, because the intruders wrecked the clinic."

Captain Hakin had collapsed two turns back, and now he barely roused when Livadhi spoke to him. "Captain . . ."

"Uhhh . . ."

"Captain, we have a legal problem: you are the only *Koskiusko* officer here; we cannot contact the others, and we need to make plans for resistance."

"We're not going to *resist*," Dossignal said. "We're going to get this ship back."

"Do . . . it," Hakin said.

"Thank you, Captain; I accept your permission."

In the next few minutes, the admirals agreed on the new command structure required by the emergency, and on goals. Then they settled to considering how to regain control of the ship.

"We need to get our combat-experienced people over into T-3 and T-4," Dossignal said. "That's where we've got part of a ship, and might with luck capture a Bloodhorde ship. The sooner we get those people off on that mission, the better."

"Through the blast and fire doors . . . ?"

"How else?"

"If they're smart—if they have enough men—they'll be watching all the access points."

"They don't," Esmay said confidently. "There were only twenty-five of them in sickbay."

"Not a complete team: they usually send a threefold pack, three tens."

"You mean we missed some?"

"No . . . some may have died aboard *Wraith*. We haven't had time to get into the foamed compartments and look. That'll be where their weapons and gear are, too."

"But the thing is, they're not going to be able to watch every place we can get through. So where *will* they be?"

"Where they're still in contact with each other, for backup," Bowry said. "If they were after the bridge—and I would be, if I were trying this trick—that means they'll be watching on Deck 11, where we might be trying to get to weapons stored in the security weapons lockers, and Deck 17."

"So . . . let's try Deck 8," Dossignal said. "Commander Takkis can get into the core, to the secondary command center, and make sure that the FTL drive isn't working under their command. The rest of us—"

"What d'you mean 'us'—you aren't going out there."

"I certainly am. I belong over there in the 14th, with my people."

On the way down to Deck 8, they saw no sign of the intruders. Most of the people here were staff or students of the Training Command, Senior Technical Schools Division. Scattered among them were elements of the ship's crew, mostly security, and researchers from the SpecMat Research Facility. They watched, wide-eyed, as the group passed, masked and armed.

Deck 8 seemed especially quiet when they came out of the stairwell. Esmay, in the lead, stopped short when she saw the first body lying sprawled in the corridor.

"Trouble," murmured Seveche, behind her.

"And we don't know if it's gas or something else," Esmay said. There was no other way from here to the firewall doors; she took a breath and edged forward, as quietly as she could.

"Dead some hours," Seska said as they came up to the body. The man had ship security patches on his shoulder, loose on one corner where someone had hacked at them but given up.

"Maybe that was one of the first," Dossignal said. "And the attacker then went on to meet the others . . ."

Esmay wished they would all shut up. She could hear nothing, see nothing. At the first compartment, she looked in. Five corpses lay sprawled on the floor, sagging from chairs onto work surfaces . . . her stomach turned; she swallowed with an effort. Whoever had come here was quick to kill.

Nearer to the core, they could see the solid wall that cut them off from the rest of the ship. Esmay knew now that this was no simple bulkhead, but instead a section of the hull itself, capable of sustaining pressure if the wing detached. It lay against a similar section of the core: two thicknesses of hull. Once these barriers came down, the only way across was by means of the override codes, which could open small airlock hatches.

Admiral Dossignal entered the code, while the others guarded. The hatch did not move. He tried again; again it would not open. "Commander Seveche," he said. "Did you hear the captain give the code?"

"Yes, sir."

"Then you try it; perhaps I misremembered."

Seveche also entered the number, but again the hatch did not open.

"Either the captain didn't remember the right sequence, or they've found a way to change it," Dossignal said.

"Or someone in the crew changed it, perhaps thinking the intruders had it," Seveche said.

"Amounts to the same thing," Dossignal said. "Now . . . There's got to be another way to get through this."

Seveche grunted. "Not without the equipment that's over

in our section, sir. Two thicknesses of hull—we might manage one, with the tools in SpecMat Research, but not two."

"What's our communications situation?"

"We can reach Admiral Livadhi on the headsets; so far I've picked up nothing from the rest of the ship. That's what I'd expect with the wings closed off; we'd need higher power."

"If we can't go inside, how about outside?" asked Captain Seska.

"Same problem, getting through the hull."

"Over on T-3 and T-4, there are airlocks on every deck," Seveche said. He had projected a map of T-1 on the bulkhead and was going through it deck by deck. "This one certainly isn't over-provided with airlocks. There's one out at the end of the Special Materials Fabrication Unit, of course, but—"

"T-1 was designed to be secure from casual interference," said Dossignal.

"So we have to go all the way through SpecMatFab and hope no one flips the switch. Right. When I design a DSR, it's going to have some add-ons."

"This one has add-ons; that's part of the problem." Dossignal looked around at his group. "We'd better get out there, then. I think we can assume that all the intruders are somewhere else, probably in the core section. Come on—" He strode off, startling them with his haste. Esmay caught a look between Captain Seska and his exec which suggested they weren't any happier than she was with the admiral's assumption that they needn't worry about the intruders. "Luckily it's on this deck," Dossignal said. Esmay wished he'd slow down and let some of his escort get ahead of him.

"Admiral—" Seveche said after a few meters. "Sir—let us catch up—"

Dossignal slowed and turned. "Mari, there's—" He gasped, and staggered. Esmay realized she'd gone for the deck just as her body smacked into it. So had Seska, Frees, and Bowry; the others stood where they'd stopped, looking around.

"DOWN!" yelled Seska, and the rest of them went down. "Admiral?"

"Alive," grunted Dossignal. "And lucky."

Esmay looked past Dossignal, up the passage, trying to guess where the shot had come from, and what kind of weapon it was. She'd heard nothing until the impact.

"Very lucky," Seveche agreed, crawling forward.

"Not for long," said a quiet voice; the figure that stepped out was a lot closer than Esmay had anticipated, and loaded with weapons. "Drop—"

She had fired almost before she knew it; the intruder's shot ricocheted off the bulkhead as her burst took him apart from neck to hip. Someone—not that intruder—screamed.

She ignored that, made herself get up and move forward, past Admiral Dossignal, through the mess of splattered blood and tissue, to check the opening from which the intruder had come. It was a small compartment lined with shelves of office supplies, and empty now.

"—Two casualties," Seveche was saying into his headset. "Deck 8, main passage—"

"You're the one who was in the mutiny," Captain Seska said to Esmay.

"Yes, sir."

"Good reaction time. My guess is this one was cut off when the doors went down; if he'd had a partner, we'd already know it."

Esmay thought about it. "Makes sense, sir." She could see nothing, and hear nothing, but the sounds their own party made. "We could get the admiral into cover in this closet. Just in case."

By the time help arrived, they had both casualties in the closet, with Esmay and the *Wraith* exec, Commander Frees, watching for more trouble. Dossignal kept insisting that he was all right, that they should go on without him, and once others had arrived, he put it as a direct order.

"I'm not fool enough to think I should go—I'd only slow you down—but you can do nothing useful here, and over there you might save the ship. I've dictated orders for the 14th—Lieutenant Suiza, take this to whatever officer is senior when you arrive. Now go."

CHAPTER SEVENTEEN

Nothing hindered their movement until they reached the access area for the Special Materials Fabrication Unit.

"You can't do that! It's in use . . . there's ninety meters of whisker in the drum now . . ." The shift supervisor for the Special Materials Fabrication Facility was a solid, graying petty-chief, who was not intimidated by a mere four officers. "You'd have to have permission from Commander Dorse, and he wouldn't—"

"Stand aside, or there'll be ninety meters of whisker and . . . I estimate 1.7 meters of you." Seska, intent on getting back to his ship, furious with more than the Bloodhorde, was past making polite requests, although he'd started with one.

"Admiral Dossignal will kill me if you get in there and destroy an entire batch—"

"No . . . the Bloodhorde will kill you. The admiral will only break you to pivot and then give you twenty years hard time if you don't get—out—of—the—way."

"Bloodhorde? What does the Bloodhorde have to do with it?"

"Haven't you heard anything?" Esmay stepped forward, trying to project harmlessness and a pure heart.

"No, I haven't. I've been monitoring a startup whisker for the past five hours and my relief hasn't shown up and—"

Esmay lowered her voice. "Bloodhorde commandos are loose on the ship, and your relief is probably dead. The only way we can fight them is to get out of T-1 and the only way out of T-1 is through here. I suggest you let us pass, and when we're safely out, let the Bloodhorde in, if they show up. Then do a breakoff early."

"But that'd be ninety meters wasted . . ."

"Excuse me," said Frees, to one side. The man's head turned, and Esmay hit him as hard as she could with her weapon. She might have killed him; at that moment she didn't care.

They barricaded the hatch to the passage as well as they could, and climbed quickly into the EVA suits in the nearby locker. They checked each others' suits before opening the first of the lockout hatches that isolated the Special Materials Fabrication Unit from the ship's artificial gravity. Inside was a metal-grid walkway ten meters long, ending in another lockout hatch. Rails ran along either bulkhead, with rings set every half-meter. They went in, closed the hatch behind them, and punched for Airless Entry. The light ahead of them turned green, and they started down the walkway.

Esmay felt herself lifting with each step, as if she were walking in deepening water. In the last meter, her steps pushed her off the walkway completely, and her feet trailed back, lured by the weak attraction of *Koskiusko's* real mass. She grabbed for a rail, and hoped her stomach would crawl back into her midsection.

"I hate zero-G," Bowry said.

"I hate the Bloodhorde," Seska said. "Zero-G is just a nuisance."

They cycled through the second lockout hatch into a long dark tube lit by the eerie purple and green glow of the growth tank. It seemed to go on and on, narrowing to a dark point far away. Here Esmay could feel no slightest hint of attraction to any mass. Her stomach slid greasily up into her throat when she moved one way, and back down her spine when she turned the other way. She tried to concentrate on her surroundings. Along one side was a narrow catwalk with a rail above it.

"Remind me again what happens if we disturb the growing whiskers," Seska said.

"They shatter and impale us with the shards," Bowry said.

"So we don't disturb them," Seska said. "Minimal vibration, minimal temperature variance—we slide on the

rail. Not thrashing around, not trying to look. Just relaxed
. . . like this." Esmay watched as he made a circle of his
suit glove loosely around the rail, and pushed off from
the lockout hatch. He slid away . . . and away . . . and
vanished into the darkness. Esmay noticed that he'd
pushed off precisely in the axis of motion he wanted; his
legs simply trailed behind him.

"I hope there's a bracket on the end of this thing," Frees
said, and did the same thing.

"Lieutenant, it's my turn to be rear guard," Bowry said.
Esmay wrapped her glove around the rail, loosened it in
what she hoped was the right amount, then kicked off.
It was a strange feeling. She was drawn along effortlessly,
as if the rail itself were moving, and she could see nothing
but the faint reflection of the greenish purple glow on
the bulkhead, a long vague blur of not-quite-color.

When she slowed, she didn't at first realize it. Then
the blur steadied . . . she thought it was motionless. Now
what? If she moved around too vigorously she could bang
into the bulkhead and disturb the whiskers. She moved
very slowly, bringing up her other hand to steady herself,
then turning to look back the way she'd come. Far away
now she could see the little cluster of lights at the lockout
hatch. Nearer—something was coming, sliding along . . .
too fast. If Bowry hit her, they'd both hit the bulkhead, if
not worse. She gripped the rail and pulled herself along
hand over hand, trying to let her body trail without twisting.

She couldn't watch and move at the same time, not
without twisting. And she didn't want to go too fast; she
didn't know how much farther she had to go. She glanced
up from time to time, matching speed with Bowry . . .
and as he slowed in his turn, she also slowed. Somewhere
ahead of her were the others; she didn't want to slam into
them, either.

"Slow now," she heard. She hoped Bowry heard it too;
but she didn't look, just put out her arm to brake against
her movement. Her legs slewed sideways, but she was able
to stiffen her torso and keep them off the bulkhead.

When she turned to look forward, she saw the narrowing rounded end of the fabrication unit, and the big round lock that allowed completed jobs to be taken out. To one side was a smaller personnel lock. Why did they even have locks at this end, when the point of SpecMatFab was its hard vacuum and zero-G? She thought of the answer almost as soon as the question. Of course they didn't want all the debris in space getting into the unit.

The personnel lock was manual, a simple hatch control that required only strength to turn. Then they were outside, clinging to the grabons and loops that Esmay thought were misnamed as "safety" features. Beside it were a row of communications and oxygen jacks.

"Top up your tanks," Seska said. Esmay had almost forgotten that standard procedure. She glanced at her readouts; it hardly seemed reasonable to spend the time now for just a few percents. But the others were all plugged in; she shrugged mentally as she pushed her own auxiliary tube into place. Her suit pinged a signal when tank pressure reached its maximum, and she pulled the connection free.

Seska clipped his safety line to the first loop and started pulling himself along, up the rounded end of the fabrication unit alongside the arching supports for the whisker transport system. Esmay followed Frees again, with Bowry behind her, stopping to unclip and reclip her line every time it ran out. When they got to the upper surface— upper as defined by the whisker track—Seska paused.

From here, the size of Koskiusko surprised Esmay all over again. The fabrication unit alone was larger than most warships, coated like them with matte black, and studded with the shiny knobs of the shield generators. Beyond it rose the angular outer face of T-1, black against the starfield, with the faint gleam of the transport track rising over its edge.

"Check," Seska said.

"Two."

"Three."

"Four."

Esmay shivered. Only four of them, out here alone on a ship so big she couldn't see most of it. . . .

"We'll take the transport line," Seska said. "It'll save us time." Nobody mentioned how much air was left; no one had to.

Esmay could see on her own suit gauges that they had spent twenty minutes cycling through locks, traversing the long tunnel of the fabrication unit, climbing up this far. And now they had to go back the same distance they'd come, cross the entire ship, find a way down to one of the locks opening into T-3's repair bay. Inside, walking along the decks, even running up and down ladders, they could have done it within the limits of a suit tank. Out here? It didn't matter—they had to. Seska clipped his line onto one of the rails of the transport line and pushed off. They followed.

Esmay had wondered how far beyond the ship's surface artificial gravity projected. As they came over the edge of T-1, with the dome of the bridge ahead of them, she could feel nothing . . . but when she looked, her legs had drifted toward its surface.

The transport track led directly over the domed core of *Koskiusko*, and Esmay thought that if she had not been both rushed and frightened, she would have enjoyed the view. The five blunt-ended wings splayed out around them, the dome itself studded with shield generator points and an array of retractable masts for communications and remote sensing. She looked for, but could not see, any other ship shapes against the stars. The escorts were out there somewhere . . . but too far to occlude a noticeable patch of the starfield.

It was easy to lose track of time in that long traverse of darkness. The glowing numerals inside her helmet flicked through the tenths of seconds, then seconds, then minutes. She did not look at her oxygen gauge; if it went too low, too fast, there would be no helpful bomb disposal team to hook up a new one for her.

"Trouble." That was Seska; Esmay looked his way. Beyond him, the starfield shifted suddenly. Her mind froze up, but even as Seska said, "They're maneuvering," she had figured it out. Someone had decided to rotate the ship . . . and that someone could not be the captain.

But it could very well be the Bloodhorde commandos, in control of the bridge.

She told herself not to panic. She told herself that despite the seeming solidity and immobility of *Koskiusko*, the ship had never been really immobile: all ships moved, all the time, and she was no more likely to lose her grip and fall off when it was under drive than when it was moved only by the old laws of physics. *Kos* wasn't a warship; it couldn't develop the acceleration of the most anemic civilian cargo vessel on insystem drive.

Bowry's voice, elaborately casual, broke into her thoughts. "Lieutenant—I don't suppose you know whether the FTL drive is irretrievably broken?"

The FTL drive. At once she knew what the Bloodhorde was going to do, and kicked herself mentally for not seeing it before. Of course they were going to take their prize away from possible rescue before trying to open it, like a jay with a sweetnut. "No, sir," she said to Bowry. "Drives and Maneuver seemed to think it was most likely sabotage, but the sequenced jumps out could have knocked something loose."

"Those escorts ought to be doing something useful," Seska said. "Like blowing us away, when they see us moving under power."

Esmay had forgotten about the escorts, too. Her mouth went dry. Here she was, clinging to the outside of a spaceship under power, which was likely to come under fire . . . her EVA suit felt about as protective as facial tissue.

"Unless our crew's doing it, and they're talking to them." Bowry didn't sound really hopeful. "I suppose they could be moving away from the jump point and closer to the escorts."

"No . . ." That was Frees. "Looks to me like we're heading for it, but on a different vector . . . without the nav computer, I can't be sure, but—didn't this jump point have four outbound vectors?"

"Yes," Seska said. "I can't judge the approach, but you're probably right, Lin. We're less than a half hour from jump, I'd guess, and a lot more than a half hour from any place we can get into the ship. This should be interesting . . . pity we have no way to record the experience of the first people to die going through unprotected jump."

"The commandos survived," Esmay said, not knowing she was going to say it. Silence followed; she assumed the others were watching the wheeling starfield that proved *Kos* was moving under power.

"They were in *Wraith*," Seska said.

"But there was a hull breach and forward shield failure. There's nothing wrong with *Kos*'s FTL shields." She didn't know anything about shield technology, except that all FTL-capable ships had FTL shields. "If we get off this thing and down onto the hull . . ."

"Good idea, Suiza."

It took almost the entire half hour to clamber down, carefully clipping and unclipping and reclipping safety lines, from the high smooth arch of the materials transport track to the hull. Here, for the first time, Esmay could feel through her bootsoles a faint lateral tug, another proof that *Kos* was moving on her own, arguing with the inertia of her former path.

They were perhaps two-thirds of the way across the bridge dome from the Special Materials Fabrication Unit, its bulge hiding from them T-1 and all but the tip of SpecMat. Suddenly, light behind them, a flare that spread into a glow overhead. Esmay ducked instinctively, and looked up. The materials transport track flared into blinding vapor at its highest point, and shed flaming pieces that streamed along a track revealing their progress.

"Let's see," Seska said. "Now we're on the outside of a ship headed for jump *and* someone's shooting at us. I wonder where the adventure cube camera crew is?"

"On the other escort, of course," Frees said. "That's why they're not shooting at us yet."

"I would wonder what else could go wrong, but I don't want to give the universe ideas," Bowry said.

Esmay grinned. She suddenly realized one other thing she'd been missing . . . humor that felt right to her.

"If they're at standard distance, they can't get mass weapons to us before we go through jump," Seska said. "And that's only an escort, isn't it? Two more LOS shots ought to wipe them out for recharge, and then we'll be gone."

"Assuming the other one doesn't fry us," Bowry said. Light flared again, and this time the haze thickened. The rest of the transport track peeled away. "Good tracking, but they'll burn out their power supply if they don't let it go." Abrupt darkness; Esmay blinked, and the stars showed again.

"If the other one wanted to, they'd have done it already. What I heard in the first conference was that one of the escorts was waffling and probably would jump out pretending to go for help."

"Desertion . . ." mused Frees.

"Butt-covering," Bowry said. "How I hate the prudent ones."

"Doing all right, Lieutenant?" Seska asked, not as if he were worried, just checking.

"Fine, sir," Esmay said. "Just trying to remember if there's an airlock access around here somewhere." Because even if they could survive jump on the outside of the ship, they'd run out of air before they finished . . . even a short jump lasted days longer than the air supply in an EVA suit.

"That's an idea," Seska said. "Get back in and go for 'em?"

"No, sir . . . not just the four of us, with only four light weapons. I was thinking, just stay in the airlock, with the outer hatch cracked so no one can get into it from inside, until we drop out of jump. Then go on."

"Might work," Seska said. "We can use suit—"

Koskiusko bulled its way into the jump transition with an uncanny slithering lurch and a vibration that ground its way through Esmay's boots into her sinuses. The stars were gone. She could see nothing beyond the readouts in her helmet and they looked very strange indeed. Her com was silent, as dark a silence as the visible dark around her. Under her, the vibration went on and on, unhealthy for the ship, for the connection of wing to core, for the stability of the drives themselves. If the drives failed, if they dropped out of FTL at some unmapped point . . .

She clung to her handholds, and tried to talk herself out of the panic she felt. Of course it was dark; they'd outrun the light. If her readouts looked strange, she could still see them. Oxygen, for instance, gave her two hours more . . . but as she watched none of the values clicked over. The time-in-suit display was frozen in place, unmoving.

She had never been that good in theory, and she knew little about FTL flight, except that there was no way to define where and when ships were when they vanished from one jump point and reappeared (later, if there had been such a thing as absolute time, which there wasn't). FTL flight wasn't instantaneous, like ansible transmission; the onboard reckoning might be anywhere from hours to days to—for the longest flight ever recorded—a quarter-standard year. Onboard, inside the hull and the FTL shielding, the clocks worked. Here . . . she forced a breath, which was not reassuring. She was breathing; she could feel the warm movement of her expiration on her cheeks. But the suit timekeeper wasn't keeping time, which meant it wasn't logging the oxygen she breathed, which meant she could run out without even knowing it.

And was it better to know when your oxygen was out? She shied away from that to a consideration of the suit comm failure. Lights and comm worked fine inside ships in FTL flight . . . why not here, if they were inside the shields?

If they weren't inside the shields . . .

A low moan came through the suit earphones, dragging on and on like a lost cow on a spring night. Esmay couldn't figure out what it was, until it ended in a long hiss. Her mind put the sounds together like pieces of a puzzle: it could have been a word, slowed down. She struggled, trying to imagine what word it could have been, but a piercing jitter followed. She nudged the suit controls, damping the sound—at least that worked. But if the suit coms didn't work, they could all get lost . . .

Something bumped the back of her helmet; she turned cautiously. It had to be one of the others. It bumped again. Now she could hear someone's voice—Seska's—as well as a faint gritty noise where their helmets rubbed together.

"Radios don't work. Have to touch heads. Hook in." He tapped her arm, and she remembered her safety line. Of course.

Esmay switched on her helmet light, and watched in amazement as the light reached slowly—*slowly*—down like the extrusion of a semisolid adhesive from its tube. When it reached the hull, the edges of the shape it made rippled uneasily, the edges a moire pattern of odd colors. Unfortunately, it illuminated no helpful markers, nothing to suggest which way an airlock might be.

"—Suiza?"

If the light moved slowly, so might comm, the radio waves distorted by whatever the FTL drive did to space and time. Esmay had a sense of waking up from some kindred slowness, as if part of her body were keyed to the velocity of light itself, and lagged far behind them.

"Here," she said to Seska. She dipped her head; the bar of light from her helmet bent slowly, undulating with the movement. She handed the end of her line to the gloved hand that appeared in the light.

"—know someone who would take one look at that and spend the next month in a trance of math, trying to explain it." That was another voice, fainter, and she worked out that it must be transmitted helmet to helmet, from the other side of Seska. "Frees linked. Bowry linked."

"—airlock? Clock's not working." Of course they had figured out the implications of that for themselves. Where was the nearest airlock? She stared into the darkness, trying to picture this part of the ship, to build up the model from her first days aboard when she studied *Kos*. There was an airlock for the emergency evacuation of bridge crew at the base of the dome, across from T-1, which meant on their present path and perhaps a quarter hour's careful traverse. In the dark she was not sure what their former path had been, but the leakage of the gravity unit helped her find downslope.

"Follow me," she said, and pointed her helmet downslope. The light beam bent, kinked like water from a moving hose, and rippled off in the approximate direction. Esmay started after it, uneasily aware that she could catch up with her own light source. Just like the idiot captains they taught about in the Academy, who had microjumped their ships out in front of their own beam weapons, and fried themselves. She glanced sideways without moving her head, and saw other streams of light like her own but slightly different in color . . . felt a touch on her back.

"—Follow you," Seska said. "Stay in direct contact."

She felt her way cautiously from one grabbable protuberance to another. It was like climbing boulders in the dark, which she'd done only that one time because it was such a stupid way to get hurt, hanging out over a dark place feeling for nubs and not knowing how far down. . . .

Here *down* was a meaningless concept, and she had no idea what would happen if she lost contact with the hull. There was no sensation of external pressure, as there would be from speed in an atmosphere, with wind battering. No, but from deep inside came another pressure, as one body cavity after another insisted that things were wrong, were bad, and shouldn't be moving this way. The worst of the vibration had evened out, it should have been better. Instead, she felt growing pressure in her skull; she could feel the roots of her teeth tickling her sinuses; her eyes wanted to pop out to escape the swelling.

She paused as she felt a tug on the line connecting her to the others. A helmet tapped hers, then steadied.

"—think maybe we're not inside the FTL shielding," Frees said. "Just the collision shields."

Of course. Her memory unreeled the correct reference this time, showing the FTL shield generators affecting a network of spacers set just under the hull covering. Of course the outer hull could not be shielded from FTL influences—it had to travel there.

It was hard not to overrun her light, but she finally figured out just how to position her head and move, so that she could see possible handholds and clip points coming up just out of reach. She passed a communications array, and remembered that it was only a few meters from the airlock entrance. But which way? And exactly how many? She paused there, wrapped her line around the base of the array (and why hadn't it snapped off when they went through the jump point?)

"It's nearby," she told the others when they'd caught up and touched helmets, for all the world like cows touching noses. "Wait—I'm going to look."

A pause. "—Shine in different directions. Might help." It would. She watched as the two beams she could see looped out on either side of hers. She gave herself five or six meters of line, and scooted out to the end of it, then began circling.

The airlock, when she found it, had a viewport beside the control panel. She clipped in to the bar meant for that purpose, peeked through, and saw only more dark. She didn't want to try turning on the interior lights—why announce to the Bloodhorde commandos where they were?

She tugged a signal on her line, and wrestled with the control panel as she waited for them to catch up. She had trouble making her light stay on the controls while she tried to operate them. The safety panel slid at last, and she looked at the directions. It had been designed for emergency exit, not entrance, so the entrance instructions were full of cautions and sequences intended to keep some idiot from blowing the pressure in neighboring compartments.

She punched the sequence that should work. Nothing happened. She looked at the instructions again. First lock the inner hatch, the button marked INNER HATCH, then the CLOSE switch. Then check the pressurization, TEST PRESSURE. She went that far then read and completed the rest of the sequence. But the lights did not turn green, and the airlock did not open.

"—Have a manual override?" Seska asked. She had not even noticed his approach, or the touch of the helmet.

She looked, and saw nothing she recognized. "Didn't find one—I tried the auto sequence twice." She moved aside.

Frees found the override, beneath a separate cover panel, with its own instructions. It was mechanical, requiring a hard shove clockwise, which freed a set of dials that had to be rotated into the number sequence printed on the inside of the cover. Seska and Frees struggled with the lever. She could imagine what they were saying. Fighting with the lever would use oxygen fast.

Esmay stared at the instructions for the automatic sequence, wondering why it wasn't working. Lock inner hatch, test pressurization, enter number of personnel coming in, key in opening sequence for outer lock. She'd done that. She went on reading, past the warnings against unauthorized use, down to the fine print, hoping to find something she'd missed that would get it open.

In that fine print, down at the bottom, the final word was *no*: NOTE: EXTERNAL AIRLOCKS CANNOT BE USED DURING FTL FLIGHT. In even finer print: *This constraint poses no risk to personnel as personnel are not engaged in EVA activities during FTL flight.*

She leaned over and put her helmet against Seska's. "Some fool must have painted this thing shut," he was saying.

"No," Esmay said. "It won't work in FTL flight. It says that at the bottom." The others stopped struggling.

"So it does," Frees said, leaning into her helmet. "On this panel too. Says we don't need it because of course we aren't out here in FTL. Silly us, being impossible."

"Wish they were right," Bowry said. "All right, Suiza—now what?"

Esmay opened her mouth to protest that—they outranked her; they were supposed to make the decisions—and shut it again, thinking. The oxygen running out, at a rate they could not determine. Time passing . . . somewhere, at least inside the ship, time was passing. Could they make it to their original goal before the oxygen ran out? Could they get in if they did? If all the airlocks were inoperable in FTL flight, they could at least use the air outlets in the repair bays . . . if those worked.

Then it occurred to her that maybe this airlock had an external oxygen feed too . . . some airlocks did, for the use of personnel stacked up waiting to use the lock. She turned back to the control panel and looked. There: traditional green nipple fitting, though only one at this lock. Would it work or was it too automatically shut off because no one would use it during FTL flight?

"Oxygen outlet," she said, and tapped Bowry, next to her, on the shoulder. He looked, nodded, and turned. She found the recharge hose on the back of his suit, and unclipped it for him.

The oxygen flowlight came on when he plugged in, so at least the ship's system thought it was supplying oxygen.

"Gauge still stuck," Bowry said. Which was going to make it hard, if not impossible to figure out when the suit tanks were recharged. "Counting pulse," he said then. "Don't interrupt."

Esmay had no faith that her own pulse was anything like normal, nor did she know how long it would take to replace an unknown consumption, even if she could use her pulse to determine duration. They crouched what seemed like a long time in silence, until Bowry said, "There. Should do it." He unplugged from the access, and said, "Your turn. If you know your heart rate, give it three minutes. Otherwise I can count for you."

"Others first," Esmay said. "They were wrestling with that lever."

"Don't be too noble, Lieutenant; we might think you were bucking for promotion." Seska moved over and plugged in, then Frees, and finally Esmay.

"Why three minutes?" Frees asked, while Esmay was still hooked up.

"Because—if I can just get it out—I've got a test that doesn't depend on the suit's internal clock. We'll need more, but I figured three minutes would give us a margin of fifteen, at least. My suit stopped registering at 1 hour, 58.3 minutes. Is that in the range for the rest of you?"

It was, and just as Esmay had counted not her pulse but seconds, Bowry said "Aha!" in a pleased voice.

"It works?"

"I think so. It would help if we could rig some way of getting us all hooked up at once, though, because calculating the differentials for the waiting periods is a bit tricky."

"Give us an estimate; it'd take too long and we don't have tools—"

"All right. Suiza, you're still hooked up—you'll need the longest time on, then it goes down. I'll count it off for you."

Esmay wondered what kind of gauge Bowry thought he'd worked out, and how long it was going to be, but she didn't want to interrupt his count. She felt vaguely silly, hanging there in the dark and silence, waiting to be told it was time to unhook herself from the oxygen supply, but tried to tell herself it was better than being dead. Finally—she could not guess how long it had been—Bowry said, "Time's up. Next?"

When they had all tanked up by Bowry's count, which Esmay could only hope bore some relation to reality, they still had to decide what to do next.

Seska took the lead. "Suiza—do you know where all the airlocks are?"

"I studied it for Major Pitak's exam when I first came aboard, but I don't really know . . . there are some I do remember. On each deck, between T-3 and T-4, for instance. Once we're on T-3, there are airlocks both inside the repair bay, and opening on the outer face toward T-4."

"We could just stay here," Frees said. "We know where *this* oxygen is."

"If we knew how long the jump transit was . . . if it's anything more than a day or so, we've got other suit limitations."

"I don't suppose you know a handy external source of snacks, water, and powerpacks?"

"And toilets?"

Esmay surprised herself with a snort of laughter. "Sorry," she said. "I believe all those substances are restricted to the interior of the ship during FTL flight."

"Then we'd better head toward the next oxygen access, and hope that we find a way inside before . . . we have to."

Navigation was going to be their worst problem. Although *Kos*'s hull was studded with more protuberances than Esmay had expected, it was still mostly matte black and unmarked. Creeping, feeling her way, across that great black expanse, she felt like a deep-sea creature, one of those her aunt had shown her pictures of. Some of those, she recalled, clustered around deep-ocean vents that provided warmth and nutrients. How did they find their way? Chemotaxis . . . however that worked. She couldn't figure out an equivalent for it on the hull of a ship in hyperspace, so just kept moving.

An abrupt change in the topography she could see signaled the dropoff, as it were, into the gulf between T-3 and T-4. Esmay struggled to think which direction to move next. Down toward the lower decks in the crease between T-3 and the core? Along the top of T-3? She didn't even know if the great clamshell gantry supports were closed around *Wraith*, or if they'd gone into jump with the repair bay open to the dark.

As if in answer to her question, light reappeared in the outer dark. At least, she supposed it was light, because her eyes reacted to it, and her brain, trying to make what she saw into the shapes she expected. It looked strange, and more like pale smoke blowing than light, thick streams fraying to looser strands as she watched, but it gave an impression of some angular bulk just off to her left, with towering plumes above. Far away, a tumbled trail of light, a badly ploughed furrow, receded redly into the distance.

They had all paused, and moved into the helmet-touching huddle. "If I were a physicist," Seska said, "I just might go crazy. Most of what we've seen since jump hasn't fit most of what I learned about FTL flight. But since I'm a mere ship's captain, I say it's beautiful."

"The gantries are up," Esmay said. "Repair bay's unsealed. If it doesn't have some kind of barrier I don't know about, we should be able to get in that way."

"Why'd they turn the lights on *now*?" asked Frees.

"Just got the separate power supply hooked up," Esmay said. "The Bloodhorde's got the bridge—they probably cut power to the wings, maybe even life support, but each wing actually has its own ship support capability."

"So we just walk over and hop down one of those openings?"

"Only if we want to hit sixteen or seventeen decks down after a 1-G acceleration. We might be able to climb down the gantry legs . . ." She'd never actually been on the gantries, but she'd seen others up there. The problem was . . . would their friends shoot them first, or give them time to explain who they were?

"Our suitcoms should work in there," Seska said. "And maybe they won't see us right away."

The walk along the topside of T-3 to the first of the openings was easier than the final traverse of the dome, but fraught with its own difficulties. The unhappy light streaming away from the openings illuminated nothing in their path, and a lot was in their path. The sheared roots of the materials transport track supports . . . cables set to brace the clamshells, counterweights for the mechanisms that raised and lowered them . . . at least something was always near at hand to clip the lines to.

Personnel access in normal operations was on the center of curved openings, now clearly downlight of the arching supports themselves. They edged along the opening, and the light changed color as they moved beside it. Even those few tens of meters of uplight . . . were too blue, and a turn of the head made it red.

The personnel lift shaft was where Esmay had remembered it should be. Far, far below, its controls locked down. She could see a section of *Wraith* with her skin off and a crowd of workers in EVA gear clustered around a bundle of crystals that ran out of sight fore and aft.

There was, at least, the comfort of a niche below the

hull line, a platform large enough for twenty or more
workers to stand waiting for the personnel lift. Esmay
started down the ten mesh steps that led down to it. On
the second step, ship's gravity caught her feet; she felt
glued to the step. By the time she got to the platform,
she felt the drag of gravity through every bone, but her
head felt clearer. Inside, the light looked normal, if less
bright than usual. She glanced around. Only some of the
lights were on, spotlighting the workers. Of course—on
internal power, they'd conserve where they could.

The others came down, one by one, carefully; none
spoke until they reached the platform. Esmay glanced
around. Oxy supply lines in the bulkhead . . . a real
bulkhead, with the green triangle for oxygen access painted
on it. A water tap. Even a suit relief valve . . . suit maintenance really hated people who turned in soiled suits.
A movement in her helmet caught her attention—her suit's
internal clock was working again, and the oxygen gauge
squirted up, then dropped, then rose again slowly to
indicate that she had 35 percent of her supply left, one
hour and eighteen minutes at current usage.

She started to speak, then realized that if the suitcoms
were working properly they could be overheard. And why
wasn't she hearing the others. Different circuits?

She found the controls in her suit and switched around
the dial.

"—Gimme *one*—just *one*—now half . . ."

Back to the other channel, the one they'd used into the
jump into FTL. "They're on a different setting, at least
some of 'em are."

"Makes sense." Seska was peering over the rail at his
ship. "How do we get down?"

"Carefully," said Frees, eyeing the emergency ladder
which led down to the first horizontal gangway on this
side of the repair bay, five decks below. "If we try to get
the lift up, they'll know we're here."

"Better report now," Esmay said. "If we hail them on
their own frequency, it might be someone I know. They
can get Major Pitak to identify me, anyway."

"You're right, but—in the grand tradition, it seems a bit tame to let them know. Adventurers who've survived unprotected FTL flight ought to do something more dramatic . . . why weren't we provided with those little invisible wire things that spies and thieves are always using to lower themselves from heights?"

"Blame the props department," Esmay said, surprising herself. They all chuckled.

"Suiza, if you ever get tired of maintenance, I'd be glad to have you on my ship," Seska said. "I wondered at first, but now I can see why the admiral wanted you on the operational end of this."

Esmay's ears burned. "Thank you, sir. Now—I'll just let them know we're here." She switched channels, and found herself listening to the end of the previous set of directions.

" . . . Now back a tenth . . . just right . . . *there*."

"Lieutenant Suiza here," she said, hoping she wasn't cutting across another transmission.

"What! Who? Where are you?"

"I'm up at the top of the bay, on the personnel platform by lift one. With three other officers: Captain Seska and Lt. Commander Frees of *Wraith*, and Commander Bowry from the Schools. I have an urgent message from Admiral Dossignal for the senior officer in T-3."

CHAPTER EIGHTEEN

"What did you think you were doing hiding out up in the rafters all this time? I was told you were going over to T-1 to some kind of conference with the admiral and Commander Seveche and other important brass." Commander Jarles, head of Inventory Control, was the senior commander aboard T-3. Esmay had met him briefly, at one of the officers' socials, but she did not know him well. Now he was angry, his stocky body thrust forward in his chair, his cheeks flushed.

"I did, sir."

"And with everything else going on, you just lazed your way the long way round? You can't tell me you got past the blast doors, or that you didn't hear the allcall telling everyone in this wing to get their tails to assembly points!"

Esmay interpreted the emphasis on "important brass" to mean that Commander Jarles of Inventory Control had had his nose put out of joint because he wasn't invited to that conference. Now he was feeling very much on his dignity.

"Sir, if I may ask—how is communication with the rest of the ship, especially T-1?"

"We've got a link to T-4, thanks to the access tunnel, but no one else. Why?"

"Then you might not be aware that the captain was gassed and in critical condition; Admiral Dossignal was injured in a firefight, and that's why the admiral didn't come along. I have his orders here." Esmay fished them out of her pocket and handed them over. Jarles pursed his lips, and gave her a nod that clearly meant *Tell the rest*.

"We couldn't get past the blast doors out of T-1," she said.

"The captain gave us the override codes, but they didn't work. The admirals felt it was imperative to get Captain Seska and his exec back to *Wraith*—the reasoning's in that order cube, sir. So we got out the SpecMatFab far end, and followed the transport track partway over the ship."

His eyes widened. "You crossed the whole ship?"

"Yes, sir. I don't know if the scans here picked it up, but the ship took hostile fire from beam weapons—the shields held, but the transport track was destroyed." She waited a moment for any questions, then sprang the big one. "Then it went into jump. That's why it took us so long to get back."

"You're telling me . . . you were on the outside of this ship . . . during jump insertion?"

"Yes, sir."

A long pause. "Lieutenant, you're either crazy or lucky or blessed by some combination of deities I never heard of. The officers with you confirm this story?"

"Yes, sir."

"All right. I presume you need a little time to . . . eat . . . or something. We've got a scratch mess set up; my clerk'll direct you. Give me a time to read these orders, then I'll want a complete report, down to each breath you took, and from the others as well. You can have an hour."

Pitak was waiting for her outside. "*Where* have you been?"

Esmay was too tired to smooth it out for her. "Crossing the outside of the ship during the fighting, the jump, and FTL flight. Thanks, by the way, to whoever turned on the repair bay lights. We were having problems up until then."

Pitak's brows went up. "Well. Somehow I suspect I'm losing you permanently for Hull and Architecture. I'll take you down for what passes for food. Where's the admiral?"

"In T-1, as far as I know—he was hurt, but alive. The captain was gassed, and maybe dying, when we left."

"And here we are, hijacked like any fatbellied trader, going someplace we don't know and into trouble we can only imagine. Much good our escorts did us!"

Esmay found a toilet, then food . . . basic mush, but it was hot and the temporary cook had spiced it with something that gave it an actual flavor. She had expected to feel better after eating, but the warmth in her belly made her sleepy instead; she felt she could sleep standing up, and maybe even walking. It made no sense . . . she woke with her cheek on the table. Major Pitak was a few feet away, talking on the com. Esmay struggled to get her head up as Pitak came back.

"You need sleep," she said. "I talked to Commander Jarles, and he said what with the jump and all he'll need longer to assess the admiral's orders. You're going down for a half-shift at least."

Esmay would have argued, but when she pushed herself up, her head swam. Pitak found her an empty space in a nearby corridor, in a row of other sleeping forms, and before she knew it Esmay was asleep on the hard deck. No dreams troubled that sleep, and she woke clearheaded.

She made her way around the other sleepers, found a working toilet and shower—it was hard to believe that with all the emergencies they still had enough extra water to use for showering, but she needed it. Then she went back to Commander Jarles's office, where she found Commander Bowry dictating his own report of their experiences.

He grinned at her, but kept talking. "—Then the lights came on, which made it easier to find our way to T-3 and the overhead access . . . whatever those openings are really called . . . Anyway, once back inside the ship, we found normal gravity, and our suit instruments began working again." He turned off the recorder. "Did you fall in a heap, too? I did, and I've just talked to Seska and Frees aboard *Wraith*—they said they'd barely gotten aboard when they couldn't stay awake. Scared hell out of their crew."

"Maybe it was being outside the FTL shields," Esmay said.

"Maybe. Maybe it was having had a long and interesting day. You know, you're really good at this kind of stuff—how'd you get stuck in a DSR, if you don't mind my asking?"

"That mutiny, probably. I'd guess they didn't want any of those involved where they'd get into similar trouble, and since I ended up commanding, they sent me as far away as possible."

"Where you promptly found a use for your newly acquired expertise. Yah. They might as well put you back in command track; you're a lightning rod."

"I was technical track before. Scan."

"You?" He shook his head. "Your advisor messed up; you're a natural, and I don't say that lightly. Put in for transfer."

"That's what my boss here said once. Major Pitak, in Hull and Architecture."

"Believe it."

She almost did. From someone like this, a seasoned veteran who had observed her . . . maybe it was true, and maybe she was not just lucky, but good at it.

Commander Jarles came out of his inner office. "Lieutenant Suiza—glad you're here." He sounded much more cordial than the day—was it day?—before. "Hope you're rested, both of you. Captain Seska says he's staying aboard *Wraith*, but Lt. Commander Frees is coming to liaise with us on a plan to retake the *Koskiusko* and fight off any attempted boarding. Lieutenant Suiza, Admiral Dossignal seems to have a lot of faith in you."

Esmay couldn't think what to say—*Yes, sir* seemed a bit too pushy—but Bowry spoke up.

"Considering that she saved the captain's life, and later the admiral's, I'd say he had reason."

"I suppose." He looked down at the files in his hand. "He wanted you to take over all security for T-3 and T-4, and said you had helped develop a plan to trap a Bloodhorde ship. Frankly, with the admiral out of communication, I'm not comfortable putting that much responsibility on a junior officer I don't know very well. I've consulted with Major Pitak, who gives you a favorable review, but I'm not sure."

"Got a plan yet?" came a voice from the door. That was Frees, whom rest and food had restored to an almost bouncy quality. "Captain Seska sends his regards, and says he's got a guess how long we'll be in FTL flight." He waited a moment for that to sink in, then waved a data cube. "Nothing wrong with *Wraith's* nav computers, though she couldn't give us any scan data. But from where we were, there are four primary mapped routes that we know—and know the Bloodhorde knows. They're on all the standard references. Two we can pretty much dismiss; they won't go back where they attacked us, because they can figure that our ships will be out there looking for them. In the same way, they won't backjump where you came from, because they don't know if there were more Fleet ships there. But there's Caskadian, which has a direct route into Bloodhorde space at Hawkhead. And Vollander, which is offset to most routes, and a long jump to Bloodhorde space . . . but direct, and a long way from any Fleet pickets."

"Put it up on the screen," Jarles said. Frees complied, and they stared at the tangle of lines, thicker or thinner with flux values, edged with colors that told which political entities were known to use those routes.

"*Wraith's* onboard systems say we went through the first jump point some 43 hours ago. We need someone from Drives and Maneuver to give us the figures on this ship's FTL drive, and then we might know which route we're on, and when we might drop out."

"How long are they for regular travel?"

"Caskadian should be about 122 hours, maybe longer given the slow insertion and assuming the same exit. Vollander would be about 236 hours."

"Long jumps—longer than we made coming in. I'd expect them to go for the short one, with so few of them aboard."

"Now on the connecting lines—how does this ship handle series jumps?"

"It doesn't. Or rather, in theory it can, and we did coming out after you, but usually there's a pause of several hours for recalibration between jumps."

"Besides," Esmay said. "They'll want to get more of their people aboard. The intruders have been working as hard as we have—without relief, and shorthanded."

"So we've got roughly sixty hours before you think we'll come out of jump, and until then all we have to cope with are the ones aboard."

"Yes, sir."

"Captain Seska wants to know how far the repairs on *Wraith* can get by then," Frees said.

Commander Jarles shrugged. "We have no access to the main inventory stores—and we can't move anything from SpecMat while we're in FTL. I suppose Major Pitak will know about the structural repairs—" Esmay decided this was no time to tell him that nothing was going to come from SpecMat by the exterior transport system until it was rebuilt.

"Sixty hours," Bowry said. "Nobody can come in from outside while we're in FTL flight—and surely those Bloodhorde are getting tired by now. There aren't that many—if we can get back in contact with the rest of the ship, we might be able to take control back."

"And get ready for whatever's waiting when we come out of jump," Esmay said. "If they're jumping to a place where they have a battle group waiting . . . how many ships would that be?"

"With the Bloodhorde—five or six, probably."

"A two-part plan," Bowry said. "Get control of this ship, and defeat whatever's waiting for us."

"For which we need warships," Jarles said. "We can't mount weapons on *Koskiusko*."

"Who's here for Weapons?" Esmay asked. "I know Commander Wyche is in T-1."

"It can't be done," Jarles said firmly.

Esmay looked at him, then glanced at Bowry. Bowry spoke up.

"I think, Commander, to make best use of the resources of the 14th, the senior person in each department should assist in our planning."

For a moment he puffed around the neck, exactly like the frogs Esmay remembered from home. Then he relented. "All right, all right."

*   *   *

When the fourth person started to remind the group that they couldn't do what they usually did, Esmay lost patience.

"Now that we know what we *can't* do, it's time to start thinking what we *can* do. Fifty-eight hours, at this point: what can we do in fifty-eight hours? Thousands of intelligent, inventive, resourceful people, with the inventory we have available, can come up with something."

"Lieutenant—" began Jarles, but Commander Palas held up his hand.

"I agree. We don't have time for the negatives. Do any of you know what the senior officers were planning in case of a Bloodhorde assault?"

Bowry outlined it quickly. "So," he finished, "I'd think that getting a Bloodhorde ship into T-4 would still work. Is there some way to get it . . . sort of stuck, so they can't move it? I think they'd come boiling out, and if they were somehow diverted away from it, some of our people could get in—if it could be unstuck . . ."

"There's that new adhesive . . ." said someone in back. "Really strong, but depolymerizes in the presence of specific frequencies of sound. We could coat the barriers—"

"That's what we need to hear. Now we know we don't have that many troops capable of close-contact fighting— someone think of a way to immobilize Bloodhorde troops, who will be wearing EVA battlesuits."

"So gas won't work," someone muttered. "If we knew the signal characteristics of the suits . . ."

"What about gluing *them* down?"

"Then our people couldn't get to the ship—the stuff stays tacky too long."

"You'll think of something," Esmay said. "Now—about getting to the rest of the ship—"

"Once we're out of FTL, we could rig a communications cable back around to T-1 . . ."

"Once we're out of FTL, the airlocks will work. And we have lots of EVA suits; our people work in vacuum a lot."

Commander Bowry nodded. "Then to head the team

that's going to get *Wraith* as ready as possible to be put out on the drive test cradle: Major Pitak, because she's Hull and Architecture."

"I'll need to pull people from—"

"Go ahead. If there's a conflict, get back to me. Commander Palas, could you head the team that will plan the capture of a Bloodhorde ship, assuming we can get one into T-4."

"Certainly. May I ask where you'll get your crew?"

"That was my first assignment from Admiral Dossignal; I'll choose a crew from those who've served aboard warships fairly recently. Lieutenant Suiza, I'd like you for my exec, when the time comes, but in the meantime, I'd like you to work on the assignment Admiral Dossignal gave you: prepare Security here to defend these wings against the intruders. I suspect they'll try to get into T-4 to prepare it for their own ships."

"Yes, sir." Esmay wondered how she could possibly get ready for both, but having argued against negative thinking, she knew better than to say anything.

◆ ◆ ◆

Vokrais grinned happily at his pack. Bloodied, bitten, but not defeated, and they had the bridge, its surviving crew demoralized and—at least temporarily—cooperative. The ship had made its jump into FTL without falling apart. The wings were locked off, helpless. Three of them had been reduced, at least largely, to unconscious dreamers and corpses. T-3 and T-4 so far held out; he'd expected more resistance there, but it didn't matter. When they came out of jump in a few hours, the ship pack would be waiting, with enough warriors to manage them. After all, they had no real weapons over there, and they were only mechanics and technicians anyway.

His people had even gotten some rest; it didn't take the whole pack to subdue these weaklings. Three of them were sleeping now. By making the bridge crew work longer shifts, they'd kept them tired enough that there'd been no sign of rebellion. He stretched, easing his shoulders. They had done everything they'd set out to do, done it better than predictions; their commander had not believed they'd be able to get the ship through jump. He was waiting for a message; he'd be delighted to get the whole prize.

Still, he hated leaving any part of the job undone. He had missed out on four years of raiding; the pack had fewer shipscars than any other of their seniority. They'd paid— paid dearly, in honor and opportunity—for the preparation necessary for this operation. He didn't want to share the glory with anyone. If he could offer his bloodbond the ship entire, he could raise his banner any time he chose, independent command.

He glanced around. Hoch looked bored; he had tormented the Serrano cub until all the fun was out of it. Three of his remaining pack would be enough to hold the bridge against the unarmed, spineless sheep that now sat the controls.

Excitement roiled in his gut again. "Let's do it," he said in his own tongue. His pack looked up, eager. Who should stay behind? As he described what they were going to do, he looked at their faces, looking for the slightest hint of weakness, exhaustion, or even worse, contentment.

First they would unlock the barriers to T-4 . . . with the crippled *Wraith* in T-3, most of the personnel would be in T-3. Could they repair *Wraith* in time? He doubted it, but even if they did it could not outfight a whole ship pack. Vokrais considered which deck they should use. According to the ship maps, Deck 17 contained hydroponics and even a few small gardens tucked among the gantry supports. Unlikely anyone would be watching for them up there, and they'd have a good view of the entire repair bay. They could work their way down, using their weapons and gas grenades to subdue anyone in their way, and drive them to a holding area at the base . . . and they had no way out. Not if he opened only the Deck 17 hatch . . . they'd be sure to close it behind them.

Corporal Jakara Ginese kept her eyes on her screens, obedient and to all appearances as scared as all the rest.

She had not indulged in the sidelong glances that got Sergeant Blanders a beating; she had not struggled when one of the Bloodhorde fondled her and told his friends what he planned to do with her later. Above all, she had not revealed, by the slightest change of expression, that she understood everything they said in their own language. While she could do nothing, she did nothing.

But now . . . she thought it over, while appearing to cower away from the leader's rough bloodstained hands. "You will be good, won't you?" he asked. "You wouldn't think of giving any of us trouble . . ." She gave a little moan, and trembled, and told herself that it would be over soon, one way or the other.

She was sitting the wrong board, though the Bloodhorde hadn't figured that out. They'd come in screaming and shooting, and by the time they'd done, what with bodies all over the floor and the noise everyone was making . . . they hadn't noticed her changing nametags with a dead woman. At that point, she wasn't sure why she'd done it. Some instinct had urged her, and when they left the communications board empty, and she moved to environmental, where Corporal Ascoff usually sat, she began to think what she could do. None of her shipmates had commented, though she'd gotten some looks . . . but after what happened to Sergeant Blanders they didn't look anywhere but at their own work.

The environmental systems board cross-linked to ship security, another board the Bloodhorde had left empty after they changed the override codes. Possibly they didn't know that; she wouldn't have known it, sitting comm as she usually did, but she and Alis Ascoff had been working the same bridge shift long enough to share details of their work. Either Security or Environmental might have reason to close off the wings from the core, or take control of life support.

If they were watching too closely—as they had with ten of them always alert, always stalking around behind people—she could do nothing. But if they left only three . . . at some point, she would not be observed for a moment, and . . . what would be the best thing to do? If she opened all the wings, would the sleepygas simply spread to the core and put everyone there to sleep?

The captain had gone to T-1 to confer with the admirals. She knew that; she'd seen the captain on the bridge shortly before the Bloodhorde commandos burst in and took over. So if the captain was still alive, he was in T-1, and maybe the admirals too. If he wasn't gassed. If he wasn't dead.

If you can't make up your mind, her mother always said, do something anyway. Luckily, the core environmental system needed frequent adjustment when it was cut off from the wings. She had explained this, earnestly, when she first needed to touch the board. The Bloodhorde had leaned over, far too close for comfort, and stared at the display a long time before giving her permission to touch it. After the tenth or eleventh change, they'd paid less attention, only asking now and then when the display showed a yellow band instead of green just how long she proposed to let it go?

The three left behind would be nervous. She listened as the others left, and did not turn around. Someone else did; she heard the blow and the angry command to get back to work. They would be watching . . . but would they understand? A yellow flicker on her board, just as before. The core, unlike the wings, did not have a large hydroponic/garden area for oxygen production and carbon dioxide uptake; oxygen was supplied from electrolysis of the water in the Deck 1 pool, and she had to keep the hydrogen collectors from overfilling. As well, she needed to put new CO_2 scrubbers online. She started to enter these commands, and as she expected one of the three came up behind her.

"What now?"

"The hydrogen, sir." She pointed. "It needs a new collector unit. And I need to put another ten CO_2 packs online."

"No tricks, understand?" The muzzle of his weapon stroked her cheek. She shuddered, nodded, and her fingers trembled as she entered the values. She heard him walk away.

The question now was, how long did she have, and how could she do the most the quickest? She would open the T-1 access, she'd decided, but not T-5, because she knew T-5 had been gassed. If she had time, she'd reset the override codes for all the wings, so that the captain or any of ship's security who were still alive and awake could use them.

"Sir!"

Admiral Livadhi looked up; one of the security guards stood panting in the doorway. "Yes?"

"Sir, the hatches are open . . . we're not cut off from the core . . ."

"All the hatches? All decks?"

"Yes, sir—at least, that's what the system says."

Livadhi looked over at Dossignal, who was hunched awkwardly in his chair. "I don't think this is *their* doing."

"No—I'd say go for the bridge, with everything we have." They had planned an assault on the bridge, but had not been able to breach the barrier.

"You can handle this end?"

"I can hardly run yours," Dossignal said, grimacing. "Having been stupid enough to get shot." Then he grinned. "Confusion to our enemies," he said.

"I intend a good deal worse than confusion," Livadhi said, and spoke into his headset. "Bridge team: go ahead."

"You stupid—!" The snarl came just before the blow that knocked her to the deck. Corporal Ginese would have been furious with herself for not remembering that the barrier status lights showed clearly on the board, if she'd been able to think. A savage kick in the ribs curled her around the pain. She said nothing. She thought, with all the intensity of her being, *Please, please, please . . . let it work. Let someone be alive there, awake. . . .*

Now two of them were on her; she heard bones snap as one of them kicked savagely at her arms, her ribs. It

hurt more than she'd expected . . . and more noise . . .
she couldn't think why it should be so noisy, all that clatter
and roar and shouting. If they were going to make that
much noise, why not just shoot her?

She hardly noticed the blows had ceased . . . then it
was quiet again. Someone wept in the distance. Nearer,
footsteps . . . she wanted to flinch away, but couldn't move.

"I think . . . she's alive," someone said.

Not one of them. Not someone from the bridge. She
opened the eye that would open, and saw what she had
hoped to see: shipmates, armed, and just beyond them,
a Bloodhorde corpse. She smiled.

✧   ✧   ✧

"They're trying to get through the barrier up on Deck
17," the sergeant minor said. "They've got the core-side
barrier open, but the interlock we put on the wingside
barrier's holding."

"Are they really committed?"

"It sounds like it."

"Then I think it's time for Brother Ass and the Cactus
Patch," Esmay said.

"What?"

"Folk tale from my home planet, slightly revised. As long
as we provide enough resistance, they'll be sure we didn't
want them there. Only we *do* want them there, because
it's our trap."

"How long do we make 'em wait?"

"Long enough to—" A shout from down the passage.
"Suiza!"

"Yes?"

"Our people have the bridge! The barriers are operable
on the old override codes!"

Esmay swung back to her comunit. "Now—let them in
now." If they knew they'd lost the bridge, they might not
come into the trap. "Be sure to lock the gate behind
them, once they're onto another deck." By all combat
logic, they should be hoping to clear T-4 from the top
down . . . if they found the top deck empty, they should
go looking for resistance.

The scan techs had installed additional surveillance near the hatch and in the passages beyond. Esmay watched as the hatch slid aside . . . the Bloodhorde commandos still wore their Fleet uniforms, now bloodstained and filthy, under light armor they'd stolen from the ship security. Helmets and respirators . . . they couldn't be gassed, but the respirators were noisy enough to affect their hearing. The helmets were supposed to compensate with boosted sensitivity . . . but that had its shortcomings. They each carried several weapons, the light arms intended to suppress shipboard violence.

"They're outnumbered, but we're still outgunned," said the petty-chief looking over her shoulder.

"Guns aren't the ultimate weapon," Esmay said. Would they choose the well-lit passage ahead, or the dim one to the left, among the garden rows? They'd had only a few concussion shells, taken from *Wraith*'s damaged starboard battery, and she hadn't been able to seed every possible route.

As she'd hoped, they headed down the dimmer passage. They moved as she remembered her father's troops moving, cautious but swift. It was on the basis of that trained advance that she'd planted the shells where she had . . . and when they passed the marked point, the shells burst around them. Esmay had the sound turned down . . . but they hadn't. They were flat on the deck, firing at nothing, and unable to hear anything but the racket they made and their own ringing ears . . . she was sure of that.

The top level of T-4 was too big for them to check thoroughly; she had counted on that, and on their reaction to resistance. From one position to another, they followed what seemed to be a retreating force of slightly lesser strength. They would be trying to pick up its communications through their helmets . . . surely they would change channels until they found it. And what they heard would sound authentic . . . Esmay had discovered that the 14th had its own Drama Club, its members eager to create and record a script full of dramatic conflict. It had multiple branches, just in case the enemy didn't follow the main plotline, and one of the communications techs cued the different segments while watching the vidscan to see what the intruders were really doing.

She keyed to listen herself for a moment.

"Hold 'em at Deck 15—we can hold 'em if they don't come down that inboard ladder—"

"Corporal Grandall, cut off that ladder—"

"—Here's the ammo, sir, but we're running—"

Sure enough, on the vidscan, the Bloodhorde had turned back, looking for, and finding, the inboard ladder. Poppers wired into sensors blew off as they started down. Smoke swirled . . . Fleet uniforms wrapped around bundles of insulation moved, fell, were dragged backwards.

"Whiteout! Whiteout! They're on the ladder—"

"HOLD them—"

"We're TRYING—NO! They got Pete!"

"—More gas masks! They're using more . . ."

It would have been fun to watch, like being behind the scenes when an adventure cube was being taped, except that more than half the sites needed someone live, on the scene, to produce a realistic effect. The enemy didn't know which targets were live, but Esmay did. She had argued at first for a less risky approach—dousing the intruders with that adhesive, if nothing else—but the capture of an enemy warship would be easier if it thought it was coming into a ship controlled by its own people.

Ideally, they'd get to the base of the repair bay just as the ship came out of FTL flight. They'd find the lockers of EVA suits; they'd open the repair bay—it was all set up for automatic use, with new—and newly aged and scuffed—control panels and instructional labels.

Esmay switched to the secure link to the bridge: they had opened a T-3 access hatch and fed an optical link through it. She knew the captain was alive, but in critical condition, now in a regen tank in Medical, which had been purged of the sleepygas. The casualty count was rising, as search teams found more and more bodies . . . most were bodies, but a few had been wounded. Barin hadn't been found yet.

A jolt like stepping off a ledge in the dark bumped her spine on the chair. She glanced at the clock. An hour early?

"Jump point exit," said someone unnecessarily. Moments later: "Caskadian System, low-vee exit."

So they were where they'd expected to be, and in one piece. A low-vee exit meant scan would clear soon, and they'd know how much trouble they were in. Esmay wondered what jump exit would have looked like from outside and shuddered. They could not have survived the whole trip outside, she was sure.

"Prelim scan: six, repeat six Bloodhorde ships. Weapons analysis follows . . ."

Now where were the Bloodhorde intruders? She looked back at the vidscan . . . at Deck 10. Too far up; she wanted them able to contact their own ships, and for that they had to be at Deck 4.

"Release, release!" she said. The communications tech nodded, and switched to the final segment: anguish, terror, harsh breathing . . . resistance melting away in panic. Predictably, the Bloodhorde team followed, and although they came out into the repair bay control compartment with some remnant caution, they didn't hesitate long.

They had made good use of their data wands . . . one pair went straight to the control centers, and the others to the EVA lockers. The communications tech put on the post-battle tape—if they kept listening, they'd hear individuals trying to find each other, trying to decide what to do, where to take the wounded.

The two who could speak—or at least understand—the Bloodhorde dialect tuned in the output of the communications desk in the repair bay. What would they say to their ships?

The Bloodhorde ship looked nothing like the sleek black ovoids of the Fleet.

"Damn converted tramp hauler," someone muttered through the comlink. Esmay wished they'd shut up, but she agreed. Slightly larger than a Fleet escort, and perhaps a third shorter than a patrol craft, its hull had a more angular outline suggesting its origin as a civilian freight carrier.

"Part of that's bare metal," someone else said. Esmay spotted the oblong patch, glinting dully in the repair bay's spotlights. The rest was probably the same organoceramic material that most ships used, its scarred uneven coloring suggesting patches of different ages and origins. Along the flank, bright-painted symbols that must mean something to the Bloodhorde. Near the nose, rows of stylized eyes and jagged teeth. She shivered.

The ship edged in, still untethered but now in easy reach of the grapples. Someone nudged her; she followed the gesture to see tiny figures in EVA gear moving on the plates of Deck One. That would be the Bloodhorde intruders, come out to welcome their friends and let them aboard. One of them moved to the control board for the grapples on her side; another stood at the controls for the other set of grapples.

She could not see their hands on the controls, but she could see the result, the shift of the grapple heads as they moved into position, and the sharp pings in her helmet as the grapples released from the heads and then impacted the ship. The sling buffer at the inboard end of the repair bay deployed, as if released by the grapples . . . they hoped the Bloodhorde would think that. She watched the intruder at the grapple controls spin around, and imagined his surprise. But nothing more happened. He made some hand signal to another of his team, out of her sight, then turned back to the controls.

The Bloodhorde ship barely moved, drawn by the retracting grapples. Esmay boosted the magnification on her helmet scan, and watched as the intruder pushed the grapple controls to maximum. She grinned through her tension. She'd thought they would do that . . . the plan would work anyway, but this was a bonus.

The ship moved faster, as all the grapples exerted full power. They must think the sling buffer would halt it if it moved too fast . . . and it would . . . after jolting the passengers a bit.

She watched in fascination as the ship moved slowly, inexorably, past the marked safety point . . . stretching out the grapples again, swinging like a ball on an elastic line. As if in automatic response, another buffer sling deployed—and another. The enemy ship rammed into them, nose first, stretching the first to its limit—one . . . two . . . bands ruptured and flung back across the bay with an indescribable noise. The impact shook the entire bay. *Now* . . . would they notice anything? The second held, and the third, barely deformed. The enemy ship shuddered, held by the buffer slings' adhesive coating and the taut grapples behind.

"We did it," she said aloud. "We got ourselves a warship!"

CHAPTER NINETEEN

"And two problems," said the woman on scan in the bridge. "Take a look—"

The second and third Bloodhorde ships kept coming, now obviously aiming for the drives test cradles.

They should have thought of that. They'd assumed the Bloodhorde would be cautious, would test with one ship until they were sure it was safe. Not their style . . . of course they'd get in close with as many as possible, and with those small ships it was not hard to maneuver in close.

"Now what, genius?" murmured Major Pitak. Esmay stared, her mind watching possibilities that flickered past more rapidly than the turning dials of a biabek game.

"We won't be able to get *Wraith* out now," someone else said. "We should have done that first—"

Wraith, trapped in the repair bay, immobile, capable of blowing itself, but probably not the rest . . . unless its self-immolation ignited the others' weaponry. Would it? Was that good enough, the best she could hope for?

No. She wasn't playing for any outcome but victory. Her terms.

"We take them both," she said. "The ones on the test cradles. Then we get *Wraith* out . . . and the other Bloodhorde ship, if we can. It's actually better—evens the odds—"

"But we don't have crews for that many—and they're not even our ships."

After the first panic had come a surge of exhilaration; she felt as if her mind was working at double speed. "Oh, yes, we do. We have thousands of the top experts on every ship system right here—right now."

"Who?"

Esmay waved her hand, indicating both wings. "Think about it. D'you really think our people can't figure out the controls on Bloodhorde ships? They're simple. D'you think our people can't offer effective resistance to Bloodhorde troops, if we turn them loose? I think they CAN. I think they WILL."

They had to. And it was better. Even if they just got two, the odds were almost even . . .

Bowry had seen it too. "We'll have to scramble, though, to get two—no, three—crews ready to board. They'll be down in less than an hour." He grinned at her. "Well, Lieutenant, I think I'll have to find another exec—you're going to have to take one of those ships yourself."

"Me?" But of course, her mind insisted. Who else? The most terrifying thing about it was that she didn't feel as scared as she should be. "Right," she said, before he could say anything else. "Which one?"

"The T-3 cradle—because I've already got a crew assembled here. Maybe Captain Seska can free some of his crew for you."

"Yes, sir." She was already thinking who she wanted.

"Whoever gets control of a ship first takes group command," Bowry went on. Esmay hadn't thought of that, but they would need to coordinate. "My advice, if you're first, is to get that thing off the cradle—don't wait for me—and fire on the first ship you can locate."

❖   ❖   ❖

Vokrais was furious. After all they had accomplished, that pighead of a ship pack commander was going to let two more shiploads board. He knew what that would mean—they'd be claiming credit for kills he and his men had made; they'd be marking loot.

"There is no need," Vokrais said. "We have this ship at our mercy. Only the troops aboard *Deathblade* are needed. What if the Familias ships are following? If you take two more ships out of formation, how will you beat them off?"

"You assured me they could not follow, having no idea where you are." The ship pack commander sounded

entirely too complacent. When Vokrais had started this
mission, the ship pack command had been promised to
his own warclan. Now it had gone to the Antberd Comity,
on whose graves he would spit if he got the chance.
Ambitious, rich with loot they never bled for, he didn't
know why the Overband let them get away with it. And
here was another one, not even an Antberd, but a hireling
. . . he had met Cajor Bjerling at the arena once, and
hadn't liked him then.

He wanted to slug someone, and unfortunately they'd
dumped the Serrano cub for safekeeping before they
came to T-4.

"I claim this ship," he said. He wouldn't get it, but at
least the claim would be registered. "I claim the blood
shed, and the riches won, the deaths and the treasures,
for the men who won them."

"It's big enough to share the glory," Bjerling said. "And
soon enough to divide the loot when the deed is done."

"The deed is done," Vokrais argued.

"You need not fear my justice," Bjerling said. "Unless
you want to challenge my honor."

Of course. In the middle of the operation he was
supposed to challenge the commander? Even if he won,
the Overband would not be pleased with him.

"I do not challenge your honor," he said. "Only remember who opened this ship like an oyster."

"You are not likely to let me forget," Bjerling said. "The
troops in *Deathblade* will await the arrival of those from
Antberd's Axe and *Antberd's Helm* before they maneuver."

In other words, Vokrais thought sourly, he would have
no chance to show the *Deathblade* troops, whose commander he knew well, how he had conquered. The others
would overwhelm everything.

"May his wife grow spines in her fur," said Hoch quietly.

"If only it were possible," Vokrais said, enjoying the idea.

"So we have to wait around for them all to land—
assuming those incompetents can actually land on the test
cradles—and get inside? Just stand here like targets?"

"He would not be ill-pleased if any of these people did

kill us—greedy swine. We shall be extremely careful, packsecond. There is no reason, with so many eager to find loot, for us to take risks."

Hoch chuckled. "Perhaps we might even disappear?"

"Not that, I think. After all, our people are in charge on the bridge. Perhaps we should go back and be sure they know who's being so helpful." Assassination on a mission was unusual, but not unheard of, and Vokrais felt in the mood to kill someone. "Let these people find their own way in; it will be good practice for them. Not all boardings are unopposed."

✧   ✧   ✧

Esmay had just made it back to T-3 when she was called to one of the communications nodes.

"I hear we're about to be trapped in here," Seska said, sounding angry.

"Not for long," Esmay said. "We're going to take the ship behind you, and the one coming in to the T-4 test cradle. As soon as we're clear, they'll warp *Wraith* out."

"Better odds," Seska said, sounding slightly less angry. "Save me one, why don't you? I presume you'll be taking one of them yourself?"

"Yes—the one behind you; Commander Bowry's already got his crew over in T-4."

"Who's going to take the one that's docked? Or were you going to leave that one where it is?"

"Leave it—we don't have the crew."

"And I presume you have a plan to get to the test cradle and board? What if they dump their troops and take off again?"

"In that case, you're not blocked, and Bowry can take the ship of theirs that's in T-4. But what we hear through their transmissions is that they're planning to stay awhile— it's made the commando leader mad—he thinks they're stealing his glory."

"Good. And good luck, Lieutenant."

Esmay went back to the command center set up in the 14th's headquarters area.

"I've got a list of volunteers for your crew, Lieutenant,"

said Commander Jarles. "You seem to be quite popular."
She wasn't sure if this was sarcasm or honest surprise.
"They're sorted by specialty, then rank-ordered by those
with experience in ships similar to the enemy's. I told them
to wait for you in R-17."

"That's wonderful, sir." It was indeed; the only problem
was knowing how many she should take.

"We've got a link now to the other wings. One of the
instructors over in Admiral Livadhi's command has done
a tactical analysis—he suggests—"

An alarm went off.

"They're going through somewhere!" Esmay said.

"They're not even off that ship yet," said Commander
Palas. "We've been watching."

"Then it's the others—the original intruders. But why?
And where?"

"Warn the bridge," Jarles said. "That'll be where they're
going—they may not know we've taken it back. Lieutenant
Suiza, pick your crew and get in position—I think we can
ignore that tactical analysis."

Esmay took the list and looked at it on her way down
to R-17. Petty-major Simkins, Drives and Maneuver, had
operated the commercial equivalent of the Bloodhorde
hulls during the three years he'd tried making it in the
civilian world. Two others had less, but some, experience
with those ships. Scan—she hoped they'd be able to take
some of their own aboard, or tight-link to *Koskiusko*'s
bridge. No one had a lot of relevant experience, but there
was a pivot-major, Lucien Patel, that the entire Remote
Sensing unit thought was another Koutsoudas. Worth a
try, anyway. For backup in scan, she picked the one person
with recent combat experience, and another because he
had both commercial and military background. Communications, that was critical . . . that one, and that one,
and a backup. Environmental she wouldn't worry about—
they'd fight in their suits, and either win this in a hurry
or die in a hurry. Weapons—she really needed good
weapons people. There were five that seemed to stand
out from the rest of the list.

When she got to the meeting place, she was startled by their response—the swift approving murmur, the eagerness on their faces. They looked at her as if she could make this mad enterprise easy. She felt her own heart lift, and gave them back the grin they seemed to be waiting for.

"Told you," she heard someone say. "She's got a plan."

Not yet, she didn't, but she did have a crew list. She read it out, and those named came forward; others looked disappointed.

"Can't you use a few more?" asked a burly sergeant who looked vaguely familiar. "If there's someone aboard, if there's a fight. I've won my share of barroom brawls."

Extras with that attitude couldn't hurt. Esmay nodded, and another half-dozen clustered around. Others lingered, but didn't come forward.

"The rest of you—if you haven't heard, some of the original intruders have gone back into the rest of the ship. And there are plenty of troops coming in. I'm sure you can think of something appropriate to do. The plans we had for dealing with the troops aboard one Bloodhorde ship now need to work for three times that number."

The really worrisome problem was how to get to the drives test cradles unobserved. Both repair bays were now open and floodlit, so that any movement across the gap might be seen . . . would be seen if the Bloodhorde were looking for it. Even though she and Bowry both had guides—specialists who were test cradle supervisors—so that they could approach the keel of the test cradle rather than its upper deck where ships rested—they would be in sight of anyone watching from the repair bays for part of the distance. Esmay did not want to trust that no one would glance over and notice a string of EVA suits going the wrong direction.

"We need something else to get their attention," Esmay said. "More smoke-and-mirrors, like we used to get the intruders well into T-4, but big enough to enthrall however many of them come out."

"If we turned the lights out, they couldn't see you as well."

"Not at first, but they probably have lights of their own. They'll be expecting something . . ."

"We're supposed to have been partially disabled . . . what if our lights go off, then flicker back on? If they've got those fancy faceplates on their helmets, that'll give 'em fits."

"I'll bet we can look really inept," someone else said. "Fluctuations in the artificial gravity, flickering lights—it could seem like the power's out of control."

"But not until we're on our way," Esmay said. "And that means after most of them are off the test cradles—the timing's going to be tight."

"Trust us, Lieutenant," said one of the people she had not picked for her crew. "We're trusting *you*."

Good point. Esmay nodded at her. "Fine—I'll leave it to you, then. Come on, folks—let's get suited up and see about wiping out a Bloodhorde battle group, or whatever they call themselves."

The Bloodhorde ships disgorged EVA-suited figures in clumps that reminded Esmay of strings of frog spawn in the lily ponds back home. Little shiny blobs, two and three together, silvery in the light from the repair bay. They kept coming and kept coming, more than Esmay would have thought would fit in such a small ship.

"Do they know how visible they are?"

"Probably. It helps them find each other, after all . . . though I don't know if other ships they attack have so much light outside. Why would they? It's depressing to think how visible *we're* going to be." EVA suits were intended to be seen; it was a safety feature.

"Too bad we didn't think to spray ourselves matte black or something."

Her gaze fell on the rolls of sheathing for *Wraith*'s denuded flanks. "The skin."

"What?"

"The sheathing . . . those rolls . . . they wouldn't shine . . . If only we'd thought of that earlier. But now they'd see us if we tried to use them."

"It's easy enough to peel off the hull," said one of the techs. "Just takes a sonic generator set at the right frequency, depolymerize the adhesive. What were you thinking, wrap it around you? It's not that flexible."

"How flexible is it?"

"It'd make a roll about this big—" The man held out his arms.

"In other words, several of us would fit into it, in our suits?"

"Oh, sure."

"Would it be any good against scans?"

"Most of 'em, certainly, small as you'd be."

But they had no time; it could take an hour to cut and roll enough tubes, and they didn't have an hour. Esmay put that out of her mind and said, "What else might give us some cover?"

"Well—we can't use the high-speed sprayers in the repair bays, 'cause they'd see it, and besides that's part of the plan—" Esmay wondered what plan, but didn't interrupt to ask. "But there's the little hand sprayers in the Small Parts Coating workbay."

One of the EVA suit techs shot down that idea—paint might eat through the fabric, and they had no time to experiment—so they'd prepared to go as they were, silvery suits and all, when one of the cooks' assistants came running up with an armload of dark green waste sacks.

"We'll look like a row of green peas," muttered Arramanche.

"Better than silver beads," Esmay said. "At least they're dark, and not shiny."

Ahead of her, the base of the test cradle loomed, clearly visible in light from the repair bay. Visible too was their shadow, enlarging as they neared. In its center was the little red blinking dot of the rangefinder on her helmet, giving her the distance and rate of approach.

"Now," said Esmay. The lights went out; she had only her helmet readout to go on, and a single chance to make any adjustments that had to be made. But presumably the

Bloodhorde attackers would be startled by the change in light—they'd be looking for people in the repair bays, where they were. Seb Coron had told her about night fighting, that no one could resist looking to see where a light had just come on, or gone out.

Nearer—five meters . . . four . . . she pushed the makeshift control and a little jet of gas spewed out; she felt the shove as if the ones behind her were leaning on her back. Three meters . . . a very slow progression to two, then one, then she tucked her head, rolled, and felt her boots thud on the hull; her knees took up the impact easily.

The base of the drives test cradle was a maze of cables and attachments, but the test cradle supervisor they'd found knew where the nearest hatch was. Once inside, they rose through the shaft with only short tugs on the line. Then they were at the upper hatch, and Esmay peered through . . . there was the Bloodhorde ship, an angular dark bulk against the starfield. She couldn't tell if it was occupied, not until she had the instruments in the test cradle up and running. That was a job for the supervisor, who grunted and fumbled around for a moment. Then—

"It's got active scan leaking all over it," he said. "Can't do much without them noticing. Good thing is, with them putting out that much, they're not likely to notice anything we put on the cable. Want me to signal *Kos*?"

"Yes."

In moments the signal came back: their arrival had been logged, and they were waiting for Bowry's report from the other test cradle. Esmay reminded herself that his team had had longer to travel, that they had crossed below the line of the Bloodhorde troops coming in. Then, when she thought she couldn't wait another moment, the signal came.

"Ready?"

"Go." This was only one tricky bit in the many tricky bits of the plan. Keeping it simple had not been an option. They needed to focus Bloodhorde attention on the repair bays, away from the assault teams who were after Bloodhorde ships. What they had to work with was more in the nature of handwaving and colored smokes than real weaponry or the skill to use it—but to the repair crews of a DSR, handwaving and colored smokes were second nature. Esmay didn't know what they were going to do, only that it would occur in sixty-second bursts of maximum distraction. They hoped.

The first of the Bloodhorde reinforcements had made it to the cradles when the lights went out. They cursed the stupid Familias sods who had not the sense to surrender without playing childish tricks, and turned on their own searchlights. The beams made harsh moving shadows of the construction machinery, the cradle supports, grapple housings, gantries and the robotics that sprouted on them like barnacles on a dock. In the vacuum of the open repair bays, the laser rangefinders left no trace; the first victims didn't even see the little colored dots on their suits for squinting into that mass of bright lights and shifting shadows. More curses in the headphones, but they knew how to deal with this kind of resistance. It was tricky, with their own ship now moored in T-4, but they lobbed in some of the little mines called bouncers, and waited until three or four of them had blown up. They had proximity fuses, but would recognize patches on Bloodhorde EVA suits, which made them only very dangerous to play with.

They came on, alert for any more direct resistance. A hundred more had made it alongside their own ship, alongside *Wraith*, when the lights came back on, flickered on and off several times, and then went out again. Helmet filters darkened, oscillated in response to the rapid changes, and finally cleared as the darkness came back. Again their own lights probed the darkness, and they remembered the confusion they'd seen. They were not novices, to be put off by such basic ploys. They didn't bunch up; they moved along in a disciplined skirmish line, until their forward elements reached the airlock at the hub end of the repair bay.

Then the big robotic sprayers, which had slid down the gantries centimeter by centimeter in the light, dropping meters whenever the lights weren't on them, rotated, aimed . . . and fired thick yellow liquid at them. It dispersed to a fine spray in the vacuum, a spray that adhered with equal rapidity to their suits, including the helmet viewplates.

Not all of them got a full dose. Some, near the nozzles, were physically thrown off their feet by the force of the spray, and of those a few managed to curl protectively into balls, so their helmet faceplates weren't entirely obscured. But it took a critical few moments to realize what had happened, and its effect. In those few moments, their formation disintegrated. A few battered and blundered their way to airlocks. But the rest were blind, their external sensors clogged with spray, in some cases stuck fast to the deck by having unfortunately stepped on a coat of spray before it set completely.

The suits were powered; they could pull free. But they couldn't see; they couldn't get the paint off with gloved hands . . . in fact, though they didn't know it, they'd have needed an unusual solvent to remove the paint without eating through the faceplate.

✧   ✧   ✧

"They're wrathy," said one of those who could understand the language coming out of those suit radios. "They're cursing the name and the war clan of someone named Vokrais." Down on the deck of the repair bay, the brilliant yellow suits seemed almost to glow in the shadowy areas. Evidently those mixing the paint had added reflectants and fluorescents to it.

"Good. How many of them did the trap miss?"

The external vidscans, hastily rigged a few hours before to cover areas not usually monitored, showed several clusters of Bloodhorde invaders around the outer edges of the repair bays.

"Perhaps fifty—a hundred—"

"Let's keep them occupied." The sprayers lifted much faster than they'd come down, the beaked nozzles rotating inward. Other machinery shifted up and down, back and forth, in an elaborate dance intended to look vaguely menacing. Would that keep the attention of the Bloodhorde from what was happening behind them? One enterprising operator detached one of the sprayers from its usual mounting, and sent it toward the repair bay opening, as if in search of more troops to spray. He ran it out on a boom, its nozzle swinging threateningly from side to side, and watched on the vidscan as the Bloodhorde troops shifted uneasily on their lines. One of them raised a weapon . . . and let off a triumphant screech of Bloodhorde when his shot holed the paint reservoir.

He hadn't thought what would happen if he succeeded: the bursting reservoir meant a cloud of dispersing paint, still tacky enough to cloud several more faceplates. More screamed curses came over the radio; the other troops lost the last remnants of discipline, and rushed into the repair bay.

Esmay pulled herself into the ship. Both outer and inner hatches were open, which argued that anyone aboard would be in an EVA suit. She edged across to the inner hatch, noting the slightly greasy feel of a substandard artificial gravity generator, and peered around. She was looking into a large open compartment with rows of upright stanchions, each fitted with a top crossbar and several loops. It looked nothing like anything she'd seen in a Fleet vessel. Then she realized how handy that apparatus would be for someone getting into an EVA suit without help. This was where the Bloodhorde troops prepared for boarding.

Where was their bridge? Was anyone there? She waved two of her people forward, and two aft. She herself went forward, behind the other two. She saw the leader's arm lift, and held her breath . . . they and Bowry's team had the only five needlers available, weapons that were safe to use in the confines of a warship's bridge.

His hand jerked twice, and then he moved forward. Esmay followed, alert for movement from any direction.

There was none. On the bridge, the Bloodhorde had left two—she had no idea what their duties had been—and both were dead.

"Let's get this ship going," she said. Someone dragged the bodies back to the big compartment near the locks; the specialists moved to their areas.

The controls looked familiar enough, despite the odd lettering on the labels.

"This'll do, Captain," said Petty-Major Simkins. Esmay started to say she wasn't the captain, when she remembered that she was . . . at least for the moment. A captain, if not the captain. Simkins was her engineering section, ordinarily in Drives and Maneuver. "It's just a basic small freighter perked up with some weaponry . . . shields aren't more than civ level. If the others' shields are no better, it'll only take a few hits." That it would take only a few enemy hits to destroy them was understood.

"Weapons?" she asked. That was Chief Arramanche, who held up a finger for a moment's more grace.

"We've got . . . almost a full arsenal of missiles, Captain" she said then. "Ample for the mission. But this thing has no beam weapons." Which meant they'd have to come close to be sure of a kill.

"Scan?" Esmay asked.

"Power . . . on . . . Captain, we're operational." Lucien Patel had a light, almost breathy voice, but it sounded confident enough. "And we have . . . there's *Kos*'s signal . . . the three other Bloodhorde ships. One's probably a pirated superfreighter, and the other's about this size."

❖   ❖   ❖

Vokrais eyed the empty curved passage uneasily. Something was different, and he couldn't be sure what.

"Which deck is this?" he asked.

"Four."

"I'm going to check the air," he said. He pulled down the mask, and lifted the helmet. The lights . . . had they or hadn't they told that bitch to cut the lights below Deck 8? He couldn't remember. The smell . . . it seemed fresher than he remembered, but that might be breathing through that mask for hours. He couldn't see or hear or smell anything definite, but he could not relax. Every since he'd found that Bjerling was commanding, he'd had the feeling that things were going wrong.

"Trouble, packleader?"

"Nothing I can taste," he said. "But—" His team was shorthanded now—they were so few, and Bjerling hated him, he was sure. If Bjerling's people killed them all, it could be blamed on the Familias troops. Who would ever know?

"We need a hostage," he said finally. "Someone Bjerling would want . . . maybe those admirals if any of them are still alive."

"The Serrano cub?" Hoch asked.

"No—if he's still alive, he's still just a cub. Bjerling will have to talk to us if we have important prisoners, and enough of his people will hear to bear witness. Otherwise . . ."

"The bridge?" Hoch asked.

"I suppose." He was in the trough of the waves now, the sky far away and the sea cold and near . . . the space between waves of battle joy, where he could feel exhaustion and hunger and realize that it wasn't over yet. "Yes. The bridge."

Running up the stairs ahead of the rest, his rage came back and the energy with it. Bjerling's sons should all have shriveled balls; his daughters should all whore for prisoners in the arena. The Antberd Comity should fall to quarrels and jealousy, its last survivor dying poor and crippled—

He saw the little pile of trash an instant too late to stop and had just long enough to recognize what it might be instead, and extend his curses to the entire Familias Regnant when the stairwell erupted in flame and smoke and he died, unrepentant.

❖　　　❖　　　❖

The question they couldn't answer ahead of time was what the other Bloodhorde ships would do. Now, as they powered up *Antberd's Axe*, Esmay kept mental fingers crossed.

"Think we ought to trust their life support?" asked one of her techs.

"No," Esmay said. "Lift off when ready, maximum acceleration—ours, not theirs."

Antberd's Axe bounded off the drive test cradle like a bucking horse; its gravity generator compensated only a little, and Esmay's knees buckled.

"Wow!" said Simkins, sitting helm. "I guess they moved the red line over . . ."

Eighteen decks of T-3 flashed past, and a howl of Bloodhorde that Esmay assumed was invective crackled from the speakers around the bridge.

"They're annoyed," said the pivot-major sitting the communications board. She was supposed to know some Bloodhorde. "They think their captain got bored and went off to play. But I now know our name: *Antberd's Axe*."

"Where's the other one?" Esmay asked. She couldn't interpret the blurry scan she saw. "Scan—?"

Bowry's voice came over her headset, scratchy but recognizable. "We're off. I'm taking the big one," he said. "Scan—"

"There!" The scan image steadied, still grainy but now she could interpret what she saw. Bowry's Bloodhorde ship, that must be, veering from hers toward the biggest blip on the screen. The Bloodhorde flagship, if they had flagships. Esmay looked for her own target, which had been parked, as it were, some thousand kilometers on the far side of *Koskiusko*, where it had a clear shot down the throat of anyone coming through the jump point.

Had it mined the jump point? She suspected not. Setting minefields wasn't a Bloodhorde sort of thing to do, even if they had put that mine on *Wraith*. It didn't matter . . . she was going there anyway. The third Bloodhorde ship, positioned insystem of the DSR from the jump point, would require a separate attack run. From where it was, missile attack would risk blowing *Koskiusko*; she hoped it was like this one in having no beam weapons.

Arramanche said, "Got it. Ready on your order, Captain."

"That ship wants to know what you think you're doing,"

communications said. "They're saying this is no time for dancing with the bear, whatever that means."

Wait, or shoot now? Her mind grappled with the geometry of it, their motion relative to *Koskiusko*, to the Bloodhorde ship, to the other Bloodhorde ship, the distance, the velocity of the weapons, the probable quality of the other ship's shields, its maneuvering ability. "Hold it," she said. "We're going closer."

Going closer was like riding a polo pony; *Antberd's Axe*, whatever its shortcomings by Fleet standards, bounced happily from heading to heading with no resistance. She had been right to close; the other ship could dodge as well . . . instead, it held its position, as if certain she was no threat.

"The big one's moving," Lucien said. "Putting out quite a plume, but Bowry should have it . . ."

"Range in, Captain," Arramanche said.

"Go ahead," she said. Arramanche hit the controls; the whole ship shuddered, with every departing missile.

"It's no wonder they don't mount beams on this thing—it'd fall apart," said Simkins.

"On track!" yelled the scan tech on *Kos*. "You've got—"

The screen flared, and their target disappeared.

"Good shot," Esmay said. "Now—let's go after that third one."

"Two down," said the *Koskiusko* contact. That must have been Bowry, in the other Bloodhorde ship. Surely they hadn't gotten *Wraith* out that fast.

"Lovely shot," Lucien said. Esmay glanced at his screen, and saw that it was now much crisper than before. Maybe he was a genius.

Their ship's artificial gravity wobbled as Simkins tried to maneuver sharply enough to get a good angle on the third Bloodhorde ship. It had boosted toward *Koskiusko*, then veered as both Esmay and Bowry went after it.

"It's launched missiles," Lucien said, just as *Koskiusko*'s scan tech told them the same thing. "Tracking . . . one flight at *Kos* and one each at us and Bowry. Lousy aim . . . you'd think with a target the size of *Kos*—"

Esmay ignored that, and told Simkins to get the last bit of acceleration out of the ship.

"We're not going to make it," Arramanche said. "It—"

Wraith's position lighted up on Lucien's scan.

"All hot," Lucien said. "I didn't know they had that much left—"

"Got him," said Seska calmly in Esmay's headset. And the entire portside array of beam weapons focussed on the fleeing Bloodhorde ship, overwhelming its shields . . . the screen flared again, a final time.

"Captain to Captain," Bowry said. "I'd say there'll be no rank-pulling on this raid, eh? One each, that's pretty fair shooting. Even if two of them were sitting ducks."

"Not our fault," Seska said. "Besides, you two had to get 'em with their own guns—that brings the challenge up to an acceptable level."

"Thank you," Bowry said.

Esmay grinned at her crew. "All right, let's get this thing back to *Kos* before someone else takes a potshot at us."

"There's nobody in this system who'd dare," Arramanche said.

Esmay brought *Antberd's Axe* back to the test cradle with no flourishes; a *Koskiusko* crew waited to talk them into the docking pad and tie the little ship down with "appropriate care." She supervised the powerdown, the locking of weapons; she made sure the two Bloodhorde corpses were bagged and turned over to the deck crew. Simkins handed her the little red key—an actual key, she was startled to note, completely unlike the command wands that Fleet used to unlock controls—and she tucked it into the holdall of her suit. Then she followed the others out of the ship, and closed the hatches herself.

When they got back to *Koskiusko*, back into aired space and out of suits that had acquired a stench all their own, Esmay thought she wanted only three things: a shower, a bunk, and word about Barin Serrano. Instead, she found herself the center of a shouting, laughing, crying, dancing mass of people. Her crew, *Wraith*'s crew, Bowry's crew, coming at a dead run through the tunnel, and at least half the people who'd been left in T-3. She was hugged, pummeled, cheered. She and the other two captains were lifted shoulder high, carried through the passages toward the core . . .

Where she saw Admiral Dossignal, standing a little lopsided, near the lift tube cluster. Seveche and Major Pitak were beside him, watching her.

The crowd slowed, still exuberant but aware of stars and their implication. Esmay managed to wriggle down, and then make her way out of the crush.

"Sir—"

"Good work, Lieutenant! Congratulations to all of you."

"Is there any word . . . ?"

"Of Ensign Serrano?" That was Major Pitak, sober-faced; Esmay braced herself for the worst. "Yes . . . he was found; he's alive, but badly hurt."

But alive. He had not died because she'd done nothing. With the knowledge that he was still alive—and surely if he was alive, he would be fine when he got out of the regen tanks—her heart lifted to impossible heights. She turned back to the crowd, hunting for those she knew.

"You did it!" she yelled at Arramanche. "You did it!" to Lucien. "We DID it!" with all the others, to all the others.

Admiral Dossignal leaned over to speak to Pitak through the din. "I think we can quit worrying, Major. I do believe life has given her that kick in the pants."

CHAPTER TWENTY

By the time Esmay finally got some sleep, while others headed *Koskiusko* back toward Familias space, her initial euphoria had worn away. She woke several times, her heart pounding from dreams she couldn't quite recall. She felt angry, but couldn't find a target for her anger. The Bloodhorde intruders were dead; no use to be angry with them. Nothing seemed right . . . but of course schedules and ship's services were still upset. Those who had been aboard *Antberd's Axe* with her came around for more congratulations; it was hard to give them the responses they deserved. She wanted to, but she felt empty of anything but unfocused irritation. When Lieutenant Bowry sought her out and told her he'd be glad to give her a strong recommendation for a switch to command track, she felt a prickle of fear.

Another sleep cycle helped, but in the next, one of the nightmares caught her again, this time vivid enough that she woke hearing herself cry out. She turned on the light, and lay staring at the overhead, trying to slow her breathing. Why couldn't she get over this? She was not that child any more; she had proven it. She had commanded a ship—*Despite* didn't count, but she allowed herself credit for *Antberd's Axe*—and destroyed an enemy vessel.

Only because it had suspected nothing; only because its captain had been stupid. Her mind led her through the many ways every decision she'd made could have gone wrong. She had been hasty, impulsive, just like that child who had run away. She could have gotten everyone killed.

Others thought she had done well . . . but she knew things about herself they didn't. If they knew everything, they'd understand that she could not really be qualified.

Like a novice rider who might stay on over a few fences, she had been lucky. And she'd been supported by skilled crew.

It would be safer for everyone if she went back into obscurity, where she belonged. She could have a decent life if she just kept out of trouble.

Admiral Serrano's face seemed to form before her. *You cannot go back to what you were.* Esmay's throat tightened. She saw the faces of her crew; for a moment she could feel the surge of confidence that had freed her to make those critical decisions. That was the person she wanted to be, the person who felt at home, undivided, the person who had earned the respect the others gave her.

They would not respect her if they knew about the nightmares. She grimaced, picturing herself as a cruiser captain who followed each battle with a round of nightmares . . . she could see the crew tiptoeing around listening to the thrashing and moaning. For a moment it seemed almost funny, then her eyes filled. No. She had to find a way to change this. She pushed herself up, and headed for the showers.

The next shift, word came down that Barin was out of regen and could have visitors. Esmay didn't really want to know what horrors he'd endured, but she had to visit him.

Barin's eyes had no light in them; he looked less like a Serrano than Esmay had ever seen him. She told herself he was probably sedated.

"Want some company?"

He flinched, then stiffened, looking past her ear. "Lieutenant Suiza . . . I hear you did good things."

Esmay shrugged, embarrassed again. "I did what I could."

"More than I did." That with neither humor nor bitterness, in a flat tone that sent prickles down her spine. She could just remember that flatness in her own voice, in that time she didn't want to think about.

She opened her mouth to say what he had, no doubt,

already been told, and shut it again. She knew what others would have said—it had been said to her—and it didn't help. What would help? She had no idea.

"I don't belong," Barin said, in that same flat voice. "A Serrano . . . a *real* Serrano, like my grandmother or Heris . . . they'd have done something."

In the split second before she spoke, awareness of what she was going to say almost clamped her jaw shut. Against the ache of that, Esmay got out the first phrase. "When I was caught . . ."

"You were captured? They didn't tell me that. I'll bet you gave 'em a rough time."

Anger and fear together roughened her own voice until she hardly recognized it. "I was a child. I didn't give anyone a hard time . . ." She could not look at him; she could not look at anything but the moving shadows in her mind as they came clear out of the fog. "I was . . . looking for my father. My mother had died—a fever we have on Altiplano—and my father was off with his army, fighting a civil war." A quick glance at his face; now his eyes had life in them again. She had accomplished that much. She told the story as quickly, as baldly, as she could, trying not to think as she told it. The runaway . . . the fat woman on the train . . . the explosions . . . the village with dead bodies she had first thought were sleeping. Then the uniformed men, the hard hands, the pain, the helplessness that was worse than pain.

Another quick glance. Barin's face had paled almost to the color of her own. "Esmay . . . Lieutenant . . . I didn't know . . ."

"No. It's not something I talk about. My family . . . had insisted it was a dream, a fever dream. I was sick a long time, the same fever my mother had had. They said I'd run away, gotten near the front, been hurt . . . but the rest of it was just a dream, they said."

"The rest of it?"

It felt like knives in her throat; it felt worse. "The man . . . he was . . . someone I knew. Had known. In my father's command. That uniform . . ."

"And they *lied* to you?" Now Serrano anger flashed in his eyes. "They lied to you about that?"

Esmay waved her hand, a gesture her family would have understood. "They thought it was best—they thought they were protecting me."

"It wasn't . . . it wasn't someone in your own family—?"

"No." She said it firmly, though she still wasn't sure. Had there been only that one assailant? She had been so young—she had had uncles and older cousins in that army, and some of them had died. In the family book of remembrance, the notations said "died in combat" but she was well aware now that notations and reality were not the same thing.

"But you . . . went on." Barin looked at her directly now. "You were strong; you didn't . . ."

"I cried." She got that out with difficulty. "I cried, night after night. The dreams . . . they put me in a room at the top of the house, at the end of the hall, because I woke them up, thrashing around so. I was afraid of everything, and afraid of being afraid. If they knew how scared I was, they would despise me . . . they were all heroes, you see. My father, my uncles, my cousins, even my Aunt Sanni. Papa Stefan had no use for crybabies— I couldn't cry in front of him. Put it behind you, they said. What's past is past, they said."

"But surely they knew—even I know, from my foster family—that children don't just forget things like that."

"On Altiplano you forget. Or you leave." Esmay took a deep breath, trying to steady her voice. "I left. Which relieved them, because I was always trouble for them."

"I can't believe you were trouble—"

"Oh yes. A Suiza woman who did not ride? Who would not involve herself with stock breeding? Who did not flirt and attract the right sort of young men? My poor stepmother spent years on me, trying to make me normal. And none of it worked."

"But . . . you got into the Fleet prep school program. You must have recovered very well. What did the psychnannies say? Did they give you any additional therapy?"

Esmay dodged the question. "I had read psych texts on Altiplano—there wasn't any therapy available there—and after all I passed the exams."

"I can't believe—"

"I just did it," she said sharply. He flinched, and she realized how he might take that. "It's not the same for you."

"No . . . I'm a grown man, or supposed to be." The bitterness was back in his voice.

"You are. And you did what you could—it's not your fault."

"But a Serrano is supposed to—"

"You were a captive. You had no choices, except to survive or die. Do you think I never tortured myself with 'A Suiza is supposed to—'? Of course I did. But it doesn't help. And it doesn't matter what you did—if you spewed your guts—"

"I did," Barin said in a small voice.

"So? That's your body . . . if it wants to vomit, it will. If it wants to leak, it will. You can't stop it." She was aware that she was talking to herself as much as Barin, telling the self that had grieved so long what it had needed to be told.

"If I'd been braver . . ." in a smaller voice still.

"Would bravery have kept your bones from breaking? Your blood from flowing?"

"That's different—that's physical—"

"Vomiting isn't?" She could move again, and now she stepped closer to the bed. "You know you can make anyone vomit with the right chemicals. Your body produces the chemicals, and you spew. A leads to B, that's it."

He moved restlessly, looking away from her. "Somehow I can't see my grandmother admiral puking all over a musclebound Bloodhorde commando just because someone mentioned the arena combat."

"You had been hit in the head, hadn't you?"

He twitched, as if he'd been poked in his sore ribs. "Not that hard."

Esmay fought down a flash of anger. She had tried; she

had told him things she had not told anyone else, and he was apparently determined to wallow in his own pangs of guilt. If someone could wallow in pangs . . .

"I just don't know if I can face it," Barin said, almost too quietly to hear over the soft buzz of the ventilator.

"Face what?" Esmay asked, her voice edged.

"They'll . . . want me to talk about it."

"Who?"

"The psychnannies, of course. Just as they did with you. I . . . don't want to talk about it."

"Of course not," Esmay said. Her mind skidded away from his assumption that she had had therapy.

"How bad is it, really? What do they say?" A pause, a gulp. "What do they put in your record?"

"It's . . . not too bad." Esmay fumbled through her memory of those texts, but couldn't come up with anything concrete. She looked away, aware that Barin was now staring at her. "You'll do fine," she said quickly, and moved toward the door. Barin raised a hand still streaked with the pink stain of nuskin glue.

"Lieutenant—please."

Esmay forced herself to take a deep breath before she turned back to him. "Yes?"

His eyes widened at whatever he saw on her face. "You . . . you *haven't* talked to the psychs, have you? Ever?"

The breath she'd taken had vanished somewhere; she could not breathe. "I . . . I . . ." She wanted to lie, but she couldn't. Not to him; not now.

"You just . . . hid it. Didn't you? By yourself?"

She gasped in a lungful of air, fought it into her chest, and then forced it out through a throat that felt stiff as iron. "Yes. I had to. It was the only way—" Another breath, another struggle. "And it's better . . . I'm fine now."

Barin eyed her. "Just like me."

"No." Another breath. "I'm older. It's been longer. I do know what you're feeling, but it gets better."

"This is what confused people," Barin said, as if to himself. That non sequitur snagged her attention.

"What do you mean, confused?"

"It wasn't just the difference in Altiplano social customs and Fleet's . . . it was this secret you had. That's why your talents were all locked up, hidden . . . why it took combat to unlock them, let you show what you could do."

"I don't know what you're talking about," Esmay said. She felt a tremor in her mind like that of stepping onto the quaking surface of a bog.

"No . . . but . . . you need help as much as I do."

Panic; she could feel her face stiffening into a mask of calm. "No, I don't. I'm fine now. It's under control; as you say, I can function."

"Not at your best. I heard about your best; Grandmother said the combat analysis was unbelievable . . ."

For a moment it seemed funny. "Your grandmother wasn't on the Board of Inquiry."

His hand flipped a rude gesture. "Boards of Inquiry exist to scare captains into heart attacks and ulcers. What I heard, through the family, was how the real commanders, who have combat experience, saw it."

Esmay shrugged. This was only slightly more comfortable than the other topic.

"And no one, Grandmother included, could understand how you did it . . . there was nothing in your background, she said."

"My father is not a bad tactician," Esmay said stiffly, aware that the reflexive annoyance was not entirely honest.

"I imagine not. But not all children inherit the talent—and those that do usually show it earlier. You didn't even choose command track."

"I took advice," Esmay said. "It was pointed out to me how difficult outsiders found it to succeed in higher command in Fleet."

"Argue all you want," Barin said, hitching himself up in the bed. This time he didn't wince. "I still say, as Grandmother said, that you were hiding something, something that kept you from showing what you could do."

"Well, it's not hidden now," Esmay said. "I did command that ship . . . actually now, two of them."

"Not that," he said.

"I told you," she said then. "It's not hidden."

"I'm not a psychnanny. D'you think my telling *you* about my experience would be sufficient?" Despite his attempt at persuasion, she heard the covert plea: he hoped she'd agree that he need not talk to anyone else about it.

"No." She took a quick breath and hurried on. "They know already; you have to talk to them. And they'll help you, I'm sure of it."

"Ummhmm. So sure that you will talk to them too?"

"Me?"

"Don't." He lay back against the pillows. "Don't play with me . . . you know you're not healed. You know you still need help."

"I . . . they'll throw me out . . . a mutineer who hid craziness in her past . . . they'll send me back . . ." She noticed after she'd said it that Altiplano had become "back" and not "home."

"They won't. Grandmother won't let them."

The sheer Serrano arrogance of this took her breath away; she laughed before she thought. "Your grandmother doesn't run everything in Fleet!"

"No . . . I suppose not. But it doesn't hurt to have her on your side, which you do. She's not about to lose an officer she considers brilliant." He sobered. "And . . . if you talked to them about your problem . . . you see, I don't know anyone else who's been . . . who ever . . ."

"You want a partner, is that what you're saying?"

He nodded without speaking. Clear in his expression was the effort it cost him to pull himself out of his own pain long enough to reach out to her.

Her heart pounded; her breath came short. Could she?

"You already told me," he said then. "It's not like it'll be the first time for you."

When you hit the ground, Papa Stefan had always said, it was too late to be scared of being bucked off. You had already survived the worst . . . now all you had to do was catch the horse and get back on.

"I caught the horse," Esmay said; she almost laughed at Barin's confusion. "All right," she said, knowing the panic would come again, but able at this moment to face the pawing, snorting shadow, to walk toward it. "I will talk to them—but you have to cooperate too. I want a Serrano ally closer to my own age than your estimable grandmother or your ferocious cousin. Is that a deal?"

"Deal. Although I'm not sure you've got the right adjective with the right relative."

Major Pitak looked up when Esmay came back from sick bay. "How's the boy?"

"Shaken up, but healing. He's got to see the psychs, he says."

"Standard," Pitak said. "Is it bothering him?"

"As much as it would bother anyone," Esmay said, and gathered her courage again. The shadow condensed from a cloud of smoke to a dire shape, snorting fire. "Major . . . back before all this happened, you said perhaps I should see the psychs . . . about what happened on *Despite*."

"Is that still bothering you?"

"Not . . . just that. I know we're shorthanded, but— I'd like to do that."

Pitak gave her a long, steady look. "Good. Go find out how long it will take, and let me know. You're in enough good graces right now that nobody's going to grudge you some help. Would you like me to call over there and find out when they can take you?"

"I . . . thank you, Major, but I think I should do it myself."

"You don't have to do everything the hard way, Suiza," Pitak said, but it had no sting.

Setting up an appointment was absurdly easy. The appointments clerk didn't ask for details when she said she wanted a psych appointment, just asked if it was urgent. Was it urgent? She could put it off by saying it wasn't . . . but putting it off hadn't solved it before.

"Not an emergency," she finally said. "But . . . it's . . . interfering with things."

"Just a moment." Of course they were busy, Esmay told herself. Barin wasn't the only one with urgent needs relating to the recent action. All those who'd been captives, she expected, and some who'd simply seen too much death, too much pain.

Another voice came over her headset. "Lieutenant Suiza . . . this is Annie Merinha. I need just a few bits of information, in order to place you with the individual most likely to help you."

Esmay's throat closed; she could say nothing, and waited for the questions as if they were blows.

"Is this related only to the recent events, or is it something else?"

"Something else," Esmay said. She could barely speak.

"I see that you were in a difficult situation aboard *Despite*, and received no psych support services subsequently—is this related to that?"

She could say yes, and be telling the truth . . . but not the whole truth. She could tell them the rest later, surely . . . but lies had started this, and she wanted it over. "Partly," she said. "There's . . . it's all mixed up with . . . with other things."

"Predating your entrance to the Regular Space Service?"

"Yes."

"There's nothing on your record . . ."

"No, I . . . please, I can't explain it . . . like this."

"Certainly." A pause, during which Esmay imagined damning check marks on a laundry list of mental illness that would bar her forever from anything she wanted to do. "I can see you at fourteen hundred today. T-5, Deck Seven, follow the signs to Psych, and ask the front-desk clerk. You're on the schedule. All right?"

It was not all right; she needed more time to get herself ready for this . . . but she could hardly complain that they were helping her too quickly.

"That's fine," she said. "Thank you."

"You'll need about two hours. We'll arrange the rest of your sessions once we've met."

"Thank you," Esmay said again.

She glanced at the time. 1030. She had that long to live as she had lived, however that was. It felt like doom coming down on her. She went to tell Major Pitak she would be gone for several hours.

"That's fine. In the meantime, I want you to have lunch with me."

Her stomach roiled. "Major . . . I'm really not hungry."

"True, but you're also tied up in knots. I'm not asking what it's about, now that you're getting help, but I'm also not letting you mope around by yourself. Soup and salad—you need something before you go over there and spill your guts. It's going to be exhausting."

Through the meal, Pitak kept up a series of anecdotes that didn't really require a response from her. Esmay ate little, but appreciated the thoughtfulness.

"Lieutenant Suiza." The clerk smiled at her. "I know you don't know me, but—we all want to thank you for what you did. *I* spent most of the time flat out, having dreams I can't even remember, no good to anyone. If it hadn't been for you—"

"And a lot of others," Esmay said, accepting the file the clerk handed her.

"Oh, sure, but everyone knows you took that Blood-horde ship and fought them off. They ought to make you a cruiser captain, that's what *I* think." The clerk looked at a screen at his desk and said, "There—the room'll be ready in just a couple of minutes. We like to freshen it up between . . . d'you want something to drink?"

Her mouth was dry again, but she didn't think she could drink; her stomach had knotted shut.

"No, thank you."

"Your first time with psych support?" Esmay nodded; she hated to be that transparent.

"Everyone's scared beforehand," the clerk said. "But we haven't killed anyone yet." Esmay tried to smile, but she didn't really think it was funny.

Nubbly toast-brown carpet ran halfway up the

bulkheads, here painted cream; a fat-cushioned couch with an afghan draped over one end and a couple of soft chairs made the little compartment look more like a particularly cozy sitting room. It was quiet, and smelled faintly of mint. Esmay, aware that she had stopped in the doorway like a wary colt halfway through a gate, forced herself to go on.

"I'm Annie Merinha," the woman inside said. She was tall, with a thick braid of light hair going silver at the temples. She wore soft brown pants and a blue shirt with her ID tag clipped to the left sleeve. "We don't use ranks here . . . so I'll call you Esmay, unless you have a favorite nickname."

"Esmay's fine," said Esmay through a dry throat.

"Good. You may not know that a request for psych support authorizes whoever works with you to have complete access to your records, including all personal evaluations. If this is a problem, you'll need to tell me now."

"It's not," Esmay said.

"Good. I called up your medical record earlier, of course, but that was all. There are some other things you need to know about the process before we get started, if you feel you can understand them at this time."

Esmay dragged her wits back from their hiding places. She had expected to have to tell everything at once . . . this was much duller, if less painful.

"The slang for most of us is psychnannies, as I'm sure you know. That's reasonably accurate, because most of us are nannies, not medtechs or psychiatric physicians. You're from Altiplano, where I believe they still call nannies nurses, is that right?"

"Yes," Esmay said.

"Do you have any cultural problems with being in the care of a psychnanny rather than a physician?"

"No."

Annie checked off something. "Now: you need to know that although our sessions are confidential, there are limits to this confidentiality. If I have reason to believe that you are a danger to yourself or others, I will report that. This includes participation in certain forms of religious or political activity which could be a danger to your shipmates, and the use of proscribed substances. Although you may choose to attempt concealment of any such activity, I must in conscience warn you that I'm very good at spotting lies, and in any event dishonesty will markedly affect the value of your treatment. Do you want to go on?"

"Yes," Esmay said. "I don't do anything like that . . ."

"All right. Now we get to the heart of it. You said you had problems connected both with your experiences on *Despite*, and with other experiences from before you joined the Service. I would have expected problems existing when you joined to have been dealt with at that time." She stopped there. It took Esmay a long moment to realize that this was an implied question.

"I . . . didn't tell anyone."

"You concealed something you knew was—?"

"I didn't know . . . at that time . . . what it was." *Only dreams, only dreams, only dreams* pounded her pulse.

"Mmm. Can you tell me more about it?"

"I thought—it was only nightmares," Esmay said.

"There is a question on the intake physical about excessive nightmares," Annie said, with no particular emphasis.

"Yes . . . and I should have said something, but—I didn't know for sure they were excessive, and I wanted to get away—to get into the prep school . . ."

"How old were you then?"

"Fourteen. The first year I could apply. They said the application was good, but to wait a year or so, because they'd already filled up, and besides they wanted me to take extra courses. So I did. And then—"

"You did get into the prep school. The dreams?"

"Weren't as bad, then. I thought I was outgrowing whatever it was."

"You didn't know?"

"No . . . they said it was only dreams."

"And now you know differently?"

"I do." That sounded as grim as she felt. She met Annie's

eyes. "I found out when I went home. After the court-martial. That it was true, it was all real, and they lied to me!"

Annie sat quietly, waiting for her breath to steady again. Then she said, "What I understand you to say is that something happened when you were a child, before you joined Fleet, and your family lied, told you it had never happened and you only dreamed it. Is that true?"

"Yes!"

Annie sighed. "Mark down another one for the misguided abusive families of the world."

Esmay looked up. "They're not abusive, they just—"

"Esmay. Listen. How painful was it to think you were going crazy because you had unreasonable, disgusting, terrifying bad dreams?"

She shivered. "Very."

"And did you have that pain every day?"

"Yes . . . except when I was too busy to think about it."

Annie nodded. "If you tormented someone every day, made them miserable every day, scared them every day, made them think they were bad and crazy every day, would you call that abusive?"

"Of course—" She saw the trap, and turned aside like a wild cow swerving to avoid a gate. "But my family wasn't—they didn't know—"

"We'll talk about it. So the first problem you have is these dreams, that turned out not to be dreams, of something bad that happened when you were a child. How old were you when it happened?"

"Almost six," Esmay said. She braced herself for the next questions, the ones she wasn't sure she could answer without coming apart.

"Do you still have the same dreams, now that you know what it is?"

"Yes, sometimes . . . and I keep thinking about it. Worrying about it."

"And your second problem has to do with your experiences aboard *Despite*?"

"Yes. The . . . the mutiny . . . I've had dreams about that, too. Sometimes they're mixed up, as if both things were happening at once. . . ."

"I'm not surprised. Although you haven't told me yet what kind of childhood trauma it was, there are parallels: in both instances you were under someone's protection, that protection failed, and someone you trusted turned out to be against you."

Esmay felt particularly stupid that she hadn't figured this out for herself; it seemed obvious once Annie had said it.

"I presume the mutiny on *Despite* involved a lot of close-contact fighting aboard?"

"Yes . . ."

"So of course the Bloodhorde intrusion here would rekindle the same feelings—and tie into the earlier trauma as well."

"I wasn't quite as scared this time," Esmay said. "Not at the time, anyway."

"Luckily for the rest of us. Now—have you ever told anyone about the events in your childhood?"

Esmay felt her shoulders hunching. "My . . . my family already knows."

"That's not what I asked. Have you ever told anyone since you grew up?"

"One person . . . Barin Serrano . . . because he was feeling so bad. About having to consult you, and . . . and what happened."

"Barin Serrano . . . ? Oh. The ensign in sickbay—he's assigned to someone else. Interesting. You're friends?"

"Yes."

"It must have been hard for you to tell him . . . how did he react?"

Esmay shrugged. "I don't know what a normal reaction is. He was mad at my father."

"Good for him," Annie said. "That's what I'd call a normal reaction. Now . . . since you've told it once, do you think you could tell me?"

Esmay took a breath and plunged into the story again. It

was no easier . . . but no harder, even though Annie was a stranger. When she faltered, Annie asked just enough to get her started again. Finally—she was sure it had taken hours—she got to the end. "I thought . . . thought maybe I'd gone crazy. From the fever, or something."

Annie shook her head. "That's one thing you don't have to worry about, Esmay. By any definition of sanity, you're well onto the sane side . . . you always were. You survived enormous trauma, physical and emotional, and although it damaged your development, it didn't stop it. Your defenses were normal ones; it was your family's response which, if it manifested in an individual, would be called insane—or at least unsound."

"But they weren't crazy . . . they weren't the ones waking up everyone in the house at night screaming. . . ." It was absurd to think of her family as crazy, those normal people walking around in everyday clothes, carrying out normal lives.

"Esmay, nightmares are not a symptom of insanity. Something awful happened to you; you had nightmares about it: a normal reaction. But your family tried to pretend it hadn't happened, and that your normal nightmares were the real problem. That's a failure to face reality—and being out of touch with reality *is* a symptom of mental illness. It's just as serious when a family or other group does it, as when one person does it."

"But . . ."

"It's hard to connect your normal family—living their everyday lives—with your mental image of insanity? I'm not surprised. We'll talk more about this, and your other problems, but let me reassure you: you are sane, and the symptoms you've had are treatable. We'll need to spend some time at it here, and you'll have some assignments to complete on your own. They should take about two hours, between our sessions, which I'm setting up twice a decad for now, every five days. Now: do you have any questions about the process?"

Esmay was sure she had questions, but she couldn't think of them. She had an overwhelming desire to lie down and sleep; she felt as tired as if she'd been working out for two hours.

"You will probably have some somatic symptoms for the first several sessions," Annie went on. "You'll be tired, perhaps achy. You may be tempted to skip meals or binge on desserts . . . try to eat regularly and moderately. Allow extra time for sleep, if you can."

CHAPTER TWENTY-ONE

All very well to say that, but what good was time for sleep if she couldn't sleep? Esmay acquired an intimate knowledge of every flaw in the surface of bulkhead and overhead, every object in her quarters. When she shut her eyes, she felt wider awake than before, heart racing. At meals, she dutifully forced down one mouthful after another, mimicking whoever sat fourth down on the left, taking a bite when he or she did. No one seemed to notice. She felt suspended in a hollow sphere; nothing seemed quite within reach.

To her surprise and relief, no one seemed to expect her to do more than routine work, even though the ship was shorthanded. Pitak handed her endless lists of inventory to check, progress notes on *Wraith*'s repair to enter into the database. She was vaguely aware that this was routine clerical work, more suited to a pivot or corporal, but she felt no rancor. The simple tasks engaged her fully, kept her busy. Whatever burst of energy had sent her across the ship, into the enemy's craft, into battle, had vanished. Someone else could figure out how to get *Koskiusko* back to Familias space, back to the rest of the Fleet deployment. Someone else could worry about *Wraith*'s repairs, about internal damage, even about casualties. She couldn't quite manage to care.

In the next session, Esmay found herself defending her family again. "They didn't understand," she said.

"You had the nightmares. You screamed so much, you said, that they banished you to a distant part of the house—"

"It wasn't banishment—"

"For a child to sleep alone that far from anyone else? I call that banishment. And you had changed in ways that

385

most adults would recognize as a response to stress. Hadn't you?"

Seb Coron had said she loved to ride, until after that. She had been outgoing, ebullient, eager, adventurous . . . but all children grew out of the easy joy of early childhood. She tried to say that to Annie, who insisted on reflecting it back to her in other interpretations. "Whenever a child's behavior changes suddenly, there's a reason. Gradual change is not so diagnostic—exposure to new experiences can mean new enthusiasms replace the old. But sudden change means something, and a child's family is supposed to notice, and look for the cause. In your case, of course, they already had a cause they knew about."

"But it wasn't connected . . . they said I'd just gotten lazy. . . ."

"Children don't 'just get lazy.' That's an adult's quick label for some behavior they don't like. You had liked riding before . . . then you quit, and forgot you'd ever enjoyed it. And you think that's not related to a sexual assault?"

"I . . . suppose it could be." Her whole body twitched, like a horse's skin trying to flick off a biting fly.

"Do you remember whether the assault was in a building or outside?"

"All the buildings were destroyed . . . at least partly. I'd found a corner . . . taller than I was, but only a little . . . there was . . . was straw, and I'd crawled into it . . ."

"What did it smell like?"

Her breath caught again . . . a whiff of that smell, not the smoke but the other smell, blew across her mind. "Barn," she said, so softly she could barely hear herself. "It was a barn. It smelled like home. . . ."

"That's probably why you were in it, your nose leading you to something that didn't scare you silly. So there, in a place you had thought safe—remember, smells go straight in to the emotional center of the brain—you were assaulted in the most terrifying way by someone whose uniform you had previously associated with safety. Is it any wonder you hated cleaning stalls later?"

Astonishment all over again. "I wasn't just lazy," she said, half-believing it. "Or being a sissy about the horses moving around. . . ."

"No—your accurate memory told you that barns weren't really safe, that bad things could happen if you were trapped in a corner. Your brain was working fine, Esmay, trying to keep you safe."

Even as her ears heard, her mind denied. "But I should have been able to—"

"Whoa." Annie held up her hand. "In the first place, you could no more change the new insight your experience gave you than a low-level computer can change the program you feed into it. The part of your brain that's concerned with survival is a very low-level computer; it doesn't care about anything but connecting sensory input to danger and food. If you'd had proper treatment early on, with neuroactive drugs, the worst of the damage could have been prevented . . . but there would always have been a trace of it. That's what life is, after all: that's why mindwipes are illegal."

"You mean I'm stuck with it forever?" If she was going to be stuck with it, why go through therapy?

"Not exactly. The kind of work you're doing now, thinking through it bit by bit, will lessen the effect. There are still drugs we can give, to stabilize your insights and put a sort of shield between your present awareness and the ingrained connections while the new connections become stronger."

"What about the nightmares?"

"Those should diminish, possibly disappear forever, though you might get a recurrence in another period of extraordinary stress. Other patterns of thought which have impeded your development—as a person and as an officer—will change with continued practice."

"I don't like the idea of drugs," Esmay said.

"Good. People who like the idea of drugs have usually medicated themselves with things that don't work and leave neurons flapping in the breeze. You don't have to like your medicine, you just have to trust me to know when you need it."

"Can't I do it without?"

"Possibly. Slower, and with more difficulty, and not as certainly. What do you think the drugs will do, turn you into one of those people in horror cubes, who drags around in an asylum in ratty slippers?"

As that was the image that had come to mind, Esmay could think of nothing to say. Her head dipped in a weak nod.

"When you're ready for drugs, Esmay, I'll tell you exactly what to expect. Right now, let's get back to the other connections between what happened and the things you quit doing, quit enjoying."

She had quit enjoying horses; that still shocked her more than the nightmares. She had not even remembered enjoying them; the image Seb Coron gave her, of a child hardly ever off her pony, felt alien. How could she have been that child, and become this woman? Yet if she believed him about the rape, she had to believe him about the pony. It would mean nothing to Fleet, she was sure, but in her own family that by itself had made her different, inferior.

Could it really be just a matter of smells, of her olfactory system going its own stubborn way, associating the smell of barns and horses with all the terror and pain of that day? It seemed too simple. Why couldn't her nose have associated all the pleasure she'd had, if that pleasure had been real?

Her nose chose that moment to comment on the smell of dinner, which she had been forking into her mouth without thinking about it. She hadn't noticed anything for days, but now a smell got through, and she realized that her mouth was full of ganash stew. She hated ganash stew, but she couldn't spit it out. She gulped, managed that mouthful, and took a long swallow of water. "Come play ball, Lieutenant?" someone asked. Who was that? Her mind thrashed around, not finding a name for the pleasant-faced young woman. Barin would have known. Barin . . . had not been around for awhile. Therapy, she reminded herself. He probably felt like she did, in no mood for games.

She needed an excuse. "No thanks," she said, putting the words together like parts of an intricate model, keeping careful control of tone and volume and pitch changes. "I need to work out—maybe another day."

From there to the gym, uncrowded in the aftermath of the battles. Everyone's schedule was upset, not just hers; she scolded herself for being absentminded and climbed on one of the treadmills. When she glanced aside, her gaze caught on the mechanism of the virtual horse. She had not been on one in her entire Fleet career; she had never considered using one. If she didn't enjoy riding real horses, why bother with a simulator?

It wouldn't smell like a real one. The thought insinuated itself, and her mind threw up a picture of Luci on the brown mare, two graceful young animals enjoying movement. Pain stabbed her—had she been, *could* she have been, like Luci? Could she have had that grace?

Never, never . . . she lunged forward on the treadmill, driving with her legs, and almost fell. The safety rail felt cold against her palms. She forced herself to slow down, to move steadily. The past was past; it would not change because she learned more, or wanted it to.

"Evening, Lieutenant." A jig, moving past her to the horse. He mounted clumsily, and Esmay could tell by the machine's movement that he had set it for basic mode, a slow trot in a straight line. Even so, he was off-rhythm, posting just behind the beat.

She could do better. Even now, she could do better, and she knew it.

She had no reason to do better. This life had no need for expertise in riding. She reminded herself of the smell, the dirt, the misery . . . her mind threw up images of speed and beauty and grace. Of Luci . . . and almost, tickling at the edge of awareness, of herself.

On the wall of Annie's room—she thought of it that way, though she had no reason to think it was really Annie's room—a flatscreen displayed a vague, misty landscape in soft greens and golds. Nothing like Altiplano, where the mountains stood out crisply against the sky, but it was a planet; she felt grounded by even that little.

"In your culture," Annie began, "part of the global definition of woman or girl is someone to be protected. You were a girl, and you were not protected."

I wasn't worthy of protection ran through her mind. She curled into the afghan, not quite shivering, and focussed on its texture, its warmth. Someone had crocheted it by hand; she spotted a flaw in the pattern.

"A child's reasoning is different," Annie said. "You were not protected, so your child's mind—protecting your father, as children do, and the more strongly because your mother had just died—your child's mind decided that either you were not *really* a girl, or you were not a *good* girl, and in either case you did not deserve protection. My guess would be that your mind, for reasons of its own, chose the 'not really a girl' branch."

"Why do you say that?" asked Esmay, who had been remembering the many times someone had told her she was a bad girl.

"Because of your behavior as an adolescent and adult. The ones who think they're bad girls act like bad girls—whatever that means for their culture of origin. For you, I suppose it would have been having affairs with anything that had a Y chromosome. You've been conspicuously good—at least, that's what your fitness reports say—but you haven't formed any lasting relationships with either sex. Also, you've chosen a career at odds with your culture's definition of women, as if you were a son rather than a daughter."

"But that's just Altiplano . . ."

"Yes, but that's where you were raised; that's what formed your deepest attitudes towards the basics of human behavior. Do you fit in, as a woman, in your society?"

"Well . . . no."

"Are you far enough from their norm to make them uneasy?"

"Yes . . ."

"At least you haven't taken the whole-bore approach: some people in your situation chose to reverse both parts of the definition and define themselves as 'bad, not-girls.'"

"Does that mean I'm . . . not really a woman now?"

"Heavens, no. By the standards of Fleet, and most of the rest of Familias, your interests and behaviors are well within the definition. Celibacy's unusual, but not rare. Besides, you haven't considered it a problem until now, have you?"

Esmay shook her head.

"Then I don't see why we should worry about it. The rest of it—the nightmares, the flashbacks from combat, the inability to concentrate and so on—are matters for treatment. If, when the things that bother you are resolved, you find something else to worry about, we can deal with it then."

That made sense.

"My guess—and it's only a guess, not an expert opinion—is that when you've got the rest of this straightened out, you'll find it easy to decide whether you want a partner, and if you do, you'll find one."

Session after session, in that quiet cozy room with its soft textures, its warm colors . . . she had quit dreading them, though she wished they weren't necessary. It still seemed slightly indecent to spend so much time talking about herself and her family, especially when Annie refused to excuse her family for their mistakes.

"That's not my job," Annie said. "It may, in the end, be your job to forgive them—for your own healing—but it's not your job or mine to excuse them, to pretend they didn't do what they did do. We're dealing in reality here, and the reality is that they made what happened to you worse. Their response left you feeling less competent and more helpless."

"But I was helpless," Esmay said. She had the afghan over her knees, but not her shoulders; she had begun to recognize, by its position, how much stress she was feeling.

"Yes, and no," Annie said. "In one way, any child that age is helpless against an adult—they lack the physical strength to defend themselves without help. But physical helplessness and the sensation of helplessness are not quite the same thing."

"I'm confused," Esmay said; she had finally learned to say so. "If you're helpless, you feel helpless."

Annie looked at the wall display, this time a still life of fruit in a bowl. "Let me try again. The sensation of helplessness implies that something could have been done—that you should be doing something. You don't feel helpless if you don't feel some responsibility."

"I never thought of that," Esmay said. She felt around inside herself, prodding the idea . . . was it true?

"Well . . . did you feel helpless in a rainstorm?"

"No . . ."

"You might be frightened, in some situations—perhaps severe weather—but not helpless. The opposed feelings of helplessness and confidence/competence develop through childhood as children begin to attempt interventions. Until you have the idea that something is doable, you don't worry about not doing it." A long pause. "When adults impose responsibility on a child for events the child could not control, the child is helpless to refuse it . . . or the guilt that follows."

"And . . . that's what they did," Esmay said.

"Yes."

"So when I got angry, when I found out—"

"A reasonable reaction." She had said this before; this time Esmay could hear it.

"I'm still angry with them," Esmay said, challenging.

"Of course," Annie said.

"But you said I'd get over it."

"In years, not days. Give yourself time . . . you have a lot to be angry about."

With that permission, it began to seem a limited anger. "I suppose there are worse things . . ."

"We're not talking about other peoples' problems here: we're talking about yours. You were not protected, and when you were hurt they lied to you. As a result, you had a lot of bad years, and missed a lot of normal growing experiences."

"I could have—"

Annie laughed. "Esmay, I can guarantee one thing about your child self before this happened."

"What?"

"You had iron will. The universe is lucky that your family

did get a sense of responsibility into you, because if you'd chosen the 'bad' branch, you'd have been a criminal beyond compare."

She had to laugh at that. She even agreed to take the neuroactives Annie said she was ready for.

"So, how's it going with the psych stuff?" Barin asked. It was the first time since his release from sickbay that they'd had a chance to talk. They had come to the Wall, but no one was climbing. Just as well; Esmay didn't feel like climbing anyway. When she looked at the Wall, she saw the outside of the ship, the vast surfaces that always seemed to be just over vertical.

"I hate it," Esmay said. She hadn't told Barin about the trek across the *Koskiusko*'s surface in FTL flight; even this topic was better. The weird effects of unshielded FTL travel did not bear thinking about. "It wasn't too bad when I started, just talking to Annie. It actually helped, I think. But then she insisted I go to that group thing."

"I hate that too." Barin wrinkled his nose. "It wastes time . . . some of them just ramble on and on, never getting anywhere."

Esmay nodded. "I thought it would be scary and painful, but half the time I'm just bored. . . ."

"Sam says that's why therapy happens in special times and places . . . because listening to someone talk about themselves for hours *is* boring, unless you're trained to do something in response."

"Sam's your psychnanny?"

"Yes. I wish you were in my group. I'm still having trouble talking about it to them; they want to make a big thing about the physical damage, the broken bones and all. That's not what was worst. . . ." His voice faded away, but she felt he wanted to talk to her.

"What was worst, then?"

"Not being who I'm supposed to be," he said softly, looking away. "Not being able to do *anything* . . . I didn't manage to put a scratch on them, slow them down, anything. . . ."

Esmay nodded. "I have trouble forgiving myself, too. Even though I know, in my mind, that it wasn't possible, it still feels as if it was my weakness—mental weakness—that didn't stop them."

"My group keeps telling me there was nothing I could do, but it feels different to me. Sam says I haven't heard it from the right person yet."

"From your family?" Esmay asked, greatly daring.

"He means me. He thinks I think too much about the family, in quotes. I'm supposed to make my own standards, he says, and judge myself that way. *He* never had a grandmother like mine."

"Or a grandfather like mine," Esmay said. "But I see his point. Would it help if your grandmother told you you'd done as much as you could?"

Barin sighed. "Not really. I thought about that, and I know what I'd think if she did. *Poor Barin, have to cheer him up, give him a boost.* I don't want to be 'Poor Barin.' I want to be who I was. Before."

"That won't work," Esmay said, out of long experience. "That's the one thing that won't work. You can't be who you were; you can only become someone else, that you can live with."

"Is that all we can hope for, Es? Just . . . acceptable?" He glowered at the deck a moment, then looked up, with more of the Serrano showing than Esmay had seen for awhile. "I'm not happy with that. If I have to change, fine: I'll change. But I want to be someone I can respect, and like—not just someone I can live with."

"You Serranos have high standards," Esmay said.

"Well . . . there's this Suiza around who keeps setting me an example."

Examples. She didn't want to be the one setting examples; she hadn't been able to live up to any. New insight pounced on that, turned it inside out, put it in the imaginary sun to air. As a child, she had copied the people she loved and admired; she had tried to be what they wanted, as much as she understood it. Where she had failed was not only not her fault—it wasn't, in the larger context of the Fleet and Familias Regnant, even failure.

Fleet seemed to think she had set an acceptable example. Now that the *Koskiusko* was back with its companions, she heard rumors of the reactions in high places. Her head cleared, little by little, from the initial murk of therapy . . . she saw that Pitak and Seveche were not just tolerating her weak need for therapy; they wanted her to take the time she needed. The ensigns and jigs at her table at mess treated her with the exact flavor of respectful attention which a lifetime's experience of the military told her meant genuine affection.

They liked her. They liked *her*, they respected *her*, and not her fame or her background, which they didn't know anyway. She was the only Suiza—the only Altiplanan—any of them had ever met, and they liked her. With reason, Annie said when she confessed her embarrassment, her confusion. Slowly she came to believe it, each day's experience layering a thin glaze of belief over the self-doubts.

From time to time she looked at the virtual horse in the gym, wondering. She had not told Annie that it had begun to haunt her. This was something she had to work out for herself. Automatically now her mind picked that thought up and played with it. Denial? No—but this was something she *wanted* to work out for herself. A choice she would make, when she was free to make it.

"I could get attached to the old girl," Esmay said, peering out the observation ports to the patterns of lights on T-1 and T-5. "She's an amazing ship." She and Barin had found a quiet corner of the crafts activity compartment; the climbing club was busy on the Wall, and Barin had confessed he felt no more eagerness for climbing than she did. She thought he looked a lot better; she knew she felt better . . . she had had no nightmares for the past twenty days and was beginning to hope they were gone forever.

"You're going to transfer to Maintenance Command?" Barin looked up from the model he was putting together, the skeleton of some exotic beast. She could not read his expression, but she saw tension in the muscles of his face.

"It's tempting . . . there's a lot more to learn here . . ."

"Fine for a sponge," Barin said, in a tone that suggested what he thought of sponges.

"Fretting, are we?" Esmay asked, wrinkling her nose at him. "Eager to get back to the *real* Fleet?"

He flushed, then smiled. "Therapy's going well, even the group part. It may even—in the very long run—turn out to be something worthwhile."

"Look out all admirals . . . someone's after your job?"

"Not quite. By the time I get to that age, there may be no slots for new admirals anyway. That's another reason to get back into my own track as soon as possible." He cleared his throat. "How's your stuff going?"

"Stuff? I'm not shy about it, Barin. The sessions have helped. I still wish I knew how much of the change was me, and how much was in those medications, but . . . they say it doesn't matter."

"So what are you going to do? Back into technical track, into scan?"

"I'm transferring," Esmay said. "If they approve, which I hope they will. So far they're being encouraging." She still found it hard to believe how encouraging. Gruff Pitak had practically leaped over the desk, and she had undeniably grinned.

"Transfer to *what*, you annoying woman?"

Esmay ducked her head, then faced him squarely. "Command track. I think it's time a few dirtborn outsiders held command."

"Yes!" His grin lit the compartment. "Please . . . when you get your first *legal* command . . . wangle me a place in your crew."

"Wangle?" She pretended to glare at him, but her face wouldn't stay straight. "You Serranos can wangle all you want, but Suizas expect to *earn* command." He made a face and sighed dramatically. "Gods help us all—we let the Suizas off Altiplano."

"Let?" Esmay reached out and tickled him. Startled, he dropped the model onto the desk.

"You touched me!"

"I'm an idiot," Esmay said, feeling herself blush.

"No . . . you're human. Overwhelmed by my charm."

Esmay laughed. "You wish!"

"Yes, I do," he said with a sudden change of expression. Slowly, he reached out and touched her cheek. "I do wish an alliance with this Suiza of Altiplano. Not just because Suiza has pulled Serrano out of trouble twice now, but because . . . I do like you. Admire you. And most desperately wish you'd like me enough to welcome me into your life." A pause she knew was calculated. "And into your bed."

Her pulse raced. She wasn't ready for this, she hadn't let herself think about it since Pitak's lecture during the crisis. Her body informed her that she was lying, that she had thought of very little else whenever she had the chance. "Uh . . ."

"Though not if the prospect disgusts you, of course. Only if . . . I never thought you'd touch me, aside from whacking me firmly with your elbow or knee in a wallball game." He was joking now, flushing a little himself, and Esmay felt moved to perform a rescue.

"I'm shy," she said. "Inexperienced to the point of total ignorance, barring what I saw on the farm as a girl, which I hope is a long way from anything you were thinking of, as it involved biting and kicking and hobbles."

Barin choked back a laugh. "Esmay!"

"Inexperienced, I said. Not, you will notice, unwilling."

In the long silence that followed, watching the shifting expressions play over his face, feeling the first feather-touch of his fingers on her face, on her hair, Esmay laid the last fiery ghost to rest.

Awards ceremonies all had the same structure; she wondered if all recipients felt a little silly, so far removed from the mood in which they'd done whatever it was that got them honored. Why the discrepancy? Why had the

Starmount stricken her to silent awe when she saw it on someone else's uniform, while she had felt first nothing much, and then a sort of shamed confusion, when she wore it herself? As Admiral Foxworth spoke briefly to each recipient, she found she could believe that the others deserved their medals—that those awards were real. It was hers that felt . . . wrong.

The sessions of therapy rose up like a mirror in her mind. From a vague shape against darkness her own face came clear, as real as any other. She was real . . . she had done what she had done, and its worth lay not in anything *they* said about it. What bothered her . . . she struggled with it, fought to bring it out where she could see. Why was it right for others, but wrong for her? *You don't deserve it*, said part of her mind. She knew the answer to that now, knew the roots of that belief and could pull up those roots no matter how often the wrinkled seed sprouted. But what else? If . . . if she became that person who could be honored, who could be recognized in public as honorable, then . . . then what? Then someone might . . . look up to her as she had looked up to that young man. Might expect her to be what the award made her seem, what they judged she was ready for.

She almost grinned, making that connection.

She could remember, down the years, from before the trouble, an instructor telling some hapless student: "Don't tell me I overmounted you: shut up and *ride*." And then he'd looked at her, the little Esmay knee-high to the tall horses, watching from the ringside, and said, "This one'll show you." He had tossed her up to another horse—the first time she'd been on a horse and not a pony. She'd been more excited than scared, too young to know she couldn't do what she was told to do—and not knowing, she'd stayed aboard. It had felt like flying, so high above the ground, so fast. She could almost feel that grin stretching her face. "Like that," the instructor had said, lifting her down. And then he'd leaned close to her. "Keep that up, little one."

She wasn't riding ponies any more. She was out in the world, on the big horses, taking the big fences—and she would just have to live up to her reputation as the horses and fences grew bigger. . . .

"Lieutenant Esmay Suiza." She stood, came forward as directed, and listened as Admiral Foxworth read the citation. She waited for him to pick up the ribbon his aide held on a tray, but instead he raised one bushy gray eyebrow. "You know, Lieutenant, I've seen the summary of the Board of Inquiry." Esmay waited, and when the silence lengthened wondered if she was supposed to answer that. Finally he went on. "The final paragraph specifically notes that you are not to be in command of any combat vessel until such time as you have demonstrated competence in relevant training exercises. Yet I find that your citation says you took command of the vessel *Antberd's Axe* which subsequently engaged enemy vessels in a hostile encounter. Your commander praises your initiative, when I would think he should condemn your blatant disregard of the findings of that Board of Inquiry." He looked at her, his face now blank of all expression. "Do you have anything to say, Lieutenant?"

All the things she wanted to say, and must not, tangled in her mouth. What was right? What was safe? What was . . . true? Finally she said, "Well, sir, my recollection is that the Board said I should not command any *R.S.S.* combat vessels until further training . . . it didn't say anything about Bloodhorde ships."

A long moment of utter silence, during which Esmay had ample time to regret her boldness and consider the power of angry admirals. Maybe she had overmounted herself, maybe the fence was too high. Then a slow grin creased his face and he looked past her to the rest of the assembly. "*And* she can think on her feet," he said. The crowd roared; Esmay felt the blood rushing to her cheeks. The admiral picked up the decoration and pinned it on. "Congratulations, Lieutenant Suiza."

On the far side of the fence, the ground was still there; she would survive this time, and she would keep riding forward. Coming back to her seat, she caught Barin's eye; he was sparkling all over with delight in her, and she indulged herself with a moment's fantasy . . . Suiza and Serrano. Yes. Oh, my, *yes.*

ABOUT THE AUTHOR

Elizabeth Moon has earned degrees in history and biology, run for public office, served as a columnist for her local paper, been an emergency medical technician in rural Texas, and completed officer's training school in the Marine Corps. Her much-acclaimed novels include *The Deed of Paksenarrion*, an epic fantasy; the "Heris Serrano" series; and two nationally bestselling collaborations with Anne McCaffrey, *Sassinak* and *Generation Warriors*. Her most recent novel was *Remnant Population*. Moon lives outside of Austin, Texas, with her husband and their son.

DAVID WEBER

continued